Sir Middling U

A NOVEL

Kevin Crowley

FriesenPress

One Printers Way
Altona, MB R0G 0B0
Canada

www.friesenpress.com

Copyright © 2023 by Kevin Crowley
First Edition — 2023

This book is a work of fiction. Names, characters, entities, places and incidents are either the product of the author's imagination or are used fictitiously. Any resemblance to actual persons, either living or dead, entities, events or locales, is entirely coincidental.

All rights reserved.

No part of this publication may be reproduced in any form, or by any means, electronic or mechanical, including photocopying, recording, or any information browsing, storage, or retrieval system, without permission in writing from FriesenPress.

ISBN
978-1-03-917500-6 (Hardcover)
978-1-03-917499-3 (Paperback)
978-1-03-917501-3 (eBook)

1. FICTION, HUMOROUS

Distributed to the trade by The Ingram Book Company

*For Catherine,
with love and gratitude*

The politics of the university are so intense because the stakes are so low.
—Wallace Stanley Sayre

Chapter 1

The old basset hound waddled into Duffy's office and collapsed on the carpeted floor. He was wearing diapers—disposable pull-ups, to be exact. They were just the thing for a leaky bladder but a tad snug for a plump, short-legged animal whose swollen genitals chafed at the unnatural confinement. A hole had been cut in the backside to accommodate the dog's tail. It only added to the indignity. The basset hound was a purebred, after all, the descendant of noble hunting dogs.

"Oh, Bertie," said Duffy, looking up from his laptop. "What have they done to you?"

The sorrowful pooch wagged his tail and rewarded himself with the pleasure of a long, slow pee.

Duffy got up from his desk and stroked the dog's velvety ears.

"So, old fella, did you bring the boss with you?"

The boss was Bertie's master, Dr. Alexander Meriwether, president of Sir Richard Middling University. To say that Meriwether was a dog lover was like saying Jane Goodall was partial to chimpanzees. The president of Sir Middling U was simply mad about dogs. He went through life blithely assuming that all of humankind had a similar affection for domesticated canines. It was no surprise, then, that he took his current dog—the beloved Bertie—everywhere he went. Students cooed with delight whenever they spotted the droopy-eyed basset hound on campus. Faculty and staff were less smitten, but as members of the academic community they made room for eccentricity.

Like many basset hounds, old Bertie was afflicted with an astonishing assortment of maladies. His plumbing, for one, was falling apart. Citing the dog's veterinarian, Meriwether described the ailment as "chronic canine incontinence." To the president's staff—who had to mop up after the leaky pooch—it was uncontrolled pissing, plain and simple. No matter what you called it, Bertie's bladder troubles had escalated in recent months. Meriwether had begun encasing the dog's hind end in Huggies, which he swiped from his grandson's diaper bag. The pull-ups did the trick and Bertie continued to attend meetings and events all around campus.

A more benign challenge was boredom. Although the old dog hated exercise, he would often wander away from the president in search of livelier company. Duffy was always a good bet. As Sir Middling's director of communications, he kept a collection of souvenir merchandise close at hand. Bertie had no interest in the scarves and sweatshirts, but he was fond of the Sir Middling mascot—a plush little muskrat with long ears, a toothy grin and an oddly placed tail that was easily mistaken for a penis.

"Here you go," said Duffy, handing over a well-worn sample. "Play with old Musky while I finish my work."

Bertie took the soft toy in his yellow teeth and began to chew and drool with quiet contentment.

As Duffy settled back into his chair, his executive assistant shot through the doorway.

"There you are!" cried Terri Coyne.

Duffy looked up. "Are you talking to me?"

Sir Middling U

"Of course not," said Coyne, as if her boss had just said the silliest thing. "Bertie wandered out of a meeting. We've been looking for him everywhere."

"Start your search here next time," said Duffy. "Bertie likes a good chew toy."

"Don't we all," chortled Coyne.

Duffy ignored the remark. After three years at Sir Middling U, he had grown used to his assistant's salacious humour and low regard for authority. Coyne was a veteran of the university, a self-described "old timer" who was perfectly at home in a world of oddball characters and quirky behaviour. Her skinny frame was topped with a billowing froth of grey hair, giving her the look of a PEZ candy dispenser. Her wardrobe—foraged from local vintage stores—was heavily weighted towards peasant skirts, embroidered blouses and bell-bottom jeans. Despite her outlier tendencies, no one had a better grasp of how the university worked than Terri Coyne. She always knew what form to fill out, which dean had clout and who was bonking whom. Such knowledge was pure gold within the byzantine groves of academe, which is why Duffy overlooked his assistant's sass and sarcasm.

"Listen, Terri," he said. "Would you ask one of the co-op students to take Bertie back to the president's office? I need to wrap up a few things before I head over there myself."

"Sure, boss. It's just the kind of experience every student needs on their résumé."

Duffy sighed. "I don't need it on my résumé either. But someone has to walk Bertie back across campus."

"He's not walking today," said Coyne. "Meriwether pulled him here in a red wagon."

"You're kidding?"

"Nope."

"That's bordering on whacko."

"I'd say whacko is in the rear-view mirror."

"Well, just get Bertie out of my office before his diaper explodes."

"Of course, sire."

Coyne herded the slow-moving hound with a light kick from her suede boots.

"There's a good doggy," she said. "Just put one fat paw in front of the other and drag your nuts across the carpet."

Bertie groaned in protest. As he shuffled out the door, the plush muskrat fell from his mouth and landed with a soggy plop.

"Don't worry about that, boss," Coyne called over her shoulder. "I'll get a co-op student to clean it up."

Chapter 2

When Coyne and Bertie were gone, Duffy turned back to his cluttered desk.

"Where was I?"

His eyes landed on a shipping envelope next to his computer. The parcel had languished there for weeks, avoided and resented like an overdue bill. Duffy let out a quiet groan. It wasn't that he disliked parcels. Quite the opposite. Parcels reminded him of Christmas, and though he was no longer a practising Catholic—or practising anything, religiously speaking—he retained a fondness for the blissful tranquility of the yuletide season. He was developing a similar attachment to sertraline, which his doctor prescribed to numb the stress and anxieties that went with being head of Sir Middling U's communications department.

What bothered Duffy about *this* parcel was that he knew what it contained: a book. He also knew the title and the name of the author, which is why he'd ignored it for so long. The package bore the logo of the Sir Richard Middling University Press—SIRMUP, in a faux Oxfordian font—and its arrival had been heralded by a flurry of texts from a chipper young publicist whose name Duffy could never remember.

- Hi James! It's me. I'm sending you a proof copy of Dr. Mittens' new volume of poetry. We'd love a promo on the website!
- Oops, forgot to mention—it's a sequel to his previous book, Shitty Weather.
- … this one's called More Shitty Weather.
- Hey James! Has More Shitty Weather arrived?

Duffy ignored the texts, just as he ignored the parcel. Communications was a catch-all function that attracted a wide range of tasks and duties, many of them dumped on Duffy by colleagues who were more skilled at avoiding hard work and sticky problems. As a result, Duffy was forever swamped by a cascade of demands. Some were straightforward, like the promotion of homecoming weekend. Others required tact, such as the time he had to inform an elderly widow that the drunken students who routinely peed on her flowerbeds had been "spoken to" but not penalized. And then there were genuine crises, like the uproar over the university's decision to bestow an honorary degree on a wealthy donor who, as it turned out, also funded a group of white supremacists. (To everyone's relief, the donor succumbed to liver cancer and the issue died with him.)

With time and experience, Duffy had learned that the most urgent demands would often be displaced by some new calamity within a day or two. As for the others, most would resolve themselves once the person making the request conceded that little of what went on at Sir Middling U was of interest to the outside world.

Of course, there were things that could not be ignored. As Duffy told his assistant manager—a former Middling Muskrats cheerleader named Sequoia Tush—the ability to distinguish between the ignorable and the un-ignorable was the mark of a good PR pro. To help make such decisions, Duffy employed what he called his Shitstorm Decision Matrix, or SDM for short. This handy tool was based on a simple premise: any request from someone who could make your life hell was a priority; all else was put-off-able. Applying the SDM to the parcel on his desk, Duffy concluded that a request from a bubbly young publicist to promote a book of mediocre poetry by a junior professor of English named Percy Mittens was *definitely* ignorable. At least for the time being.

As he sipped his morning decaf, Duffy's thoughts turned to a more immediate concern: a last-minute summons to meet with President Meriwether at 10 o'clock. Duffy didn't know what the meeting was about. But whatever the topic, he was determined to ask for an update on his proposal to add community relations to his list of responsibilities. The request would result in more work—the last thing he needed—but it would also elevate his job title to assistant vice-president.

Duffy, who was about to turn twenty-nine, had recently begun listening to a podcast on career management. Each episode was linked by a common theme: any millennial who wasn't already on the fast track to a corner office would soon be trampled by the galloping speed of social and technological change. Jolted by the thought of Gen Z-ers nipping at his heels, Duffy rose from his desk with fresh resolve to press Meriwether for an update. He slipped into his black leather motorcycle jacket—"pre-distressed" at the factory, according to the label—and slung a matching satchel over his shoulder. As he hustled out of his office, he stepped blindly onto Bertie's sodden muskrat.

"Christ almighty!" he yelped.

Coyne, who happened to be walking by, smirked.

"Could be worse," she said. "Just be thankful Bertie wears diapers."

Chapter 3

As he strode towards Founders Hall, Duffy pulled a black watch cap over his curly red hair and leaned his tall, thin frame into the bleak November day. The toque and the leather jacket were part of a look he had cultivated during his undergraduate days. Back then, he was a skinny philosophy student who played guitar in a Bruce Springsteen cover band. The leather jacket, watch cap and five o'clock shadow (an orange fuzz, really) were meant to make him look less like an altar boy, which at the time he still was. The ensemble had fooled no one, especially the young women Duffy had tried to date. It did, however, bolster his confidence enough to get him through university and the general malaise of youth. Duffy had revived the rock 'n' roll look a few years later when he went to work for Sir Middling U. The get-up was intended to establish a distinctive style (advice from another career guru) and separate himself from the male faculty, many of whom seemed to think that rumpled dress shirts, ill-fitting sports coats and dun-coloured slacks reinforced their academic *bona fides*.

The watch cap also had its practical uses, especially on days like this. A shroud of dark clouds had settled in over Sir Middling U and an icy wind nipped at cheeks and ears. The dismal weather intensified the funk that always gripped the campus at this time of year. Assignments were due, exams loomed and marking piled up; the Student Counselling Centre extended its hours, and the cafeteria removed all knives from the cutlery trays.

From Duffy's office, Founders Hall was a ten-minute walk along a route that took him through the quad and past a larger-than-life statue of Sir Richard Middling, the university's namesake. Sitting astride a powerful stallion, the bronze Sir Richard gazed resolutely towards the horizon—or at least as far as the Main Library, a mountain of dull concrete that blocked all views of the university sports fields and the picturesque Yawnbury River beyond.

The library building had been erected in 1981, a provincial election year in which the government announced the miraculous discovery of millions of unallocated dollars buried deep within the public works budget. The money was hastily spent on capital projects in a few closely contested ridings. Sir Middling's new library sprouted up like a spring weed, with less than twelve months separating the preliminary design from the grand opening. It joined the university's other unremarkable buildings, which were scattered around the campus like a field of glacial erratics.

As Duffy approached the statue of Sir Richard, his eyes were drawn to the horse's massive scrotum. The bronze bollocks were canary yellow today. A week earlier, they had been sky blue; before that, sunset orange.

The "painting of the balls" was a Sir Middling tradition that dated back to the installation of the statue in 1921. The ongoing prank was carried out late at night by students who, often drunk or high, took cans of spray paint to the horse's giant nut-sack. The caper was repeated so often that the campus maintenance crew waited until summer to remove the layers of paint. The exact day of the cleaning had been kept secret ever since a reporter from the student newspaper, *The Rat's Ass*, had snapped a photo of two workmen vigorously scrubbing the horse's bronze junk. The editor invited readers to submit captions and memes—an inspired bit of fun that still ranked as the most successful social-media campaign ever associated with Sir Middling U.

The university administration turned a blind eye to the ball painting. It was juvenile, of course, but harmless in the grand scheme of things. In fact, the vice-president of fundraising and alumni relations, J.J. Jones, was an enthusiastic supporter of the ritual. A former lineman on the Middling Muskrats football team, Jones protected the ball-painting tradition as if it were a rookie quarterback. In his view, the petty vandalism was a cherished bond that connected students to alumni and helped raise a steady flow of donations from aging Muskrats.

"No matter what colour those balls are painted, they're always gold to me," Jones liked to say.

He wasn't alone. A cabal of activist professors also encouraged students to deface the horse's ball-bag, albeit for a different reason. Members of this group, who called themselves *Le Collectif radical*, liked to sport red liberty caps at protests and post-rally cocktails. They believed the statue of Sir Richard glorified the country's colonial past. Standing at their lecterns like Jean Valjean on the Paris barricades, they urged students to take up the spray-paint canister like a revolutionary's cudgel and wield it against the misguided veneration of racism, oppression and the tedious conventionality of neoclassical equestrian statuary. A new member of *Le Collectif* once suggested that the group could do more for diversity through the faculty hiring committees than it could by painting the balls of a bronze horse. The pragmatic young upstart soon found his liberty cap missing and his name stricken from the group's email list.

Richard Middling—"Brave Sir Dickie" to students and those with a sense of irony—had been a prairie boy who went on to become a militia officer, politician and businessman. He'd risen to fame (or notoriety, depending on your point of view) by leading Canada's first-ever battle on foreign soil: a bloody assault on a battalion of Boers who were dug in along the banks of a river crossing called Paardeberg Drift.

Major Middling entered the history books on a hellishly hot South African morning in February 1900. Delirious with typhoid, he'd risen from his sickbed and strolled recklessly along the front lines, shouting incoherent orders and waving his arms like one of the baboons that were forever pilfering his food rations. Witnesses said that the frenzied major bolted over a rocky outcrop and ran screaming towards enemy lines. His men, loyal to a fault, grabbed their rifles and followed. The Boers cut down half the Canadians but somehow missed the madman leading the charge. Another platoon of Canadian troops—pink-cheeked farm lads and rough-hewn lumberjacks—followed their comrades into the breach, overrunning the perplexed Boers with lightning speed and backwoods savagery. After the surrender, Middling was found sitting in the middle of the river, frothing at the mouth and singing "The Maple Leaf Forever." Invalided back to Canada, he received a hero's welcome. He entered federal politics, became a minister without portfolio and was a vocal supporter of residential schools for Indigenous children. He later made a fortune selling bullets and bombs to the army during the First World War. For his contributions to the Dominion and the Commonwealth, Major Richard Middling was proclaimed a Knight Commander of the Order of the British Empire.

As Duffy passed the statue of Brave Sir Dickie, his eyes drifted from the horse's yellow undercarriage to a different kind of graffiti painted across the animal's bronze rump: the phrase *Amalgamate Now!* stenciled in neon green.

Duffy was tempted to dismiss the slogan as just another student cause, like last year's campaign to create a crosswalk for the Canada geese that mobbed the Sir Middling campus. (Not only did the geese decline to use the street crossing, several ganders launched a ferocious attack on the young do-gooders who tried to herd them across it.) As Duffy gazed at the words painted on the bum of the horse, something made him pause and take notice. He had seen a similar call to action on social media, each post tagging the university and the provincial Ministry of Higher Education. His PR instincts aroused, Duffy took a picture of the message emblazoned across the backside of Sir Dickie's horse and added it to a file on his phone titled *Issues Management*.

When Duffy arrived at Founders Hall, he noticed that the accessibility ramp was torn up and roped off. A sign attached to the railing read, "Ramp temporarily disabled." Duffy winced. He pulled out his phone and sent himself a reminder to have the wording revised. Then he bounded up the steps and through the main doors. As he stood in the lobby cleaning his fogged-up glasses, his ears were assaulted by a familiar noise: the wrathful voice of Professor Sylvia Kiljoy, crashing and banging like rolling thunder along the musty corridors of the old administration building. As head of SMUFA—the Sir Middling University Faculty Association—Kiljoy had a regular meeting with the university president. "My weekly flogging," Meriwether called it, usually over a tumbler of single malt in the faculty club. From course loads to class sizes, there were few topics upon which Kiljoy could not work up a righteous fury. As Duffy made his way along the corridor, the union chief's voice grew louder, barreling towards him from somewhere within the executive suite. As if on cue, the door to the reception area suddenly burst open and the whippet-like frame of Sylvia Kiljoy raced out.

"Good morning, professor," said Duffy.

Kiljoy gave him a withering glare. "Piss off!" she snapped without breaking stride.

Duffy watched with detached curiosity as the president of the faculty association sped down the hallway like an angry race walker, her narrow hips swinging wildly and her cork sandals thumping the carpet. When she rounded a corner and disappeared, Duffy entered the executive suite and presented himself at the reception desk.

"Hello, Moneypenny," he said with a feeble attempt at a Scottish accent.

Sophie Munn, President Meriwether's executive assistant, indulged him with a smile. "Good morning, James. M will see you in a moment."

It was a flirtatious jest, shared only when no one else was present. Duffy and Munn had discovered a mutual interest in James Bond movies when a Sir Middling film professor named Audrey Sherble published a book called *Secret Agency: Sex, Seduction and Female Empowerment in the Spy Genre*. The book attracted a flurry of media interest with little effort on Duffy's part. The buzz petered out, alas, when reviewers discovered that *Secret Agency* contained plenty of references to things like objectification theory, fourth-wave feminism and cinematic phenomenology, but not a single photograph. It hadn't helped that Dr. Sherble refused to do interviews. "My work speaks for itself," she'd declared. And indeed it did. After garnering a few headlines in online journals such as *e-femera.com*, the book faded from the realm of public discussion. If nothing else, however, it did have a lasting influence on how James Duffy and Sophie Munn greeted one another in the outer office of President Alexander Meriwether.

"What was Kiljoy worked up about?" asked Duffy, sitting on the edge of Munn's desk *à la* Sean Connery.

"Who knows? She didn't stop to chat."

"Really? I find that shocking. A sweet gal like Sylvia Kiljoy not stopping to ask, 'What's new?' or 'How's it going?' She must be having an off day."

"I'm waiting for her to have an *on* day," said Munn. "Now, in you go. Dr. Meriwether has a full morning and I'm trying to keep him on track."

"Right you are, Moneypenny," said Duffy, flashing what he hoped was a playfully rakish smile. He lifted himself off Munn's desk, opened the door to the president's office and passed on through.

On the other side of the threshold lay Bertie, who had been returned to his master by an obliging student just moments earlier. Duffy stepped over the bloated hound and approached Alexander Meriwether. The president was leaning his hefty frame over a round meeting table. The palms of his hands lay flat on the polished surface and a newspaper was spread out before him like a nautical chart. In fact, the whole office had a maritime look. Meriwether was a naval historian with a penchant for explorers, chief among them Captain James Cook. The walls of his office were adorned with antique maps and paintings of tall ships. A metre-long replica of *HMS Endeavour* sat atop an oak sideboard, forever in irons despite its billowing sails. A former naval officer himself, Meriwether spoke with the good-natured bluster of a man who downplayed his own abilities while taking the measure of others. He'd spent several years aboard an Iroquois-class destroyer before enrolling in graduate school, and there were few things in academic life that could rattle his famously even temper.

"Ah, James!" said Meriwether, looking up over his reading glasses. "Thanks for coming. What do you make of the mayor's speech last night about rezoning the Village? Is she just humouring the developers or is she really giving in?"

The Village was the student ghetto situated just west of Sir Middling U. At one time, the neighbourhood had been a real village on the outskirts of the town of Yawnbury, its small houses filled with the families of tradespeople and labourers. As the years passed and the community expanded, the aging owners sold their modest abodes to small-time landlords, who, in turn, enlarged the dilapidated dwellings without actually fixing them up. Student tenants didn't seem to mind. Most were keen to rent anything within a block or two of the university; the shabbier the house, the less they worried about the wear-and-tear of weekend parties.

Lately, however, a new generation of landlords were growing more ambitious. A few were tearing down the houses and replacing them with multistorey apartment buildings. There were even rumours of a foreign consortium amassing dozens of properties and planning the redevelopment of entire blocks. Sir Middling's academic leaders weren't sure what to make of the situation, but instinctively, they resisted anything that smacked of change.

"The mayor has to give something to the developers," Duffy said after a moment's thought. "They can make her life more difficult than we can."

"True enough," said Meriwether. "Give some thought to how we communicate our position to the mayor. Let her know that we're *leaning* towards opposition."

Duffy smiled. The president of Sir Middling U was famous for hedging his bets, a talent that both impressed and amused his director of communications.

"How firmly are we leaning, sir?" asked Duffy.

The cheeky tone of the question was not lost on Meriwether. Perhaps it was the old man's naval training, or maybe his upbringing in a large family, but the president of Sir Middling U was a tolerant leader who liked a little fun in his conversation—it took the edge off tense situations and encouraged subordinates to speak their minds.

"Semi-firm," replied Meriwether. "Like a good Wensleydale cheese."

Duffy allowed himself a chuckle as he scribbled this new task into his notebook.

"Now, over to you, James," said the president. "Anything I need to be aware of this morning?"

"Well, sir, I was wondering if there's anything new on amalgamation."

"Why do you ask?"

"For starters, the phrase *Amalgamate Now!* is painted on the backside of Sir Dickie's horse. There's also chatter on social media using the same slogan."

Meriwether shook his shaggy, bull-like head.

"Tweets from twerps!" he said. "Listen, James, I've told you before: amalgamation is a non-starter. Bud Walters at the Ministry of Higher Education has been pushing that nonsense for years. Every time he drafts a report, we give his boss an earful and the whole notion gets put on a dusty shelf. Trust me, no minister wants to be the guy or gal who closed a university."

"Not close it, sir. Just merge it with the ambitious polytechnical college in the next town."

If Sir Middling U had a nemesis, it was the Henfield Institute for Polytechnical Education. HIPE, as most people called it, was located in the neighbouring community of Henfield, a twenty-minute drive from Yawnbury. The two schools had been rivals since the day HIPE opened in 1946. Not quite a university, it had been intended to serve the employment needs of Second World War veterans and the booming post-war economy.

Administrators at Sir Middling U resented the flood of federal and provincial cash that poured into the polytechnic from the get-go. Meanwhile, the executive team at HIPE fumed like a younger sibling at Sir Middling's condescending attitude. As the demand for skilled labour took off, HIPE embraced the new era with the swagger of a gifted youth. It kept abreast of employment trends, adding applied programs like data processing, microelectronics and advanced manufacturing. In response, Sir Middling U doubled down on traditional theory-based education. The fates of the two schools were sealed in 1990 when the government extended daily train service from the provincial capital to

Henfield, but not as far as Yawnbury.

"*Alea iacta est*," the president of Sir Middling U, a classics scholar, had conceded at the time.

"Not only that, but the die is cast," replied the president of HIPE, an engineer.

Over the years, a succession of HIPE presidents had lobbied the government to elevate the polytechnic to university status, a promotion that would increase its funding and prestige. The province, however, was reluctant to add to its swollen roster of existing universities, each of which had an insatiable appetite for public funding. The Ministry of Higher Education compromised by *treating* HIPE as if it were a university—acknowledging its growing reputation for applied research, consulting it on system-wide planning and including the HIPE president in the minister's quarterly conference call with the heads of all the universities in the province.

Grateful but not satisfied, HIPE proposed an amalgamation with Sir Middling U—a reverse takeover in all but name that would give the polytechnic its coveted new status without increasing the number of universities in the province. Sir Middling U railed against the scheme whenever HIPE raised it. Most politicians remained non-committal—"devoutly agnostic," as one wag put it. Nonetheless, the skyrocketing cost of post-secondary education prompted a growing number of elected officials to quietly discuss amalgamation over late-night drinks.

"Absorb us or close us, it amounts to the same thing," Meriweather replied to Duffy. "There's an election next year. No government would want to head to the polls after killing off a century-old institution, especially one that has produced three federal cabinet ministers *and* a Supreme Court justice."

Three junior cabinet ministers, thought Duffy, and a lecherous old judge who had a coronary while humping the wife of a colleague in his private chambers. But Sir Middling's director of communications knew better than to make light of the university's most successful alumni in front of the president, a man who prized such graduates for the rarity they were.

"Yes, of course," said Duffy. "But perhaps we should work up a strategy just in case. The government is questioning the value of a liberal arts degree. If they keep banging the amalgamation drum, people are bound to start listening."

"Have you been talking to Kiljoy?" asked Meriwether. "That's exactly what she was just on about."

Duffy's eyes popped as if he'd been goosed with a cattle prod. He and Kiljoy had been engaged in a verbal tug of war throughout his time at Sir Middling U. *The Rat's Ass* had once published a cartoon of this very image. At the time, Duffy and Kiljoy were dueling spokespeople in a fractious round of contract negotiations. The cartoon had been an amateur sketch—two skinny, mannish-looking figures pulling on opposite ends of a rope—but the point was clear.

In most disputes with the faculty union, Duffy was simply doing his job as a functionary of the administration. There were times, however, when he genuinely believed in the arguments he was asked to make. The thought that he and Kiljoy might agree on something was a discombobulating shock, like seeing your grandmother naked.

"No, sir, I haven't been talking to Professor Kiljoy," said Duffy. "But I am curious to know why she's suddenly concerned about amalgamation."

"It's the Amalgamate Now zealots over at HIPE. They've been pushing Bud Walters to write a new report."

"*Has* Walters written a new report?"

"Yes," acknowledged Meriwether. "Bud is set to retire from the ministry in February. This is his last kick at the can. But report or no report, amalgamation won't fly. It's toxic for politicians. Always has been, always will be."

When it came to politics, Duffy knew better than to speak

in absolutes. Still, he gave the president's opinion a moment of respectful thought.

"I'm sure you're right, sir. All the same, I'd like to sketch out an issues-management plan."

The president lowered himself into his desk chair and folded his hands on top of his impressively round belly.

"All right," he conceded. "But on one condition: You keep it quiet. I don't want anything to fuel the rumour mill."

Too late for that, thought Duffy, recalling the sight of Professor Kiljoy roaring out of the president's suite.

"Is there anything else, James?" asked Meriwether.

"Well, if you don't mind me asking, sir, have you had a chance to read my proposal about adding community relations to the communications portfolio?"

"And boost your title to assistant vice-president?"

"Yes, that too," admitted Duffy.

Meriwether leaned forward and gave a thoughtful nod.

"The idea has merit," he said. "But budgets are tight. The deans are clamouring to have all spending increases stay on the faculty side. Arts wants more sabbatical leaves, Science is pushing for a new faculty lounge and the dean of Grad Studies wants to double her travel budget."

"I understand," Duffy lied.

"Good. Because when it comes to budgeting, support staff need to remember that students are Sir Middling's top priority."

Duffy failed to see how any of the deans' demands would benefit students. But before he could ask for clarification, Meriwether turned back to his newspaper and began humming happily to himself.

Duffy took his cue. As he stepped around Bertie and made for the door, a familiar knot began to twist and coil deep within his guts. Was it the spectre of amalgamation? Or perhaps regret over not pushing harder for his promotion?

Probably both, he decided.

As he often did when leaving the executive suite, Duffy slipped an antacid tablet into his mouth and headed for the nearest washroom.

Chapter 4

Nearly a decade before he joined Sir Middling U, Duffy had studied philosophy at a small Jesuit-run college. In his fourth year, he applied to a master's program in journalism at a larger university in the city.

"You want to be a *news reporter?*" one of his undergrad professors had said, as if the mild-mannered student standing before him—an altar boy, for heaven's sake—had confided an interest in the pornography business.

Duffy was undaunted. He enjoyed philosophy but felt a strong pull towards the applied side of life. Journalism seemed like a good way to feed his intellectual curiosity while doing something active and useful. One of his uncles had been a war correspondent who died while covering a coup in Central America. Duffy overlooked the fact that the uncle, a *bon vivant* named Jocko Muldoon, had drowned after a night of binge drinking with fellow journalists. (Old Jocko had stumbled west towards the harbour instead of east to the press-pool hotel.) The misadventure only fueled a fantasy in which Duffy saw himself as a globetrotting foreign correspondent, bravely reporting on wars, revolutions and natural disasters.

As it turned out, Duffy's membership in the fourth estate was short-lived. After earning his MA, he served a three-month internship at the largest newspaper in the province. Unable to convert the experience into a staff job, he accepted several contracts as a junior producer for public radio. The work did not involve the kind of gritty, in-depth reporting that he had hoped for. Instead of prowling the urban netherworld for stories about grifters, gangsters and gun molls, Duffy arranged interviews with cookbook authors, garden experts and the organizers of the Santa Claus parade. The few stories that he did report—citizen-in-the-street interviews about tax hikes, the weather and gasoline prices—resulted in a portfolio that, in the words of one old-school editor, was "goddamn embarrassing."

The most memorable piece in Duffy's story collection was an audio clip about North Shore Norman, a prognosticating groundhog that was dragged from its late-winter hibernation each year to look for shadows. What made Duffy's report stand out was Norman's reluctance to leave his comfy cage—that and the cussing that flew from its owner's mouth when the surly marmot bit the old codger's finger clean through to the bone.

"I'll kill the little bastard!" the man had screamed on live radio.

Duffy's producer cut the feed short but not before the noon-hour audience of seniors, pre-schoolers and stay-at-home parents were treated to a string of salty language rarely heard on mid-day radio. The ensuing uproar kept the station's audience-affairs producer busy for three full weeks. The clip itself was saved and replayed internally every Groundhog Day for the dark amusement of the broadcaster's national newsroom.

When a career in journalism looked doubtful, Duffy accepted an offer to join the political staff of the minister of higher education. The big man himself, a loud force of nature named Gerry Blowhardt, had been a land developer before winning a byelection in a suburban riding north of the city. A high school dropout, the minister knew more about zoning bylaws and subdivisions than he did about education and research policy. To compensate, he surrounded himself with what he called "college kids"—eager young graduates who could help him navigate the rarefied world of higher education. The minister was fond of telling his team that everything he knew about university came from the movie *Animal House,* a quip that seemed less funny to Duffy the longer he worked for the Honourable Gerry Blowhardt.

As a recent graduate who had spent five years breathing the stale air of academe, Duffy was keen to create meaningful change. In his experience, many in the university world seemed to cling to structures and practices that were decades, if not centuries, out of touch with student needs. At team meetings, Duffy would give voice to his ponderings: Why, he would ask, do universities seem to value research more than teaching? How can institutions that whine about chronic underfunding afford a four-month summer break? And why was it easier to find electives like *Deconstructing The Amazing Race* than ones that taught basic career skills?

Duffy understood the importance of research and scholarship, and he appreciated the value of critical thinking and a liberal arts education. But wasn't there room in a four-year degree for more courses that would help a graduate pay off their student debt?

Most of Duffy's co-workers dismissed him as an impractical do-gooder—a philosophy grad trying to make actual use of his studies. But a few colleagues detected an earnest sincerity in his grumbling. They suggested he develop a proposal. Buoyed by their encouragement, Duffy outlined a draft plan that would provide additional government funding to any university that created more career-oriented courses, especially in the arts.

Blowhardt said he loved the idea—"Goddamn brilliant, kid!"—but what he really needed his team to focus on was a request by the largest university in the province to build a stadium on a satellite campus in the minister's riding.

"The only fucking thing that matters right now is getting the fucking funding for the fucking stadium," declared Blowhardt. "Do I make myself clear?"

Perfectly fucking clear, thought Duffy.

The minister's staff secured the stadium funding through a strategy of backroom deal-making and supportive articles in the media. Duffy had played only a minor role, but the experience proved valuable. He discovered a knack for writing media pitches that actually resulted in news coverage. In recognition of this talent, the minister's press secretary—a scrappy politico named Jill Kaiser—assigned Duffy to a more senior task: drafting a communications plan to re-announce a round of infrastructure funding that the government had already unveiled a year earlier.

"The trick to these *encore* announcements is to make them sound like new money," said Kaiser.

"Isn't that a bit deceptive?" asked Duffy.

"This is politics, dickhead, not the Kumbaya club."

Duffy, who had learned guitar by playing "Kumbaya My Lord" at Sunday mass, quickly got over his misgivings about the encores. The Kumbaya crack, however, stung for some time.

After giving his assignment a few days' thought, Duffy recommended that the re-announcement events take place in July and August—the dog days of summer when the legislature was in recess and reporters were desperate for something to write about. The first project to be re-announced was an addition to the Main Library at Sir Richard Middling University. Blowhardt insisted on a grand affair. "A big fucking circus, with me in the centre ring," he'd said. Duffy's role in the circus was to drum up an audience of reporters, photographers and TV cameras. He accomplished this by promising photo ops, interviews with the minister and free deli sandwiches.

Blowhardt had visited Sir Middling U just once in his life, a drunken road trip to party his brains out at the infamous tail-gate parties that took place around the university's homecoming football game. Kaiser, who struggled to contain her boss's penchant for boorish yarns, urged him not to mention this experience to his hosts at Sir Middling U. Like many universities, Sir Middling's homecoming reputation was a source of embarrassment and community tension. "Five thousand drunk Muskrats fighting, fornicating and flashing their tits," as the local police chief described it. The orgiastic spectacle attracted more news coverage for Sir Middling U than any of its research, teaching or student accomplishments.

"It drives the administration apeshit," Kaiser told Duffy. "So, if you hear the minister talking about tail-gate parties, change the subject."

To the surprise of many, the funding re-announcement went off remarkably well. Minister Blowhardt told those who asked that, yes, he had visited Sir Middling U once before, but sadly, he had been ill at the time and didn't remember much. The encore kickoff was covered by *The Rat's Ass*, the local cable TV station, a citizen vlogger and *The Yawnbury Yowler*, the town's daily newspaper. The event also attracted a summer intern from *The Dominion Press*, a national news-sharing agency. The eager young trainee filed a short item that was quickly gobbled up by copy-starved editors far and wide. Within minutes, the story appeared on the websites of the province's biggest newspapers, television stations, radio broadcasters and online news sites—a degree of coverage that was rare for both Sir Middling U and the minister of higher education.

At the post-event reception, the provost of Sir Middling U approached Duffy and handed him a glass of white wine.

"You're the man I want to talk to," said Dr. Rose Samaroo.

Duffy was smitten. The provost was elegant and fetching, a tall woman with dark hair, high cheekbones and a delightful hint of the Caribbean in her voice. Her beauty was enhanced by a keen intelligence that blazed behind dark brown eyes.

"My spies tell me that you're the talented individual who arranged for today's news coverage," she said.

"It was a team effort," replied Duffy, hoping modesty would sound gallant.

"Well, I hear you've done this before. Media relations seems to be your forte."

"I've certainly spent my share of time in newsrooms."

"Really? Tell me more."

Duffy felt busted. What the hell was he thinking? All told, his newsroom experience amounted to less than ten months. He took a gulp of wine—much larger than intended—and the sparkling liquid shot out of his nose like water from a whale's spout.

"Oh, my!" said Samaroo. "Are you all right?"

"Yes," spluttered Duffy, searching his pockets for a tissue.

Samaroo produced one from a leather briefcase that was as slim and chic as its owner.

"Thank you," said Duffy. "I should never drink and brag at the same time."

Samaroo laughed. "Listen," she said, touching Duffy's elbow with the fingertips of her left hand. "I have something I'd like to discuss with you. Let's find somewhere to chat."

She led Duffy to the side of the room and motioned for him to take a seat at a small, linen-covered table. Her eyes locked onto his and she leaned towards him, making Duffy feel like the most important person in the room.

"I have a vision for this university," she began. "Sir Middling U is a traditional liberal arts college. And with just five thousand students, it's a pretty small one at that. The comprehensive universities look down on us and the research universities barely acknowledge our existence. I plan to change that. I want to invigorate Sir Middling's potential and lead it into the twenty-first century. I've assembled a working group of forward thinkers. We're quietly putting the pieces in place to transform Sir Middling U into an exemplar of the new liberal arts university."

Duffy didn't hear a word Samaroo said. He was entranced by the silky cadence of the woman's voice. His face collapsed into a dopey grin. As Samaroo spoke, Duffy gazed with dewy eyes upon the exquisite features of her face. When she stopped speaking, he continued to gape, waiting for the soothing voice to resume its intoxicating whispers. It took him a moment to realize that Samaroo had asked him a question. But what had she asked? Duffy was mortified. He struggled to think of something to say—something to validate the faith that this extraordinary woman seemed to have in his media skills. His mind remained painfully blank as the seconds ticked by.

Samaroo saved him. "It's a lot to take in," she said. "Let me cut to the chase. We've developed the concept; now we have to sell it. What we need is a communications pro who can build the university's profile and change the way people think about Sir Middling U. I have a hunch, James, that you're the man for the job."

Duffy flushed with surprise and excitement. An exhilarating mix of joy, self-esteem and unforeseen possibilities rippled pleasantly through his veins. He had rarely been chosen for anything—not for road hockey teams, not for the high school musical, not even for a spot on the altar-boy roster at Our Lady of the Immaculate Conception. (He was put on a backup list—the "B Team," as the parish priest called it—and was only promoted when several of the first stringers failed to show up for training.)

A giddy sense of arrival made Duffy tingle from head to toe. But just as suddenly, the thrill turned to panic. Had he misunderstood what this bright, beautiful woman was trying to tell him? He needed clarity but feared asking for it. The ball was in his court. Samaroo was waiting, again, for him to respond.

"Are you offering me a job?" he blurted out.

"I can't quite do that," Samaroo said with a coy tilt of her head. "The university has its hiring protocols. What I can do is urge you to apply. I'll let the hiring panel know that you're my preferred candidate. Interested?"

"Absolutely," said Duffy. "What exactly is the position?"

"Director of communications, reporting to me as university provost. You would play a senior role in what I promise will be a priority project for this university. It's a great opportunity for someone looking to move up in the world of public relations."

Duffy was mesmerized. Was this happening? A real career job? Samaroo broke the spell by standing up and offering him her hand. He grasped it lightly, delighting in the sensual feel of the woman's soft, warm skin.

"One other thing," said Samaroo. "Sir Middling U is more than a place to work. It's a community. Every member is valued, from the lowliest caretaker to the most accomplished scholar. We respect and support all of our students, staff and faculty. I think you'll find it a very nurturing environment."

Duffy wondered if such a collegial workplace existed. His experience on the political side of government was more like a jungle—a survival game with only two kinds of players: predators and prey. Sir Middling U, on the other hand, seemed like the kind of haven where competence, hard work and decency were appreciated.

"Sounds almost too good to be true," he said.

"It's what a modern workplace *should* be," said Samaroo. "Call my office tomorrow. My assistant will give you all the information you need."

She gave Duffy one last enchanting smile before slipping off like a cloud on a summer day.

Six weeks and three interviews later, Duffy received a phone call from the assistant to the provost of Sir Middling University. The director of communications job was his. Could he start in two weeks?

Duffy had daydreamed about this call ever since he'd met

the beguiling Dr. Samaroo. He wished it were her on the phone making the offer. But no matter. He would be spending plenty of time in her wondrous presence before long.

"Yes," Duffy replied to the executive assistant. "Please tell Dr. Samaroo that I'm delighted to accept the position and look forward to starting in two weeks."

He savoured the moment, lost in a soft-focus memory of Rose Samaroo. When the image dissolved, he moved on to more prosaic tasks. The first was to call his boss, Jill Kaiser, to let her know that he was quitting his job in the minister's office.

"I've already forgotten you, Duffy," snapped Kaiser. "Just clean out your desk and leave your security pass at reception. I've got a ministry to run."

Duffy laughed, but to be truthful, he was a little hurt.

"What, no goodbye drinks?" he asked in a lighthearted tone.

The line just buzzed. Kaiser had already hung up.

On the appointed day, Duffy presented himself bright and early at the office of the provost of Sir Richard Middling University.

"James Duffy, reporting for duty," he said to the executive assistant, a middle-aged woman with pin-hole eyes and a look of mild disdain on her doughy face.

"There's been a change in plans," said the assistant, who, according to a name plate on her desk, was Miss Ottie Crump, BA. "You'll be reporting to Dr. Clive Blunt, the vice-president of university services."

"Pardon me?"

"There's been a change in plans," Crump repeated. "You'll be reporting to Dr. Clive Blunt, the vice-president of university services."

"There must be a mistake," sputtered Duffy. "I'm the new director of communications. I've been hired to work with Dr. Samaroo."

"There's no mistake," Crump said with a growing hint of

annoyance. "Like I said, twice, there's been a change in plans."

"Where is Dr. Samaroo?"

"Packing up her office."

"Why?"

"You weren't told?" asked Crump, as if it were Duffy's responsibility to be aware of such things.

"Told what?"

"Dr. Samaroo has accepted an appointment as vice-president of strategy at the Henfield Institute for Polytechnical Education. Her duties here have been spread among several vice-presidents. Dr. Blunt will be overseeing the Communications Department."

Duffy was stunned.

"But what about Dr. Samaroo's vision for a new kind of liberal arts university?" he said. "What about the working group of forward thinkers?"

"You'll have to ask Dr. Blunt about that."

The look of dismay on Duffy's face mirrored the shock and disappointment rippling through his soul.

"It's just that no one told me," he muttered weakly.

"Please don't blame me," replied Crump.

"I'm not," said Duffy. "It's a bit of a surprise, that's all. Is Dr. Blunt expecting me?"

"Dr. Blunt is away at a conference for the rest of the week."

"Should I be meeting with someone in HR?"

"I suppose you could start there," said Crump. "Best to book an appointment first."

"They don't know I'm starting today?"

"How should I know?"

Duffy took a deep breath and tried to compose himself.

"Do I have an office?" he asked.

"I assume so. The Communications Department is over in Alumni Manor." Crump handed Duffy a campus map. "If you hurry, you might catch your predecessor before she leaves."

"I didn't know I had a predecessor," said Duffy, his voice limp with defeat. "Dr. Samaroo made it sound like the job was brand new. To be honest, I'm feeling pretty dejected."

"Welcome to Sir Middling U."

Duffy had the presence of mind to call over to Alumni Manor to see if the outgoing communications director, a woman named Grace Boyle, was still there.

A voice like dry gravel answered the phone. "Comms Shop. What'cha want?"

"Is that Grace Boyle?"

"No, it's her father. Who's this?"

"My name is James Duffy. I'd like to talk to Grace Boyle."

"Just pulling your leg, Jimbo. I'm Grace Boyle. You the new guy?"

"Yes. *James* Duffy. I was hoping to drop by and say hello before you left."

"Well, I've got a lot to do this morning. Come by this afternoon. I'll be liquored up by then, and believe me, that's when I'm at my best."

Duffy let out a timid chuckle and agreed to meet the outgoing director at three o'clock.

Grace Boyle was an ex-journalist whose yellow teeth and weathered face bore testament to a lifetime of cigarettes, whiskey and late nights. She had lobbied hard for early retirement after ten years at Sir Middling U and was now sprinting to the exit before anyone had second thoughts about letting her go.

Boyle met Duffy at the entrance to Alumni Manor. As they wound their way through a labyrinth of newly renovated offices, Duffy's spirits lifted. The sleek desks, ergonomic chairs and funky collaboration spaces were a pleasant change from his previous office. The furnishings at the Ministry of Higher Education were far more respectful of the public purse. Some of his former colleagues claimed that the ministry's battered desks and chairs were army surplus, cast off from an abandoned radar facility above the Arctic Circle. By comparison, the furniture in Sir Middling's Alumni Manor looked straight out of a Scandinavian design catalogue.

"Wow," said Duffy, gesturing to a glassed-in meeting room with lounge chairs and an espresso machine. "I think I'm going to like this place."

"Don't get too excited," said Boyle. "This new stuff is for the fundraising team. The furniture budget ran out before they got to the comms office."

She led Duffy down a narrow hallway that ended in a window-less space about the size and feel of a high school locker room. There were four old desks in the centre, arranged in a single block. A fifth desk sat alone near the front of the room. Above it, a sign hung slightly askew from the ceiling. It featured a row of changeable white letters on a black background. The message read, *Abandon hope all ye who enter!*

Boyle saw the troubled look on Duffy's face. "Lighten up," she said. "It's a joke."

"For me?"

"Sort of. We dust it off whenever someone new joins our little cell block."

Duffy gazed around the spartan room. "Where's the staff?"

Boyle looked at her watch. "It's nearly three-thirty. I'm guessing they called it a day."

"Really? That seems a bit early."

"Depends on how you look at it," said Boyle. "If you stay till four-thirty, some procrastinating peckerhead is bound to rush in here with a last-minute request. If you want to dodge overtime, you gotta slip out early."

Duffy nodded as if it all made perfect sense.

Boyle walked to the back of the office and disappeared through a darkened doorway. Duffy heard the flip of a switch and the pop and buzz of a fluorescent light bulb coming to life.

"Ta da!" said Boyle, suddenly illuminated by a harsh, flickering light. "This hole-in-the-wall is all yours."

Duffy's mouth fell open. The office was long and narrow—a hallway (he later learned) that had been walled up at one end with a stack of filing boxes. A crack of light shone across the top row where the boxes didn't quite reach the ceiling. Voices could be heard on the other side—laughter and pleasant banter from people who were, no doubt, enjoying their Scandinavian furnishings. As Duffy's eyes adjusted to the dim light, he took stock of his new office. In the shadows at the far back was a graveyard of derelict office equipment: old computers, printers, typewriters, film projectors and copiers, the taller pieces poking up like gothic tombstones on a foggy night.

There was an office desk at the front. It was covered in newspapers, file folders and an assortment of other detritus that included a half-eaten apple, an issue of *Cosmopolitan* magazine and a cracked coffee mug. Farther along, the yellowed leaves of a forsaken philodendron drooped sadly over the edge of the desk, as if the plant had given up all hope of ever being watered again. The entire scene was bathed in the eerie blue light of a computer monitor, the screensaver of which displayed a pair of well-oiled bodies entwined in a sensual embrace.

"Sorry about the mess," said Boyle. "The maid quit a month ago."

She lit a cigarette and took a long, satisfying drag.

"Surely you're not allowed to smoke in here?" said Duffy.

"What are they going to do? Expel me?"

Cigarette in hand, Boyle looked Duffy up and down. The tough-cookie expression that was baked into her leathery face softened just a little—a look of empathy, if not kindness.

"Let me give you some advice, kid," she said. "Universities have their own caste system. Academic leaders and faculty members are the privileged elite; support staff and managers are the poop-stained wretches. To survive, you've gotta suck it up and live with the bullshit."

Duffy pondered this dismal assessment. It was at odds with Rose Samaroo's glowing description of the Sir Middling community. But then again, Samaroo had gotten the hell out of Dodge.

"Where do the students fit in?" asked Duffy.

Boyle gave a cynical snort, which ignited a coughing fit. The hacking quickly grew worse, rattling up from deep within the woman's boney, tobacco-clogged chest. Duffy grew alarmed. He wondered if his soon-to-be-retired predecessor was having a seizure. He grabbed a bottle of water from the cluttered desk and offered it to Boyle. She waved it off. The coughing seemed to peak, and just as quickly, began to subside to a phlegmy rasp. Boyle wiped her eyes and stubbed out her cigarette.

"I gotta switch to filter tips," she said.

Duffy smiled uneasily. The two of them stood in silence—the earnest newcomer and the world-weary veteran, close to one another yet poles apart. Boyle took a swig of water and cleared her throat.

"Come on," she said. "I'll show you what's what."

Over the next ten minutes, she explained her filing system, gave Duffy a written guide to his new responsibilities and said that his executive assistant, Terri Coyne, could explain the rest. Finally, Boyle picked up her coat and handbag. She looked into Duffy's eyes and touched his cheek lightly with the tips of her nicotine-stained fingers.

"Don't let the bastards get you down."

With that, she left.

Duffy stood in the silence of his hallway office. The air was sour with the smell of cigarettes, whiskey and the drugstore fragrance worn by the woman who had occupied this space for nearly a decade.

"What the fuck have I done?" he said.

Chapter 5

As Duffy walked back from his meeting with President Meriwether, he found himself thinking of Dr. Rose Samaroo. She had now been at the Henfield Institute for Polytechnical Education for more than three years. As the vice-president of strategy, she would be the driving force behind HIPE's efforts to amalgamate with Sir Middling U. Duffy hadn't seen the impressive Dr. Samaroo since his final interview for the role of director of communications. He wondered if she even remembered him.

When he reached the Communications Department, he found himself standing in the space where the door to his office should have been. The door had been missing for the better part of a month, carted off by a three-person crew from building maintenance. The foreman, a lanky sort with the name "Lloyd" stitched above the breast pocket of his overalls, insisted that the door's rusty hinges could only be fixed in his workshop.

"She's some squeaky," he'd said in a voice that made Duffy think of cod, dories and quaint seaside houses. "I'd recommend a full tear-down back at the shop. Might as well do the job right, eh b'y?"

Duffy had acquiesced. He believed in building relationships with the rank and file—the ones, he liked to say, who really ran an organization. But after nearly four weeks without a door, Duffy's solidarity with the rank and file had begun to erode. Calls to the maintenance shop went unanswered, and Lloyd didn't seem to have a university email account.

Duffy asked Terri Coyne for advice.

"How do I get hold of someone in building maintenance?"

"Who ya looking for?"

"A guy named Lloyd. He sounds like he's from Newfoundland."

Coyne laughed.

"What?" said Duffy.

"Lloyd has never been to Newfoundland in his life."

"He sounds like he has."

"He's from Yawnbury. He just puts on the Newf accent to mess with people."

"Why would he do that?"

"Just bored, I guess."

"Well, how do I get hold of him?"

"He won't get back to you without a kick in the ass. You've gotta go down to the maintenance shop and bust some balls."

Duffy wasn't the ball-busting type, but he was keen to get his door back. He decided to walk over to the shop and see if Lloyd had made any progress. He arrived mid-morning and knocked on the door. No one responded. Duffy knocked harder. Still no answer. He went around to the garage door and peered through a grime-covered window. Inside, two men in overalls were playing ping pong on a narrow table. When Duffy looked closer, he saw that the table was an office door. The name plate read: *James Duffy, Director of Communications*.

"Can I help you?" said a gruff voice.

Duffy jumped like a spooked cat. He spun around to find Lloyd standing a few feet away, holding a tray with four cups of coffee.

"I was just wondering when I might get my door back," said Duffy.

Lloyd cocked an eyebrow. "What door?"

"The door with the squeaky hinges. The one you took from my office in the Communications Department last month."

Lloyd nodded thoughtfully. "I don't know anything about that."

"I can see the door in your workshop," said Duffy. "Two of your guys are using it as a ping-pong table."

"Is that so? Well, even maintenance workers deserve their fifteen-minute break."

"Of course, they do. But here's the thing: I need my door back. Any idea when that might happen?"

"Depends on what's wrong with it."

Duffy bit his lip. "The hinges squeak."

Lloyd gave him a look that said, "You're about as useless as tits on a bull." But when the maintenance foreman spoke, what he said was: "Squeaky hinges, eh? Did you try a little WD-40?"

Duffy wondered if Lloyd, whose Newfoundland accent had vanished, was trying to wind him up. Then he remembered something from an HR workshop called *Dealing With Challenging Colleagues*. "Never assume ill intent on the part of your conversational partner," the trainer had lectured. Duffy took a deep breath and gave Lloyd the benefit of the doubt.

"No, I didn't," he said. "But now that the door is in your shop, would you mind oiling the hinges for me?"

"Could do," replied Lloyd. "But you'll have to a submit a work order. You office folks aren't the only ones who've got processes."

Duffy dug deep into his diminishing supply of restraint and mustered a polite smile.

"My assistant submitted the work order nearly two months ago," he said. "In fact, you led the crew that came to my office and took my door away. You even made me sign a form authorizing its removal."

"Well, then, we're in good shape," said Lloyd. "I'll get one of the boys working on it straight away."

"All I want is my door back," said Duffy, a little more sharply than he intended.

Lloyd's face went a shade darker. "Easy on the snark, mister. You'll get your door back just as soon as we can manage it. Now, if you don't mind, the boys are waiting for their coffee. Have yourself a good day."

Lloyd kicked the shop door open with the toe of his work boot and walked on through. A moment later, Duffy heard a burst of laughter from the men inside.

The sight of the coffees reminded Duffy that he hadn't finished his morning decaf. Rather than head back to his office, he decided to grab a couple of lattes and pay a visit to one of the few friends he had among the faculty of Sir Middling U.

Dr. Fifi Dubé was a bright young scholar who studied the political economy of climate change. While earning degrees from McGill, Harvard and the London School of Economics, she had published numerous articles and a well-received book, all before her twenty-seventh birthday. She was collegial, hard-working and brilliant—a winning combination that deeply annoyed her faculty colleagues.

The only reason Fifi was working at Sir Middling U was to be close to her ailing mother. Iris Dubé had struggled with asthma her entire life. Now in her early sixties, she was additionally burdened with congestive heart failure. Her declining health, coupled with the recent death of her husband, had prompted Iris to return to Yawnbury, the home of her youth. Iris's dearly departed spouse—Fifi's stepfather—had been a petroleum consultant named Frank Dubé. He and Iris had lived their lives moving from one oil-rich country to the next so that Frank could help kings and dictators turn fossil fuel into gold. Owing to her parents' constant travels,

Fifi had done most of her growing up in boarding school. It was the perfect training ground, she later said, for learning to navigate the arcane rules, petty jealousies and spiteful politics of academic life.

Taking the job at Sir Middling U was a major detour from Fifi's expected career path. No one had been more confounded by the choice than her advisor at the London School of Economics. "Are you bloody mad?" the eminent scholar had exclaimed. "I only mentor one post-doc at a time. You going off to Sir Back-and-Beyond makes me look like a damn poor judge of horse flesh!"

Fifi was undeterred. Her decision to move back to Canada and seek academic work at Sir Middling U was part of a *crise de conscience* that had flared up following the sudden death of her stepfather. (The Dark Lord, as Fifi called Frank Dubé, had slipped on a puddle of motor oil in an otherwise immaculate street in Kuwait City, striking his head and passing away two days later.) Fifi realized that if she didn't make up for lost time with her mother, it would soon be too late. She joined Sir Middling U on a post-doctoral fellowship. Over the next twelve months, she applied for several tenure-track positions but was turned down for each. As a consolation, one of the hiring panels upgraded her contract to a limited-term faculty appointment, which the department chair said (without a hint of irony) would "add some meat" to Fifi's CV.

Fifi had gone straight to her office and punched a hole in the wall.

"I love my mother," she later told Duffy. "But I wish Iris would either get better or kick the bucket so I can get the hell out of this two-bit prep school."

Fifi and Duffy had first encountered one another during a meeting of Sir Middling's equity, diversity and inclusion committee. Duffy had asked a question—far too politely in Fifi's opinion—about why the university had no plan to implement the education-related recommendations of the Truth and Reconciliation Commission on Indigenous residential schools.

"Mr. Duffy is calling bullshit on this committee!" Fifi had declared. "And I agree. When it comes to social justice, Sir Middling U flits from one crisis to another without making good on any of its commitments!"

Duffy had been mortified. His motivation had been far less altruistic than Fifi seemed to think. He had simply seen Sir Middling's lack of action on Truth and Reconciliation as a missed opportunity for some good PR. But given the ferocity of Fifi's support, he'd decided that this was not the time to set the record straight.

Over the next few months, he and Fifi crossed paths several times at Sir Dickie's, the campus grad pub. Before long, they were meeting for coffee at least once a week. Duffy assumed that "Fifi" was a nickname, since the diplomas that hung on her office wall certified that F.I. Dubé had been awarded a Bachelor of Arts, a Master of Arts and a Doctor of Philosophy, each *summa cum laude*.

"So," Duffy said one day, "does 'Fifi' come from your initials?"

"Nope."

"A nickname?"

"Sort of."

"Something cute that your dad used to call you?"

"My stepfather wasn't a nickname kind of guy."

"Okay, I give up."

Fifi put down the book she was reading and looked Duffy square in the eye.

"It's my burlesque name," she said. "I perform in an all-woman troupe called The Fabulous Ladies. You should come to one of our shows."

Duffy's pale cheeks flushed as red as a cathouse garter. He nodded thoughtfully, hoping to appear more sophisticated than he was.

"You know, I've never actually seen a burlesque show," he said.

"All the more reason to come to one of our gigs," replied Fifi. "It'll make you laugh *and* give you a boner—the perfect night out."

Duffy's mouth dropped open.

"Shocked?" asked Fifi.

"A little," admitted Duffy. "You're pulling my leg, right?"

"Nope. I really am part of a burlesque troupe. We dance, tell naughty jokes and get pretty darn naked. Most people find it funny *and* arousing."

Duffy scoured his brain for a witty reply, but his Catholic upbringing sprang into action like an involuntary muscle. Racy repartee was beyond his reach. He tried to smile but his lips seemed to work on just one side, producing a look of virginal embarrassment. Fifi was delighted.

"You were in a cover band," she teased. "Didn't you do the whole sex, drugs and rock 'n' roll thing?"

Duffy let out a nervous chuckle. "We smoked a little weed, but the sex was mostly wishful thinking."

"Geez, I would never have guessed," said Fifi. More seriously, she added, "Just to be clear, I'm not coming on to you. I prefer women, at least in bed."

It took a moment for Duffy to digest this remark. If he were more quick-witted he might have replied, "I prefer women *both* in bed and out." But he was not that droll, and not that worldly. He just sat there, eyes blank and mouth open. Fifi's words would prowl through his conflicted mind for a very long time. It wasn't that he was shocked by her sexual preference; it was the frank mention of sex itself, and Fifi's evident comfort with it.

Nearly three years on, Duffy had still not summoned the courage to see Fifi perform with her burlesque troupe. And despite his lively imagination, he was in no hurry to do so. He enjoyed Fifi's company and didn't want any of his personal hang-ups to spoil their friendship.

The two of them first bonded over their mutual newness to Sir Middling U and a shared inclination to see academic culture as theatre of the absurd. Although Fifi was a passionate advocate for social justice, she had no patience for the kind of hollow antics that groups like *Le Collectif radical* got up to. Once, when members of the group had marched into a meeting of the university senate wearing their red liberty caps and academic robes, she and Duffy giggled so loudly that President Meriwether, who was chairing the meeting, asked them to leave.

Duffy often popped in on Fifi during the workday. He knew her teaching schedule and tried to respect it. But on this morning, after his meeting with Lloyd from building maintenance, he cut things a bit tight. He showed up at Fifi's office just before her eleven o'clock class. The door was partially open, so he gave a courtesy knock and walked in.

"Hey, Feef, what are you hearing about amalgamation?" he asked, handing her a latte and dropping his skinny bum into a battered old club chair.

"Not now, Duffy. I've got to teach in ten minutes."

"I won't make you late. Just tell me what you're hearing about amalgamation?"

"You *will* make me late, Duffy."

"Give me the Coles Notes version. Is the faculty association talking about amalgamation with HIPE?"

Fifi stood up. She was tall and fit, her physique accentuated today by black leggings, a short grey skirt and a snug-fitting burgundy turtleneck. Her jet-black hair was pulled up in a messy bun, which added to her imposing presence. She knew exactly how to use her height and figure to deal with those who annoyed her, be they insufferable colleagues, whiney students or friends who couldn't take a hint.

"I'm leaving now, Duffy," she said. "Meet me at Sir Dickie's at three."

For the second time that morning, Sir Middling's director of communications watched a formidable woman stride away from him with purpose and confidence.

Chapter 6

Back in his office, Duffy was working his way through a list of emails when his junior manager, Sequoia Tush, appeared in the doorway. She was staring at her phone, absorbed with something on the screen.

"Hey, James," she said. "There's a weird social-media post that tags Sir Middling U."

"What does it say?"

"It's … I dunno. Kinda like poetry."

Tush handed her phone to Duffy. He stared at the screen for a moment, trying to make sense of the post. Then he read it out loud: *"Cumulo-nimbus/ You hoary tease/ Birth your love storm for all to see. @MoreShittyWeather, @SirMiddlingU, #poetrylovers."*

Duffy handed the phone back. "You're right. It's poetry—very bad poetry."

"Should we worry about it?" asked Tush.

"Only if we care about the reputation of Sir Middling's English lit program."

"*Do* we care about its reputation?"

Duffy had to think about it.

"Well," he said, "the English Department gave the author of that poem a tenure-track job, so *they* don't seem to care. But let's keep an eye on it. Most poets are troublemakers at heart."

Duffy arrived at Sir Dickie's Pub fifteen minutes early for his three o'clock meeting with Fifi. The lunch crowd had moved on and the late-afternoon drinkers had yet to drift in. The only patrons were a few older faculty members and a handful of grad-school idlers, none of whom were sufficiently engaged in the life of the university to pester Duffy with a request for communications help.

One person he hoped to avoid was Sylvia Kiljoy. The grad pub served as a kind of clubhouse for the executive of the faculty association. It was a place where professors could approach their union leaders to grouse about the intolerable hardships of academic life. Spending time in Sir Dickie's was also a way for the union executive to "show the flag," as Kiljoy put it. Flag-showing had become a necessity due to the growing influence of *Le Collectif radical*, whose members believed that the faculty association was doing too little to impede the work of the university administration.

It wasn't Sylvia Kiljoy, however, who approached Duffy at his favourite table at the back of the pub.

"Hey, James!" said a cheery voice.

Duffy looked up to see the joyful face of the young publicist from the Sir Middling University Press.

Oh, crap, he thought.

Duffy usually sat with his back to the wall in public places. It was a habit picked up from his father. James Duffy Sr. had fled the Troubles in Northern Ireland as a young lad and somehow managed to become a policeman in Canada. "Keep your back to the wall," the old man liked to say, "and you'll never get caught with your pants down." It was one of the many bits of wisdom that his father—a "real talker" in the opinion of Duffy's mother—shared with his only son. Few of these tips made much sense, but Duffy remembered all of them and practised most. Today, however, he had lowered his head—and his guard—to read messages on his phone.

"Did you get the proof copy of Dr. Mittens' new volume of poetry?" the publicist asked.

Duffy didn't like to lie, but he wasn't above it either. His PR instincts kicked in and he played for time.

"I *think* I did," he said. "I get so much mail, you know, and things are pretty busy right now. Remind me: What's the deadline?"

"Dr. Mittens is still reviewing the printer's proof but we're hoping to get some advance buzz. We've started a social-media campaign, and we'd love for you to post a news release to the website!"

Duffy nodded thoughtfully. He was hoping that the publicist, being young and chatty, would keep blathering on, thus saving him from making a rash commitment. When the woman stopped speaking and waited for his reply, Duffy began to wonder if he had underestimated her.

"Well," he said, giving in to the silence, "I did see one of Dr. Mittens' social-media posts. Was that some of his poetry?"

"Yes!" exclaimed the publicist. "That was my idea. You know, tease the audience with a few choice lines to build excitement."

"I see," said Duffy. "What's the response been like?"

"You know social media. Haters like to hate. But we have had a couple of positive comments."

"Really?" said Duffy, a little too surprised.

A shadow of hurt passed over the publicist's face. Duffy felt bad. He was about to agree to promote the book on the university website when, to his relief, Fifi walked up.

"Oh, my! Here's Dr. Dubé," he said, leaping to his feet and reaching to take Fifi's coat.

"Hello, Dr. Dubé," said the publicist, shaking Fifi's hand with professional vigour. "We met at the marketing meeting for your new book on climate-change policy."

Fifi didn't recall the young woman. She looked to Duffy for an introduction, but he refused to make eye contact.

"Well, it's nice to meet you … again," said Fifi.

"This is a bit of a coincidence," said the publicist.

"Is it?"

"Yes! I just submitted all the paperwork to have your book considered for the Macphail Prize for Public Policy. The Confederation Society will be announcing the shortlist before Christmas."

"That's very kind," said Fifi. "Thank you."

"Well, SIRMUP is very proud to be your publisher!"

The publicist turned to Duffy. "James, I'll send you a new publicity shot of Dr. Mittens. Let me know if you need anything else to promote *More Shitty Weather*."

Duffy replied with a weak smile.

"I better get going," said the publicist. "I have a meeting with the editor of *The Rat's Ass*. I'm hoping he'll do an interview with Dr. Mittens this week. Catch you both later!"

When the young woman was out of earshot, Fifi said, "My, isn't she the positive young thing?"

"Yes, the perky publicist," said Duffy.

"You don't remember her name, do you?"

"No, as a matter of fact, I do not."

"Why don't you ask her?"

"We've met too many times. It'd be embarrassing."

"More embarrassing than that awkward little moment just now?"

"I'll ask Terri," said Duffy. "She knows everyone at the university."

"God, you're hopeless."

"At least I know I'm hopeless. You've got to give me marks for self-awareness."

"No, I don't," said Fifi. "But if I did, you'd get a C minus. Now, what did you want to talk about?"

Duffy told her about the *Amalgamate Now* slogan on social media and the backside of Sir Dickie's horse. He also mentioned his encounter with Sylvia Kiljoy at Founders Hall.

"I told Meriwether I'd look into the amalgamation chatter," he said. "What's the faculty association saying?"

"I'm not close to anyone on the executive, Duffy. You know that."

"But you must hear stuff."

"Well, I heard our faculty rep talking about your old pal Rose Samaroo. Sounds like she's the one pushing HIPE to take over Sir Middling U."

"Take over?"

"Amalgamate, take over—it amounts to the same thing, especially when one university is far more ambitious than the other."

"HIPE isn't a university, at least not technically," said Duffy. "That's what the amalgamation proposal is all about."

"It might as well be a university," said Fifi. "Its faculty produce more research than my colleagues here at good old Sir Middling U."

"That may be true, but back to my question: What does the faculty association think about amalgamation?"

"Jesus, Duffy! I just told you that I'm not close to anyone on the executive."

"Right, sorry. I'm just bird-dogging for Meriwether."

"You mean you're sucking up to Meriwether so you might get promoted to assistant vice-president."

"Is it a sin to have ambition?"

"You tell me. You're the Jesuit-educated philosophy grad."

"I just don't want my career to stagnate," said Duffy.

"Yet here you are at Sir Middling U."

"Ouch. You really know how to hurt a guy."

"I'm just getting warmed up."

"That's what scares me," said Duffy. "How about we get back to amalgamation? Meriwether thinks it would be political suicide for any government to kill off a hundred-year-old institution."

"Alex is sticking his head in the sand," said Fifi, who had begun rooting through her backpack for a lozenge. She had quit smoking recently; sucking a tart candy was her new addiction.

"Look at it from a politician's perspective," she continued, warming to the political economy of the subject. "You could save a hundred million bucks or more every year by simply folding two nearby universities into one. That's a lot of money that could be spent on other priorities, like healthcare or early childhood education. When you think about it, amalgamation is a no-brainer."

"What's in it for HIPE?"

"The usual, I'd guess. More funding and more prestige. Samaroo must be thinking that some of the savings will go to HIPE. And if amalgamation does happen, she'll be the golden girl on the fast track to a president's office somewhere."

Duffy sighed. "Well, when you put it like that … "

"What other way is there to put it?"

"Aren't you worried about losing your job?" asked Duffy.

Fifi let out a snort. "I'm on contract, remember? And I'm trying to get the hell out of this joint."

"Well then, what about *my* job?" said Duffy. "And what about all the other staff and faculty jobs? Where's the famous Fifi Dubé sense of solidarity?"

"Hey, I don't want anyone to lose their job. But as a political economist, I see the utility of amalgamation."

"I thought you were a social-justice warrior?"

"I'm an advocate for social justice. There's a difference."

"Which is?"

"Buy me a drink sometime and I'll explain it to you."

Duffy smiled. "You know, Feef, I like it when you talk like a hard-ass dame."

"I *am* a hard-ass dame, Duffy, and it scares the shit out of you."

"That's true, but can't a guy fantasize?"

"You fantasize too much and act too little. And speaking of

hard-ass dames, why don't you just talk with Kiljoy about amalgamation? Sounds like the two of you might be on the same side for once."

Duffy lay his head on the table and groaned. "You don't talk *with* Sylvia Kiljoy. She talks *at* you, and harshly, especially if you're a mere staff member."

"Buck up, old boy, and turn on that Irish charm you're always bragging about."

Duffy looked up. "You mean like, *Don't be a feckin' eejit, woman!*"

Fifi smiled.

"Now *that's* the spirit, boyo!"

Chapter 7

Before booking an appointment with Sylvia Kiljoy, Duffy decided to run it by his boss. Although he met more regularly with President Meriwether, he reported to Dr. Clive Blunt, Sir Middling's vice-president of university services.

Blunt's field was economics. An introvert, the dismal science suited him perfectly. He loved research, hated teaching and was rarely available to the grad students he supervised. As an administrator, he gravitated towards budget setting, process development and logistics planning. Social situations caused him panic; casual chit-chat was beyond his comprehension. Once, at a meet-and-greet with the parents of scholarship winners, Blunt had abruptly walked away from a mother who was telling him how proud she was of her son for winning the Golden Scholar Award despite the boy's challenges with dyslexia. The dean of Arts, who'd witnessed the incident, tried to comfort the mother. "Don't worry," he'd said. "We don't let Dr. Blunt anywhere near the students."

After more than two decades in higher education, Clive Blunt looked very much like what he was: an awkward, forty-something academic who had once been tall and thin, but after years of labouring at a computer, had developed a thick waist, narrow shoulders and pronounced slouch. Over this ungainly frame he draped a modest supply of department-store slacks, dress shirts, ties and sports jackets, all in various shades of brown. To his credit, he had learned not to pair white sports socks with dark dress pants—a sartorial basic that eluded many of his male colleagues.

As the most senior faculty member involved in budget setting, Blunt wielded considerable power over deans, department heads and the handful of Sir Middling professors who applied for research funding. His temperament had a modest range, hovering between impatient and petulant. Faculty and staff mocked him in private and walked on eggshells in his presence.

Despite his soft-skill deficit, Blunt had ambitions to succeed Alexander Meriwether as president of Sir Richard Middling University. Without question, he was a competent manager. He could be relied upon to keep the institutional machinery grinding along at a steady if uninspired pace, and there was never any danger of change or innovation on his watch. What he failed to grasp, however, was that a good university president was first and foremost a people person—the organization's chief diplomat, cheerleader, relationship-builder and all-round glad-hander. Left-brain bureaucrats like Blunt could manage the day-to-day operations of a university, but it took a socially astute both-brainer like Alexander Meriwether to cultivate the kind of goodwill and connections needed to keep the school well thought of and well funded.

Of the many departments entrusted to Blunt's care, the one he least understood—and least cared for—was communications.

"Your unit is a cost generator," he'd told Duffy during their first meeting. "I don't see the need for it myself. Anyone with a university education should be able to communicate. We all have email, do we not?"

Duffy had replied with a nervous chuckle. He tried to explain the value of strategic communications: promoting the university, keeping staff and faculty informed, dealing with the media, responding to crises, attracting good students, and cultivating positive relations with alumni, donors, government officials and the community.

"Good Lord!" Blunt had responded. "What will you try to persuade me of next? Marketing and social media?"

Duffy hid his alarm with an amiable smile. "No need to dive into the deep end just yet, sir. Let me pull together some examples of what I'm talking about."

"Knock yourself out," said Blunt. "But whatever you come up with, just email it to me. I have too many meetings already."

It was six months before Duffy met with his boss again. As per HR policy, the two were required to discuss Duffy's probationary review in person.

"Looks like you'll be staying on," Blunt muttered as he handed Duffy a copy of his performance review.

Duffy glanced at the two-page form. There were checkmarks beside each box, but no comments. "I think we were supposed to complete this together," he said.

Blunt's face grew pinched, like a migraine was coming on.

"Add whatever comments you like," he said, rubbing both temples with his fingers. "Just don't ask me to waste any more time on it."

Duffy had learned to adapt to his boss's misanthropic quirks by requesting meetings only when the topic could be dressed up as a non-communications matter. Another approach was to ambush Blunt as he exited the weekly meeting of the president's executive team. Duffy deployed both tactics to raise the subject of amalgamation.

"Good morning, doctor," he said as the door to the executive meeting room swung open and Clive Blunt walked out.

"What is it, Duffy? I'm in a hurry."

"Of course, sir. I'd like your thoughts on a matter of institutional strategy."

"Strategy?"

"Yes. Have you heard anything about HIPE pushing for amalgamation?

"I thought this was about strategy."

"It is, sir. There's chatter on social media and some graffiti around campus. I'm pulling together a few talking points in case the media start asking about it."

"If the media call, just tell them it's none of their business."

"Right. Well, that's certainly one approach," said Duffy. "We might also try to control the narrative. The key is to prepare our messaging ahead of time so that we can get it out quickly."

"Oh, Duffy, there you go again with your communications nonsense. If it's strategy you want, then here's my advice: Just ignore the media until they go away."

Duffy wasn't entirely opposed to the ignore-it-till-it-goes-away approach. But he had run amalgamation through his Shitstorm Decision Matrix and determined that it *was* a topic that needed addressing.

"I see," he said. "Well then, sir, would you mind if I had a chat with Dr. Kiljoy? I'd like to get a sense of what the faculty association is hearing."

"I'd rather you didn't," said Blunt. "That's above your pay grade."

"Of course. It's just that Dr. Meriwether asked me to brief him on the amalgamation chatter, and he wants to know what SMUFA is thinking."

Blunt clenched his jaw. Of the many people he hated to deal with, Sylvia Kiljoy was at the top of his list. The two had known and disliked one another for nearly twenty-five years. They were both U.S.-born economists who had met as undergraduates at a small college in Maine. For the next four years they'd competed for the same scholarships and part-time research jobs. Later, to their mutual annoyance, they were both accepted into the same master's program at the same state college in the American mid-west. Their rivalry had only grown worse, spilling into the open and disrupting the entire department. The program chair threatened to expel them both if they didn't reach an accord.

After several rounds of mediation, Blunt and Kiljoy agreed to avoid one another while completing their MAs. They also promised to apply to different universities for doctoral studies. The respite that followed lasted a full five years. Then, as fate would have it, each landed a tenure-track position at Sir Middling U when a pair of economics professors—Scottish-born twins—decided to move back to the old sod to be nearer kith and kin. Kiljoy and Blunt tried to set aside their grievances, but once again, they were competing for the same research funding, teaching assignments and committee appointments. The tension eased a little when both secured tenure, but decades later, they still sniped at one another like teenaged siblings.

"All right," Blunt said to Duffy. "You take the meeting with Sylvia. But just find out what SMUFA has been hearing. Do not commit me to anything. Understood?"

"Perfectly."

The conversation seemed to be at an end, yet Blunt lingered a moment.

"Do you really think the media will be interested in amalgamation?" he asked.

"Yes," said Duffy, happy to be on home turf. "It's just a matter of time. Sooner or later some reporter is going to get curious about the amalgamation chatter on social media, or someone with an agenda is going to point it out. Either way, we need to develop talking points ahead of time."

"Well," said Blunt, "if Sir Middling U needs a spokesperson, I'm prepared to step forward."

Duffy cringed. Despite hours of media training, Clive Blunt still spoke to reporters like a Dickensian headmaster scolding a slow-witted student. The man once chastised a television journalist so harshly that Duffy tip-toed in front of his boss, took over and answered the remainder of the questions. Deeply relieved, the young reporter continued the interview as if nothing peculiar had just happened on live TV.

"We're still in the early stages of the amalgamation issue," said Duffy, choosing his words carefully. "I'd recommend that I handle the initial interviews. If it looks like the government is serious about merging HIPE and Sir Middling U, we can designate a more senior spokesperson."

Blunt nodded his approval. "Well, if you need me to speak to the media, just tell me when and where, and I'll set them straight."

God help us, thought Duffy. But instead of saying so, he gave Blunt a pleasant nod and watched his boss stride off like a man with important things to do.

Chapter 8

"Quick question, Duffy."
"Shoot."
"Are you banging Sophie Munn?"
Duffy, who was jogging alongside Fifi, came to an abrupt stop. They were running a three-kilometre trail that took them around the Sir Middling U sports fields, along the banks of the Yawnbury River and down to the boathouse where the university rowing crew kept its racing shells. Fifi, who was in better shape, liked to talk as they ran. Duffy, who possessed a narrow chest and gangly physique, did not. He bent over, put his hands on his knees and gulped the crisp fall air.

Duffy admired and dreaded Fifi's frankness in equal measure. Sometimes it was refreshing, like when she called out the hypocrisy of a pompous colleague. At other times it was like getting caught scratching your privates. At least today they were alone on the trail. Not that an audience would have stopped Dr. Fifi Dubé from blurting out a cringe-making question or observation. She liked to play to a crowd, which helped explain her interest in teaching and burlesque.

"No, I am not banging Sophie Munn," said Duffy. "Why?"

"A friend of mine wants to know."

"What friend?"

"Nobody. By the way, Sophie's got nice boobs and a great ass."

Duffy agreed, but he wasn't about to share his opinion with Fifi.

"There's more to Sophie than you think," he said. "Did you know she speaks Spanish and spent a year travelling through South America?"

"*Sí, por supuesto. Es una chica impresionante.*"

"No one likes a show-off," said Duffy. "And besides, I thought that you of all people would focus on a person's substance, not their tits and ass."

"Moderation in all things, buddy boy. I admire substance *and* a nice butt."

Duffy started to walk again. The autumn clouds were breaking up and the sunshine warmed his face.

"So, who's this guy who's interested in Sophie?" he asked.

"Who said anything about a guy?"

"Okay, who's this *person?*"

"Ooooooh! Are you jealous?"

Duffy could never win with Fifi. "Are you sure you're a real scholar?" he asked. "You know, with a PhD and a funny hat? Sometimes I wonder."

"I'm the real deal, all right," said Fifi. "You just can't handle complexity."

Duffy wondered if this was true. Fifi, on the other hand, embraced complexity *and* ambiguity, like a flower welcoming both sunshine and rain.

"Let's change the subject," he said.

"Okay. Have you talked to Kiljoy about amalgamation?"

"Tomorrow. I had to clear it with Blunt first."

"When you see her, ask what the faculty association is doing about that peckerhead Rufus Lillidew. And while you're at it, ask Blunt the same question."

"What's Lillidew got to do with amalgamation?"

"Nothing. But he's bringing another far-right speaker to campus to defend the Sir Dickie statue."

Sir Richard Middling's support of racist policies, along with his role in imperialist wars and colonial violence, had escaped scrutiny for decades. There was the occasional criticism by a graduate student, usually over a pitcher of beer, but nothing backed up by a passionate desire to right Sir Dickie's many wrongs. Nothing, that is, until a young historian named Magda Zwick had penned an article in *The Rat's Ass* that described the statue of Sir Richard Middling as "an iconic representation of hegemonic masculinity, the adulation of war and the veneration of the phallus."

"Even the man's horse has an oversized cock," she'd written.

The article, along with others of a similar vitality, earned Zwick a tenured professorship at a newer university, one with a greater tolerance for progressive views and female competence. Her departure from Sir Middling U might have brought an end to the reappraisal of Sir Richard's legacy had it not been for the same tide that had lifted Zwick to greater things: a rising concern across North America and Europe over the glorification of political and military figures. For the first time, Sir Middling U was on the leading edge of a trend.

"Listen, Feef," said Duffy. "I sympathize with those who see Sir Dickie as a symbol of oppression, but Lillidew's entitled to his opinion too. This is a university, after all. You know, a forum for competing ideas and critical dialogue."

"Don't be glib, Duffy. And don't lecture a gay woman with a PhD about freedom of speech."

"Hey, I'm just playing devil's advocate. If you don't mind a lowly staff member saying, it seems a bit hypocritical to stop someone from speaking just because you don't like what they have to say."

Fifi glared at Duffy. "Well, if you don't mind a scholar who has studied these issues saying, it shouldn't be about half-baked opinions. It should be about rigorous research and fact-based dialogue. Lillidew has brought zero substance to the discussion—just platitudes about cancel culture, woke politics and reverse discrimination. History needs to be re-examined in a scrupulous and objective way. This is a university, after all."

Good point, thought Duffy. He would never admit it to Fifi, but he loved to see her debating skills in full flight. She had a remarkable intellectual range. One minute, she was happy to talk tits and ass; the next, she was dismantling a colleague's flimsy arguments. This little skirmish with Duffy was a mere warm-up for someone of Fifi's abilities. Still, there was a point in all their discussions when Duffy had to decide whether his friend was angry or simply enjoying the verbal ping pong. He decided there was a definite note of irritation in Fifi's voice, so he shifted the conversation to someone they both disliked.

"Who did Lillidew invite to campus this time?" asked Duffy.

"Harrison Dewlap."

Duffy nodded. "You're right, Dewlap is a dink."

"He and Lillidew are both dinks," said Fifi. "In fact, they're the worst kind of dinks: *pseudo-intellectual* dinks."

Dr. Rufus Lillidew was a professor of political science. While participating in a student-radio debate several years earlier, he had become enraged over what he described as a "wave of wokeness" washing over university campuses and drowning out conservative voices.

"We live in an age of affirmative intolerance!" he'd thundered into his microphone.

No one quite new what *affirmative intolerance* meant, least of all Lillidew himself, but the expression had gone viral on social media. Pretty soon the internet was full of memes, GIFs and merchandise emblazoned with the words. Many on both the right and the left adopted the slogan as their rallying cry, accusing one another of co-opting its true meaning. One person who'd embraced the conservative interpretation was Harrison Dewlap.

A blogger, part-time pastor and frequent pundit on Christian radio, Dewlap claimed to have a PhD in theological anthropology. When pressed by a journalist, he'd been forced to admit that what he had was an honorary doctorate from an evangelical seminary in the Netherlands (which, as the journalist pointed out, did not have the authority to bestow graduate degrees). That didn't stop Dewlap from using the title of "Dr." to support his books and speaking engagements. He usually appeared at Bible colleges and gatherings of the religious right, but he occasionally wangled an invitation to speak at a public university like Sir Middling U.

"So, what's Dewlap going to talk about when he's here?" asked Duffy.

"He's got a new book out called *A Monumental Disgrace: The War Against History*. It's basically a bigot's defence of military and colonial statuary."

"Have you read it?"

Fifi glared at Duffy again. He realized, too late, that he had tacked and jibed once too often and was now heading back towards choppy water.

"Of course, I read it," said Fifi, her voice smouldering with a mix of scorn and defensiveness. "I'm a professional scholar. I do my research before I shred the so-called arguments of a hatemonger like Harrison Dewlap."

Duffy wanted to leave it there, but he felt bad about making light of a topic that Fifi cared deeply about. As a communications man, he gravitated to surface-level banter—a safe zone where he was unlikely to offend others, or worse, commit himself to a firm position. It was a far cry from the earnest, debate-loving philosophy student he'd once been, but it was an approach that had served him well in his chosen career.

"Listen, Feef," he said. "Rather than shut Dewlap and Lillidew down, why not hold an alternative event with a panel of real scholars? I'm sure it would draw a bigger crowd than what Dewlap's going to get, and better news coverage."

Fifi's glare softened. "Not a bad idea. But you need to put some skin in the game. I'm tired of people proposing ideas but not sticking around for the heavy lifting. You get Blunt and Kiljoy to back the event and maybe I'll forgive you for all the stupid things you just said."

"Whoa!" said Duffy. "I'll raise the idea with them, but you're the one who has to pitch it. It'll have no credibility coming from the PR guy. Why don't you kick the idea around with the student and faculty diversity groups and come up with a plan."

The scowl on Dubé's face gave way to a smile.

"Duffy, you're not as shallow as you let on," she said.

"Thank you."

"But you know what?"

"What?"

"You better make a move on Sophie Munn before someone else does."

Chapter 9

When Duffy received Blunt's blessing to speak with the president of SMUFA, he emailed Sylvia Kiljoy to request a meeting. Two days later, her executive assistant responded.

"Dr. Kiljoy is extremely busy," wrote Theresa Kenilworth. "Tell me what you want and I'll decide if it's worth mentioning to her."

Duffy had learned over time that there was a certain kind of university staff member who, like servants in a royal household, adopted a tone more superior than that of their academic masters. When he encountered such haughty minions, he reminded himself that within the labyrinthine corridors of academe, one is always playing the long game.

"Thanks for your email!" he replied, deploying an exclamation mark like a cheery smile. "Dr. Blunt has asked me to speak directly with Dr. Kiljoy. A half hour should suffice, preferably this week. Would you please set that up? Many thanks!"

The assistant responded a day later: "Dr. Kiljoy has fifteen minutes this Thursday at four o'clock. Be punctual."

So much for cheery punctuation, thought Duffy.

As he prepared to leave for his meeting with the head of the faculty union, Duffy realized that he had never been to the SMUFA office. He checked the campus directory to confirm its location. When he'd first joined Sir Middling U, the faculty association had been clamouring for space in Founders Hall. ("To be closer to the power centre," Kiljoy had argued.) After occupying their new premises for six months, the union executive decided they weren't "comfortable" with how often they crossed paths with administration officials in the corridors and washrooms of Founders Hall. ("It's like they're spying on us," Kiljoy had complained.) To mollify the faculty association, Clive Blunt persuaded his colleagues on the president's executive team to pay for another SMUFA relocation. He took budget money earmarked for a long-promised staff lunchroom and used it to move the SMUFA office back to its original space, beside the Sir Middling U faculty club.

Three years on, Duffy had lost track of the various moves.

"Terri, is the faculty association still located next to the faculty club?" he asked.

Coyne looked up from her computer. "It was yesterday."

"You couldn't just say, 'Yes, James, it's still there'?"

"When it comes to the faculty union, I don't assume anything."

"That's actually a good point."

As Duffy pulled on his leather jacket, Coyne wheeled her chair in front of the door to block his exit.

"Before you enter the lion's den," she said, "do you know how to pronounce the name of Kiljoy's receptionist?"

"Of course," said Duffy. "It's Theresa Kenilworth."

Coyne smiled and shook her head as if to say, "Oh, you poor schmuck."

"Her first name is spelled *Theresa*," she said. "But she pronounces it the Italian way."

"What?"

"Apparently the Italians say, '*Teh-**ray**-zzza*.'"

63

"*Tay-reeza?*"

"No, no," said Coyne. "Emphasize the middle syllable and linger on the last: *Teh-**ray**-zzza.*"

"*Teraz-uh?*" said Duffy.

"No!" scolded Coyne. "Put the emphasis on the 'ray' and linger on the 'zzza.' *Teh-**ray**-zzza.*"

"*Tay-ray-za?*"

"*Teh-**ray**-zzza.*"

"Hmmm," said Duffy. "I don't think that's how the Italians pronounce Theresa."

"Maybe not, but that's how *Signora* Kenilworth pronounces it."

"I didn't know she was Italian."

"She's not. But she visited Rome once on a tour of Europe. When she got back, she began saying *ciao* and calling herself *Teh-**ray**-zzza.*"

Duffy shook his head, a mix of disbelief and amusement.

"Any other words of wisdom before I leave?" he asked.

"*Buona fortuna!*"

For the entire fifteen-minute walk to the SMUFA office, Duffy practiced saying *Teh-**ray**-zzza*. When he arrived, the first thing he saw was the executive assistant's nameplate on her desk: *Theresa Kenilworth, BA.*

"Hi, Theresa," said Duffy, the English pronunciation flying across his lips before his brain could pull it back.

Kenilworth scowled with storm-dark eyes—the only thing about her that looked remotely Italian.

"I'm sorry," said Duffy. "It's *Teh-**ray**-zzza*, right?"

By the icy cast of the woman's glare, Duffy guessed that forgiveness was not part of her social tool kit. The executive assistant picked up her phone, pressed an extension number and, in a frosty tone, said, "Dr. Kiljoy, your four o'clock is here."

Duffy looked for a seat as far from the reception desk as possible. He spotted a stylish leather chair that reminded him of the new furniture in the Fundraising and Alumni Office. He picked up a newsletter from the coffee table. It was a copy of *Rage!*, the faculty association's monthly bulletin.

The top story was an update on SMUFA committee appointments. It seemed that no one wanted to volunteer for the Student Mentorship working group. On the other hand, the Protest and Strike Readiness committee had more members than it needed. Elsewhere on the front page was the union president's monthly column, *Let Them Howl!*

"I'm angry!" it began. "Angry over injustice! Angry over privilege! Angry over the administration's refusal to raise faculty salaries in line with university inflation!"

Duffy chuckled. "University inflation" was a term used by faculty unions and administrators to explain to government why the cost of running a university always rose faster than the consumer price index. What Duffy admired, at least from a PR perspective, was that university inflation was partly fueled by the generous pay hikes awarded to full-time professors with each new contract. In addition to cost-of-living increases, faculty compensation included opaque bump-ups such as "progression through the ranks." All in, the combination had goosed salary increases above the CPI for several years running.

As he read Kiljoy's column, Duffy chuckled less and thought more about what Fifi had said about the cost savings to be had through amalgamation. His thinking was interrupted by a drill-sergeant voice.

"Let's not dilly-dally, Red," Kiljoy barked from her doorway. "I have work to do."

Duffy hadn't been called Red since elementary school. His old gym teacher had used that moniker as a shame-and-control tactic. Duffy wasn't a particularly wilful child, but his bright hair—more orange than red—had marked him for abuse. He assumed that Kiljoy's use of the same nickname was a similar attempt to knock him off balance and gain some sort of advantage.

"Let's make this a stand-up meeting," the union leader said as she closed the door behind Duffy. "I find meetings go faster if we don't get too comfortable."

Kiljoy took up a command position behind her desk, chin raised and arms crossed over her narrow chest. "So, spit it out," she said. "Why are you here?"

"In a word, amalgamation," replied Duffy, mustering what he hoped was a collegial smile.

"Go on," snapped Kiljoy.

"There's a fair bit of chatter on social media."

"And?"

"I'm doing an environmental scan for Dr. Meriwether to get a sense of how serious the issue is."

"And what have you learned?"

Duffy cleared his throat. "Well, that's why I'm here," he said. "I'm hoping we can share information. You know, sort of collaborate."

Kiljoy's eyes narrowed. "You go first. What have you got?"

Duffy took a moment to regroup. This was not going the way he'd hoped. He studied Kiljoy's face, searching its hardened landscape for an indication of how much she knew about the HIPE amalgamation drive. The woman's pronounced cheekbones and hawk-like nose reminded him of a photograph he had once seen of a beardless Abraham Lincoln. The image knocked his train of thought off the rails. He felt himself twitch, as if he were waking up from a disturbing dream.

"Hello? Hello?" said Kiljoy, snapping her fingers in front of Duffy's face. "Are you still here?"

"Yes, of course," he stammered. "I was just marshalling my thoughts."

"Let me save you the trouble. As usual, you know pathetically little about the topic at hand. I'm willing to share what the faculty association is hearing, but only up to a point. If I get the slightest sense that you and your pals at Founders Hall are keeping anything from me, I'll launch a social-media storm that will paralyse the administration for the next three months."

"Fair enough," replied Duffy, who saw nothing fair about it. "So, what can you tell me?"

Kiljoy let some air out of her aggressive stance. She uncrossed her arms, let her shoulders relax and dialled down her bellicose tone from ten to eight.

"Rose Samaroo has been working with Bud Walters at the Ministry of Higher Education," she began. "They're trying to persuade the government to let HIPE swallow Sir Middling whole. Samaroo hired a consulting firm to work up a financial analysis, which they're calling the Walters Report. It claims that amalgamation could save more than a hundred million dollars annually in labour costs and operational efficiencies. Samaroo hopes the savings will be split between HIPE and the province. The result would be one well-funded university in place of two underfunded ones, with plenty left over for the government to spend on other priorities."

"Holy hell!" gasped Duffy. "How many jobs would be lost?"

"Nearly half of Sir Middling's faculty through buyouts and early retirements. HIPE can't just eliminate academic programs all at once; they'll need to wind them down over two or three years to let our students finish their degrees."

"What about support staff?"

"Seventy percent laid off in the first year, and more after that."

"Wow," said Duffy. "How far along is this?"

"I've heard that Samaroo and Walters have made two presentations to government: one to the deputy ministers of higher education and finance, the other to the premier's chief of staff."

"What's the government saying?"

"The deputy ministers love it—one less university to deal with, plus a huge pot of budget savings. But they're not the ones who have to worry about the political fallout. That's what the premier's major-domo is trying to work out."

"Giles Prigg?"

"Yes," replied Kiljoy. "You know him?"

"A little. We crossed paths when I worked in the minister's office. He's very smart."

"Cunning is the word I'd use."

Duffy nodded his agreement. "So, doctor, do you have a copy of the Walters Report?"

Sylvia Kiljoy eyed Duffy suspiciously, deciding just how much to share with this errand boy from the dark side.

"Not officially," she said. "HIPE and the government have it locked down tight."

"But someone's out there stirring it up on social media," said Duffy.

"That could be Samaroo. She's probably trying to build support with business leaders and taxpayer groups. Meanwhile, the premier's office is staying mum while it figures out the politics."

"That sounds about right," said Duffy. "What's the faculty association thinking?"

"That we don't want to get screwed."

Duffy was pleased to hear the SMUFA view put so plainly, but he tried not to let it show. Kiljoy—whose rust-coloured pantsuit and nest of grey hair declared how little she cared for appearances—had no such inclination.

"Listen, bucko," she growled, standing ramrod straight again. "You tell Meriwether and Blunt that we're in this together. They either shit or get off the pot."

"Meaning?"

"Meaning we need a joint strategy, *pronto*."

Duffy was startled by how fast Kiljoy had reverted to her take-charge self. He was also alarmed by the thrill of excitement it stirred in his loins. The union president was a plain-looking woman, somewhere in her mid-forties, but her fierce vitality exuded more than a hint of erotic allure.

"I'll get right on it," Duffy found himself saying.

"You do that, Red."

As Duffy turned to leave, he remembered his promise to Fifi.

"One other thing," he said. "What does the faculty association think about Professor Lillidew bringing Harrison Dewlap to campus?"

"Rufus Lillidew is a lightweight stooge, and Harrison Dewlap is a bigoted con artist. What more is there to say?"

"Some faculty are angry that one of their colleagues is bringing a guy like Dewlap to speak at Sir Middling U."

"I don't like it either," said Kiljoy. "But there's this thing called freedom of speech. It's generally thought to apply on university campuses, even at this institution."

"Yes, of course. I'm not talking about cancelling the Dewlap lecture. In fact, there's a proposal floating around to hold an alternative event—a panel discussion with more reputable scholars. Would SMUFA support something like that?"

"Normally, yes," said Kiljoy. "But haven't we got enough on our plates right now? The very people Samaroo is courting in business and government probably agree with the likes of Dewlap and Lillidew. They already see Sir Middling U as a third-rate university full of social-justice warriors. Now is not the time to pick a fight over a side issue."

Duffy was taken aback. "I don't think many faculty members would consider social justice a side issue."

Kiljoy's menacing gaze drilled deep into Duffy's pale blue eyes.

"Listen to me, mister PR man," she said, wagging a bony finger in Duffy's face. "I've spent my career fighting for social justice. But what's needed now is *realpolitik,* not group hugs and hot cocoa. Stay focused on amalgamation, Red. If we don't stop that, social justice is the least of our worries."

Duffy felt chastised, and a little aroused. He slid his satchel around to the front of his pants.

"I understand," he said.

"Good. Now scram. I've got grown-up work to do."

Chapter 10

As Duffy was driving to work the next day, the co-hosts of the *Yawnbury in the Morning* radio show were engaged in their usual empty-headed banter.

- "Hey, Jane, the weatherman—or should I say, weatherperson?—is calling for some of the white stuff."
- "Oh, Don, you're such a dinosaur!"
- "Guilty as charged, amigo!"
- "Well, Señor Don-o-saur, I don't care if you're politically incorrect—just let me keep my fireman calendar!"
- "Oh, Jane, you naughty girl!"

Duffy jabbed at the on/off button until the radio went silent. The inane chatter drove him crazy, but it was the mention of "white stuff" that had sent a chill up his spine. He had nothing against winter. In fact, there were few things he loved more than a simple walk in gently falling snow. It was tranquil and soothing, far more effective at calming a troubled mind than any of his anxiety meds.

Duffy's only problem with winter was that one of his duties was to monitor the forecast for the kind of major snowstorm that might require the campus to close.

In his first year at Sir Middling U, he'd been surprised to learn that the university had no protocol for deciding when to shut down due to winter storms.

"We just kinda wing it," the director of operations had said.

Being new and eager, Duffy set out to draft a bad-weather policy. He contacted several other universities to find out how they handled snowstorms. With examples in hand, he developed a set of procedures to help Sir Middling U's senior leaders decide when to close the campus. He sent the draft to Blunt but received no response. Two weeks later, he asked Sophie to add his proposal to the agenda of the next meeting of the president's executive team. More silence. After a month, Duffy decided to proceed as if the protocol had been approved. When the first snowstorm of the season was forecast, he re-sent the procedures to Meriwether, Blunt and the director of campus operations, along with a short note: "I suggest a conference call at 5:30 a.m. to make a decision about the day ahead." The email drew a quick response from Meriwether. "Love the proactive approach! I'll delegate the decision-making to Clive. Good luck, gents!"

Blunt was furious. As he often did, he aimed his anger at the director of communications.

"Don't you *ever* show initiative again, James!"

Things went from bad to worse. Blunt ignored Duffy's advice about the impending winter storm. Instead of closing the university, he kept it open. By mid-morning, a once-in-a-decade blizzard had buried Yawnbury under a metre of snow. The storm of outrage that followed—from faculty, students and parents—was far worse than the blizzard itself. The next time the weather office mused about dicey weather, Blunt vowed not to repeat his mistake. Without consulting Duffy or the director of campus operations, he decided to close the university pre-emptively. The next morning, dawn broke clear and sunny. Many in the Sir Middling community welcomed the day off; others—including professors who had scheduled exams, and co-op students with on-campus job interviews—did not. Social media hummed with ridicule and fury, and Blunt was deluged with angry calls and emails. He assigned Duffy the job of responding to all of them.

"Since you're so keen on protocols," snarled Blunt, "explain your weather policy to *these* people!"

Fueled by the memory, Duffy's anxieties began to simmer as he pondered the radio host's "white stuff" remark. He drove onto the university campus and parked his old four-door sedan—a "grandpa special," as Fifi called it—near the library. As he walked to the Communications Department, his gaze alternated between the late-fall sky and the weather app on his phone. There was no sign of snow in either place. Still, Duffy knew that he had crossed a critical line in his mental calendar. The prospect of snowstorms would haunt his days and disturb his sleep for the next four months.

"You have a visitor," said Terri Coyne.

"Friend or foe?" asked Duffy as he entered the office and took off his jacket and wool cap.

"Who can tell around this place?"

As Duffy passed through his doorless doorway, he found Bertie sitting in his chair and drooling on his desk. A string of milky slobber hung from the soft folds on each side of the basset hound's sorrowful face. Directly below his droopy jowls, a pool of spittle was gathering on top of the unopened parcel that contained Percy Mittens' volume of poetry. The package seemed to have been positioned strategically to catch the steady drip of saliva.

"I'm so sorry, James!" said Sophie Munn, rushing in with a roll of paper towels. "Bertie wouldn't get out of your chair, and he kept slobbering all over your desk. I just ran out to get something to mop it up with."

Duffy picked up the parcel by one corner; a string of drool slid off and pooled on his desk.

"Sorry about that too," said Sophie. "I needed something to catch the drip."

"No worries," said Duffy. "It seems Bertie is a good judge of poetry."

Sophie gave Duffy a quizzical look. He just smiled and pulled up a chair for her to sit on. He thought about lifting Bertie out of his own chair but decided that it might provoke more drool, or worse. Instead, Duffy slid two unopened boxes of alumni magazines next to his desk and lowered his bum on top.

"This is a nice surprise," he said. "Bertie has been to my office a few times, but I believe this is your first visit, Ms. Munn."

"You've never invited me," said Sophie.

"Well, as you can see, it's not the kind of place you bring a lady."

Sophie studied the long, dimly lit office. Her eyes came to rest on the strip of light near the ceiling at the far end of the room.

"Is that wall really just a stack of boxes?"

"Yes, it is."

"And the boxes don't quite reach the ceiling?"

"That's right."

The look on Sophie's face wasn't what Duffy had expected. He'd thought she would be amused or even sympathetic—*Oh, you poor dear!*—but instead, she looked slightly appalled, as if she'd just learned that Duffy was a fan of muscle shirts and monster trucks.

"Not very *feng shui*, is it?" she said.

Duffy gazed around his office. He had occupied this space for three years, long enough to forget how truly awful it was.

"Maybe it's too *feng shui*," he said. "I mean, isn't *feng shui* about arranging your personal space to reflect your inner self?"

"Not exactly," said Sophie. "It's about harmonizing a space and making it as auspicious as possible for the person who occupies it."

Duffy looked at Bertie, who continued to drool on the wad of paper towels.

"How about old Bertie here?" he said. "He looks pretty content. Do you think he's oriented in a harmonious and auspicious manner?"

"Don't be silly," said Sophie.

Duffy patted Bertie on the head. "Did you know that a basset hound's ears are called 'leathers'?"

"No, I didn't," replied Sophie. "And by the way, Bertie and I are here on business."

Duffy stood up and pulled the dog's floppy leathers out to each side.

"Go ahead. We're all ears."

Sophie gave Duffy a long-suffering look. It was spontaneous and natural, an expression that men had been inspiring in women for millennia. Duffy took the opportunity to admire Sophie's oval face, flawless skin and brown eyes. Her father's ancestors were Scots Gaelic; her mother was the child of Greek immigrants. The combination of light and dark enchanted Duffy. He thought about Fifi's advice. Maybe he *should* man up and ask Sophie out. Duffy was screwing up the courage to suggest dinner Friday night when Sophie explained the reason for her visit.

"Dr. Meriwether asked me to take Bertie for a walk and to see what you've learned about amalgamation."

"Ah, yes," said Duffy, sitting back down. "Well, I spoke to Sylvia yesterday."

"Sylvia?"

"Kiljoy," he said, feeling a blush of embarrassment rise in his cheeks.

"I don't think I've ever heard you call her Sylvia before."

Duffy tried to laugh it off. "Well, believe it or not, we actually had a good conversation."

"Really? Do tell."

Duffy tried to read between the lines, but Sophie's expression remained as sweetly inscrutable as ever.

"It seems Rose Samaroo has been pitching the government on amalgamation while using Bud Walters for cover. HIPE hired some big-city firm to cost out the savings, which could be more than a hundred million dollars a year. The premier's office is weighing the politics."

"What does *Sylvia* think?"

Duffy sensed a hint of subtext in Sophie's use of the union leader's first name. Best to ignore it, he decided.

"Kiljoy says she's willing to work with the administration. She's seen the Walters-HIPE report. It says amalgamation could eliminate fifty percent of Sir Middling's faculty over a few years, and seventy percent of staff and managers right off the bat."

"Wow," said Sophie. "Dr. Meriwether will want to hear this right away. He has a few minutes over the lunch hour. I'll book you in for twelve-thirty. How much of this do you think he knows already?"

"He's got a lot of contacts in government and at HIPE, so I'm sure he knows more than he let on the other day. I think he's hoping it'll go away if we just ignore it."

"What do you think?"

"If Samaroo's math is correct, we're in trouble. It'll be hard for government to resist saving a hundred million dollars a year."

"Have you talked to Dr. Blunt yet?"

"No, but this is going to get weird. Imagine me, Blunt and Kiljoy all working together."

Sophie gave a knowing nod. Then she looked at Bertie. "Speaking of weird, what's that sound?"

Duffy leapt up and lifted the old dog off his chair. Bertie's penis had escaped the pullups and was spraying urine left and right.

"For Pete's sake!" said Duffy, looking for somewhere to put the canine water hose.

He set Bertie down on a pile of Sir Middling U sweatshirts that were used by the marketing team for photo shoots. When he looked up, Sophie was holding the shipping envelope that contained Dr. Percy Mittens' book of poetry. It was soaked through.

"I hope this isn't important," she said.

"Not to me," replied Duffy.

Chapter 11

Dr. Rose Samaroo made a habit of arriving late to meetings. Not too late, just enough for her entrance to be noticed.

As she glided towards a table at the back of the HIPE faculty club, her lunch companions had plenty of opportunity to admire her long, graceful strides. All three set their drinks down and stood up as Samaroo approached.

"My dear Rose," said Ed Palavoy, president of the HIPE faculty association. "Fashionably late as usual."

"*Strategically* late," said Samaroo.

The others chuckled.

"Ah, there's nothing quite like the subtle jab of a stiletto," said Dr. Hugh Endicott, president of HIPE.

"Oh, Ed and I are old friends," said Samaroo, giving Palavoy a tepid pat on the hand. "We have our management-union battles, but we keep it professional."

"Of course, we do," said Palavoy, summoning a smile as bright and insincere as the one that adorned the face of his elegant colleague.

The other guest, Bud Walters, was no stranger to office politics. He had spent much of his career jousting with colleagues in the Ministry of Higher Education. Those battles, however, were mere squabbles compared to the guerrilla warfare waged in most universities. Insults and slights, both real and perceived, could simmer for years in academia, spawning alliances, intrigues and reprisals as intense as those of medieval Venice.

"What is it they say?" mused Walters. "Academic politics are so fierce because the stakes are so small?"

"Something like that," said Endicott. "But the issue we're here to talk about is an exception."

"Indeed," said Samaroo, patting Palavoy on the hand again. "Ed here is hoping that if he plays ball on amalgamation, we might just find him a more lucrative job in administration."

"That's *not* what I meant," said Endicott. "Ignore these two, Bud, and bring us up to speed on amalgamation. What does the province think of our proposal?"

"Yes, Bud, what's the latest?" asked Samaroo, leaning past Palavoy to address Walters. "My contacts in the premier's office keep me informed, but I'd *love* to get your take on things."

Walters was determined to stay out of whatever battle was brewing between Samaroo and Palavoy. He turned to Endicott and said: "I'll cut to the chase, Hugh. Earlier this week, I met with the deputy ministers in finance and higher education. They're still on board. And they're keeping their ministers out of the loop, at the request of the premier's office. But the real news is on the political side: the premier's chief of staff is now leaning towards amalgamation."

"Leaning?" said Palavoy. "What does that mean?"

Walters took a sip of his gin and tonic. "Giles Prigg has done a preliminary review of the politics. It seems that CLAP, the Corporate Leaders Advisory Panel, is supportive. But there's concern at the municipal level. The Post-Secondary Mayors'

Alliance got wind of our report. Now every university town in the province is worried that the amalgamation of HIPE and Sir Middling U is just the tip of the iceberg. A university provides a community with a thousand or more well-paying jobs. It also generates millions of dollars in annual economic spinoffs. No mayor is going to give that up without a fight."

"Is the premier considering other amalgamations?" asked Endicott.

"Possibly. Which brings me to my other piece of news: Prigg plans to appoint a special advisor to evaluate the HIPE-Sir Middling proposal. The advisor's mandate also includes a review of the whole post-secondary system."

"Good Lord!" said Endicott. "Why?"

"Ass-covering," said Samaroo. "A special advisor can float trial balloons. The premier can disavow the ones that get shot down and take credit for the ones that stay aloft."

"Exactly," said Walters.

"I'm okay with a special advisor as long as it isn't some jumped-up little twit from ERPI," said Endicott. "Those guys love to mess with things."

The Education Research Policy Institute— ERPI for short—was a private think tank that looked for ways to align public education with economic prosperity. University faculty and administrators dismissed ERPI as being far too practical, but they rarely said so in public. The institute was, after all, financed by the same business leaders who donated to capital campaigns and university research.

"God forbid that it's Dev Sharma," said Samaroo.

"Who's Dev Sharma?" asked Palavoy.

"He's the ERPI meddler who came up with the idea of tying university funding to accountability agreements," said Endicott. "A real stickler for transparency."

Walters took another sip of his G and T.

"Well, Bud, spit it out," said Palavoy. "Who's the special advisor?"

"It's only speculation at this point," said Walters.

"Well then, who's the frontrunner?" asked Samaroo.

"Dev Sharma."

Samaroo closed her eyes and lowered her head. Endicott slapped the table with his right hand and said, "Damn!" Walters finished his drink.

"What's Sharma's background?" asked Palavoy.

"He's a number-cruncher with an online PhD," said Samaroo. "He couldn't get a faculty position at a university, so he ended up at ERPI. God knows what he and his buddies smoke down there, but they certainly put the 'high' in higher education."

The quip fell flat, something new for Samaroo. She didn't like the silence that followed.

"Well," she conceded, "I suppose ERPI serves a purpose."

"There's more to Dev Sharma than you seem to think," said Walters. "The guy studied statistics and economics at U of T, and has an MBA from McGill. You can snigger at his PhD, but he earned it while working full-time as an advisor to the federal minister of science and technology. He turned his doctoral thesis into a well-received book, and he's published a number of policy papers about the role of higher education in economic prosperity."

"That may be," said Samaroo, "but if he hasn't worked in the academy, his accomplishments won't carry much weight with the professoriate."

Walters let out a wry chuckle.

"Excuse my bluntness," he said, "but neither the government nor the voters give a hoot about what the professoriate thinks. And if Dev Sharma comes up with a way to save millions of taxpayer dollars each year, they'll care even less."

Samaroo felt the sting of rebuke; Endicott jumped in before she could fire back.

"Bud, your candor is a virtue," he said.

"All part of the service," said Walters, rattling the ice in his empty glass.

Samaroo composed herself. "Let's get back to business. What does the Sharma appointment mean?"

"It means we may have lost control of Frankenstein's monster," said Endicott.

The faculty-club lunch wrapped up sooner than expected. Endicott and Palavoy rushed off to other meetings.

"Do you have time for a coffee?" Walters asked Samaroo.

"No, but I have time for you," she replied, her grace and diplomacy fully restored.

"So, you've forgiven my bluntness?"

"Almost," said Samaroo.

"Good. Because I must say, Rose, that you're one of the most intelligent and skilful administrators I've ever had the pleasure to work with."

"Why, thank you, Bud."

"Which is why I'm going to be frank with you again," said Walters, leaning forward as if to share a secret. "I've been proposing university amalgamation for twenty-five years. I've put my career on the line for it time and again. And do you know why? Because I care deeply about higher education. It has the unique potential to transform society for the better. Unfortunately, it's not living up to that potential. A bloated inertia has seeped into the system and gummed up the works. Amalgamation could help clean up the engine and get the pistons moving again. It could focus attention and resources on the essentials: cutting-edge research, quality teaching, career-oriented education. But to pull it off, it has to be done for the right reasons. So, Rose, my question for you is this: Why are *you* so keen on amalgamation?"

Samaroo, who could feign a good heart-to-heart with the best of them, wasn't expecting the impassioned tone in Walters' question.

"Well, Bud, that *is* candid."

"And your answer?"

"Because I think it's the right thing too," she said firmly. "HIPE is a good polytechnical institute, but it has the potential to be a great applied-research university. Not just a Canadian MIT, but outstanding in its own way—a trailblazer with a brand so distinct it defies comparison. I want to see it at the top of the QS and *Times Higher Ed* rankings some day. I want people in Silicon Valley and Boston and London to hear the name HIPE and nod knowingly. But to get there, it needs more money—*a lot* more. It also needs a world-class leader with extraordinary vision and drive."

"And you're that leader?" asked Walters.

Samaroo pulled her shoulders back and raised her chin like a monarch gazing upon her realm.

"Yes, Bud, I am."

Walters leaned back and smiled.

"Rose, that's exactly what I wanted to hear."

Chapter 12

Duffy could not remember ever meeting with Alexander Meriwether twice in one week. When he entered the president's office and found Clive Blunt there as well, he felt like Obi-Wan Kenobi sensing a disturbance in the Force.

"Hello, James!" said Meriwether. "Mind old Bertie, will you? The poor fella has some sort of bladder infection."

Duffy looked down to see the pitiable dog lying on the carpet and wearing diapers again.

"He's been dripping like a faucet," said Meriwether. "Goes through pullups faster than I can steal them from my grandson."

Duffy walked past the swaddled dog and took a seat across from Blunt.

"So, James," said Meriwether. "Catch us up on amalgamation. Sophie says you've had a chat with Sylvia Kiljoy."

"Yes, sir. We met yesterday."

Duffy proceeded to share what the faculty association president had told him, including her offer to join forces.

"I see," said Meriwether. "Does Sylvia have a copy of the

Walters Report?"

"She knows what's in it, but she was a little coy about whether she had a copy."

Blunt let out a harrumph. "We need to see that report," he demanded, as if it was Duffy's fault for not securing a copy already. "I don't like being a step behind the faculty association." He turned to the president. "Alex, there must be someone you know at the legislature who can get us a copy?"

"I certainly know people who could help," the president said. "The question is, Will they? Amalgamation is a hot potato. The government will have every copy of the report screwed down tight."

Duffy saw an opportunity to impress Meriwether and improve his chances of becoming an assistant vice-president. "I still have contacts in the minister's office," he said eagerly. "I'd be happy to reach out and see about getting a copy."

"Excellent," said Meriwether. "Just keep it discreet."

"What do we do in the meantime?" asked Blunt.

"Let's book a meeting with Sylvia," said Meriwether. "I'd like to read the Walters Report before we talk to her, but we may not have time. I'll ask Sophie to arrange a little chinwag."

"All right then," said Blunt, getting up to leave. "I have to get back to a budget report."

Duffy raised his hand. "I have one other matter, if you don't mind," he said. "I was wondering if either of you had any thoughts about the Harrison Dewlap lecture. Professor Lillidew is bringing him to campus next month to talk about historical monuments. Dewlap is bound to defend the statue of Sir Richard, and that's going to stir up a hornets' nest."

Blunt rolled his eyes and shook his head.

"No one takes Rufus Lillidew or Harrison Dewlap seriously," he said.

"I'm not so sure," replied Duffy. "Dewlap has a lot of followers on social media, and he knows how to whip them up. If that

85

happens, our students and faculty are going to make an issue out of his lecture—and that means more calls to remove the statue of Sir Richard and change the name of the university."

"That's exactly my point," said Blunt impatiently. "We don't want it to become a media issue, especially right now when we're dealing with this amalgamation nonsense. Just make the Harrison Dewlap kerfuffle go away, Duffy. Isn't that your job?"

Duffy hoped that Meriwether would chime in. When the president didn't, Duffy decided it was high time to be frank, if not bold.

"Just so we're clear," he said. "There *will* be media coverage of the Dewlap lecture; Lillidew will make sure of that, and so will opponents like *Le Collectif radical*. We need to develop our messaging ahead of time so that we're not scrambling to react to someone else's agenda."

Duffy stopped speaking to give Meriwether a chance to weigh in. When the president remained silent, Duffy plowed on.

"There's talk of holding an alternative event," he said, neglecting to add that it was his idea. "A panel discussion involving scholars with more credibility than Dewlap. From a PR perspective, I think the university should promote it. We could frame our support as the administration's willingness to engage with tough issues. It would also demonstrate Sir Middling's relevance—just the thing we need to fend off amalgamation."

The look on Blunt's face combined a childish pout with repressed adult fury.

"Oh, Duffy, you haven't got the wit to understand the complexity of the situation," he said. "Now is not the time to attract attention. We need to focus on saving the university from amalgamation, and that means quietly showing the government how vital Sir Middling is to the post-secondary system."

"By ignoring one of the most topical issues in higher education?" said Duffy.

"Don't be so dramatic," snapped Blunt. "Sir Middling U has always aimed to be squarely in the middle of the pack, neither leading nor trailing on any matter of substance. You could even say that's our *brand*, to borrow a buzzword from your world."

Duffy tried to imagine activating such a brand. Instead of chanting, "We're No. 1! We're No. 1!" students could yell, "We're in the middle! We're in the middle!"

He decided that now was not the time to argue the point.

"I *do* understand the complexity," said Duffy, struggling to keep his tone civil. "But the media are going to hammer us about Dewlap and the statue issue, whether we like it or not. If we keep our heads down and pretend the controversy doesn't exist, they're going to hammer us even harder. I'm proposing a way to mitigate the reputational damage *and* demonstrate Sir Middling's relevance. But we can only do that by setting the agenda, not reacting to it."

Meriwether finally spoke. "I see your point, James, but it's not without risk. If there is one thing I've learned as an academic leader, it's to avoid risk."

"Thank you, Alex," said Blunt, sitting up a little taller. "So, it's agreed: we let the Dewlap tempest blow past without comment, and we focus on showing the government how relevant we are."

Duffy wondered if Blunt had any idea how foolish he sounded. By taking no action on one of the most significant post-secondary issues of the time, Sir Middling U would somehow prove its relevance? As Duffy digested the irony, he wrestled with his own timidity. How far should I push the issue? he thought. On the one hand, he was certain that ignoring the coming storm was fraught with peril. On the other, he didn't want to say anything that would jeopardize his chance for promotion.

He turned to the president and chose his next words with care. "I hear you, Dr. Meriwether. There are certainly lots of factors to weigh, and communications is just one of them. Would you mind, though, if I drafted some messaging, just in case? As you say, it's about minimizing risk."

"Deftly played, James," said Meriwether, giving Duffy a slap on the knee. "By all means, draft some messaging. Just don't share it without my say-so."

"Yes, sir."

Blunt glared at Duffy like an old dog who'd just lost a bone to a precocious pup.

"A word of advice, James," he said sternly. "Values and principles are all well and good, but a true administrator knows when to be practical."

"Neither lead nor trail?" said Duffy.

"Exactly," replied Blunt.

Chapter 13

Duffy went straight back to his office and scrolled through the contact list on his phone. He hoped that Jill Kaiser—now chief of staff to the minister of higher education—would take his call. They hadn't worked together in three years. Duffy had tried to keep in touch, but Kaiser never seemed to get his messages.

He dialed her number. After six rings, he was about to hang up when his old boss came on the line.

"Hey, Pete, thanks for calling back," said Kaiser.

"Hi, Jill. It's James Duffy."

"Oh hell," she said. "I thought it was a policy guy from finance."

"How's life with the new minister? Is Anne Moreno as good as she seems?"

"Better. But get to the point, Duffy. I'm busy."

"Okay. It's about the Bud Walters Report."

"Amalgamation? Fuck me. I should have known."

"I need a copy of the report."

"No way. It's locked down. Every copy is numbered, and each one has a unique sentence to distinguish it from all the rest.

Any copy I sent you could be traced back to me like DNA at a crime scene."

"There's always a safe copy, Jill. You taught me that. Besides, our faculty association managed to get hold of one. The report's out there, and the media are going to be calling both of us any day now. Send me a copy and I'll coordinate messaging with you."

"Goddamn it, Duffy! How did the union at Ass Scratch U get hold of the report?"

"It's Sir Middling U, actually. Our faculty association got a copy because they work closely with the faculty association at HIPE. Union solidarity and all that."

There was silence on the line. Duffy wondered if his old boss had hung up or simply walked away. He'd seen her do both before.

"Jill, are you still there?"

"Of course, I'm still here, dickhead. What makes you so sure the media are going to get wind of this?"

"There's amalgamation talk on social media and graffiti on the butt of Sir Dickie's horse."

"I'm not even going to ask what that means," said Kaiser.

"It means it's out there, Jill. People are talking about the amalgamation report. It's only a matter of time before the media start calling."

Duffy could hear another conversation going on in the background at Kaiser's end, punctuated by a burst of laughter.

"Would you morons shut the fuck up!" Kaiser yelled, with no attempt to cover her phone.

"Everything okay, Jill?"

"No, Duffy, it's not. And you just turned my day from shit to full-on diarrhea."

"So, nothing's changed in your world?"

"That's right. I'm still up to my ass in fuck-wads like you."

"But I'm one of the good fuck-wads, right?" said Duffy, a note of genuine hope in his voice.

"Shut up and listen," said Kaiser. "I'm going to have someone courier you an early draft of the Walters Report. There are no major changes between it and the current working copy, but it's not as traceable."

"You're an amazing human being, Jill."

"Don't be such a suck up, Duffy. Now, in return for this huge favour, I need two things from you. First, you call me the second you hear anything about amalgamation in the local media down there in Hicksville. And second, do *not* mention my name or brag about how you got a copy. If you do, I will get you fired from that backwater shithole and make sure you never get a decent job again. *Capische?*"

"No, but I understand."

"Don't try to be funny, Duffy, because you're not. You'll get the report tomorrow."

"Listen, Jill, I really appreciate it. Honest. Hey, next time I'm in the city—Hello? Jill?"

Duffy's next call was to Sophie Munn.

"Office of the President, how may I help you?"

"Hey, Sophie, it's me."

"Me who?"

"The suave guy over in Communications."

"I know a guy in Communications, but I'm not sure I'd describe him as suave."

"You might if you went out for a drink with him."

"Sounds like you're asking me out."

"This Friday. Drinks and tapas at Don Lorenzo's."

"Sorry. I'm booked Friday."

"Really?"

"Yes, James, really."

"Right, of course. How about Saturday night?"

"Busy again. But you can take me to brunch on Sunday."

Brunch was good, thought Duffy. Daytime was better than

nighttime for a first date—no post-dinner expectations, no "come up for a nightcap" awkwardness. Not that Duffy would mind if Sophie did the asking; he just didn't want to initiate things himself. Dating was a minefield, even when you were perfectly clear in asking permission. Duffy was totally on board with clarity—Can I kiss you? Do you want to have sex?—but it was still tricky, no matter what people said. Fifi would call him a wimp, but she would also be the first to call him to account.

"Perfect," he told Sophie. "Let's meet at the Art Haus Café at eleven. I'll make a reservation."

"They don't take reservations."

"Right. Well, let's just meet there and hope for the best."

"Is that why you called? To ask me out?"

"Yes, of course," Duffy fibbed. "That and another thing: Would you tell Dr. Meriwether that I'll have a copy of the Walters Report tomorrow?"

"Wow! How did you pull that off?"

"Hey, come on, I'm a man with connections."

"Really? Can you get me tickets to see Beyoncé?"

"No, but I can get passes to the next Muskrats basketball game."

"Sorry, not my cup of tea. Why don't you take your new friend, Sylvia?"

Duffy went silent. Why do women do this? he thought. Sophie was just teasing him, of course, but she was obviously paying attention to his interaction with other women. That's a good thing, isn't it? Still, he hated navigating this kind of fog-cloaked terrain. What was wrong with good old-fashioned clarity? Like, Do you have the hots for Sylvia Kiljoy?

On second thought, maybe clarity was overrated.

"I don't think Kiljoy's a sports fan," replied Duffy.

"Really? She's got a dominatrix thing going on, don't you think?"

Dominatrix thing? Where the hell is this coming from? Now Duffy had the image of a leather-clad Kiljoy stuck in his head. He wouldn't be able to look at the president of the faculty association the same way again.

"That's an intriguing thought," he said. "But I'd rather not dwell on it."

"Hey, that gives me an idea," said Sophie. "We should go see Fifi Dubé's burlesque show sometime. I hear she's performing at Fetchez la Vache later this month."

Good Lord, thought Duffy. What is Sophie doing? An odd feeling filled his chest and throat, a tingling infused with lust, guilt and confusion. It was like the time his grade-seven teacher, Sister Renata, had fainted and the whole class had gotten a glimpse of her panties as she lay on the floor. The young nun's underthings were bright red, a detail that had remained alive in Duffy's memory ever since.

"Burlesque isn't my cup of tea," he said.

"Really? I thought a man as suave as you would have a regular table at Fifi's show."

The tingling got worse; the ground beneath Duffy's feet turned from solid rock to fine sand. Does Sophie think I'm attracted to Fifi too? Is that a good thing? He decided to turn the tables.

"Fifi asked me if you were dating someone," he said.

"Did she? Well, well. What did you say?"

"I said I didn't know. Are you?"

"Hey, a gal needs to keep up a little mystery, right?"

Duffy wasn't good with mystery, especially when it came to relationships. He thought of women the way Churchill had thought of Russia: a riddle, wrapped in a mystery, inside an enigma. The truth was, Duffy thought about women all the time: Sophie, Fifi, Kiljoy, Sister Renata, the barista at Sir Dickie's.... It was an enjoyable pastime, but not very instructive. Women (and his infatuation with them) remained a beguiling conundrum for Duffy.

"How did this conversation take such a weird turn?" he asked.

"It doesn't seem weird to me," said Sophie. "You asked me out, finally, and I accepted."

Duffy felt like he was playing chess with a grandmaster, and getting his ass whipped.

"Yes, of course," he said. "And on that pleasant note, I should get back to work."

"Okay," said Sophie. "So, I will tell Dr. Meriwether about the Walters Report, and you will meet me for brunch Sunday morning at the Art Haus Café."

This is where Duffy would normally have put on a Scottish accent and said something like, "Ah, Moneypenny, you're the only girl for me." But he was too unsettled to flirt.

"Sounds good," he said. "Thanks."

"Thanks?"

"I mean, you know, thanks for letting Alex know about the report."

"And?"

"And I can't wait to see you Sunday."

"Nice save, Mr. Suave."

Chapter 14

The Bud Walters Report arrived by courier the next afternoon. Duffy pushed aside all of the papers on his desk, including the coffee- and urine-stained parcel from Sir Richard Middling University Press. He tried to open the report package with the blade of his Swiss Army knife, a prized possession that he always kept close at hand. The knife had been a gift from his father, part of the old man's "always be prepared" approach to life. The classic red-handled utility tool had been Duffy's constant companion since he was twelve. He had used it to cut fishing line, sharpen pencils, trim guitar strings and chop marijuana leaves. Once, he'd even used it to scare off an aggressively drunk fan who'd mounted the stage during one of his cover-band gigs. Mostly, however, Duffy used the knife as a worry stone, clutching and rubbing the smooth handle when his anxieties were running high.

The courier envelope was made of tougher material than Duffy first realized. He was having trouble slicing through it with the knife blade, so he pulled out the tiny scissors and cut it open, snip by snip. The Walters Report slid out and landed on his desk.

It was shorter than he expected: just eighteen pages, each stamped CONFIDENTIAL. The report contained text, financial tables, staffing charts, enrolment projections and a summary of the original legislative acts that gave birth to HIPE and to Sir Middling U.

The cover page bore a title that Duffy couldn't help but admire for its opacity: *Cost and Resource Coalescence in the Post-Secondary System (CARCPSS)*.

"CARC-PISS!" he said out loud for his own amusement.

Just then, Terri Coyne appeared in his doorway.

"Did you say, 'carp piss?'" she asked.

Duffy looked up from the report.

"No, I didn't," he said. "And when I'm sitting at my desk, please pretend that *if* I had a door, it would be closed."

"Okay, grumpy pants," said Coyne. "But when I hear you talking to yourself about carp piss, I worry that you might be losing it."

Duffy made a sweeping motion with his right hand. "That's me closing my door," he said.

Coyne flipped him the bird. "That's me saying goodbye."

Duffy turned back to the report and began reading the executive summary. It confirmed what Kiljoy had told him earlier in the week: folding Sir Middling U into HIPE would save the government more than one hundred million dollars annually, after buyouts and other one-time costs. Savings of this magnitude could be used to fund other government priorities *and* help make HIPE an international-calibre university. The report proposed eliminating 50 percent of Sir Middling U's faculty over a five-year period; the number of support staff and managers would be cut by 70 percent through layoffs in the first year alone, with more to follow in year two.

"Jesus, Joseph and Mary," muttered Duffy.

He picked up his phone and called Fifi.

"Hey, Feef. Have you got twenty minutes?"

"No. Who is this?"

"Seriously. You'll thank me."

"Yeah, okay. I'm in my office."

"See you soon."

Duffy slipped into his jacket and rushed out of the Communications office. Halfway down the hall he realised that he'd left the Walters Report behind. When he went back to fetch it, he found Coyne sitting at his desk, munching on an apple and flipping through the amalgamation proposal.

"This is a bummer," she said without looking up.

"Yes, it is. But the real question is this: Do you often sit at my desk reading documents that are marked confidential?"

"Most of your stuff isn't this interesting," said Coyne.

"So, you *do* sit at my desk and read stuff?" asked Duffy.

"Of course. How else would I know what you're working on?"

"Maybe you could wait until I told you what I thought you needed to know?"

"Ha! That's a good one. You don't tell me anything."

Duffy liked Coyne, most of the time. She was even-tempered, did his budgeting and HR paperwork and generally kept the office running. She was also the central clearinghouse for campus gossip. As Sophie had once said, "If Terri Coyne doesn't know about it, it didn't happen." Duffy valued having a well-informed assistant. Information was power, after all. But sometimes, like right now, he knew it was a disaster waiting to happen.

"Listen, Terri. My bad for leaving the report out in the open. But it *is* confidential and you really can't tell anyone about it."

Coyne pinched her thumb and forefinger together and made a zipping motion across her lips. "You can trust me, boss."

"I guess I have to, at least with this. But I'm serious, Terri. You can't tell *anyone* about this report. It's just a draft, and it probably won't go anywhere. If rumours start to spread, it'll cause a shitstorm for all of us."

"Of course, my liege."

Duffy took the report and slid it into his satchel. As he was about to head out again, Coyne said, "You know what they say about revolutions and amalgamations, don't you?"

"No, Terri, I don't. What do they say?"

"They shoot the officers first."

Duffy knocked on Fifi's office door.

"It's locked," she shouted. "Give me a second."

Duffy could hear what sounded like furniture being moved and an indistinct shuffling. A minute later, the lock clicked and the door swung open.

"Come on in," said Fifi, a little out of breath.

Duffy stayed rooted to the threshold.

Fifi was dressed in black tights and a sports bra, a combination that accentuated her lean body and put her taut midriff on full display. Her feet were bare and her neck glistened with sweat. She had turned away from the door and was bent over, rolling up a foam mat; her shapely bottom was hard to ignore. When Duffy didn't come in, Fifi looked up and saw a mix of distress and lust lighting up his pale cheeks and blue eyes.

"For God's sake, Duffy. I was just doing yoga."

"In your office?"

"I had divisional council this morning and missed my yoga class."

Duffy stayed where he was. Fifi put her hands on her hips and shook her head.

"You look like one of the losers who sit at the back of a burlesque show—the kind who like to watch but are too chicken to sit in the front row."

"Sorry," said Duffy. "I just wasn't expecting to see you half naked in your office."

"I'm not half naked. I'm wearing workout gear."

"To me, you look half naked."

"Well, isn't that typically male?"

"I suppose it is. But I am male, after all, and pretty typical."

"That's no excuse for being a gormless voyeur. Get in here and shut the door."

Fifi grabbed a hoodie and started to pull it on. She stopped suddenly and threw it on the desk.

"You know what, Duffy? I shouldn't have to cover up in my own office just because you get horny and uncomfortable looking at a woman in workout clothes. You wanna look at my ass and boobs? Go right ahead."

Chastened, Duffy walked in and sank into the old club chair.

"So, perv, why are you here?" asked Fifi.

"Two reasons. First, I got my hands on a copy of the Bud Walters Report."

"Wow, I'm impressed."

"Really?"

"Well, *mildly* impressed. Who'd you get it from?"

"I can't say. Just a contact."

"Oooh, the voyeur has contacts," Fifi mocked. "Well spit it out, bucko. What does it say?"

"You were right. There's a lot of money to be saved by amalgamating the two universities."

"How many jobs will be lost?"

Duffy didn't answer. A bead of sweat on Fifi's neck had caught his eye. The glistening droplet was trickling slowly towards her breastbone. From there, Duffy imagined, it would have an unimpeded run to the considerable cleavage that rose up from the top of Fifi's sports bra.

"Oh, for God's sake, Duffy!" said Fifi, grabbing the hoodie from her desk and pulling it on.

"Sorry," he said meekly. "There was a bead of sweat… "

Fifi shook her head, a gesture of despair and resignation.

"What was the question again?" asked Duffy.

"Jobs, horny man! How many jobs will be cut?"

"About what Kiljoy said. Fifty percent of faculty by attrition over five years, and 70 percent of support staff and managers in the first year."

"Those cold-hearted bastards," said Fifi. "So, Sir Middling U would just disappear into the belly of the beast?"

"Pretty much. The report says HIPE owns plenty of undeveloped land for expansion, so they wouldn't need to keep the Sir Middling U campus. It recommends demolishing the buildings, selling the land and using the proceeds to top up HIPE's endowment."

"Holy crap!" said Fifi. "I didn't think about the land. They want to wipe out any reminders of Sir Middling U."

"Why would they to do that?"

"Cultural genocide, my friend. The conqueror eliminates all physical, cultural and symbolic representations of the conquered. That way there's nothing left for the vanquished to regroup around. Eventually, people will just forget that Sir Middling U ever existed."

Duffy pondered this for a moment.

"They could demolish the buildings, I suppose. None of them have heritage designations. But they wouldn't be allowed to demolish the statue of Sir Richard Middling and his horse. That was a gift from the Middling Trust, and the last of the Middlings—a great-granddaughter, I think—still keeps in touch with the university's fundraising office."

Fifi started to laugh.

"What?" asked Duffy.

"Don't you see the irony? The one thing that should be torn down—the statue of the university's bigoted namesake—could be the only thing left standing."

"Let's not give HIPE or the government any ideas," said Duffy. "If they latch onto the social-justice angle, they might argue that amalgamation is as much about righting a wrong as it is about cost savings and efficiency."

"But you *do* think the statue should come down, right?" asked Fifi.

"I'm leaning that way," said Duffy, borrowing a phrase from Alexander Meriwether. "But I'd prefer that the issue of Sir Dickie's legacy be dealt with on its own, not co-opted to help justify amalgamation."

"A little wishy-washy, Duffy, but your moral compass is definitely improving."

"I'll take that as a compliment."

"What was the second thing you wanted to tell me?"

"I spoke to Kiljoy, Meriwether and Blunt about the Harrison Dewlap lecture."

"And?"

"They're okay with the idea of an alternative event, but they won't endorse it."

"Let me guess. They don't want to draw attention to Sir Middling U while the amalgamation talk is heating up?"

"That's about it," said Duffy. "For what it's worth, I tried to convince them that the Dewlap lecture is going to attract negative press anyway, so they might as well do the right thing and support the panel discussion."

"And they still didn't go for it?"

"Nope. Meriwether said to let you know that he isn't opposed to the panel discussion, he just doesn't want the university to promote it publicly."

Fifi's eyes blazed. "Meriwether is a classic political weasel. You know, *not necessarily conscription, but conscription if necessary.*"

"Is that Churchill?"

"No, Duffy. That's Mackenzie King! Don't you know your Canadian history?"

"Not well enough, apparently."

"What did you study again?"

"Philosophy and journalism."

"Oh, right. My condolences."

"Listen, Feef, I did try to convince them. The more I think about this Dewlap lecture, the more I think it's going to blow up on the university."

"I couldn't care less if it blows up. What I care about is diversity and inclusion, intelligent and informed debate, and taking an honest look at our history and our monuments to make sure we're honouring the right things."

"I hear you."

Fifi took a long look at her friend.

"I'm not sure that you do," she said, sounding more concerned than critical. "You're looking at the statue and namesake issue from a PR perspective, like it was just another issue that needs to be managed. I don't think you get what it means for minority groups whose ancestors were violently oppressed by the historic figures we glorify. These folks—our students and colleagues—have to walk by a memorial to Sir Richard Middling every day. Middling was a colonial war hero, a guy who went on to support the separation of Indigenous kids from their parents, and who got rich from a war in which millions of people were slaughtered. He was an influential man who had the power to help people. Instead, he used that power to hurt them. As individuals and as a university, we need to be more sensitive to that fact. Promoting an alternative discussion on monuments is the least we can do."

Duffy felt guilty, but he wasn't sure why. It was a familiar feeling. As a boy, his mother had called him a "worrier." Her solution, once Duffy was old enough to receive the sacrament of penance, had been to send him off to confession at the parish church. "Talk to Father Tom," she'd say. "It'll ease your conscience." The problem was, a talk with Father Tom only made things worse. The old priest, who'd played Junior A hockey before answering "his calling," was famous for berating penitents as if they played for the opposing team. "You did *what?!*" he would shout, no matter how venial the sin Duffy had whispered through the confessional grill. "Well, at least you're seeking God's forgiveness. For your penance, say ten Our Fathers and ten Hail Marys. And for heaven's sake, keep your hands off your pecker!"

Unlike Father Tom's scolding, Fifi's lecture did help, at least a little. Duffy could see the statue and namesake issue in a clearer light. A veil seemed to be lifting, like morning fog off the Yawnbury River. Duffy realized that Fifi was right: he had been acting like a thoughtless PR hack, ignoring his own sense of right and wrong, thinking only about his career. *When did I become this guy?* he wondered.

"I hear you," he said to Fifi. "And I'm embarrassed for treating this whole issue so lightly. The panel discussion is absolutely the right thing to do. I'll push Meriwether and Blunt harder. And if they don't come around, I'll find a way to promote the event myself."

"This could mess up your chances of becoming an assistant vice-president."

Duffy acknowledged the risk with a slight nod of his head.

"Hey, Feef," he said. "When did it become so hard to be a decent person?"

"It's not hard, Duffy. It just takes practice."

Chapter 15

Duffy handed copies of the Walters Report to Meriwether and Blunt. The three of them were seated in green leather club chairs that were arranged in a semi-circle around the bay window in the president's office. Rain was beating against the leaded glass; a current of chilly air made an end run around the old window frame and came in at the edges.

Sophie arrived with a tray of tea, milk and the president's favourite cookies: Scottish shortbreads.

"Nothing helps me think like tea and bickies," said Meriwether, who had spent a post-doctoral year at King's College London.

The group sat in silence, reading the amalgamation report, sipping tea and nibbling cookies.

Duffy didn't see Bertie, but he could smell him: a mix of urine and stale flatulence. He wondered if the old hound had crawled under the president's desk and died. A familiar whimper dispelled that notion. Duffy spied Bertie peeking out from beneath a wool blanket on the sofa across the room. The sight of the doleful pooch made Duffy think that the dog's malodourous scent, like the faint whiff of pipe tobacco, would live on in the carpet and furniture of this room long after the animal's demise.

Meriwether finished reading the report and tossed it on the coffee table with a flourish.

"Those devious buggers!" he said. "It's certainly the core of what Walters has been peddling for years, but HIPE's hired guns have really dressed it up."

"Who did they use?" asked Blunt.

"A public affairs agency in the city—Hooey, Haze and Bluster," said Duffy. "The premier's office uses them all the time."

"I'd say the cost savings are inflated by forty or fifty per cent," said Meriwether, looking to the economist in the room for confirmation.

"They're inflated," said Blunt. "But less than you might think. I'd say they're in the ballpark."

"How do you figure that?" asked Meriwether.

"Our annual operating budget is about a hundred and fifty million dollars. Seventy percent of that is spent on salaries and benefits. If amalgamation cuts fifty percent of faculty and seventy percent of support staff in the first year, that's a savings of about sixty million dollars annually. Add in the future cuts to faculty and staff, plus operational efficiencies, and you're getting close to a hundred million dollars a year."

"My Lord!" said Meriwether. "One hundred million a year?"

Duffy leaned forward. "Sir, the good news is that feelings beat facts."

Blunt's nostrils flared like a stallion enraged by a frisky colt. "What on earth does that mean?" he asked, appalled by Duffy's glib dismissal of all that Blunt held dear. "Numbers are facts—solid, reliable, immutable. They are the foundation upon which sound decision-making is made. *Feelings* have no place in the running of a university."

"Whoa, Clive," said Meriwether." We're just thrashing out ideas here. Before you demolish poor James, let's give him a chance to explain himself."

"My apologies, Dr. Blunt," said Duffy. "All I mean is that this is more about politics than dollars. Facts and numbers certainly play a role, but the government's decision will come down to one thing: Do the cost savings outweigh the potential for public outrage and a loss at the polls?"

"Go on," snarled Blunt.

"We need to control the narrative. We need to portray the hundred million dollars as a cost, not a saving. I'd recommend a campaign to get the Town of Yawnbury on side by showing how the community stands to lose hundreds of jobs and millions of dollars a year in economic spinoffs."

The scowl on Blunt's face faded to a petulant frown.

Duffy continued. "We can also work with SMUFA to rile up faculty associations right across the province—position the HIPE-Sir Middling amalgamation as a blatant attack on university professors everywhere."

Meriwether clapped his hands. "Yes, of course! The Domino Theory!" he said, warming to the military aspect of the proposal. "If Sir Middling falls, who's next?"

"Exactly," said Duffy.

"A hearts-and-minds sort of thing?" asked Blunt, a little unsure of the concept.

"Yes, Clive," said Meriwether, passing the plate of shortbread cookies around. "Hearts and minds, indeed!"

Duffy took a cookie and placed it on his saucer. The gesture aroused Bertie. The poor dog struggled to get free of his blanket, which had become wrapped around his plump torso. Bertie began to snort and twist like a man in a straitjacket. Eventually, he rolled free and promptly fell off the sofa, landing with a heavy thud. The dog lay motionless, gathering his wits. Meriwether got out of his chair and brought a shortbread over to the old hound. Bertie perked up and took the cookie gently from his master. He held it a moment, as if he wasn't quite sure what to do next. The shortbread stuck out from his fleshy jowls like a small cigar. Then, as if remembering an old trick, Bertie gave a slight flick of his head and the cookie disappeared into his mouth. He began crunching on it slowly, still sprawled on his side.

Duffy turned his attention back to the humans in the room.

"We'll need to sketch out a strategy," he said. "We should talk to Dr. Kiljoy first, then consult with the mayor and the local MPPs. We need to get them all on board and singing our song before this hits the news."

"Won't Samaroo have done that already?" asked Blunt.

"I expect she has," said Meriwether. "But as James said, HIPE is talking about taking something away from the community; we're talking about saving it. I'd say we have the easier sell."

"So, what's next?" asked Blunt.

"Let me set up some meetings to bring town council and the mayor up to speed," said Duffy.

As he got up to leave, he looked to Meriwether. "Sir, have you heard anything from the president of HIPE?"

"Nothing direct. Hugh Endicott is a sly rascal. He'll let Rose carry the torch until he sees how this is going to play out. You don't become a university president by taking chances."

Just then Bertie let out a long, sonorous fart.

My feelings exactly, thought Duffy.

Chapter 16

When Duffy got back to his office, he found Fifi sitting on his desk surrounded by a dozen students and faculty members. There were too few chairs to accommodate the group. Some were standing, some were seated on boxes, and a few of the more flexible ones were on the floor, practising the lotus position.

Duffy knew most of the professors. They were decent, thoughtful educators. Like Fifi, they steered clear of *Le Collectif radical* and its clownish brand of activism. Still, they believed that universities had a duty to lead society in matters of diversity, equity and social justice. Duffy also recognized a few of the students, including the president of the Association of Black Students and the chair of the Indigenous Students Society. He also recognized a kid with a shaved, tattooed head from the Student Front Demanding Justice—a kind of junior affiliate of *Le Collectif*. The kid, who called herself Rebel, had picked up the electric guitar that Duffy kept behind his desk and was strumming the unplugged instrument tunelessly. The guitar was a mid-level Fender—not worth much, money-wise, but rich in sentimental value. Duffy had bought it as a teenager with money saved up from a part-time job, and he was particular about who played it. He closed his hand around the fretboard to stifle the racket, then gently lifted the guitar out of Rebel's hands and returned it to the stand behind his desk. When the guitar was safely beyond the reach of the young student, Duffy turned to the group.

"Well, hello," he said. "I don't think I've ever had this many people in my office before."

"Get used to it," said Tessa Burns, a PhD candidate who headed the Association of Black Students.

"That sounds ominous," said Duffy.

"Depends on how you look at it," said Morris Hill, a professor of Indigenous and North American Studies, who had settled comfortably into Duffy's office chair.

"How are *you* looking at it, Dr. Hill?"

"With determination and steely-eyed resolve."

Duffy nodded. "And what are you determined and steely-eyed about?"

"Harrison Dewlap," said Hill. "Or as we like to say, Harrison Shit-for-Brains."

Duffy smiled uncertainly. Hill was one of the most accomplished scholars at Sir Middling U. He had degrees from the University of British Columbia, the University of Arizona and Cornell. He had founded Sir Middling U's Indigenous Studies program in the 1980s, one of the few programs at the university that had garnered national respect. Hill also had a wicked sense of humour, one so dry that Duffy was never sure if he was angry or just busting balls.

"Fifi told us about your idea for an alternative panel discussion," said Hill.

"And what do you think?"

"I think it's a smart approach. But I also think you failed to deliver the university's support."

Duffy respected Hill, so he pushed back. "Hey, I'm on your side. I'm the one who came up with the idea, and I wasn't just trying to manage an issue."

Fifi cleared her throat and shot Duffy a look.

"Well, not entirely," said Duffy. "I mean, it's my job to protect the reputation of Sir Middling U. For me, that aligns with social justice. I think the university has an obligation to support equity and diversity. That includes a candid discussion about Sir Middling U's namesake. And believe me, I made that point to President Meriwether, Dr. Blunt and Dr. Kiljoy."

"I appreciate that," said Hill. "But we need them to step up and demonstrate their commitment *now*, not just when it's politically safe to do so. Education is the most powerful tool we have for helping all members of society. A panel discussion with credible scholars is great, but it would be even better if the leaders of this university stood up and supported it publicly."

"I don't disagree," said Duffy. "But let's be frank. A panel discussion on monuments will end up focusing on the statue of Sir Richard Middling and whether the university should change its name. That's an important discussion to have. But it's a matter of timing. The administration is juggling several tough issues right now and they'd appreciate a little breathing room on this."

"What other issues?" asked Tessa Burns.

"I can't go into that," said Duffy. "But as I've told Dr. Dubé, I'll do whatever I can to help promote the alternative panel discussion myself. I just can't bring the president or the VP of university services into it."

"That's not good enough," said Burns.

"Perhaps not," said Duffy. "But what more can I do?"

"Help get us a face-to-face meeting with Meriwether and Blunt so that we can make the case ourselves," said Hill.

Duffy gazed at the faces in the room. Fifi stood at the back with her arms folded across her chest. She didn't say a word, but Duffy knew what she was thinking: Well, buddy boy, are you a man or a mouse?

Duffy, whose anxiety meds caused his thoughts and spoken words to blend together occasionally, especially when he was under stress, suddenly said, "I'm a man!"

Twelve sets of eyebrows shot up as people looked to one another to make sense of what Sir Middling's director of communications had just said.

Fifi rolled her eyes. "I think what my friend is saying is that he's a genuine ally and he'll give it another shot. Isn't that right, James?"

"Y-Yes, exactly," stammered Duffy.

"And what if they turn us down again?" asked Burns.

"I'll keep asking."

"Thank you," said Hill. "Tessa, Fifi and I will continue to lobby the president for a meeting ourselves. But if we don't make progress, we'll be back. This group loves a good sit-in, and so does the media."

"In that case, I'd better get more chairs," said Duffy.

Hill smiled and shook Duffy's hand. "Fifi was right. You're not as weaselly as you look."

As the group filed out, Fifi lingered behind. "Not bad, Duffy," she said. "Just keep walking the talk, okay? You might just come out of this a better person."

"I know. That's what scares me."

Chapter 17

The Art Haus Café was located in an old hardware store next to the Art Haus Theatre in downtown Yawnbury. Most people thought that the theatre was a repertory cinema with a funky name. In fact, it was just a plain old movie house named after the German immigrant who opened it in 1952, Artur P. Haus. Everyone was amazed that the current proprietor—Artur's son, Karl—managed to keep an independent movie theatre going. It turned out that plenty of people were willing to wait a month or so to see a first-run movie if it helped them avoid the crowds that mobbed the chain cinemas on weekends and discount Tuesdays. (It didn't hurt that the Art Haus also had a permit to sell wine and beer.)

Karl Haus had made only a few renovations to the hardware store next door before opening it up as a café. The real-estate agent who'd sold him the building had said that the exposed brick, plank floors and tin ceiling gave the place an "authentic" look. Karl wasn't sure what that meant, but he took the agent's word for it. A review in *The Rat's Ass* had described the café's ambience as "saloon meets grandpa's workshop." The reviewer conceded, in *Rat's Ass* fashion, that the coffee was "drinkable" and the breakfast prices "not bad." Before long, the Art Haus Café was a regular haunt for students, professors and the few aspiring artists who called Yawnbury home.

Duffy arrived early for his brunch with Sophie. He chose a table at the back where two large windows let in a generous amount of morning sun. The natural light flattered the exposed brick and coaxed a rustic coziness from the humble surroundings.

Duffy ordered a flat white—a new addition to the café's menu. It came in an oddly shaped pottery mug, which the café manager (Karl's youngest son) had introduced along with lattes, espressos and Americanos. Karl wasn't keen on the specialty coffees, and he liked the pottery mugs even less. But he was easing into retirement, and if his son wanted to mess with a good thing, well, the lad was free to make his own mistakes.

Duffy liked the variety of coffees, but he was in Karl's corner on the mugs. The wavy lip on the one he was given caused the froth from his flat white to run down the left side of his mouth. He was dabbing at an errant drop of foam when Sophie walked in.

"Need a bib?" she asked with a cheeky smile.

"At least I didn't use my sleeve," replied Duffy. "A word of warning: Karl's son is experimenting with hand-made mugs."

Duffy stood up and pulled a chair out for Sophie. He enjoyed watching her slide out of her coat, a camel-coloured military cut with three rows of brass buttons down the front.

"That's beautiful. Is it new?"

"Yes, as a matter of fact. Full marks for noticing."

"Ah, Moneypenny, how could I not notice?"

"Charming, James, but your accent needs work. You should talk to Angus Banks in modern languages."

"Oh, come on. You could at least pretend I sound like Sean Connery."

"Is that what you want? For me to stroke your ego with false praise?"

"Of course. I make no apologies for being male."

"Well, a real man would get me a cup of coffee," said Sophie, again with the cheeky smile.

"My pleasure," said Duffy.

He looked around for the waitress. There was only one—a young woman whose puffy eyes, uncombed hair and wobbly gait suggested a late night followed by an early morning. Duffy gave her an awkward little wave.

"I think subtlety is lost on Ms. Hangover," said Sophie.

"You're right," said Duffy.

He got up and walked over to the waitress.

"Excuse me, miss. Do you think you could bring my friend a flat white when you get a chance?"

The waitress fixed Duffy with her red-veined eyes. "Do you think you could just wait your turn?" she snapped.

"Whoa. I'm just asking for a flat white."

"Back off, mister," the waitress growled. "I'm not in the mood."

"Yes, I see that, but I was just asking for—"

"I don't get paid enough for this bullshit!"

A male customer, whose massive chest and biceps stretched his T-shirt like an overfilled balloon, leapt to the waitress's defence.

"Hey, buddy, leave the young lady alone!"

"I was just asking for a flat white," said Duffy.

"Well, you don't have to be a prick about it. I think the lady deserves an apology."

Duffy hated drama, and he loathed the possibility of violence. Turning to the waitress, he said, "I'm sorry for politely asking you for a cup of coffee. It will never happen again."

Just then, Karl's son strode out of the kitchen. "What's the problem, Misty?"

"This dork thinks he should get served ahead of everybody else," said the waitress.

"Is that right?" said Karl Haus Jr., whose pallid cheeks and bloodshot eyes suggested that he'd been at the same all-night drink-a-thon as the waitress.

"Listen, pal," he said to Duffy. "Take a seat and wait your turn, or get the hell out!"

"Of course," said Duffy. "I was way out of line. Sorry for the trouble."

The waitress turned to the beefcake customer. "Thanks, mister. Can I get you a flat white on the house?"

Duffy retreated to his table at the back of the café.

"What the heck happened?" asked Sophie.

"Just a little misunderstanding."

"What did you say to that poor girl?"

"I asked her, very politely, to bring you a flat white."

"You must have said more than that."

A serious tone had crept into Sophie's voice. Duffy sensed the mysterious power of the sisterhood coming to life. Against his better judgement, he plowed on in his own defence.

"Honestly, Sophie, all I said was, 'Excuse me, miss. Do you think you could bring my friend a flat white when you get a chance?'"

"Well, maybe you triggered a bad memory," said Sophie.

"Like partying all night and having to work in the morning?"

"Hey, mister, it's hard work waiting tables. You get hassled by all sorts of assholes."

"You mean those annoying jerks who politely ask for a cup of coffee?"

Duffy knew he'd gone too far, but he was feeling aggrieved.

Sophie shook her head and sighed. "Oh, James, just get over it."

Duffy's better judgement kicked in. "You're right. I'm fostering bad energy. I'll let it go." He closed his eyes and took a long, deep breath. Then he opened his eyes and let it out.

"That's what my yogi taught me to do," he said with his own cheeky smile.

"And what does your yogi recommend on the menu?" asked Sophie.

"He always orders off-menu," said Duffy. "But I wouldn't try that today. In fact, I think we may need to go someplace else. That waitress isn't going to serve us for hours. And when she does, she's going to spit in my eggs."

Sophie sighed. "You're probably right. Boy, you sure know how to show a girl a good time."

"All part of the Duffy charm."

As he was getting up from the table, a voice called to him over his left shoulder.

"My, my, Mr. Duffy, you still know how to attract attention."

It was Rose Samaroo.

"Oh, hello, doctor. You saw that, did you?"

"Saw it? I couldn't miss it. What did you say to that young lady?"

"Nothing really. I think she's just hung over."

"Well, I concur. She was quite hostile to my friends and me when we asked for more foam on our *cappucini*."

Samaroo gave Duffy the megawatt smile that had weakened his knees and fired his loins three years earlier. He smiled back like a schoolboy with a crush on his teacher.

Sophie stepped forward and broke the spell. "Hi, Dr. Samaroo. I'm Sophie Munn."

"Yes, of course," said Samaroo. "How is my dear friend, Alex Meriwether?"

"Just fine," said Sophie.

Samaroo turned back to Duffy and laid a hand on his forearm.

"I'm *so* glad that I ran into you, James. Could I bend your ear about something?"

Duffy felt a wave of *déjà vu*, recalling his first encounter with Samaroo.

"I hear that you're part of the Sir Middling team reviewing the Bud Walters Report," she said.

Duffy was alarmed. How does she know that? Then he thought of what he had told Jill Kaiser less than a week earlier: HIPE and

Sir Middling U were just twenty kilometres apart and their faculty members talked all the time.

"Yes," said Duffy. "Quite the proposal you've put forward."

"We like to think of it as a partnership between HIPE and Sir Middling U."

"I don't think I saw that in the report."

"Well, I can *assure* you that HIPE sees it as a partnership. The two institutions have collaborated on so much over the years. A closer relationship just seems to be the natural progression."

Duffy was unaware of any collaborations between the two schools. But he decided it was wiser to listen than to talk.

Samaroo continued. "I wanted to let you know, colleague to colleague, that I plan to invite President Meriwether and his team to sit down and discuss our mutual future," she said. "I'm sure we all want what's best for the two institutions. And I think we'd all agree that it's better to have those conversations early in the process—*before* the media get wind of the story."

Duffy agreed, but he chose his words carefully.

"I'm sure Dr. Meriwether would love to hear from you," he said.

"Please let him know that I'll be in touch."

Samaroo shook Duffy's hand as if they had just agreed on some sort of deal, then walked off to rejoin her friends.

Duffy was still watching her go when Sophie stood up and handed him his leather jacket.

"Who knew that a date with James Duffy would be filled with so much drama?" she said.

"I'm sorry, Sophie. I didn't know Samaroo was here."

"Don't apologize. You're not the first man—or woman—to go all dopey in the presence of Mistress Samaroo."

"I thought I resisted her charms pretty well."

"Ha!" said Sophie, slipping into her own coat.

"Well, she is something, isn't she?" said Duffy.

"Yes, she is," replied Sophie. "I respect her, but I can't say that I trust her."

"She's definitely complex."

Sophie gave Duffy a shove.

"What's that for?" he said.

"Would you say that about a successful man?"

"What do you mean?"

"Would you call a man 'complex' just because he was smart, handsome and ambitious?"

Duffy thought about it. "Only if he smelled as good as Rose Samaroo."

Sophie punched him again, much harder this time.

"Okay, I get it," he said. "Why shouldn't she use all of her smarts and talents to get ahead? And if men are blinded by her looks and charm, shame on us."

"There's hope for you yet, James."

"Why do people keep saying that?"

"Do they?"

"Lately, yes."

"Maybe people care about you more than you think."

"Does that include you?"

Sophie took Duffy's hand and squeezed it. "Possibly. But right now, all I want is coffee and a croissant."

"Well, Moneypenny, would you settle for decaf and bagels at my place?"

"Only because I'm starving."

As they were leaving the Art Haus Café, Duffy noticed a small poster tacked to a coming events board beside the door:

More Shitty Weather
A Poetry Reading
By Dr. Percy Mittens
FREE CHEESE!
Nov. 29, 8 p.m.

Sir Middling U

Duffy pointed to the ad.

"It could be worse," he said. "I could have invited you to that."

"At least there'd be food."

Chapter 18

Duffy arrived at his office at eight o'clock on Monday morning. Terri Coyne was already at her desk.

"Morning, Terri. How was your weekend?"

"Good. Yours?"

"Not bad."

"I heard you caused a ruckus at the Art Haus Café," said Coyne, giving Duffy a sly grin.

"Oh, for goodness sake," he said. "Is this town really that small?"

"Smaller, actually."

"Well, for the record, the waitress was hung over and she took it out on me."

"Waiting tables is hard work; you deal with a lot of assholes."

"So I've been told," said Duffy, continuing on to his office.

Coyne stood up and followed him. "I'm glad you had a good weekend," she said, "because today's off to a rocky start."

Duffy held up a travel mug. "Can I have a sip of coffee first?"

"Sure. I'll fill you in while you feed your addiction."

"It's decaf."

"Yeah, that's what they all say."

Duffy poured his coffee into a ceramic mug that bore the cartoon image of the Sir Middling mascot. Like the plush toy, the facial expression on the coffee-cup muskrat was both goofy and maniacal.

"Did you know that muskrats mate underwater?" said Coyne.

"What?"

"I read it somewhere: muskrats like to be partially submerged when they do the dirty deed. They also hook up with multiple partners."

"And you're telling me this why?"

"I think it explains the crazy look on old Musky. It also begs the question: Why choose a promiscuous rodent for a university mascot?"

It was a good question, thought Duffy, but not one he cared to explore at the moment.

"Can we get back to why my day is off to a rocky start?"

"Sure. First off, the chair of Communications Studies, Dr. Adorno, is pissed at you. Seems that a maintenance crew showed up at his office on Friday with a door. The nameplate read: Professor James Duffy. The crew said they were told to install it in the boss's office over in communications. When Adorno pointed out the misunderstanding, the lead hand said he'd have to leave the door there because his work order said nothing about taking it elsewhere."

"So, my door is with the chair of Communications Studies?"

"Real slapstick, eh? Kinda like the *Who's on First* routine. By the way, Dr. Adorno is also cheesed that you're calling yourself a professor."

"But I'm *not* calling myself a professor."

"I know," said Coyne. "But come on, you have to admit that it's funny."

"If it happened to someone else, yes, it would be hilarious. But the academic chairs already hate me."

"They don't hate you. They just don't respect you."

Duffy took a mouthful of coffee. It was already cold.

"Did you explain to the chair that the door isn't my fault?" he asked.

"Ha! Good one: *Chair! Door!*" said Coyne, who, from Duffy's perspective, was having way too much fun with the mix-up.

"Just answer the question," he pleaded.

"No, I didn't get a chance to explain the situation to Adorno. He just left an angry message on your phone."

"On my phone?" said Duffy, more annoyed than surprised. "You have access to my voicemail?"

"Of course. I'm your executive assistant. I assumed you'd be okay with it."

"We'll discuss that later," said Duffy. "Right now, we've got to fix this door thing. First, call that Lloyd guy in maintenance and tell him to go get the door from Communications Studies and bring it over here. And second, call Adorno's EA and let her know that we're sending someone over to get the door."

"His EA is a *he*. Dana Salt."

"Dana could be a woman's name."

"Trust me. Dana Salt is definitely a man," Coyne said with a knowing wink.

"I don't want to know why you're so certain of that," said Duffy. "Just get me Dr. Adorno's phone extension."

"Why?"

"Because I'm going to call him and apologize for the door fiasco."

"Apologize for something that wasn't your fault? Where's your self-respect?"

"It vanished when I took this job."

"At least you still have your sense of humour, and thank goodness for that."

"Why?"

"There's more."

Duffy took a deep breath.

"Okay, hit me."

"Dr. Lillidew is also mad at you."

"Why?"

"He said a bald-headed kid from some student association confronted him about the Harrison Dewlap lecture. Apparently, the student said that you called Lillidew a racist. The kid also said that you were helping sabotage the lecture by holding an alternative event."

"Are you kidding?" said Duffy.

"Nope. Lillidew said that he and Dewlap are considering suing you for libel. Or was it slander? I never know the difference."

"Good grief."

"What's that line you always say? No good deed goes unpunished?"

Duffy rubbed his temples with the tips of his fingers. "Is Lillidew's message still on my phone?"

"It wasn't a call."

"What do you mean?"

"Lillidew was here this morning when I arrived."

"Really? That's a surprise. Guys like him usually go straight to your boss."

"That's where he's headed now."

"To Blunt's office?"

"Yup."

"Of course he is," said Duffy, letting his head sink into his upturned palms.

"You don't think Blunt will defend you?" asked Coyne.

Duffy snorted. "Now *that's* funny."

"Well, I guess that's why you get paid the big bucks."

"How do you know how much I get paid?"

Coyne glanced at her watch.

"Oh my, look at the time. I better make that call to the maintenance shop."

"How was the date?"

"Feef, I have a bone to pick with you."

"Okay. But first tell me about brunch with the lovely Sophie Munn."

"It was good."

"I heard you took her back to your place for a midday canoodle."

"Canoodle? What are you, a hundred years old?"

"Okay then, a nooner, some afternoon delight, a post-brunch scrunch. Do you like any of those better?"

"No. How did you know we went to my place?"

"Come on, Duffy. You took a date to the Art Haus Café—the whole campus knows."

"Fuck me."

"Did she?"

"No, as a matter of fact. Sophie got a call just as we pulled up to my apartment building. Her aunt had some kind of seizure. I drove Sophie over to the hospital."

"Bummer. Does Sophie even have an aunt?"

"What do you mean?"

"Sounds like an excuse, don't you think?"

"No, it sounds like what it was. And besides, how could Sophie time a fake call like that?"

"We women have our ways."

"You're just messing with me, Feef."

"Yes, I am. But it still sounds like an excuse. Promise me something?"

"What?"

"Tell me the minute you get into Sophie's pants."

"Knock it off, will you? You're ruining this for me."

"Okay, but you *do* want to have sex with her, right?"

Duffy's cheeks went as red as his hair. "I would like to have sex with her as part of, you know, some kind of relationship."

"What if Sophie just wants to fuck?"

"Enough, already!" he shouted. "This is *not* why I called you!"

"Chillax, bro," said Fifi, pleased to have gotten a rise out of Duffy. "Why *did* you call me?"

"Like I said, I have a bone to pick with you."

"Pick away."

"Some student told Lillidew about the alternative event and said that I called him a racist."

"So?"

"So Lillidew wants to sue me, and he's complaining directly to Blunt. He's trying to turn this into an academic-freedom thing."

"First of all, it's a freedom-of-speech thing, not an academic-freedom thing. And second, grow a pair, will you? You should be wearing this like a badge of honour. You're standing up to racism; you're a role model for ally-ism. When the dust settles, you'll have your self-respect *and* the respect of others. Man up, Duffy, and embrace the opportunity."

"But I didn't call Lillidew or Dewlap a racist!"

"Hmmm, you may have implied it. But even if you didn't, you should have. Stay strong, my friend, and remember: 'Never explain, never retract, never apologize.' "

"Let me guess, Mackenzie King?"

"No, you moron. Nellie McClung, the pioneering Canadian feminist!"

"Right, of course: 'Get the thing done and let them howl.' "

"Exactly."

"So, how did Morris Hill make out with Meriwether and Blunt?" asked Duffy.

"You haven't heard?"

"Heard what?"

"Come on, Duffy. You work for Blunt, and Meriwether is always confiding in you."

"The first part of that statement is true but meaningless; the second part is not as true as you think."

"Well, Morris said he hasn't heard back from Meriwether or Blunt."

"Really? When did he call them?"

"Four days ago."

"That's not good, especially with Lillidew going apeshit," said Duffy. "Listen, Blunt is probably going to haul me into a meeting today. If I still have my job, I'll push him hard to meet with you, Morris and Tessa."

"You really think Dr. Pouty has the backbone to do the right thing?"

"I'm not sure what the right thing is in this case. You've got to admit, it's a bit of a tightrope for administration."

"Oh, geez, you're sounding like a bureaucrat again."

"Listen, Feef, it's easy to think these things are clear cut when you're not responsible for managing the whole university."

"Hey, I get complexity, remember? And I'm not talking about cancelling the Dewlap lecture. I support freedom of speech; I believe that the university should be a forum for competing ideas. But I don't see how that prevents the president and his VP of diddly squat from supporting a scholarly discussion about how we memorialize historic figures."

"Meriwether and Blunt see it differently."

"That's horseshit. This is the perfect time to show the government what Sir Middling U stands for and why it shouldn't be assimilated into the Borg."

"The Borg?"

"You know, the evil homogenous collective in *Star Trek*."

"*The Next Generation*, right?"

"Yeah."

"Good analogy."

"I think it's a metaphor, actually."

They were both silent for a moment.

"Listen, Duffy. I've got to say this straight out: I think you're letting this assistant vice-president thing mess up your judgement. No promotion is worth sacrificing your principles."

"I'm not sacrificing anything. I'm just trying to find a middle way."

"Now you're back to sounding like a wishy-washy weasel."

"That's kind of insulting," said Duffy.

"That's what friends are for," replied Fifi.

"I'm calling a time out. Count to sixty and then bring it on again."

Duffy had been reading about the Buddhist concept of the middle path. He had first encountered it in his undergrad studies, along with the Greek concept of moderation in all things. He had been thinking about both recently, a by-product of his tentative exploration of meditation and non-chemical remedies for anxiety. Fifi was supportive, even if she wasn't a middle-path person herself.

"… fifty-eight, fifty-nine, sixty," she said. "Game on!"

Duffy picked up where he'd left off.

"I'm with you on this, Feef. Really, I am. Let me talk to Blunt again. I'll do my absolute best to get him and Meriwether to meet with you guys. But do me a favour, will you?"

"What?"

"Find that student—she calls herself Rebel—and tell her to stop saying I called Lillidew a racist."

"Okay, but you're throwing away an opportunity to build credibility with right-thinking people."

"Never explain, never retract?"

"And never apologize!"

"You know, that doesn't sound very middle path-ish," said Duffy.

"So, you'd rather be like Blunt? Neither lead nor trail?"

"I'm just saying that maybe there's a time and a place."

"Not when it comes to doing the right thing, bucko."

Chapter 19

Duffy had barely finished his call with Fifi when his phone began to vibrate. It was an email from Blunt's executive assistant.

"Dr. Blunt requires your presence immediately. Kind regards, O. Crump."

Duffy groaned. Terri Coyne heard him from across the office.

"Was that old Crumpy?"

"Yes."

"She called twice while you were on the phone with Dr. Burlesque. Sounds like you're going to get your arse flicked with a wet towel."

Duffy drank the last of his coffee, then put on the jacket he had just taken off. He wound his scarf loosely around his neck and donned his black watch cap.

"If I don't come back, throw out all my things except the guitar."

"Can I have your chair?"

"Yes. But only if I don't come back."

"Break a leg."

"Blunt will probably do that for me."

Once again, Duffy set out for Founders Hall on a dreary late-November morning. The dark clouds seemed to press down on the campus and there was a raw nip in the air. Duffy pulled his scarf up to his nose and wished he had brought gloves.

As he approached the statue of Brave Sir Dickie, he felt a flutter of anticipation. What colour would the horse's balls be today?

Robin's egg blue, it turned out.

Duffy glanced at the horse's rump. The *Amalgamate Now!* slogan was painted over with a new exhortation: *Bite me, boomers!*

As a career-minded millennial, Duffy empathized. Boomers tended to hang on to their jobs until the bitter end, especially at Sir Middling U. The pay was good, the benefits generous and the expectations low. Why not ride the gravy train to the end of the line? Well, thought Duffy, because we millennials want to move up the ranks. We want to run things. We want your boomer jobs. And besides, we just don't like you.

The inner monologue put a smile on Duffy's face. "No harm in making yourself laugh," as his father liked to say. Standing alone in the quad, Duffy felt a pang of sentimentality. If Blunt fired him, this would be his last chance to soak up the campus atmosphere. He gazed around like a first-time visitor. The view, however, tilted towards the dispiriting: a weathered old statue, a few leafless maples and a wall of drab, red-brick buildings. Would Duffy miss this place if Blunt fired him? Or if Sir Middling U merged with HIPE? He tried to summon a sense of attachment and nostalgia, but all he felt was the damp autumn chill.

Then, suddenly, a wellspring of giddiness gushed forth and flooded his senses. Duffy raised his fist to the dark sky and yelled, "Bite me, boomers!"

As if on command, rain crashed down in buckets. Duffy looked around sheepishly. It was still a little early in the morning for students and faculty to be out and about, but there might be a few staff members scuttling between buildings. Alas, only Brave Sir Dickie and his horse had witnessed Duffy's outburst.

He bent his head and trudged on.

The office of the vice-president of university services was on the main floor of Founders Hall, just down the corridor from the president's suite.

Duffy stopped in front of the door, shook the rain out of his hair and removed his jacket and scarf. They were both dripping wet. He rummaged through his pockets and found an old tissue. He tried to dry his face with it, but the worn fibres quickly disintegrated. Tiny fragments clung to his unshaven cheeks like flakes of snow. Duffy rubbed them off and ran a comb through his hair. Then he opened the door and entered the office like a fugitive surrendering to police.

"Hello, Ottie," he said to Blunt's executive assistant.

Crump looked at him over her reading glasses.

"I see the rain has started," she said, as if Duffy were to blame. "No umbrellas in the Communications Department?"

"Not in our budget, I'm afraid."

"Take a seat. Dr. Blunt will be with you shortly."

Duffy parked himself on one of the wooden chairs in the corner of the waiting area. Rainwater leaked from his trousers and formed a small pool around his shoes. Water also seeped from his mop of red hair, creating rivulets that ran down his pale forehead and cheeks. He eyed a box of tissues on Crump's desk.

"May I have a couple of those to dry my face?" he asked.

"There's a box in the washroom down the hall," said Crump, not bothering to look up from her computer screen.

The woman had been cool towards Duffy since the day he started at Sir Middling U. He wondered if Crump blamed him for the departure of Rose Samaroo and the instalment of Clive Blunt as her new boss. If so, Duffy felt her pain.

He decided he could live without a tissue. Instead, he scrolled through the messages on his phone. One was a social media alert. Duffy clicked it open and read the post.

"With tongues of lightning and thunderous groans/ The wild storm shakes our bed with lusty squalls/ Till heaven erupts and we, entwined, sink deep in love's sweet slumber. @MoreShittyWeather, @SirMiddlingU, #poetrylovers."

"Good grief," he said.

Just as he was about to look at the comments below the post, Blunt opened his door. He pointed at Duffy and summoned him with a theatrical curl of his index finger.

As Duffy passed Crump's desk, the executive assistant grinned like a gleeful onlooker at a public hanging.

"Have a nice meeting," she said.

Blunt's office had all the personality of a dentist's waiting room. The walls were decorated with degrees, certifications and plastic-framed posters declaring a range of platitudes. One featured a photograph of a kitten dangling from a clothesline, below which ran a caption: *Hang in there, baby!*

Duffy pondered the incongruity of such a poster hanging in the office of a cranky, humourless bureaucrat like Blunt. He also wondered what a psychologist would make of the painfully bland office and its gallery of trite sayings. Then again, what would a psychologist make of Duffy's own clutter-filled hallway office?

As he took a seat, he noticed a book on the side of Blunt's desk. It was a training manual called *Tough Conversations*. Duffy had his own copy—it came with an HR course that taught managers how to deal with problem employees. Seeing it splayed open on his boss's desk, Duffy prepared for the worst.

"I'm going to be clear and candid," Blunt began, parroting a line that Duffy recognized from Chapter One of *Tough Conversations*.

"Dr. Lillidew came to see me this morning. He is extremely angry with you, James. And from what he tells me, I don't blame him. Dr. Meriwether and I explicitly ordered you not to meddle with the Dewlap lecture."

"I haven't been meddling with anything, sir," replied Duffy. "Some of the faculty and students came to see me to express their concern about a man like Dewlap being invited to campus. They asked for my thoughts. I suggested they hold an alternative event. My thinking was that it would be more constructive than a protest, and less likely to create headlines in the media."

"Rufus says you called him a racist."

"Absolutely not."

"Are you calling a distinguished faculty member a liar?"

Duffy had never heard anyone refer to Dr. Rufus Lillidew as distinguished. He was tempted to point this out but thought better of it. Instead, he stole a glance at Blunt's copy of *Tough Conversations* and tried to recall something useful. What did it say about sticking to facts? Yes! *Stick to Facts and Focus on Solutions,* Chapter Two.

"I hear you, Dr. Blunt," replied Duffy, using another phrase from the HR manual. "And I believe we both want the same outcome: to keep the Dewlap lecture on the down-low while focusing our time and energy on amalgamation."

"If you hear me so well, Duffy, why does Dr. Lillidew think you called him a racist?"

"I assure you that I did not call him a racist. It's a misconstrued version of a conversation I had with the faculty and students who came to see me. I have witnesses—genuine faculty members—who can vouch for what I said."

Duffy had no idea what his witnesses might say. From his last conversation with Fifi, it would probably be something like: "Of course, Mr. Duffy called Lillidew a racist. Sir Middling's director of communications is a *mensch* with *cojones* the size of those on Sir Dickie's horse." The prospect of such testimony made witness-calling a dangerous gamble, Duffy concluded. Fortunately, his boss moved on.

"I still want you to apologize to Dr. Lillidew," said Blunt.

"I can't apologize for something I didn't say," replied Duffy. "But I could apologize for the misunderstanding. Would that suffice?"

Blunt pursed his lips and narrowed his eyes like he'd just swallowed a spoonful of cough medicine. He had hoped to bully Duffy into making a simple, clear apology. But little of what went on at Sir Middling U was simple or clear.

"I guess it will have to do," said Blunt, who didn't sound happy about the compromise. "But make your apology today. I want this over and done with ASAP."

"Yes, sir," said Duffy.

Before Blunt could end the meeting, Duffy seized the moment to raise a related issue. "While we're on the topic of statues," he said, "I understand that Dr. Hill reached out to you for a meeting."

"What of it?"

"Well, strategically speaking, it might be constructive for you and Dr. Meriwether to meet with Dr. Hill, Dr. Dubé and Tessa Burns from the Association of Black Students. It would help lower the temperature on the Dewlap lecture *and* demonstrate the administration's willingness to listen to the Sir Middling U community."

"Out of the question!" snapped Blunt. "If we meet with them, they're going to ask me to make a show of support for their alternative event, and when I say I can't do that, it's only going to make things worse."

Blunt leaned across his desk and pointed a finger at Duffy. "Let me be clear, James: you need to get with the program. You are not doing yourself or your career any favours by pushing back on the wishes of President Meriwether and myself."

"I understand, sir," said Duffy. "The thing is, I have a lot of experience with reputation management. But I'm not much use to you or the president if I can't be candid. We know that Sir Richard Middling's legacy is problematic. The university's mission statement commits us to using education as a tool for supporting equity, diversity and inclusion. I think that you and Dr. Meriwether have a real opportunity here to bring that commitment to life by simply meeting with Morris, Fifi and Tessa."

Blunt's lips vibrated in a twitchy pout. He was belly breathing—one, two, three, four—and stealing quick glances at his copy of *Tough Conversations*.

"The answer is still no," he said firmly. "The organizers of the alternative event are free to hold their panel discussion, just as Dr. Lillidew is free to invite outside scholars to speak on campus. Neither event requires the support of the president or myself."

Duffy nodded—a flag of truce, if not surrender.

"I won't press my counsel any further," he said. "But to be clear, faculty and students will almost certainly hold a sit-in here at Founders Hall. To be prudent, we should think through the university's response ahead of time. The media will definitely cover a sit-in and they'll want a comment from us."

"What other options do we have?" asked Blunt.

"Such as?"

"Preventing students and faculty from entering Founders Hall, or having campus police remove them if they do?"

Now it was Duffy's turn to bite his lip and do a little belly breathing.

"I wouldn't recommend either of those things," he said. "The protesters will alert the media to whatever they're planning. The last thing we want are photos and video of a shoving match on the steps of Founders Hall. Or worse, police dragging students down the hallway in front of the president's office."

"You're not giving me any options, James," huffed Blunt.

"I suppose you could lock Founders Hall in advance of a sit-in," said Duffy. "But that would make it look like the administration is under siege—and that's the last thing we want right now, isn't it?"

"That's it? No other options?"

"We could pray for a snow day."

A spark of hope warmed Blunt's cold eyes. "Is there any snow in the forecast?"

"I was only kidding," said Duffy.

Blunt scowled. "Check the forecast anyway."

"I'll do that. But can we settle on a Plan A, just to be safe?"

"All right," said Blunt, the frustration in his voice giving way to weariness. "Draft a communications plan in case there's a sit-in. But *do not* deploy it until I've signed off. Understood?"

"Yes, understood."

"One other thing," said Blunt. "I'd like you to spend less time on these negative distractions and more time promoting the university's accomplishments. Sir Middling U is always hiding its light under a bushel basket."

When the wattage is this low, thought Duffy, there's no need for a basket.

"Point taken, sir," he said. "But to be fair, my team and I *do* try to promote Sir Middling's achievements."

"Is that so? Then why haven't I seen anything about Dr. Mittens' new volume of poetry on the website? He says you're ignoring his publicist."

Duffy should have seen this coming. Mittens was the kind of guy who would complain to your boss rather than speak to you directly. Duffy made a mental note to add this "Mittens Factor" to his Shitstorm Decision Matrix.

"Promoting the book is on my to-do list," said Duffy, a response that sounded lame even to him.

"Move it to the top," ordered Blunt.

Duffy felt his spirits sink further. "Are you sure that a book called *More Shitty Weather* should be my top priority right now?"

"What are you talking about?" asked Blunt.

"Dr. Mittens' new book of poetry. It's called *More Shitty Weather*."

"Good grief!" exclaimed Blunt. "I had no idea. Percy didn't mention the title."

"Perhaps his book is one light we should keep under a bushel," said Duffy.

"Yes, well, perhaps. But my point still stands: I want you to spend more time telling the world about all the wonderful things we do here at Sir Middling U."

"Yes, sir," said Duffy, pretending to scribble the request in his notebook.

As he got up to leave, Duffy felt a deeper appreciation for the kitten on the clothesline.

Hang in there, baby!

Chapter 20

Giles Prigg was a paradox to friends and foes alike. Tall, slim and immaculately coiffed, he dressed in bespoke suits and Italian-made shoes. The effect, reinforced by a graciously superior manner, was more European financier than Canadian civil servant. He was a pragmatist—*dogmatically flexible*, as he liked to put it—who had little time for hardliners at either end of the political spectrum. Although he preached the value of win-win negotiations, he was a shrewd strategist who always seemed to get what he wanted. Prigg believed that principles were fluid, that the public good was a flexible concept, and that politics was the art of getting re-elected. The premier made him chief of staff because he was clever, ruthless and effective; his party colleagues hated him for the same reasons.

For those who failed to grasp Prigg's particular brand of genius, it was a mystery why he'd chosen Dev Sharma to advise the government on university amalgamation and system-wide reform.

Sharma was baffled himself.

As vice-president of the privately funded Education Research

Policy Institute, he was known as a zealous reformer whose opinions were controversial but maddeningly well researched.

"I make no apologies for being a pointy-headed empiricist," he often said in response to his detractors.

Despite the metaphorical shape of his head, Sharma found it perplexing that his fiercest critics were fellow PhDs who presented themselves as objective scholars, scientists and researchers. Faculty officials attacked his character more than his proposals, dismissing him as a technocrat who lacked proper reverence for the practices and traditions of "the academy."

"I won't let some efficiency wonk tell me how to spend my time," declared one professor, a sociologist who wrote a travel blog while spending a paid sabbatical exploring country pubs on a walking tour of Wales. (A jealous colleague had shared the blog with Sharma, who'd used it as Exhibit A in an op-ed that questioned the rigour of sabbatical oversight.)

Sharma arrived for his meeting with Giles Prigg carrying a battered old briefcase stuffed with charts, graphs and reports. He set the bulging bag on a coffee table and released the clasp that held the overstretched sides together. The case burst open, flinging loose papers into the air like a confetti cannon.

"My apologies!" exclaimed Sharma as he snatched at the fugitive documents. "I like to come prepared."

"Indeed," said Prigg, who watched with amusement as the flurry of papers descended like giant snowflakes.

Sharma's idiosyncrasies had announced themselves even before his briefcase exploded. In addition to the swollen valise, he was carrying a bright red parka over one arm and a pink umbrella in his free hand. His sport coat seemed several sizes too big; the knot in his tie looked like a sailor's half hitch; and the gap between his brown slacks and hiking boots exposed a pair of lemon-yellow socks.

"Well, you certainly know how to make an entrance," Prigg said with genial aplomb.

Sharma smiled uncertainly while stuffing papers back into his briefcase.

"Why don't we start with a cup of tea?" suggested Prigg.

The coffee table between the two men held a contemporary tea set—the pot tall and slender, the cups delicate and shallow. Prigg pushed Sharma's overflowing briefcase to one side before pouring out two cups of tea and sliding one towards his guest.

"Let me start by summarizing the challenge," said Prigg, taking a seat on an elegant suede-covered sofa. "Our government appreciates the value of higher education. Research and teaching drive the knowledge economy; the knowledge economy creates jobs and prosperity; and jobs and prosperity win elections. That said, the cost of running universities continues to grow faster than inflation. To quote my dear grandmother, we spend more on the cow than we get for the milk. The question, therefore, is two-fold: First, how do we create a financially sustainable post-secondary system? And second, how do we do so without diminishing the quality?"

Sharma rubbed his hands together in anticipation of a meaty discussion.

"So, this is bigger than the one-off amalgamation of HIPE and Sir Middling U?" he asked eagerly.

"Much bigger," replied Prigg. "Bud Walters and his friends at HIPE have tabled an interesting proposal. But does it make sense to amalgamate two universities without a system-wide strategy in place?"

"The short answer is no. The long answer is more complex."

"That's why you're here, Dev," Prigg said with an easy smile.

Sharma shifted to the edge of his seat and leaned forward. "There's certainly an opportunity to control costs through amalgamations," he said. "But a one-off is just a tactic, not a strategy. Let's set amalgamation aside for a moment and zero in on some fundamental issues."

"By all means," said Prigg.

"Universities need to be refreshed and rebalanced. Some schools are very innovative, others not so much. Broadly put, the system lumbers under the weight of entrenched practices, runaway salaries, administrative bloat, productivity issues, a flawed funding system and questionable constructs like tenure and the four-month summer hiatus."

"Provocative," Prigg said admiringly. "But I'm not sure you're 'zeroing in' yet."

"Sorry," said Sharma. "I tend to get carried away."

He took a sip of tea and began again.

"Let me start with costs. There are a lot of things driving up university expenses. But the biggest operating cost for universities is labour, and faculty compensation is the biggest portion of total labour costs."

"What about support staff and senior admin?"

"Their combined compensation is significant. But let's focus on the academic side for now. Total faculty compensation has been rising by more than the simple cost-of-living increases that universities and faculty unions like to highlight when they settle a contract. What's rarely mentioned are additional drivers—things like 'progression through the ranks'—which can quietly boost salary increases above the rate of inflation."

"Ah, yes, *progression through the ranks!*" said Prigg, wagging an index finger for dramatic effect. "Now there's an expensive mystery."

"It's certainly worth examining in more detail," replied Sharma.

Prigg smiled mirthlessly while scribbling a note into his leatherbound diary.

"Another issue is faculty workloads," said Sharma.

"What about them?"

"Studies suggest that full-time professors in this province teach an average of about three one-semester courses over the typical eight-month academic year. That's essentially two courses in the fall and one in the winter term."

"But they do research in addition to teaching?"

"This is where things get fuzzy. Universities talk about a 40-40-20 split—the notion that faculty spend about 40 percent of their time teaching, 40 percent on research and 20 percent on what they call 'service.'"

"Service?" said Prigg, his right eyebrow arching like a cat.

"Committee work, administrative duties, conference planning—that sort of thing. The problem is, without a clear definition—and with little effort to quantify it—it's difficult to measure how much service is really being done."

Prigg gave a dismissive snort. "Every managerial and professional job has service-type expectations. But it doesn't reduce your workload; it simply adds to the length of your workday."

"I'm not saying it's right or wrong," replied Sharma. "My point is that few universities provide the public with meaningful data about productivity, especially in terms of faculty service and research activity."

Prigg was mulling this over when Sharma suddenly slid off his chair and began crawling towards a meeting table in the centre of the room. The researcher had spied one of his errant sheets of paper, which had settled beneath the table after escaping from his over-filled briefcase.

"Everything all right, Dev?" inquired Prigg.

"Yes," said Sharma, waving the recovered document like a prize. "What were you saying, Giles?"

Ever the gracious host, Prigg carried on as if his guest were not lodged beneath a meeting table.

"I was about to ask a question: How do I put all of what you've said into perspective for my colleagues?"

Sharma swivelled around and crawled back to his chair. He gave a little grunt as he pulled himself up and sat down. After taking a breath, he said, "You tell them that by modernizing the system, the government can save millions of dollars *and* increase the quality of research and teaching."

Prigg set his teacup on the coffee table. "So, what's preventing this modernization?"

"Inertia, in my opinion," said Sharma. "Many in the academy dislike change, and they're fiercely protective of their autonomy. Their usual line is, 'Trust us, we know best.' And in many cases, they do. But as a publicly funded system, it's a dinosaur mired in a tar pit of expensive, opaque and outdated practices."

"*Postsecondarisaurus*," quipped Prigg.

Sharma chuckled. "I may steal that!"

"By all means," replied Prigg. "So tell me, Dev, how do we go about fixing things?"

"First, document the problems and missed opportunities with plenty of data. Second, hold a meaningful round of consultations. And third, develop a strategy with clear goals, measurable objectives and significant penalties for any university that doesn't deliver change."

"What kind of penalties?"

"Freeze their funding."

Prigg smiled. "Anything else?"

"The real trick will be implementation. You'll face a lot of resistance—protests, work to rule, plain old tantrums. I suggest you push back with data on teaching loads, compensation increases and research activity."

Prigg leaned back, looking very pleased with things.

"What next?" asked Sharma.

"What I'd like you to do, Dev, is put everything you've told me into a succinct briefing note—no more than three pages. I'll need it by early next week."

Sharma, who prided himself on quality and thoroughness, thought he'd misheard.

"Boil it down to three pages?" he asked incredulously.

"Yes. And include your top three recommendations."

Sharma shook his head and let out a low, burbling noise.

"No, no, no," he said. "Three pages is barely enough for an abstract. This is a complex issue, Giles. There's an entire nexus of challenges. Even if I had twenty pages, I'd just be skimming the surface."

"I understand," replied Prigg, his voice calm and reassuring. "But all I need right now is an executive summary—an appetizer, not a seven-course meal. Remember what The Bard said: *Brevity is the soul of wit.*"

"Shakespeare gave those words to Polonius to say, and Polonius was a pompous fool who ended up with a dagger in his chest."

Prigg chuckled. "Nonetheless, give it the old college try. My assistant will get in touch about our next meeting."

Sharma gave a nod of reluctant agreement.

Prigg stood up and shook his guest's hand.

"It's been a pleasure, Dev."

"Likewise," replied the researcher, a little uncertainly.

"One more thing," added Prigg. "Keep our conversation to yourself, will you? No need to feed the rumour mill."

"Of course."

Prigg smiled benignly as he watched Sharma gather his things and leave the office. He then poured himself another cup of tea and sat down at his desk. The meeting couldn't have gone better. Sharma would soon provide him with a bouquet of eye-popping trial balloons. Once in hand, all Prigg had to do was let go of the strings and see which way the wind blew them.

Chapter 21

Beyond the study of economics, Clive Blunt and Sylvia Kiljoy shared few interests in common. Their mutual dislike, which had aged like cheap wine, was now a vinegary animus from which neither could abstain. As Duffy sat between them in the president's office, he felt like a bartender trying to keep two drunken regulars from taking a swing at one another.

"How much longer do we have to wait for Alex?" complained Kiljoy.

"Patience has never been your strong suit," said Blunt.

"At least I get things done."

"You tear things down; I build things up."

"What self-deluded horseshit."

The sniping between Blunt and Kiljoy reminded Duffy of the lifelong bickering that went on between his two sisters. They couldn't help themselves; after decades of knowing one another, it was simply how they communicated.

"Has Dr. Meriwether been in touch with anyone at HIPE?" asked Duffy, hoping to change the topic.

"A short chat with Hugh Endicott," said Blunt. "He also spoke to the premier's chief of staff."

"What did Prigg have to say?" asked Kiljoy

"Alex said he was evasive. Amalgamation is just a 'blue-sky' discussion at this point, according to Giles."

"Do you believe him?"

"Not for a second."

"Good," said Kiljoy. "I've always thought Prigg was a snake. A clever snake, mind you, but still a snake."

"What about Rose Samaroo?" asked Blunt.

"Snake-like, for sure. But I have a grudging respect for her."

"How so?"

"She's succeeded in a man's world."

"Yes, looks and charm," said Blunt.

"That and more—much more," said Kiljoy. "She's smart, she's determined and she knows what she wants. If Rose Samaroo were a man, she'd already be a university president somewhere."

Blunt let out a harrumph.

"Oh, poor Clive," Kiljoy cooed mockingly. "If only you were a woman, you'd be a president somewhere, eh?"

A pout formed on Blunt's beet-red face. He picked up his phone and began scrolling through his messages.

Duffy tried to picture the two of them as undergrads. Kiljoy likely got the better of Blunt; she had the quicker wit and sharper tongue. Blunt probably had a higher IQ, but his lack of emotional intelligence would have held him back. Their peers and professors probably disliked them equally.

Fifi had a theory that Blunt and Kiljoy had dated for a while. Duffy couldn't see it, but he had to admit that the depth of their dislike for one another might be rooted in romance.

"It all makes sense if you think of them as former lovers, not just academic colleagues," Fifi had once said.

"I don't want to think of them that way," Duffy had replied.

Of course, that's exactly how Duffy now thought of Blunt and Kiljoy. The effect was like PTSD: Duffy didn't just remember the image that Fifi had planted in his brain, he relived the trauma itself.

Eventually, the bear-like frame of Alexander Meriwether ambled through the door and the tension in the room dissolved.

"Sorry to keep you waiting, folks," said Meriwether, accompanied by a waddling Bertie. "I was speaking to Rose Samaroo. She wants to meet."

"When?" asked Kiljoy.

"ASAP."

"What's the format?" asked Blunt.

"Informal. The four of us and four from their side."

"Who are their four?" asked Duffy.

"Rose, Hugh Endicott, Ed Palavoy and their communications person."

"That's Kerri Quartermain," said Duffy. "She's a piece of work."

"Explain," ordered Kiljoy, sounding once again like a general grilling a subordinate.

"I worked with her in the minister's office," said Duffy. "She doesn't have much communications experience, but she talks loudly and often, so people think there's more to her than there is."

"Let's move on," said Meriwether, a little impatiently. "The meeting will be a preliminary chat to let both sides feel one another out."

"Or feel us up," said Kiljoy. "If we let our guard down, HIPE is going to screw us over."

"Do you have to be so vulgar?" asked Blunt.

"Too salty for you, Clive? Better toughen up because we're in for some rough trade."

"Oh, for God's sake," said Blunt. "Can we please talk about strategy?"

Duffy jumped in. "I'd suggest we finalize a holding statement. The media may start calling any time. Frankly, I'm surprised they haven't already."

"Have you started a draft?" asked Meriwether.

"Yes, sir," said Duffy, who had his laptop open on his knees. "I'll send it to all of you now."

Blunt and Kiljoy flipped open their laptops; Meriwether looked over Duffy's shoulder and read the statement out loud:

> *Sir Richard Middling University has played a vital role in the province's higher education system for more than one hundred years. From time to time, discussions arise about how this role should evolve. Sir Middling U wishes to assure the community that our future is bright. We look forward to the next century with pride and confidence.*

"It doesn't say a damn thing," said Kiljoy.

"Yes, it's perfect," said Meriwether.

"Shouldn't we mention the word 'amalgamation'?" asked Blunt.

"Certainly not," said Meriwether. "From now on, the 'A' word is banished."

"Why?" asked Blunt.

"Because the more we say it, the more it sounds inevitable."

"Exactly," agreed Duffy. "We want to control the narrative—and our version of the narrative does not include the 'A' word."

There was a knock at the door. Sophie Munn came in. "I'm sorry for interrupting, Dr. Meriwether, but there's a story on *The Daily Clamour* website that you should all see."

Duffy had the site bookmarked on his laptop. He clicked the link and a large headline popped up:

Province Eyes University Amalgamations
HIPE and Sir Middling U first to merge, sources say

"I guess the media didn't get the memo about the 'A' word," said Kiljoy.

There was silence in the president's office for a brief moment. Then a chorus of ring tones filled the room and everyone grabbed their phones.

"Dear Lord," said Meriwether. "It's the chair of the board."

"I've got the dean of Arts calling," said Blunt.

"I've got a text from the head of the provincial faculty association," said Kiljoy.

Duffy's phone also went ping, ping, ping as the texts and emails from reporters piled up.

"We stick to the holding statement until we know more!" said Duffy, jettisoning his usual deference. "And don't talk to any reporters. Just send them to me."

"What else do we need to do?" asked Blunt, a squeak of panic in his voice.

Duffy, whose deadline experience and crisis-management training leapt to the fore, felt a thrilling rush of adrenaline.

"I have draft statements for faculty, staff and students, as well as for the Board of Governors. I'll update them right now and send them out. We'll also activate the phone bank in the fundraising office to answer calls from parents, donors and alumni."

"Good thinking," said Meriwether.

"I've also got a social-media plan ready to go," said Duffy. "We'll launch it now. I suggest we all meet again in one hour."

"Batten down the hatches, folks," said Meriwether. "We'll be sailing through rough seas for the next few days."

Kiljoy packed up her laptop and began to leave. As she passed Duffy, she leaned down and whispered into his ear, "Good thing you've got control of the narrative, Red."

Meriwether invited Duffy to work out of the boardroom next to his office for the rest of the afternoon.

"That way we can update one another quickly," said the president.

Duffy called his assistant manager, Sequoia Tush.

"Put today's date on all the draft statements and send them out ASAP. If you get any media calls, just forward them my way. And tell J.J. Jones that we need to borrow his fundraising call centre. I'm setting myself up in the boardroom over here."

Duffy had rehearsed such procedures with Tush a half dozen times or more, but this was her first exposure to live fire. He hoped the drills had sunk in.

He grabbed his laptop, phone and notebook and walked out of the president's office and into the adjacent room. It was called the Old Boardroom even though it was the only boardroom in Founders Hall. Its long oak table could accommodate sixteen people—quite a few but not enough for the current size of the university's Board of Governors, which now met in Utility Hall, a multi-purpose auditorium that was also used for town halls, staff training and therapy dog sessions for anxious students.

Duffy preferred the Old Boardroom, which had changed little since it was built in 1923. Wood-paneled and high-ceilinged, the room was adorned with the faded portraits of past presidents and board chairs, all but of one of whom were male Caucasians. There was a distinct odour that clung to the room no matter how vigorously the cleaners scrubbed the carpet and leather upholstery. Like the air in an old church, it was a stale, perfumy scent that invoked the solemnity and ritual of another era.

Duffy and Fifi had once debated the origin of the smell.

"Male hegemony," said Fifi.

"Cigars and whiskey," countered Duffy.

"Same thing."

Sitting on one of the original red-leather chairs, Duffy could almost hear the old governors debating women's suffrage, the role of the monarchy and the merits of Canada's old Red Ensign flag. He ignored their whispers and set up his mobile workstation: laptop, cellphone, chargers, notebook, pen and a bottle of water. He dialed voicemail and was told that he had seven messages, including one from Jill Kaiser in the office of the minister of higher education.

"Call me now, asshole!" her message said.

Duffy decided he better read the story in *The Daily Clamour* first. It was relatively short—ten paragraphs—but it nailed all the details from the Walters Report. It also quoted two anonymous sources.

"Amalgamation is an intriguing proposal," said one. "But does it address the root issues that threaten the sustainability of our post-secondary system?"

Someone's floating a trial balloon, thought Duffy. Before he could flesh out the implications, his phone began to ring. It was a call from a friendly reporter at one of the big-city radio stations.

"Hello?" said Duffy.

"Hey, Dufster, it's Cal Hornby at CHOY-AM. So, amalgamation, eh? What can you tell me, buddy?"

"Listen, Cal, I'll send you a statement, but that's all I've got for you right now."

"Oh, come on, pal. I need some audio."

"Okay, I'll read you the statement."

"You da man, Dufster. Give me a second to get set up."

Duffy could hear some clicking and rustling in the background.

"Okay," said the reporter. "We're rolling. Do your thing, my man."

Duffy cleared his throat and read the statement right through to the end.

"That's it, Cal," he said.

"What about the last sentence?"

"What last sentence? I read you the whole thing."

"The copy I've got ends with the line, 'If that changes, we'll provide an update.'"

"What? Where did you get a copy of the statement?"

"From your president. When you didn't answer my text, I

emailed him and he sent me the statement."

"Read me the last three sentences, will you, Cal?"

"Sure, buddy: 'Sir Middling U wishes to assure the community that our future is bright. We look forward to the next century with confidence and pride. If this changes, we'll be in touch.'"

Duffy let his head hit the table. Meriwether loved to tinker with every statement that Duffy wrote. He must have added that last line as an afterthought.

"Listen, Cal. Can you do me a favour? Can you leave the last line out and just go with what I read to you?"

"Yeah, I guess so. But not every reporter is as understanding as I am. If your prez sent his version to anybody else, they're going to have some fun with it."

"Believe me, I know. Thanks, Cal."

Duffy got up and went looking for Meriwether. He found him in the outer office, talking to Sophie. Bertie was at his side.

"If he poops again," the president was saying, "take a good look at the consistency of his stool and let me know if things are firming up."

"Sir, can I talk to you for a moment?" asked Duffy.

"Oh, hello, James. Yes, of course. Let's go into my office."

"Before you go, sir," said Sophie, "might I suggest that the co-op student take Bertie for a walk and report back on his stool? You know that I love Bertie, but looking after him takes me away from my other duties."

"Yes, of course, Sophie. You're absolutely right. My apologies. You're a skilled executive assistant, not a dog-sitter."

As Meriwether turned to enter his office, Duffy gave Sophie a discreet thumbs up. In reply, she pulled a face that suggested an imminent breakdown.

Inside the president's office, Meriwether sank into the sturdy chair behind his desk.

"Catch me up, James."

"We've put out the holding statement and I've started to respond to the media. One reporter said he'd already received the statement from you."

"Yes, yes. A few reporters emailed me directly, so I passed the statement along. Just keeping up relationships."

"Well, sir, I wonder if you wouldn't mind just sending those emails and voicemails to me for answering. That way I can keep track of how many media requests we're getting and whether we've responded to all of them."

"Ah, yes, metrics and protocol. Perfect. I'll have Sophie direct everything to you. Mustn't micromanage."

"Thank you, sir. One other thing. Apparently, the statement you've been sending out is slightly different than the one we agreed on earlier."

"Is it?"

"Yes, sir. There was an additional line tacked on the end."

"Ah yes! I thought it needed a little something to wrap it up, a bow on the package if you will."

Duffy pulled up the president's version on his laptop and read it out loud.

"Oh, good grief!" said Meriwether, realising how the added line sounded. "The media are going to make hay out of that. I do apologize, James. I thought I was helping, but clearly you knew what you were doing from the get-go. *Mea culpa*. Won't happen again."

"Thank you, sir. Have you heard from anyone at HIPE or the government?"

"Hugh Endicott swears the leak didn't come from his end. And I've placed a call to the ministry but haven't heard back."

Duffy shared his suspicion that the story in *The Daily Clamour* was a trial balloon planted with the media by someone in government.

"Yes," concurred Meriwether. "It sounds like someone is test-driving an idea. If that's the case, there may be a bigger plan afoot."

"Yes, sir."

"I'll give Giles Prigg another call and see what I can find out."

"I'll check with the minister's office," said Duffy. "I have to return the chief of staff's call anyway."

"Before you go, James, would you ask Sophie if the co-op student has walked Bertie yet? And if he hasn't, would you mind walking Bertie yourself? I don't think Sophie is a dog person."

Chapter 22

Duffy spent the rest of the afternoon returning media calls and providing updates to Sequoia Tush. By the time he was done, the sun was setting and the encroaching darkness had filled the Old Boardroom. When he looked up from his laptop, he was startled by the gloom. In the light of day, the boardroom looked clubby and comfortable; at dusk, it was the perfect place for a haunting. Duffy imagined the ghost of some long-dead dean bemoaning the calibre of students these days. Sufficiently spooked, he began fumbling for the lamp at the centre of the table. A knock at the door sent a current of terror up his spine.

"Jesus!" he yelled.

The door opened and Sophie stepped in.

"Are you okay, James?"

"Yes, sorry."

"Turn on the table lamp."

"I'm trying. Hold the door open so I can see what I'm doing."

Duffy found the lamp and gave the chain a sharp tug. The sixty-watt bulb threw off a stingy amount of light, just enough to draw attention to the dark corners of the room.

"Were you asleep?" asked Sophie.

"No," Duffy said defensively. "I was focused on my laptop and didn't realize how dark it was getting."

Sophie crossed her arms and grinned.

"I scared the shit out of you, didn't I?"

"Yes, Moneypenny, you did."

Sophie glided over to the table. Duffy usually noticed what she was wearing because everything looked so lovely on her slender body. Today, however, he had been distracted by the turmoil over *The Daily Clamour* story. It wasn't until now that he noticed her outfit: a white cotton blouse, houndstooth slacks and black leather ankle boots.

Audrey Hepburn, he thought, remembering his father's favourite actress.

Sophie walked around to where he was sitting and lifted herself onto the table with a light bounce. She sat there, lovely legs swinging playfully.

"Make yourself at home," said Duffy.

"Hey, it's quitting time. Everyone but you is clocking out."

"No rest for the wicked," he said. "By the way, thanks for the heads-up about the amalgamation story. How did you come across it?"

"You're not the only one who follows the news."

"I know. But I get paid to follow it."

"Well, I *do* read the papers. But to be honest, a friend of mine at *The Daily Clamour* sent me the amalgamation story."

"Oh yeah? Who's the friend."

"Tony DaSilva. He's an assignment editor."

"I've heard the name," said Duffy. "How do you know him?"

"We travelled through South America together."

A pang of jealousy shot through Duffy. He knew it was stupid. He and Sophie had gone out exactly once, and that had been cut so short that it didn't really count. Yet here he was getting worked up over a guy Sophie had known five or six years ago. Get a grip, he thought. How would James Bond play this? Urbane and sophisticated, of course.

"A male travel companion, eh?" he said. "Safer that way."

"Actually, he was my boyfriend at the time," said Sophie. "For a while, I thought he might be the one. My dad told me to go on a long trip with him to find out for sure."

Duffy felt a tightness suddenly coil in his gut. He struggled to keep up his Bond-like poise.

"Sounds like your dad is pretty open-minded."

"He is. So's my mom. They quit their jobs and travelled around Europe in the eighties to see if they were a good fit for marriage."

Duffy thought of his own family. They could abide excessive drinking, misogyny and homophobia. But for some reason, premarital sex was too much to bear.

"Your parents sound more liberal than mine."

"They're pretty cool," said Sophie, smiling at the thought of them.

"So, what happened with Tony?"

"I met someone else. The three of us travelled together for a while, but it got awkward. Tony went off and finished the trip on his own."

"Two guys and a beautiful woman. Yes, that would be awkward."

"Two women and a guy, actually."

It took Duffy a moment to comprehend the gist of Sophie's clarification. Then it was like someone had pulled the plug on his power supply; his brain slipped into a fog and his smile went slack on one side.

"Are you okay, James?"

Duffy grabbed his water bottle and took a swig.

"Oh, James ... you're weirded out, aren't you?"

"Um, no, not really," he lied.

"You *are* weirded out."

"Surprised, that's all. You know, I really like you, and I thought we had a connection, and well, I guess I misunderstood the signals."

"What signals were you picking up?"

"That you were interested in me, you know, in a hand-holding and kissing sort of way. Those kinds of signals."

Sophie took Duffy's right hand in both of hers.

"I do like you, James, and exactly how you want me to like you. But I'm bisexual—I like women too. That's who I am. I thought you knew."

"How would I know that?"

"Because you're friends with Fifi. When you said she asked if I was going out with anyone, I thought for sure you knew that I was bi."

"No, I didn't," said Duffy, taking another sip from his water bottle. "I'm a bit of a hayseed when it comes to these things."

"Well, you're a cute hayseed."

"Cute enough to kiss?" The words popped out of Duffy's mouth like they had a will of their own. He was embarrassed. But before he could apologize, Sophie slid off the table, bent down and positioned her lips just a breath away from his.

"Let's see," she said with a sultry smile.

She gave Duffy a long, sensuous kiss, sliding both of her hands around his neck and caressing the back of his head where the hair was long and soft. Then she eased away and looked into his eyes.

"Yes, cute enough to kiss."

"I liked that," Duffy said with a directness that surprised himself.

"You should," said Sophie. "I'm a good kisser. But that's it for now. I've got errands to run. I'm free this Friday. Think of something fun to do and let me know where to meet you. We can get to know each other better, without any weirding out."

She gave Duffy an impish smile, then turned around and left.

Yes, definitely Audrey Hepburn.

Duffy sat in the dim light of the Old Boardroom, enjoying an inward glow that kept the gloom at bay. He felt better than he had for some time. He saw a path forward with Sophie—a path through unfamiliar territory, perhaps, but a path nonetheless.

"I better not fuck this up," he said.

Chapter 23

The meeting with HIPE was held in Ye Olde Henfield Inn, a neutral location where both institutions held their contract negotiations with employee unions. Kiljoy and Palavoy knew it well, but the others only by reputation.

The Olde Hen, as locals called it, was the venue of choice for student proms, sports-club dinners and those looking to stretch their wedding-reception dollar. At first glance, the hallways and event spaces appeared to have weathered such storms surprisingly well. It was only when you looked closer that you noticed the mould, chipped paint and carpet stains.

"It's a little down at heel," observed Blunt.

"It grows on you," said Kiljoy.

"Literally," Meriwether said with a laugh. "By the way, have I ever told you about the time I mistook a brothel for a guest house while on shore leave in Singapore?"

Blunt and Kiljoy were both about to reply "yes, many times," when Duffy entered the room.

"HIPE is running late," he said, brandishing his phone as if it were proof. "They're also bringing their lawyer."

"The sneaky buggers want to outnumber us from the start," said Kiljoy.

"Now, now, folks," said Meriwether. "Remember, this is just an informal chat, a little reconnoitering to get the lay of the land. We need to keep our emotions in check."

"Of course, Alex," said Kiljoy. "I was just stating the obvious. The HIPE gang are duplicitous weasels. First, they pitch amalgamation behind our backs, and now they're trying to outgun us at the table. Believe me, it's useful to be clear-eyed about how they operate."

"Point taken," said Meriwether.

There was a knock at the door; Rose Samaroo poked her head in.

"Is this the party room?" she asked with a bright smile.

"Indeed, it is," Meriwether replied cheerfully, his diplomatic skills leaping into action.

He stood up and shook hands with each member of the HIPE team: Samaroo, Hugh Endicott, Ed Palavoy, Kerri Quartermain and the university's lawyer, a hefty man named Parker Pratt.

"We ordered coffee and tea," said Meriwether. "And it looks like they threw in some fresh fruit and muffins. Please help yourselves."

The HIPE team removed their coats and nodded their greetings to Blunt, Kiljoy and Duffy.

"Why don't we jump right in," said Meriwether, putting on his reading glasses and pulling out a brief agenda.

Kerri Quartermain cleared her throat and raised her hand. Duffy had almost forgotten how annoying she could be. Her appearance was deceiving. A frumpy dresser with a lumpy physique and doughy face, Quartermain gave the impression of being a second- or third-string staffer, someone who booked the rooms and ordered the coffee. Duffy had never heard her say a necessary or insightful thing, yet she had a way of showing up at high-level meetings and inserting herself into important discussions. Now, having garnered everyone's attention, she stood up and addressed the table.

"Thank you," she said, as if acknowledging applause. "I don't know you as well as you know one another, so allow me to introduce myself. I'm Kerri Quartermain. I recently joined HIPE as assistant vice-president of communications. Previously, I was a deputy advisor to the minister of higher education. My knowledge of the inner workings of government is thorough and up to date. Please feel free to use me as a sounding board whenever you have questions about what the premier's office might be thinking. Thank you."

Same old Kerri Q, thought Duffy.

"Yes, well … thank you, Ms. Quartermain," said Meriwether. He then looked to Parker Pratt in case the HIPE lawyer also felt compelled to introduce himself further. Pratt gave a smile and a modest wave, a gesture that suggested he was perfectly fine to remain silent.

Before Meriwether could continue, however, Hugh Endicott chimed in.

"Excuse me, Alex. Before we get rolling, I just want you to know that I've asked Rose to be our point person on these discussions. HIPE's a big place, and I've got a lot on my plate. Rose has a great handle on this file, and of course, you've all worked with her before."

Meriwether nodded. He was about to get things back on track when Samaroo stood up.

"Thanks, Hugh. And good morning, everyone. I want to thank you all for making the trip to Henfield to meet with us. It's eleven-fifteen now, and some of us have a hard stop at noon. To move things along, I've taken the liberty of drafting a one-page summary of the Walters Report, which Kerri will now hand out."

Kiljoy leaned in close to Duffy and whispered, "Watch and

learn, Red." She sat upright and rapped the knuckles of her right hand on the table several times.

"Point of order, Madam Speaker!"

Samaroo stopped speaking in mid-sentence. Quartermain dropped the handouts; the sheets of paper fluttered and sailed off in all directions.

"Who put you in charge, Rosy?" Kiljoy said tersely.

"I beg your pardon?"

"Who put you in charge?" repeated Kiljoy. "I came here for a dialogue, not a lecture. I've read the HIPE proposal and I have questions. If you plan to scram at noon, I want answers, not empty message-speak."

Samaroo composed herself. She was no longer smiling, but she was back in the zone.

"Ah, the voice of organized labour," she said. "I admire your candour, Sylvia. First of all, it's not HIPE's proposal; the report was written by Bud Walters at the Ministry of Education."

"That's not entirely true, is it Rosy?" said Kiljoy.

"Sylvia, please!" said Meriwether. "I appreciate your concern, but let's keep this civil."

"Thank you, Alex," said Samaroo. "I understand that this is a sensitive topic. Emotions are bound to run high. But as we all know, Bud Walters has proposed the concept of amalgamation many times before. He sought our views, and we were happy to provide them."

"And you spent a whack of HIPE dough to hire a big-city public affairs firm to work up a cost-savings projection that supports your case," said Kiljoy.

"That particular engagement yielded a broad array of data that will be helpful with a number of projects," replied Samaroo. "And yes, some of the data was useful to Mr. Walters in outlining his proposal."

"If that's true, why didn't you tap into the stable of geniuses

Sir Middling U

you've got in HIPE's business school?" said Kiljoy. "It pains me to say it, but HIPE has some damn good math people."

Samaroo turned to the rest of the table. "Listen, folks, I'm happy to answer questions as long as they're constructive. Alex and Clive, what would you like to know?"

"I'd like to know why you didn't give us a courtesy heads-up about this proposal," said Blunt. "You worked with us at Sir Middling U for nearly ten years, Rose. You were a trusted colleague."

"Well, Clive, if you want frankness, I'm happy to oblige," said Samaroo. "I tried my best to drag Sir Middling University into the twenty-first century, but you and your colleagues resisted every step of the way. Introduce business courses for arts majors? No. Offer entrepreneurship courses to math and science students? No. Add more online course offerings? No, again. Sir Middling U is hopelessly mired in a swamp of inertia. On the other hand, I am a champion of forward-thinking change. I have no patience for excuses or whiners. Why didn't I consult you? Because I want to aim high and get things done. And I refuse to apologize for that."

Samaroo sat down and returned the glares coming at her from the Sir Middling side of the table.

"Well, that was entertaining," said Meriwether. "I'm not sure who to give the Oscar to."

"Solid performances all round," said Endicott, raising his hands in a mock clap.

"Listen, people," said Meriwether. "This is a sensitive topic, and people are passionate about their views. But I urge you all to let go of past resentments and focus on the task at hand. I'd also like to point out that we both have faculty, staff and students who are anxious to know what the Walters Report means for them. For their sakes, let's agree to focus on what's best for both institutions."

"I appreciate the sentiment, Alex," said Endicott. "But that's a tall order, considering the proposal that's on the table. We plan to push hard for amalgamation. There *will* be job losses, but we think the long-term benefits outweigh the short-term pain."

"That's because you'll get the benefits and we'll get the pain," said Kiljoy.

"I hear you," said the president of HIPE. "But the job numbers in the report are open for discussion. Sylvia, you've bargained enough collective agreements to know that trade-offs make the world go round. Amalgamation is going to happen. The question is: What are we each willing to give up to get the best deal for our people?"

Meriwether jumped in before someone else from the HIPE team could take the floor.

"We both have a lot to think about, and it's getting close to noon," he said. "Might I suggest that Rose and I touch base next week to see if there's a desire to meet again? This time with an agreed-upon agenda and a more business-like mindset?"

"I'm always open to dialogue," said Samaroo.

Silence filled the room. Parker Pratt looked around the table to see if anyone else was planning to speak.

"Is there something you wanted to add, Mr. Pratt?" asked Meriwether.

"Yes, Mr. President, there is. As HIPE's legal counsel, I just want to remind everyone about our obligations under the government's access-to-information legislation."

"Yes?" said Meriwether.

"Well, the amalgamation report is bound to attract media interest. Some of the more aggressive reporters may file access requests to obtain any documents pertaining to our internal reports and discussions."

"And?"

"And you might think twice about what you say in emails or scribble in your notebooks."

"What are you getting at, Mr. Pratt?"

"He's telling us how to do an end-run around the

access-to-information law," said Kiljoy.

"Goodness, no," said Pratt, flustered by the accuracy of the allegation. "I'm simply reminding this group of the relevant legislation and our obligations under it. The vectors here are communications, transparency and prudence."

"What on earth does that mean?" asked Meriwether, who thought he knew all about vectors from his naval navigation training.

Pratt's face looked like a ripe tomato popping out of a button-down shirt. Kerri Quartermain rescued her colleague.

"Thank you, Parker," she said. "Before we all leave, I'd like to give you a heads-up that my office has just issued a news release about this morning's meeting. It emphasizes HIPE's sincere desire to work collaboratively with Sir Middling U as we make progress towards amalgamation."

"Oh, come off it, Kerri!" said Duffy. "It's not collaboration if you tell us after the news release has gone out."

"Save your breath, Red," said Kiljoy. "These fuckers are playing for keeps."

Chapter 24

There were two surprises waiting for Duffy when he arrived at work the next morning. The first was his office door, which lay on its side against the wall next to his desk. There was a note taped to its handle:

> *Professor Duffy,*
> *Me and the crew came by to install your door. Didn't want to hang it without you here to supervise (you being a stickler and all). Get Terri to book a new install date, okay?*
> *Lloyd*

Duffy removed the note from the doorknob and let out a long sigh.

The second surprise lay on his desk. It was a package, identical in size and shape to the one that contained *More Shitty Weather*. It, too, came with a note.

Hi James!
Good thing you didn't promote Dr. Mittens' book yet! Some joker inserted the f-word into several poems after we proofed the galleys. Dr. Mittens thinks it was one of his grad students. Can you believe that? Anyway, here's a new proof copy. Give it a read and let me know about that promo on the website!
P.S.: The social media campaign is generating some great buzz!

There was a signature at the bottom of the note, but Duffy couldn't make it out. Shmarly? Charmela? Zmerjo? He held the paper sideways and upside down; neither angle made the name any more legible. Duffy smiled, nonetheless. Ignoring the original parcel had worked out. The old Shitstorm Decision Matrix was still in tune, despite the fact that Mittens had complained to Blunt. Rather than tempt fate, however, Duffy decided to open the new package.

There was no art on the cover of the printer's proof, just the title and the author's name.

More Shitty Weather
By Percy Q. Mittens, PhD

For no particular reason, Duffy took out a pen and wrote three words between the title and the author's name.

More Shitty Weather
A Poetic Parody
By Percy Q. Mittens, PhD

As Duffy finished his scribbling, Coyne stuck her head into his office.

"I see you got the book," she said.

"Yes. *More Shitty Weather 2.0.*"

"Did you hear that Professor Mittens did a pop-up poetry reading in Sir Dickie's Pub last week?"

"No," said Duffy. "How did it go?"

"It was tequila Tuesday. The crowd pelted him with slices of lime."

"That's a bit harsh."

"Apparently Mittens threw a lime rind back at the crowd and hit some girl in the eye. His publicist had to hustle him out before the girl's boyfriend put the boots to him."

"Poetry's a rough business," said Duffy.

"Especially when you mix it with tequila."

Just then, Duffy's phone began to ring. He shooed Coyne out of his doorway before picking up.

"Hello," he said.

"It's Fifi. I haven't heard from you for a few days. What's going on?"

"Lots," said Duffy, plopping down in his office chair. "Where do you want me to start?"

"With Meriwether and Blunt. When are they going to meet with me, Morris and Tessa?"

Given his failure on that front, Duffy shifted into delay mode.

"Why don't I start with me and Sophie?"

"I already know all about that."

"You do?"

"Of course. You weirded out when Sophie told you she was bisexual."

"For the record, I did not weird out. And how the hell do you know about that?"

"Us gals stick together."

"I can't believe Sophie told you."

"She didn't."

"Then how do you know?"

"She told a friend of mine."

"Did she tell you we're going out Friday night?"

"Of course. You better pick something fun. Hey! I know just the thing. *Rocky* is playing at the Art Haus Theatre this weekend!"

"*Rocky*?"

"Yeah, it's hilarious. Sophie will love it!"

Duffy liked boxing. It was one of the few interests he shared with his father. The old man had boxed with the police athletic club during his days as a young flatfoot. He tried to get his son to take it up, but Duffy was too thin and gangly. "A giraffe with mittens," the old man had said. Still, father and son enjoyed watching matches on TV and going to boxing movies together. They'd loved the first two *Rocky* pictures, but after seeing DeNiro in *Raging Bull*, neither could bear watching Stallone plod around the ring like a lead-footed ape.

Duffy didn't remember *Rocky* being hilarious, as Fifi described it, and he didn't peg Sophie for a boxing fan. But what did he know?

"*Rocky* sounds good," he said. "If you think Sophie will like it."

"Of course, she will. Go to the ten o'clock show. I'll be there with a few friends. We can sit together."

Duffy wasn't keen on a group date, especially one that included Fifi and her rowdy friends. He wanted Sophie all to himself. But he also wanted her to enjoy the evening. The smart thing would be to ask Sophie what she'd prefer.

"So," said Fifi, "what did Meriwether and Blunt have to say about a meeting?"

"Blunt won't budge, and Meriwether is following Clive's lead. Blunt says the Dewlap lecture and the panel event are routine activities for a university, and he doesn't want to get drawn into a debate about statues while amalgamation is in the news."

"Well, he's going get drawn into it whether he likes it or not. We're going to see to that. Blunt and Meriwether might as well get on the right side of this from the start. They're going to look like gormless bureaucrats when we hold a sit-in and the TV cameras start to roll."

"I told him that, Feef. I mean, I didn't call him a gormless bureaucrat, but I made it clear that the university was going to take a beating if it didn't show support for a credible debate about the statue and namesake issues."

"And?"

"And Blunt's head remains firmly in the sand."

"Well, Duffy, you better start writing a media statement because Founders Hall is going to fill up with protesters over the next few days."

"I've already written two statements."

"Two?"

"A first-day statement that says, 'The university cannot take sides.' And a second-day statement that says, 'After careful thought, the university supports the panel discussion on historical monuments.'"

"Ha!" said Fifi. "Do you think Blunt and Meriwether will cave that quickly?"

"Who knows? Depends on how bad they look in the media."

"We can make them look plenty bad."

"I know. That's why I wrote the second-day statement."

Duffy had two meetings later that morning. The first was the Risk Assessment and Management Operations Sub-Group; the second was the University Procurement Oversight Committee. Both reminded him of the Easter Vigils of his childhood, those interminable services presided over by a sonorous old priest who kept forgetting where he was in the liturgy. Father Tom, smelling of Listerine and Crown Royal, would apologize and start over again. It was a sort of Groundhog Day penance that kept the faithful in the airless confines of Our Lady of the Immaculate Conception for the better part of three hours. To Duffy's mind, the long-ago vigils and his present-day meetings shared much in common. Except now there were no pews to lie down on, no siblings to pester, and no father to rescue him with the whispered reprieve, "Let's you and me get some air, eh, son?"

To deal with the monotony of the university meetings, Duffy would often type up a fabricated version of the discussion and email it to Sophie.

- Dr. Spleen, I know we've already spent sixty minutes defining our terms, but I'd like to unpack the notion of diluted risk depreciation a little more.
- Certainly, Ann. Is it the amortization formulae or the fungible investment analysis that you'd like to revisit?
- It's the word 'fungible' that really turns me on. Can you probe that in greater depth?
- Of course. It may cut into our lunch hour, but it's time well spent.

When his last meeting came to an end, Duffy raced to the cafeteria to catch the final serving of lunch. He grabbed a chocolate milk and the only remaining sandwich—a soggy egg-salad on plain white bread. Duffy took his humble repast to a table at the back of the dining hall, where he cleared away the remains of someone else's lunch and sat down.

Halfway through the sandwich, his phone rang.

"Hey, James, it's Sophie. I heard you want to see *Rocky* Friday night?"

"How did you hear that?"

"A friend of Fifi's told me."

"I think you and Fifi have too many friends."

"Want to hear something else?"

"Sure, especially if it comes from one of your friends."

"Fifi asked me why I was attracted to you."

"What did you say?"

"I said because you're funny and you look like Prince Harry."

"Hmmm. Isn't he going bald?"

"Not as much as his brother."

"Right. Anything else that attracts you?"

"You once played in a Springsteen tribute band."

"Well, when you put it like that, I do sound pretty cool."

"It'd be even cooler if you got the band back together."

"I might just do that."

"There's something you need to do first."

"What?"

"Get over whatever hang-ups you have about my sexuality. It's not like I'm going to fool around on you, James. If we're dating, I'm all yours."

"Why do you think I have a hang-up about this?"

"Because your eyeballs popped out like Bart Simpson when I told you. And because Fifi says you've got a lot of Catholic stuff to work through."

"The Catholic stuff is probably true. But the bisexual thing, well, it's not so much a hang-up as it is a lack of familiarity. I don't think I know any other bi people."

"Yes, you do. You just don't realize it."

"Really?"

"Really."

"Sophie, I'm sorry if I seem judgemental. It's not that I think it's weird; it's just that it's new to me. Can you be patient while I get used to it?"

"Yes, but my patience has limits. This is your chance to date a good woman and stretch your mind a little. Heck, you might even get laid."

"And here I was just hoping for another kiss."

"See? You are funny. Now you just have to pass the *Rocky* test."

"Why do I get the feeling there's an inside joke here?"

"Don't worry, it'll all make sense Friday night."

"What does that mean?"

"It means come by my place at nine o'clock and we'll walk over to the Art Haus together."

"Sounds good. By the way, Fifi said she's going with some friends. Do you mind sitting with them?"

"Of course not. Her troupe's hilarious."

"You think The Fabulous Ladies will be with her?"

"Probably. *Rocky* is right up their alley: the campy costumes, the sexual innuendo, the music."

The penny finally dropped, hitting Duffy right between the eyes like a piece of flying toast.

"Sophie, we're not talking about *Rocky* the boxing movie, are we?"

A peal of laughter filled Duffy's phone. It went on and on, up and down, a rowdy rollercoaster of mirth. Duffy detected more than one voice on the line—at least two but possibly three or more.

"Slut!" yelled someone.

"Asshole!" shrieked another.

Duffy recognized the insults. He had seen the *Rocky Horror Picture Show* when he was an undergrad. He remembered the audience participation—the costumes, the lighters and the insults, the last of which were flung with raucous ferocity at the characters on the screen.

"Okay, you got me," he said. "Well played."

It took a minute for Sophie and her friends to stop laughing.

"Oh, Duffy, I'm sorry, but that was *sooooo* much fun!"

"Who's with you, Sophie?"

"Fifi and a couple of friends."

"HI, DUFFY!"

"Hi, Feef. Can you put Sophie back on the phone?"

There was a shuffling sound, like the phone was being passed around, and then Sophie came back on.

"Hey, James, are you mad?"

"No. I enjoy being the butt of a good joke."

"We thought you could take it. We wouldn't have done it otherwise."

"I'm not sure that's a compliment."

"Believe me, it is."

"So, you and Fifi are friends?"

"Of course. We're on, like, two or three committees together."

"And when Feef asked me if you were dating someone, that was all about getting me to ask you out?"

"Something like that."

"Hilarious," said Duffy, a trace of annoyance in his voice.

"Oh, Duffy, take it a like a man."

Or like a woman, thought Duffy. He regretted it instantly. Was that an offensive thing to think? Or just a meaningless mental quip? Duffy had no idea, but it had struck an emotional trip wire in his brain. For about the millionth time in his life, he felt the torment of a tightly wound conscience surge through him like a spring river. He closed his eyes and took a long, deep breath.

"Are you still there, James?" asked Sophie.

"Yes," he replied. "Listen, I just want to say that I'm glad you're taking a chance on me."

"Me, too," replied Sophie. "Just be here Friday night at nine. And dress up!"

"Can I go as Rocky Balboa?"

"As long as the boxing trunks are skin-tight and covered in glitter."

"I was afraid you'd say that."

Chapter 25

Dev Sharma was as good as his word. He delivered a three-page summary to Giles Prigg exactly one week after their first meeting.

The document included a concise description of the key issues, just enough facts to cause some shock and awe, and an appendix with links to half a dozen research studies. Best of all, from Prigg's perspective, it included three hot-button recommendations:

1. *Cap total increases in faculty and administrative compensation at no more than the consumer price index.*
2. *Require all full-time faculty who are not actively producing research to teach a minimum of four courses per year.*
3. *Demand annual cost-reduction and revenue-generation strategies from each university.*

Prigg was delighted. It was exactly the kind of stink bomb he was hoping for.

"This is perfect, Dev. Now, leave it with me. I'll share it with a few trusted colleagues to get the conversation started."

Sharma looked like a man who had something to get off his chest.

"What is it, Dev?" asked Prigg.

"Listen, Giles. As a research professional, I feel uncomfortable authoring such a brief report on such a complex topic. It barely skims the surface. I'd hate for that document to make its way into the public domain without a more substantial backgrounder to give it the context it needs."

"What would make you feel better, Dev?"

"Well, I'd like to start work on a more detailed report. I have all the research; I just need time to write a first draft."

"How much time?"

"A couple of weeks."

Prigg put his hand on Sharma's shoulder and gave the younger man a reassuring smile.

"Sure, Dev. Let's make it part of the engagement. I'll have my assistant update your contract to include a thorough background report. How does that sound?"

"Better."

"Good. Now, I've got to run and I'm sure you're itching to start writing your opus. I'll check in with you in a week or so to see how it's coming along."

"There's one other thing," said Sharma. "Is the minister of higher education aware of the work you've got me doing? I have a lot of respect for Anne Moreno. I'd hate for her to think I was going behind her back."

"Of course, she is, Dev. My office does this kind of exploratory work for every minister in cabinet. It gives them cover and protects their relationships with key stakeholders, like unions and industry groups."

"Ah, yes. What you political types call 'plausible deniability,' " said Sharma, a hint of cynicism in his voice.

"Call it what you like. It's how the sausage gets made."

The two men shook hands. Sharma picked up his briefcase and made his way out of the office of the premier's chief of staff. When he was gone, Prigg walked into the outer office and handed a thumb drive containing Sharma's report to a young man sitting at the reception desk.

"Todd, there's a document on this drive that I'd like you to paste onto the letterhead of the minister of higher education. Add the word 'Confidential' at the top and print it out for me."

As Prigg walked back to his office, he turned and added, "Give me back the thumb drive when you're done."

"Certainly," said Todd. "Do you want me to keep a copy on file?"

"Absolutely not."

Chapter 26

When Duffy arrived at his office, Terri Coyne was sitting at his desk, reading the latest copy of *The Rat's Ass*.

"Comfortable?" he asked.

"Yeah, I am, thank you. You've got the best chair in the office. With my back troubles, I could really use one of these."

"I'll see if I can find the money in our budget," said Duffy.

He hung up his leather jacket and checked the office coffee maker. The pot was empty. He examined its grimy insides, trying to decide if it really needed a wash before brewing another pot.

"Hey, James," said Terri. "Have you ever heard of a club called the Student Front Demanding Justice?"

"Yeah. It's the youth brigade of *Le Collectif radical*."

"Well, it looks like they're trying to mess with that racist you called out."

"What are you talking about? I haven't called anyone a racist."

Terri pointed to the story that ran across the front page of the student newspaper.

Professor to Bring 'Racist' Speaker to Campus
Students and faculty plan solidarity protest

"You've got to be kidding!" said Duffy.

"Read farther down," said Terri. "They quote you calling Rufus Lillidew and this Dewlap fella a pair of racists."

"Oh, for fuck's sake!"

"Are you allowed to call someone a racist?"

"I didn't call anyone a racist. Some little rat from the Student Front dreamed that up and spread it around."

Duffy's phone rang. It was Blunt.

"Have you seen *The Rat's Ass* this morning, James?"

"Just now. To be clear, I did not call anyone a racist. The reporter didn't even contact me for comment. They got it all from that student I told you about. I'll call the editor right now and get him to remove the section about me from their web version."

"What about the print version?"

"That's trickier, but I'll try to get the editor to pull back as many copies as he can."

"Have you talked to Rufus Lillidew yet?"

"I have an appointment with him this morning."

"Beg his forgiveness, James, and put this fire out, *pronto!*"

When Blunt had hung up, Duffy called *The Rat's Ass*. The editorial staff always worked late the night before the paper came out, so he wasn't surprised when no one answered the newsroom phone. He tried the editor-in-chief's mobile. It rang ten times before a painfully hungover Mike Zivchek picked up.

"Mike, it's James Duffy."

"Who?" the editor said groggily.

"James Duffy, Sir Middling's director of communications."

"It's like fucking nine a.m.," groaned Zivchek.

"Mike, listen to me carefully. You're in real shit. I mean *serious* poop. I have never called Rufus Lillidew or Harrison Dewlap a racist. And your reporter never called me to ask about it. Lillidew and Dewlap are probably going to sue your pants off. And if they don't, I will."

"Oh, crap. Is this for real?"

"Yes, Mike, this is a real adult-type situation—you know, the kind with consequences and all. Now, I can't tell you what to do, but if you were my little brother, I would advise you to get out of bed right now and remove that paragraph from your online story. Then I would urge you to race around campus and get rid of every copy of today's paper you can find. Then I'd say, 'Mikey, you should apologize to Dr. Lillidew and Harrison Dewlap immediately.'"

"Not so fast, Mr. Duffy. You're *The Man*—the voice of the administration. The Student Newspaper Society warned us about guys like you. Listen, no offence, but I gotta talk to our lawyer first."

"You do that, Mike. But the sooner you get moving, the less likely you'll get sued."

"What about the editorial?"

"What editorial?" said Duffy, flipping to the opinion pages at the back of the newspaper.

The headline on the lead item read:

Dufus Lillidew Strikes Again!

"Yeah, you might want to run that past your lawyer too," said Duffy.

He hung up. What next? He tried to decide if he should post a message to social media denying the quote in *The Rat's Ass*. Would it help? Or would it just pour gasoline on the fire? He decided the misquote was too serious to ignore. He popped an antacid tablet and began typing:

Re: @theRatsAss statue story: I did NOT say what the

@theRatsAss said I said. The editor admits the error and apologizes.

The last line was premature, but Duffy felt his denial needed some oomph. He hit "post." As he searched for Rufus Lillidew's email, his phone began to buzz. His social-media post was already attracting comments.

- So, dickhead, you support these racist profs?
- What a typical PR scumbag! You said it, you own it!
- You want cancel culture? Cancel my donation to Sir Middling U!

"Oh my, aren't you the popular one!" said Coyne, who had drifted back into Duffy's office and was scrolling through social media on her phone.

Duffy looked up. "It's going to be another crappy day in the Communications Department."

"Is there any other kind?" said Coyne.

She gave Duffy an enigmatic smile and then walked back to her desk, humming a Springsteen tune. It sounded like "Badlands."

Duffy looked at his old guitar, which was propped up behind his desk.

Maybe I *should* get the band back together, he thought.

Chapter 27

The building that housed Sir Middling U's Humanities and Social Science Department was aptly named. The Academic Complex was a maze of zigzag corridors, circular passageways and locked doors. Even the most frequent visitors would get lost now and then, searching for a way out and finding only dead ends.

"Just like an arts student," quipped one English major.

The tangled network was the product of a seemingly endless project to improve the physical connections between three separate wings, each constructed in a different era and style. Every time one director of physical resources retired, his or her successor would try to address the design flaws with ever more eccentric walkways and tunnels. Each addition generated a new layer of directional signage; so much, in fact, that the lobby of the Academic Complex looked like a gallery of wayfinding art.

Duffy was looking for Room 2C-17. Logic would suggest that it was on the second floor of the C wing, but the campus map said it was on the third floor of the A wing.

"Excuse me," Duffy asked a passing student. "I'm looking for the office of Professor Rufus Lillidew?"

"You mean *Dufus* Lillidew, the racist prick?" said the young woman. "Just down the hall on the left."

"Thank you."

Duffy walked a little farther and turned left. One office door stood out: it was covered in an overlapping mass of political cartoons. Taped to the centre of this paper quilt was Sir Middling U's policy on freedom of speech.

Duffy steadied himself, straightened his shoulders and knocked on the door.

"Enter!" said a voice full of thespian vitality.

Duffy fumbled beneath the mat of cartoons for the doorknob. He found it, gave a vigorous twist and let himself in. The office was long and narrow. At the end of it stood a very tall, very slender man. Duffy, who had never met Lillidew in person, was surprised by the professor's appearance. His head, which reminded Duffy of an Easter Island *moai,* was topped with a shock of grey hair. A pair of round spectacles perched on his beak-like nose, and a closely clipped goatee covered his chin. He wore a high-collared dress shirt, a cravat and a frock coat. Taken together, the man looked like an actor about to perform in an Edwardian play—a farcical satire, no doubt.

"Dr. Lillidew?" said Duffy.

"In the flesh!" declaimed the thin giant. Lillidew extended a long arm and shook Duffy's hand. "You must be the public relations man who likes to call people names."

Duffy, who had consulted his copy of *Tough Conversations* prior to coming over, smiled nervously. "Yes and no," he said. "Yes, I'm the university's director of communications. And no, I haven't been calling you or Harrison Dewlap any names."

"I hear otherwise, but please sit down."

Lillidew began to steam milk with a compact espresso maker that sat on a small bar fridge beside his desk.

"Coffee?" he asked. "I make a real *macchiato*—double espresso with what the Italians call a 'stain' of steamed milk on top."

"Sounds great."

"It's one of my vices. The foreman in building maintenance keeps telling me that I'm not allowed to have this machine in my office, but he comes by every Monday morning for a latte and a chat."

"Lloyd?"

"Yes, Lloyd Schmidt. He's a set builder in the community theatre that I direct. You know, I once persuaded him to play a Lost Boy in a Peter Pan panto. He wasn't half bad."

"If only he could fix doors," said Duffy.

Lillidew cocked his large head to one side. "Not sure I follow."

"Just a little battle of wits I'm having over a squeaky door hinge."

Lillidew smiled politely and went back to steaming the milk.

Duffy looked around the office. Despite the many privileges afforded to academics, few were given decent offices. Most worked in cubbyholes that had barely enough room for a desk and two chairs. Lillidew's office was larger than most—perhaps owing to the man's size—but it was certainly not spacious. To reach his desk, the professor had just enough room to pass between a modest bookcase on one side and a waist-high filing cabinet on the other. The walls were filled with posters and black-and-white photographs of serious-looking white men—Lillidew's academic heroes, no doubt.

The most unusual thing about the office was a sentence stencilled in black that ran around the top of the room's four walls. It read: *A man has no more right to an opinion for which he cannot account than to a pint of beer for which he cannot pay.*

"Do you like the quote?" asked Lillidew. "It's attributed to a rather obscure historian and essayist named George Malcolm Young."

"The Victorian?"

"He wrote about Victorian society, but he was bit of a polymath: history, literature, education—whatever he turned that curious mind of his to."

Duffy knew a little about Young from his undergrad days. One of his professors, a Jesuit who taught a course on intellectual history, had a similar interest in the man. Duffy shared this recollection with his host.

"Now *that's* interesting," said Lillidew, handing Duffy a steaming cup of Italian coffee. "A PR man with a Jesuit education, eh? Talk about competing ideals! I've always found the Jesuits fascinating—rigorous inquiry yet obedience to the Pope, truth-seeking mixed with casuistry, social justice versus social order, the marriage of action and intellect. Marvelous stuff, isn't it?"

"You forgot the bit about helping the poor and marginalized."

"Yes, well, of course," said Lillidew, a little defensively. "The Jesuits are a complex lot."

There was that word again: *complex*. It seemed to go hand in hand with *ambiguity*, thought Duffy. It reminded him of a question on his fourth-year epistemology exam: *Life is complex, but is it necessarily ambiguous?* His answer had earned him a C-plus, a mark that helped nudge Duffy away from philosophy and towards journalism.

Lillidew sat down, resting his cup of coffee on a large, bony knee.

"So, James, you think it wrong of me to bring a provocative speaker such as Harrison Dewlap to campus?"

"Not wrong, just unhelpful," replied Duffy. "I mean, surely you could find a more credible speaker than Harrison Dewlap?"

"Perhaps. But would that do as much good? By being provocative, Dr. Dewlap spurs people to challenge his arguments and articulate their own beliefs. Isn't that what's supposed to take place on a university campus?"

"If he was speaking as part of a debate, I'd agree. But you're giving him a platform to spout some pretty extreme and hurtful views, without anyone there to challenge him."

"There'll be a Q and A at the end of his lecture."

"That's better than nothing, I suppose. But it's not a rigorous debate among experts."

"Professors routinely invite guest speakers to campus; the format doesn't have to be a debate."

"But this isn't some sterile academic topic," said Duffy. "This involves the daily experience of real people. Sir Richard Middling was a powerful man whose actions caused hurt and pain to some of the most vulnerable people in society. Each time a student from a marginalized group walks past the statue of Sir Dickie, it's a reminder that society still glorifies bigots and oppressors."

"That's quite the speech," said Lillidew. "What did old Ignatius say? 'Give me the child for the first seven years, and I will give you the man.'"

"I'm no longer a Catholic," replied Duffy.

"But still a Jesuit."

Duffy conceded the point with a smile. Although he had dreaded this encounter with Lillidew, he found himself enjoying the discussion. It reminded him of his undergraduate days, debating lofty topics with classmates and teaching assistants, back when he had time and energy to care about such things.

What happened to that younger me? he thought.

The question gave Duffy pause. He needed a moment to regroup. He took a long sip of his *macchiato*. It was very good. He could see why Lloyd—amateur thespian and professional maintenance foreman—dropped by every Monday.

"Professor, you're giving me too much credit," said Duffy. "I'm just a PR guy trying to keep the university from getting slammed in the media."

"You know, James, I've devoted the better part of my career to the study of free speech and rational argument. I respect the right of any individual or group to express their opinions. And contrary to what you might think, I am passionate about intellectual rigour and informed debate. But we live in an era in which free inquiry is being chased out of the academy by an intolerant form of postmodern ideology. Heaven help the independent thinker who dares question the new orthodoxy of grievance, victimhood and wokeness. Such a person is shouted down and ostracized by a truth-and-light brigade that is every bit as intolerant as the right-wing bogeymen they rail against. These social-justice vigilantes have many of us cowering in our cubicles. By simply asking questions, we're condemned as racists and flayed on social media. Believe me, James, there is intolerance across the entire political spectrum."

"I hear you," said Duffy. "But isn't that all the more reason to bring credible scholars to campus to debate a range of viewpoints? I mean, why invite a polemicist like Dewlap to campus? His opinions have been discredited time and again. And when he's challenged, he resorts to ridicule and name-calling."

"It's *Dr.* Dewlap," said Lillidew. "And as I said, a provocative speaker can be very effective at getting people to clarify their own opinions."

The professor pointed to the words that circumnavigated the walls above them. "I think Mr. Young would agree with me."

"Maybe he was just too cheap to buy a round," said Duffy.

Lillidew chuckled and took a sip of coffee.

"Listen, professor," said Duffy. "I'm not a scholar. I'm just a communications guy. My gut tells me that bringing Harrison Dewlap to campus will do more harm than good."

"And I disagree. But speaking of communications, will you be promoting Dr. Dewlap's lecture with a university news release?"

How did I not see that coming? thought Duffy.

"After all," continued Lillidew, "if it was a human-rights lawyer coming to speak, or a diversity scholar, you'd certainly issue a news release to promote their talk. And you wouldn't insist that the lecture be changed to a debate format."

Duffy felt the ice grow thin beneath his feet. He may have had a Jesuit education, but he was never the quickest wit on the debating team. Still, he tried a quick pivot-and-bridge gambit.

"That may be so," he said. "But a lot of academics question the quality of Dewlap's work and whether he even qualifies as a scholar."

"He has a PhD, which is more than many guest speakers have."

"An *honorary* doctorate, if I recall," said Duffy. "But you've given me food for thought."

Lillidew set his coffee cup down and leaned back in his chair.

"James, didn't you come here to apologize?"

"To a degree," said Duffy. "I want to be clear that I did not call you a racist. But I acknowledge that whatever words I used prompted at least one student to claim that I did. That misunderstanding led to the inaccurate reporting in *The Rat's Ass*. I've taken steps to have that story corrected. So, yes, I apologize for the role I played in the misunderstanding that led to that article."

"Thank you," said Lillidew. "I appreciate the clarification and the courage it took to come see me this morning."

"So, you're not going to sue me?"

"Oh, I'll sue you if I can," Lillidew said brightly. "I've already spoken to a lawyer. But if you didn't call me a racist—or, to be precise, if I cannot *prove* that you called me a racist—then in all likelihood I will not pursue legal action."

"Thank you."

"Don't thank me yet. More coffee?"

Chapter 28

Sylvia Kiljoy sat alone in the president's office, waiting for Alex Meriwether and Clive Blunt. Rain lashed the windows, reminding her of a damp but glorious study-abroad term spent at Oxford's Magdalen College.

"*Maw*-d'lin College," she said, pronouncing it in the Oxfordian fashion. "*Maw*-d'lin, *Maw*-d'lin, *Maw*-d'lin."

The door opened and Clive Blunt walked in.

"Were you singing, Sylvia?"

"No. Just talking to myself."

Part of Blunt's irritation with Kiljoy was rooted in her refusal to be embarrassed. No matter what Kiljoy said or did, she maintained an air of shameless aplomb. Like Fifi Dubé, she believed in the power of militancy, whether it was feminism, labour activism, or messing with a puffed-up twit like Clive Blunt.

Kiljoy pulled a report out of her backpack and began to read. Blunt took a seat opposite her and scrolled through the messages on his phone.

There was a knock at the door and Sophie Munn came in.

"Dr. Meriwether shouldn't be long," she said. "Can I get you a cup of tea or coffee?"

"Green tea, if you have it," said Kiljoy. "Nothing if you don't."

Blunt just waved a hand dismissively and continued checking his messages.

"Do you take your green tea clear?" Sophie asked Kiljoy.

"Is there any other way?"

"I have a friend who likes hers with a splash of milk and a drop of honey."

"Even herbal tea?" Kiljoy said with an arched eyebrow.

"Yes."

Kiljoy gave a snort of derision.

"Clear it is, then," said Sophie, straining to maintain her smile.

As she was about to leave, Bertie squeezed past her legs and entered the president's office. The old hound doddered over to Kiljoy and Blunt, where he lowered himself in a pudgy heap and let out a staccato of soft farts.

"Good Lord, that animal stinks!" said Blunt.

"It's a dog, Clive."

"My point is that it *stinks*."

"Why don't you give Bertie a bath? That would be a more constructive way to suck up to Alex."

"Mind your own business, Sylvia."

Kiljoy put down the report she was reading. "Clive, do you really think you'd make a good university president?"

"As a matter of fact, I've been encouraged to give it careful consideration."

"By whom? Your mother?"

Blunt lowered his phone and returned Kiljoy's challenging glare.

"What's wrong with ambition, Sylvia? I'm a solid administrator, good with budgets, and I understand the post-secondary system inside and out."

"What about inspiring people and making them feel good about their work?" asked Kiljoy. "What about leading the executive team and herding the deans? What about glad-handing with board members, donors and alumni? What about chatting with students and their parents? You dislike all of those things, Clive. And what's more, you're terrible at them."

"What have any of those things got to do with being president?" Blunt asked with a look of genuine bewilderment.

"That's *exactly* my point, Clive. You don't understand the role of a university president!"

"You're just bitter and jealous, Sylvia."

"Okay, Clive, here's a little quiz to see if you have what it takes to become president of Sir Middling U."

"Fire away."

"Question One: Where is Alex's son doing his PhD?"

"Which son?"

"He only has one."

"Why on earth would I need to know something like that?"

"Question Two: Who is Sir Middling's biggest donor?"

"I have no idea."

"Question Three: How did the Middling Muskrats football team do this year?"

"That's irrelevant."

"Question Four: Which of the deans lost a spouse to cancer last year?"

"Enough!" cried Blunt. "You've made your point."

"Question Five: When did you last get laid?"

"Don't be crude, Sylvia. Let me ask you a question: Was that fun?"

A look of resignation softened Kiljoy's hawkish features.

"No, Clive, it wasn't," she said. "As much as you annoy me, I feel an obligation towards you, like a big sister protecting her socially inept brother. So, I'm going to be completely honest with you—"

"Like you weren't being honest before?"

"Here goes: Clive, you're a good economist and a competent budget chief, but you would be a failure as president. You'd come to hate the job, and people would hate you. For your sake, and the sake of everyone associated with Sir Middling U, please don't throw your hat into the ring."

Blunt's face trembled with anger and hurt.

"Sylvia, of all the nasty things you've said to me over the years, that was the most hurtful. I don't think you're a bad person, but you're certainly capable of being cruel."

Silence descended on the room. The two colleagues accepted its familiar embrace. Kiljoy returned to her report; Blunt went back to his phone.

A few minutes later, there was a knock at the door. Sophie appeared again, this time bearing a single cup of tea. She set it down beside Kiljoy.

"Green tea," said Sophie. "Double strained for extra clarity."

Kiljoy reached for the cup without taking her eyes off the report she was reading.

"Can I get you anything else?" asked Sophie.

"No," replied Kiljoy, without looking up.

"Well, then, off I go," said Sophie, stifling an urge to scream.

Neither Kiljoy nor Blunt seemed to notice.

A few minutes later, Blunt looked up from his phone. "Sylvia," he said tentatively. "I'd like to have a word in confidence before Alex arrives."

"You mean a secret?"

"I mean a discreet word between old colleagues," said Blunt. "This amalgamation business is getting serious. No matter what happens, I think Sir Middling U will look quite different by the time the dust settles. Surely the two of us agree that faculty are the heart of the university. Support staff can be replaced, but if Sir Middling U is to survive as a distinct academic entity, we must do all we can to keep the professoriate intact."

"What are you trying to say, Clive?"

"That we need a negotiating strategy: What are our top priorities? What are we willing to trade away?"

"You sound like Hugh Endicott."

"It's worth discussing."

Kiljoy leaned forward and set her elbows on her bony knees. "I'm listening."

"The Walters Report suggests reducing the number of Sir Middling faculty by half and the number of support staff by 70 percent. I suggest that we let Rose Samaroo know that we'd be willing to negotiate a change in that ratio in favour of keeping more faculty jobs."

"What do you have in mind?"

"That we offer early retirement and buyouts to any Sir Middling faculty member who wants a package, and that we keep all those who choose to stay."

"What about support staff?"

"We leave that battle up to the staff union. Let them negotiate with HIPE and the province."

"So, the blood isn't on our hands?"

"Don't be dramatic, Sylvia. As academic leaders, it's our duty to make the tough decisions—to establish priorities and safeguard the most essential elements of the academy."

Kiljoy leaned back in her chair. "Are you planning to share this idea with Meriwether?"

"Not yet. I wanted to get your thoughts first. We may want to make a soft approach to Rose—a discreet hint rather than an explicit offer—just to gauge her reaction."

"Open up a backchannel? How very cloak-and-dagger, Clive."

"But do you agree?"

"I'm willing to sound Rose out. But I'm not committing to anything yet. I don't like the idea of abandoning our staff, at least not the unionized ones. They could be very helpful to Sir Middling faculty in an amalgamated world."

The door opened and Alex Meriwether walked in.

"Sorry I'm late," he said. "I was just on the phone with my son. He wanted some advice on his PhD thesis."

"How's Malcolm enjoying UBC?" said Kiljoy, casting a smug glance at Blunt.

"Loving it. Thanks for asking, Sylvia."

Meriwether took off his suit jacket and lowered himself into his office chair.

"So, how's the strategy coming along?"

"We have a few ideas," said Blunt. "But let me ask, do you still plan to meet with Rose?"

"We haven't set anything up yet. Do you have some thoughts?"

"Well," said Kiljoy, "Clive was just saying that perhaps he and I should meet with Rose first to mend fences. You know, given the tone of the first meeting."

Meriwether raised an eyebrow. "I must say, I'm surprised," he said. "Pleasantly surprised. None of you got along when Rose worked here. Last week's meeting was like watching an old Road Runner cartoon."

"What's changed is the urgency of the situation," said Blunt. "If nothing else, last week's meeting showed us just how determined HIPE is."

Meriwether rested his elbows on his desk and intertwined the fingers of both hands. This prayer position, as his staff called it, was the president's preferred posture for serious thought. Sometimes, as he did now, he closed his eyes to aid his concentration.

Blunt and Kiljoy exchanged glances.

Several moments passed in silence. The aroma coming off Bertie grew more intense. Kiljoy gave the sleeping mound a nudge with the side of her cork sandal. Bertie groaned, and then a stream of urine leaked out around the edges of his bloated diaper.

"For goodness' sake!" said Kiljoy. "Alex, your dog is peeing on the carpet."

"Oh, my poor Bertie!" cried Meriwether, snapping to attention and springing out of his chair. He grabbed a roll of paper towels and a spray bottle of carpet cleaner and went to work with surprising swiftness. He then removed the diaper, dried the dog's privates with a soft cloth and guided the hapless animal with gentle hands to a plastic-lined dog bed.

"My apologies," said Meriwether, his voice both sad and weary. "Perhaps it's time to release old Bertie from his misery. But I just can't bear to do it. Not yet."

The president leaned his wide bum against his desk and crossed his arms over his thick chest.

"Back to business," he said. "I agree with your plan. It would be useful to smooth things over with Rose. And going forward, I insist that you both keep our discussions with HIPE as constructive as possible."

"Of course, Alex," said Kiljoy. "Clive and I promise to be at our diplomatic best."

Meriwether looked skeptical. "In all the years I've known the pair of you, I have never heard you sound so aligned. Are you scheming something?"

"Of course not," said Blunt. "We just want to sound Rose out on a few things. We need a better idea of what HIPE is willing to negotiate, and we'll have more success if it's just the three of us in the room."

"Just don't make things worse," said Meriwether.

Kiljoy and Blunt got up to leave. As Kiljoy reached the door, she looked from Bertie to Meriwether. Then she moved back towards the desk and laid a hand on the president's shoulder.

"It might be time, Alex."

Chapter 29

In the two weeks since the amalgamation story had broken, Duffy had dealt with more than twenty media calls. He'd also sent several internal emails to the Sir Middling community, a disparate group of two hundred and fifty faculty members, four hundred staff and five thousand students. Duffy tweaked the wording for alumni, donors and parents, and he developed a shorter version to respond to the storm of questions and comments brewing on social media. His messaging, however, was growing stale. Duffy hadn't heard from Blunt or Meriwether in nearly a week, despite repeated requests for an update. As the days passed, the university's statements riled more people than they reassured. The jungle, as Duffy called social media, smelled a wounded animal.

- *Get your sh@#t together Sir Middling U and defend our school!*
- *The balls on Sir Dickie's horse must be red*

with embarrassment!
- *I'm sure you're busy getting amalgamated, but can you send me stuff about residence food plans?*

Just as the media coverage seemed to be cooling down, it burst back into flames. Someone began leaking updates about HIPE's conversations with the government. Kerri Quartermain denied any involvement, but she was happy to give reporters a comment whenever they asked.

"I'm not sure where you're getting your information," she was quoted in one story, "but I can confirm its accuracy. The Bud Walters proposal is bold and visionary. It's a brilliant playbook for saving taxpayers millions of dollars while helping HIPE achieve its destiny as a world-class post-secondary institution."

Fuck me, thought Duffy. Few reporters bothered to ask Sir Middling U for a comment, and Blunt forbade him from calling the media proactively. Duffy quietly ignored the command, but the reporters rarely used the comments he gave them.

"If you'd say something newsworthy—like, 'HIPE is a self-serving piece of crap'— then I might consider quoting you," said a reporter from *The Daily Potshot*, a provincial tabloid.

With no such quotes to give, and no new information to share, Duffy could only offer limp platitudes in response to the angry questions flooding in via email, telephone and social media.

"Shouldn't the university be developing a plan or something?" asked Sequoia Tush, his junior manager.

The question brought Duffy up short. He realized that, while being kept out of the loop himself, he had done little to keep his own staff informed. He printed off a copy of the communications plan he had written and went through it with Tush.

"This is cool!" she said, chomping on a wad of bubble gum. "Can I do some of the media interviews?"

Duffy smiled politely. "Why don't we start by having you sit in on the media training that I've planned for the executive team."

"I could play the reporter!"

"Hmmm, let me think about that," said Duffy.

Undeterred, the ex-cheerleader pressed on. "Here's another idea," she said. "Why don't we include the Sir Middling Muskrats cheer at the end of all of our media statements?"

"What do you mean?"

"You know: 'Go Muskrats Go—Chomp, Chomp, Chomp!' "

Duffy was about to dismiss the idea. Then he thought about how bland and useless his existing messaging was. If it didn't put his audience to sleep, it pissed them off.

"You might be on to something," he said. "Here's what I'd like you to do, Sequoia. Go back to your desk and write me a new statement. Think about how you would tell your friends about Sir Middling U's point of view. Be creative, but no foul language."

"Like, don't say, 'Hey, fellow Muskrats—we don't know any fucking more than you do?' "

"You read my mind."

"I didn't have to. You've been talking out loud to yourself quite a bit lately. Terri is kind of worried."

Duffy hoped that Tush was joking, but the look on her face suggested otherwise.

"Thanks for letting me know," he said. "Communications can be a stressful occupation. I need to find a better way to handle the pressure."

"Let's see if I can cheer you up with some new messaging!"

Duffy watched his young assistant stride back to her desk, full of youthful energy and unfounded confidence. He felt bad that he hadn't done more to mentor her. Then it occurred to him that she was a Gen Z-er who would likely replace him in a couple of years.

Duffy returned to his emails. There was one from J.J. Jones that caught his eye:

"CALL ME!!!"

Sir Middling U

The Department of Fundraising and Alumni Relations had its own communications coordinator, so Duffy had few dealings with its vice-president. All the more reason to call Jones back, he thought.

Duffy picked up his phone and clicked on Jones' number.

"J.J. here."

"Hey, J.J., it's James Duffy."

"You mean 'Lame' Duffy," don't you?"

Jones loved his jock talk, which always had a testosterone-fueled edge to it. Duffy detected an extra dose of manliness today.

"Whoa, Jonesie, my man, what's up?"

"You're a red-headed pussy!" the vice-president yelled into the phone. "Sir Middling's amalgamation statements suck. We're getting our ass kicked. You need to go on the offensive, buddy! You need to blitz the fuckers!"

Duffy explained the lack of new information and how, in the hyper-cautious world of university communications, one seldom blitzed anyone, even if they were a fucker.

"My team and I are working on a new statement," he said, adding that he would have to run it by Meriwether and Blunt for their approval.

"Christ almighty!" said Jones. "You know what my coach used to say, Duffy? 'Never explain, never retract, never apologize. Just get the thing done and let them howl!' "

Duffy was impressed.

"Wow," he said. "You know your Nellie McClung."

"Who?"

"Nellie McClung. The woman who said, 'Never explain, never retract, never apologize.'"

"That was my football coach, Willy Bronk."

"Well, Willy must have known his feminist history."

"What the hell are you talking about?" asked Jones.

That got weird quickly, thought Duffy. Time to change

the subject.

"Listen, J.J.," he said. "I hear you on the messaging. I'll do what I can to punch it up."

"Punch it up and knock 'em down, buddy. And while you're at it, step on their goddamn throats!"

"And kick 'em in the nuts?" suggested Duffy.

"YES!" said Jones. "Go get 'em, Muskrats!"

Duffy found it hard to argue with Jonesie's logic. If you don't stand up for yourself, no one respects you, right?

After the call, Duffy took a shot at drafting a more assertive message while he waited to see what Tush came up with. He wasn't going to blitz the fuckers, but he did channel the spirit of J.J. Jones as he crafted a new statement.

> *Enough is enough!*
>
> *After weeks of trying to work collaboratively with the Henfield Institute for Polytechnical Education, it's time to take off the gloves and fight tooth-and-nail for our survival. Sir Middling U has been one of Canada's finest post-secondary institutions for more than a century. Our graduates hold positions of influence in education, non-profit service and arts management. We will not abandon them or the community of Yawnbury. Rest assured, Sir Middling U is here to stay!*

As an afterthought, he added the words, *Go Muskrats Go— Chomp, Chomp, Chomp!*

Duffy emailed the statement to Meriwether and Blunt before his better judgement had a chance to kick in.

Blunt responded immediately: "Are you high?" he wrote. "James, we are *not* negotiating amalgamation in the media. Stick to the original statement."

An hour and a half went by without any word from Meriwether.

Duffy decided to respond to Blunt.

"I appreciate your point of view, sir. But the fact is that we're getting hammered in the media. Alumni and donors are begging us to push back. They want a strong statement that says we're committed to saving their alma mater. While Sir Middling U remains silent, HIPE is only too happy to comment. Our stakeholders want to know where we stand."

This prompted Meriwether to finally weigh in.

"I'm going to come down squarely on the fence. James, draft a new statement. Remove the bombast and baloney. Just say we're working hard to save Sir Middling U. At the same time, I agree with Clive. We will not negotiate amalgamation in the media. Rather, we will continue to work towards a solution behind the scenes."

Having stuck his neck out this far, Duffy decided to push for more information.

"Understood, Dr. Meriwether," he wrote. "However, are we now 'negotiating' amalgamation or fighting against it? And may I ask for an update on the behind-the-scenes activity? It would help me to revise the statement."

Duffy received no reply.

As the afternoon wore on, his frustration evolved into resentment. What use was he if both his boss and the president kept him in the dark and spurned his advice? At four p.m., he sent his bombast and baloney statement to the vice-president of fundraising and alumni relations.

"Hell yeah!" Jones replied. "That's what I'm talking about!"

Duffy checked his social-media feed a few minutes later. Sure enough, there was a post from @Muskrats, Jones' account.

> @SirMiddlingU kicks amalgamation butt! Check it out Muskrats at www.supportmuskrats.ca

The link took readers to Duffy's statement, which Jones had posted to Sir Middling U's fundraising and alumni webpage. As Duffy re-read it, he thought of something else Jones liked to say: "It's better to beg forgiveness than to ask permission."

Duffy hoped it was true.

Chapter 30

Duffy's phone rang at seven-thirty the next morning. It was Blunt's executive assistant, Ottie Crump. He wiped the sleep from his eyes and shook his head like a boxer getting ready for the next round.

"Good morning, Ottie. Listen, if this is about J.J.'s post—"

"What are you talking about?"

"Isn't that why you're calling?"

"No. I'm calling about the fifteen people sitting on the floor in Dr. Blunt's waiting room, and another thirty outside in the hall."

"Are Morris Hill and Fifi Dubé there?"

"Yes, they are. And so is a young woman named Tessa Burns. They're all glaring at me as I speak."

"Don't worry, they're non-violent."

"That's easy for you to say."

"Are there any reporters or TV cameras there?"

"Not that I see."

"That's good. Is Dr. Blunt in his office?"

"No. He has his regular meeting with the deans over at Selby House."

"That's good too. Send him a message and tell him not to come back until he hears from me."

"Okay. Are you coming over here?"

"Yes. I'm on my way."

"Is there anything I should do in the meantime?"

"Order decaf coffee from the cafeteria. Lots of it. And give everyone as much as they want."

"You're kidding, right?"

"Not at all"

"Why should we give them coffee?"

"To keep their bladders so full that half the group will be in the washroom at any one time. And the decaf won't get them too jumpy."

Duffy thought he heard a chuckle.

"I'll order the coffee, but I'm charging it to your office," said Crump.

"Just for the record, Ottie, did I hear you laugh just now?"

"Goodbye, James."

Duffy's next call was to Fifi.

"Hey, Feef."

"Hey, Duffy. Thanks for the coffee."

"My pleasure. I hear you and Morris are leading an old-school sit-in."

"Yes, we are. Come on over. I saved you a spot."

"I'm on my way. When do the TV cameras arrive?"

"That depends."

"On?"

"On whether we get a meeting with Blunt and Meriwether."

"So, if you don't get a meeting, you'll call the media?"

"You're not as thick as they say."

"I'm not like anything they say," said Duffy, invigorated by having a concrete issue to manage. "You should know that by now."

"Oooh, pushback!" said Fifi. "You're definitely growing a spine."

Duffy smiled. He knew that Fifi didn't bust just anyone's balls. She might call them a moron or a jerk, but she only chirped people she respected.

"Hey, Feef?"

"What?"

"You're a good person."

"Yes, I am. And I'm going to sit on the floor of this waiting room until we get a meeting."

"I'm working on it."

As Duffy was leaving his apartment, he called Sophie.

"Hey, Sophie. Is Dr. Meriwether there?"

"Hello to you too."

"Sorry. It's just that something urgent has come up. Fifi and Morris Hill have launched a sit-in in Blunt's office."

"Just the two of them?"

"No. They brought about forty-five friends. I need to talk to the president."

"Alex is off campus for the day," said Sophie.

When she didn't elaborate, Duffy felt his latent impatience rise to the surface.

"Well, can I reach him by phone?"

"Better let me do that."

"Listen, Sophie, it's urgent," said Duffy, his voice growing strained. "Can I just call Alex myself?"

"How about *you* listen?" replied Sophie. "Trust the judgement of the president's executive assistant and let her make the call."

Duffy relented. "Of course," he said. "My bad."

"That's better," said Sophie. "Now, before I hang up, I have a personal question: Do you have your *Rocky* costume for Friday night?"

Damn! thought Duffy. With everything going on, he'd forgotten the costume.

"Absolutely," he lied. "My tailor's making me a bespoke corset."

"Ha! I can't wait to see you in it."

Duffy's mood lightened.

"How about you?" he asked. "What will you be wearing?"

"You'll have to wait and see. But I think you'll approve."

Duffy let out a two-note wolf whistle. "You've planted an image in my mind that's going to stay there for a long time."

"That's the idea."

Duffy laughed. "I'll be in Blunt's office," he said. "Call me as soon as you connect with the president."

"Go. I'll call Dr. Meriwether now."

It was another cold, damp morning. Duffy was shivering by the time he reached campus. He dialled Blunt's number as he walked towards Founders Hall.

"Hello, doctor. It's James."

"What the hell's going on in my office?" Blunt demanded.

"A few faculty members and about three dozen students are staging a sit-in. Dr. Hill, Dr. Dubé and Tessa Burns still want a meeting with you and the president."

"Duffy, how many times do I have to tell you?" Blunt scolded. "Neither the president nor I is going to meet with anyone about the Dewlap lecture."

Duffy pressed on.

"Here's the thing, Dr. Blunt. Statue controversies are a big deal right across North America and beyond. If you or Dr. Meriwether don't meet with Morris, Fifi and Tessa, they're going to call in the media, and this will make headlines from here to Red Neck, U.S.A. I know that you and the president feel strongly about your position, but please, meet with the three of them. You don't have to promise anything—just have a respectful exchange of views. That way, they feel heard and the sit-in breaks up before the TV cameras get here."

"What TV cameras?" asked Blunt.

"That's why protesters hold sit-ins. To get publicity."

"Sounds like blackmail."

"Let's call it a negotiating tactic," said Duffy. "I think it's better to agree to the meeting than to see the sit-in all over the news."

"What does the president think?"

"He's off campus for the day. Sophie is trying to reach him."

"Listen, James. Alex has put me in charge of this file, and I still say no to the meeting. Feel free to let Morris and Fifi know that my position remains unchanged."

Duffy realized that he was sailing upwind; what he needed to do was tack.

"Then we'll have to prepare for media interviews."

"What interviews?"

"If the sit-in drags on, the protesters will have the media all to themselves. They'll make the administration look like insensitive apologists for colonialism. We'll need to do media interviews to explain our position."

"You said we'd do written statements, not interviews."

"The situation is evolving," replied Duffy, exasperation seeping into his voice. "Written statements will only go so far. If there's a stalemate, things will get ugly fast. Parents, alumni and donors will start calling. Everyone, including the media, is going to ask tough questions—things like, 'What kind of university is Sir Middling if its leaders won't talk about important issues?' "

Blunt made an odd sound, a combination of *harrumph* and *snort*.

"You're stuck on the worst possible outcome," he growled. "We need to approach this incrementally. I believe that if we keep our heads down for a day or two, the worst will blow over."

"With all due respect, sir, the evidence suggests otherwise. Statues have been torn down across North America and the UK. We can still avoid violence, but it has to start with a meeting."

"Did you say violence?"

"If people start vandalizing the statue of Sir Richard, tempers could flare," said Duffy. "It has happened elsewhere."

"You should call Chief Fields in Campus Security right away."

"I messaged her first thing this morning," said Duffy. "It's part of our emergency protocols. Gail and I have run protest simulations before. Her team will take a community policing approach: a limited presence, regular discussions with the sit-in leaders, and friendly chatter with the protesters."

"Then I see no reason to talk about violence."

"I don't expect any today," said Duffy. "It's tomorrow or the next day, when both sides start getting tired and angry. There's a well-documented pattern to how these things play out."

"Just keep me posted. And send over whatever statement you propose giving to the media."

"Sir, I'll follow your direction. But I wouldn't be doing my job if I didn't say one more time that a meeting with Morris, Fifi and Tessa is our best chance of avoiding a media storm."

"Duly noted," Blunt said with finality. "Now, if you don't mind, I have a sabbatical-approval meeting to get back to."

Duffy stopped in the quad to gather his thoughts. The air was frigid and a light drizzle was coming down. Brave Sir Dickie and his horse were coated in a delicate veil of ice.

"What you need is an invisibility cloak," Duffy told the horse and rider.

As he went over the situation in his mind, he knew that things weren't looking good. But they weren't terrible, either. At least not yet. Duffy had stuck his neck way out with Blunt. But he felt confident. He remembered another one of his father's sayings: "It's never wrong to do the right thing." Then again, his father also liked to say, "When the shit flies, duck."

As Duffy approached Founders Hall, he spotted a potential source of flying excrement. A group of people were standing next to the stairs that led up to the old administration building. Several held placards: *Protect Freedom of Speech! Live Free or Die! Cancel cancel culture!*

The protesters were all men. Judging by their ages, Duffy figured three to be students and three to be junior profs. Each had short hair, glasses and overcoats—the kind of uniform that suggested the Campus Evangelical Society or the Student Conservative Club (there was overlap between the two). A seventh man towered above the rest.

As Duffy approached, Dr. Rufus Lillidew stepped forward and handed him a pamphlet.

"Ah, the public relations man cometh!" intoned Lillidew.

"Hello, Doctor. What brings you to Founders Hall on this cold, wet morning?"

"Harrison Dewlap's lecture is just a week away. I thought we should ramp up the publicity since your office won't be providing any."

Duffy glanced at the leaflet. "Any particular reason you started the campaign here today?"

"Not really," said Lillidew. "I just thought we might see President Meriwether or Vice-President Blunt."

"No other reason?"

Lillidew eyed Duffy suspiciously. "Are you a cop as well as a PR man?"

"Of course not," Duffy said, trying to sound more amiable. "It's just that Dr. Meriwether is off-campus for the day, and Dr. Blunt has his regular Tuesday meeting with the deans over at Selby House."

Is it possible, thought Duffy, that Rufus Lillidew has no idea about the sit-in taking place just up these stairs?

Apparently, it was.

"Well, thanks for that bit of intel," said Lillidew. Turning to his acolytes, he said, "Fellas, let's take this show over to Selby House."

Duffy watched the little group troop off through the drizzle towards the quad. Their rain-soaked placards were beginning to droop. Duffy felt as if a small meteorite had just shot past the Earth, missing by inches, and he'd been the only one to see it.

When Lillidew's posse had disappeared around the Main Library, Duffy sprinted up the steps and speed-walked his way towards Blunt's office. As he turned left off the main corridor, he could see the crowd of protesters seated in front of the Office of the Vice-President of University Services. A forest of signs sprouted above their heads. Some of the signs were being waved slowly, like trees in the wind; others were being pumped up and down like pistons. Just beyond them was a man with a TV camera on his shoulder. Standing beside him was a square-jawed reporter named Kirk Appleton. Both were attached to the Babbler News Corporation's national newsroom; their presence at Sir Middling U meant that someone at head office thought the sit-in was big news.

"Fuck me sideways," muttered Duffy.

He stopped short and pressed himself flat into the nearest doorway to avoid being part of the video shot. The image of the university's communications director marching towards the protesters, notebook in hand, was not the sort of B-roll he wanted to give the reporter.

Duffy called Fifi.

"Hey old buddy," she said. "Where are you?"

"I'm in the hallway, trying to avoid Kirk Appleton. Fifi, you promised no cameras yet."

"I didn't call him. I think it was some twerp from *Le Collectif*. There's a couple of them here wearing serapes and red toques."

"It doesn't matter who called. There's a national TV reporter here. This isn't going to help you get a meeting with Blunt. In fact, he'll probably burst a blood vessel."

"Did you tell him that a camera would likely show up?"

"Of course."

"Then you've proven to him that you know what you're doing. That's a good thing, my man."

"It doesn't feel good."

"It will when Blunt caves in and we get our meeting."

Just then, the door that Duffy was leaning against opened from the inside. He tumbled backwards onto a hard, shiny floor.

"What the hell, Duffy!" screamed a middle-aged woman standing over him. It was the assistant registrar, Suzie Fish. Still holding the phone to his ear, Duffy squirmed like a turtle on its back. From his upside-down view, he could see a line of white sinks along one wall and a row of toilet cubicles down the other.

"Duffy, what's going on?" asked Fifi.

"Looks like I fell into the she/her washroom."

As he struggled to get up, Duffy was greeted by several young protesters who had leapt to their feet and raced down the hall to investigate the commotion. They each had a cellphone camera pointed at him.

Oh, crap.

Duffy summoned a smile for the wall of citizen journalists. Then he picked up his notebook and walked down the hall to Blunt's office, giving Kirk Appleton the B-roll shot he'd hoped to avoid.

Inside the waiting room, Duffy picked his way through the protesters, pushing past placards and backpacks to reach Fifi, Morris and Tessa.

Hill wore an enormous smile. Tears of laughter were streaming down Fifi's face. Tessa just shook her head.

"What's so funny?" asked Duffy.

Fifi handed him her phone. The screen displayed a video of Duffy lying on his back in the women's washroom, next to Suzie Fish. The angle made it look like he was peeping up the woman's skirt.

"That didn't take long," he said.

"What the hell were you doing?" asked Tessa.

"I leaned against the wrong door."

Duffy sat down on the floor. He tried to cross his long, thin legs, but they stuck out like the two ends of a wishbone.

"We're in a pickle," he said. "Alex has put Blunt in charge of the statue file, and Blunt is still refusing to meet with you."

"That's fine with us," said Hill. "This is an issue the public needs to hear about. The Harrison Dewlaps of the world aren't just supporting symbols of an oppressive past; they're prejudiced against anyone with a different lived experience and a different worldview. This sit-in will help educate people and change a few minds."

"What is it you want from Blunt and Meriwether?" asked Duffy.

"It's not what we want from them; it's what they need from us."

"And what's that?"

"A little encouragement to do the right thing. The university can safeguard free speech *and* create space for social justice at the same time. The two aren't incompatible."

"I wish it were that simple," said Duffy. "Amalgamation complicates things."

Tessa leaned forward. "What you're saying," she said, "is that the VP and the president are worried that the Dewlap lecture, coupled with all this activism, makes Sir Middling U look like a flaky waste of taxpayer money?"

"Something like that."

Duffy looked around the room. A reporter from *The Rat's Ass* had slipped in and was taking photographs. Another reporter, whom Duffy didn't recognize, was chatting with a couple of students. Everyone was talking and laughing and drinking coffee. Even Ottie Crump was chatting happily with a handsome young Spanish lecturer from the Languages Department.

Hill looked at Duffy. "If you don't mind me saying, James, you're trying to manage something that can't be managed. Just let things unfold. The sit-in and Dewlap's lecture are going to make headlines. I'm optimistic that the outcome will be positive."

"I wish I had your faith, Dr. Hill."

The professor patted Duffy's shoulder. "If I'm wrong, it's my tenure you'll envy—not my faith."

Chapter 31

The sit-in was heading into its third day. Chief Gail Fields, the head of university security, allowed supporters to bring food and drink to Founders Hall. The special constables inspected each item before conveying it to the protesters inside. Several pans of hash brownies went missing en route. The treats were never recovered, but a few protesters noticed a distinct mellowing in their uniformed minders. Meanwhile, a crowd of sympathizers had begun a secondary demonstration in the quad. The painting-of-the-balls had evolved into a general smearing of red dye over the entire statue of Sir Middling and his horse. Someone had also thrown a few sturdy ropes around Sir Dickie's neck, a menacing sign of things to come. Meriwether was still off-campus; Blunt continued to work remotely from a spare office in Selby Hall.

The news coverage of the sit-in had started off on a light note. Duffy's slapstick spectacle in the women's washroom was the highlight of the first day. The broadcast media missed getting their own footage of the communications director floundering on the floor, but they ran a montage of amateur video from social media.

The Rat's Ass published a photograph that seemed to show Duffy peeking up Suzie Fish's skirt, with a headline that read: *PR Perv Crashes Sit-In!* The family friendly *Yawnbury Yowler* ran a photo of student protesters huddled in the hallway, eating donuts and happily showing off their cups of free coffee.

By the second day, local reporters were outnumbered by journalists and self-styled video influencers from the city. Many were positioning the Sir Middling U sit-in as the latest flashpoint in a broader social conflict over statues and the glorification of a questionable past.

The media were bombarding Duffy with interview requests. The latest statement from the university said that the sit-in and the Dewlap lecture were proof that Sir Middling U supported free speech and the expression of competing ideas. On a lark, Duffy added the line suggested by Sequoia Tush (Go Muskrats Go! Chomp, Chomp, Chomp!), which was enthusiastically embraced by students and alumni on social media.

- *Chomp and stomp @SirMiddlingU!*
- *Fight like a cornered muskrat! @SirMiddlingU*
- *Is a muskrat just a little beaver? @confused*

A distinguished art historian, quoted in several news stories, addressed the broader significance of the sit-in:

> *Statuary is intrinsically political. Like the names we put on public infrastructure, statues are symbols that represent what the dominant social group chooses to glorify at a particular point in time. By remaining silent about the sit-in, Sir Middling U's administrative leaders seem oblivious to the depth and universality of the ideas being debated on their own campus.*

"Hoo-ha!" Fifi said after reading the quote to Duffy.

Duffy emailed the article to Blunt and Meriwether. Neither responded. Meanwhile, he instructed Sequoia Tush to add more staff to the phone-bank team to answer the torrent of calls coming in from alumni, donors and parents.

Social media continued to be a PR nightmare. An arena of thoughtless anarchy at the best of times, it had descended into a free-for-all of lies, exaggerations and vicious attacks, with Sir Middling U's name at the centre of it all. Anyone foolish enough to wade in with an opinion got savaged by the anonymous mob. Few comments were rooted in fact; it was gladiatorial combat for the proudly ignorant.

Duffy chose to deal with it by flooding Sir Middling's social channels with feel-good stories and photographs: service dogs on campus, puppies in Sir Middling U T-shirts and the university's annual toy drive for the pediatric wing of the Yawnbury Community Hospital. The warm-and-fuzzy campaign did little to offset the negativity, but it allowed Duffy to tell Blunt that he was doing something to counter the tsunami of criticism on social media.

"Is this what you call a media shitstorm?" asked Tush.

"Yes, it is," said Duffy.

"Cool."

Chapter 32

While Duffy was struggling with the media beast, Clive Blunt and Sylvia Kiljoy had a video meeting with Rose Samaroo.

"Before we begin," said Blunt, "I want you to know, Rose, that we are not recording this meeting, and there's no one else in the room with us. I trust you can assure us of the same?"

"Yes, Clive. I'm all alone with my laptop and a pack of rice crackers."

"Thank you. First, I want to express our regret about the tone of our last meeting."

"Apology accepted," said Samaroo.

"We expressed regret; we didn't apologize," snapped Kiljoy.

"I see. Well then, regret acknowledged."

"Rose, we'd like to pick up on something that Hugh Endicott said towards the end of the meeting," continued Blunt.

"Which was?"

"Hugh said the job numbers in your amalgamation proposal were open for discussion. He also urged us to consider what we might be willing to give up to secure the best deal for our respective constituents. Sylvia and I would like to sound you out on both points."

Samaroo smiled and leaned closer to her screen. "We're starting to deal, are we? What did you have in mind?"

"I think we all agree that faculty are the heart of the academy," said Blunt.

"And students," added Samaroo.

"Well, yes, of course. But at the moment we're just talking about personnel. If we agree that the academic mission is our priority, then it's our duty to retain as many Sir Middling faculty members as possible in an amalgamated university."

"Go on."

"The HIPE Report—"

"The *Walters* Report," interjected Samaroo.

"Forgive me," said Blunt. "The Walters Report proposes a 50-percent reduction in the number of Sir Middling faculty. What we'd be willing to consider—and I stress the word *consider*—is a proposal that offers buyouts and early retirement packages to all Sir Middling faculty. Any professor who declines such an offer would be permitted to keep their position."

Samaroo clasped her fingers together and struck a thoughtful pose. She looked graceful and intelligent. Blunt and Kiljoy resented her for it.

"How many Sir Middling faculty members are likely to stay on?"

"We think about 30 percent might take a package, which would mean that 70 percent—about one hundred and seventy-five faculty members—might stay on."

"What about support staff and managers?"

"We'll leave that discussion to you, the government and the Sir Middling staff union," said Blunt.

"So, you want to offload the dirty work on HIPE?"

"That's the price you pay for getting what you want," said Kiljoy. "And besides, Rose, if you pull off amalgamation, you're a shoo-in to be a university president somewhere."

Samaroo's smile tightened. "Anything else on your wish list?"

"Yes," said Blunt. "We think it's important, for alumni and donor relations, to retain the Sir Middling name. So instead of dropping the name entirely, we propose that Sir Middling U be referred to as a college within the amalgamated university."

"Given the sit-in at your campus, we might be doing you a favour by getting rid of the Sir Middling name," said Samaroo.

"Our fifty thousand alumni, many of whom are donors, would disagree," said Blunt.

"Well, I'm sure we can work something out. But I can't guarantee that the Sir Middling campus will be kept."

"Understood," said Blunt.

"So, what's next?" asked Kiljoy.

"Let me run our discussion by Hugh. I'll touch base with you in a few days. After that, I propose that we all sit down again and start to work out the details."

"What about the government?" asked Blunt. "When do we update them?"

"Let's wait until after our next meeting, once we have our ducks lined up," said Samaroo.

"One more thing," said Kiljoy. "Today's conversation has to be kept quiet. I don't want that quarter horse of yours racing to the media to leak our discussion."

"Her name is Quartermain," said Samaroo. "And don't worry, I'll keep her reined in."

Samaroo called Giles Prigg.

"Sir Middling wants to deal."

"Well, well," said Prigg. "That was fast. Fill me in."

Samaroo summarized the proposal put forward by Blunt and Kiljoy.

"Oh, my," said Prigg. "Rats on a sinking ship. Doesn't Sir

Middling U pride itself on being a caring community?"

"Every university claims to be a caring community," said Samaroo. "But when it's put to the test, the reality can be quite different."

"And I thought politics was a cynical business."

Samaroo ignored the remark. "What do you think of their proposal, Giles?"

"Well, we can crunch the numbers later, but we both know that the real savings are on the faculty side," said Prigg.

"But it's a start, right? Once we amalgamate, we can reduce the number of remaining Sir Middling faculty through attrition and an early-retirement incentive."

"Perhaps," said Prigg, careful not to commit to anything just yet.

"One other thing," said Samaroo. "Blunt wants us to refer to Sir Middling U as an affiliated college. He says it will keep alumni engaged, which means the most loyal Muskrats might continue donating to a combined HIPE-Sir Middling University."

"Muskrats?" asked Prigg.

"That's what their alumni call themselves," explained Samaroo.

"How quaint. Well, Rose, what do you think about retaining the Sir Middling name?"

"Let's keep it as a bargaining chip, something to give up if we need to."

"Shrewd," said Prigg. "Still, we might be doing the Sir Middling community a favour by getting rid of the name and banishing that monstrous statue to a warehouse somewhere."

"I made the same point. But it's a hot potato right now. We're better off letting it burn their fingers, not ours."

Prigg chuckled. "Another good point," he said. "So, what's your next step?"

"I'm going to brief Hugh on the meeting. Then we'll sit down with Sir Middling U again in a week or so to start hammering out a revised proposal."

"Excellent work, Rose."

Samaroo knew that Prigg was a fox with a tiger's appetite. He listened more than he spoke, and his plans were layered with Machiavellian intrigue.

"So, Giles, what have you got for me?"

"Profound respect."

"Respect is nice, but I'd prefer an update. What is the cabinet thinking about the Walters Report?"

"They'll think what I persuade them to think."

"I admire chutzpah, Giles, but I wrote my doctoral thesis on hubris. People don't like to get played. Please don't jeopardize this amalgamation."

"Not to worry, Rose. I'm simply preparing the ground for the battle that lies ahead."

"A cabinet debate on amalgamation?"

"God, no," said Prigg. "I'm talking about next fall's election."

"I don't follow."

"The merger of HIPE and Sir Middling U is a worthy endeavour. But it's just one milestone in a longer journey. Our party can only implement change if it stays in power. The bigger question is simple: Will post-secondary reform help us win re-election?"

"So, you're floating the idea and seeing how it polls?"

"Something like that."

"But you still support our plan to make HIPE a world-class university?"

"Absolutely. What's more, I'm fairly confident it will happen."

"Just *fairly* confident?" asked Samaroo.

"Under-promise and over-deliver. That's the secret to my success," replied Prigg.

"Just remember the *deliver* part, Giles."

"Ah, Rose, you should run for office."

"Is the premier's job open?"

"Not yet. But that's an interesting idea."

Samaroo's quip about the premier's job gave Prigg an unexpected jolt.

His motivation throughout the amalgamation charade had been to prevent the minister of higher education—the talented Anne Moreno, PhD—from taking a run at his boss's job.

The sitting premier, Teddy Banks, was a jovial, well-tanned backslapper who looked good on television and could knock an after-dinner speech out of the ballpark. But he had no vision and no ability to lead a cabinet full of young sharks and old rivals. Poll after poll showed that if Banks remained leader, the party would get trounced in the next election.

Prigg needed his boss to stay in the premier's office just long enough for Prigg to get a better handle on which cabinet member had the best shot at leading a palace coup. Once he had narrowed the field, Prigg would develop a strategy to ingratiate himself with the frontrunner.

There was no question that Anne Moreno would make an excellent premier. And that's precisely what bothered Prigg. She was too smart, too strong and too well-liked for him to control.

When he got off the phone with Rose Samaroo, Prigg took a copy of Dev Sharma's report—the one printed on the letterhead of the minister of higher education—and stuck it in a plain manila envelope. On his way to lunch, he stopped by the post office and bought a packet of stamps. He affixed them to the envelope, scribbled the name and address of *The Daily Clamour's* university reporter on the outside, and slid the envelope into a mailbox.

It hit the bottom with a smack.

"Kaboom!" said Prigg.

Chapter 33

The news stories about the sit-in and the Dewlap lecture began to pile up. The media's natural inclination was to champion the Davids of the world, not the Goliaths. This meant that most of the sit-in coverage portrayed the protesters as righteous underdogs fighting a tone-deaf bureaucracy. A few reporters asked the mayor of Yawnbury and the local member of provincial parliament for comment. Both swiveled and swirled, then issued nearly identical statements that said the issue was one for the Sir Middling community to resolve.

Blunt refused to budge from his no-meeting and no-interview stance. He told Duffy that he intended to work from his temporary office at Selby House until his communications director "fixed" the sit-in.

President Meriwether wasn't much help either. In an email to Sophie, he wrote, "Tell James that Clive is in charge of the protest situation and the amalgamation file. Let James know that I trust Clive's judgement in both of these matters."

Sophie forwarded the email to Duffy, who read it three times.

"Shit on a stick," he said, his usual profanity softened by an increased dose of anxiety medication.

Duffy was working out of Blunt's office to be close to the sit-in and the president's suite. He asked Sophie to urge Meriwether not to go to his office while the sit-in was underway. He needn't have bothered. The president had not been seen on campus for days, an absence noted by the deans and other senior administrators.

"What a time to go AWOL," muttered one.

"Perhaps he has a mistress," whispered another.

"Maybe he just likes to see Clive twist in the wind," said a third.

Whatever the reason, the president's disappearance baffled Duffy. He didn't believe for a minute that Meriwether trusted Blunt's judgement with serious issues. In fact, Duffy had always felt that Meriwether did little more than tolerate Blunt, like a teacher who puts up with the class keener because the little brown-noser is willing to clean blackboards and run errands. Meriwether would grudgingly acknowledge Blunt's budget skills, but he kept him away from donors and government officials, and tended to step in himself whenever one of the deans had a bee up their nose. As for media issues, the president relied on Duffy to contain controversies and serve as Sir Middling U's spokesperson.

Why on earth, then, would Meriwether put Blunt in charge?

As Duffy was mulling this over, his phone rang.

"Hi James, it's Sequoia."

"What's up?"

"Professor Lillidew is in the quad giving a TV interview to Kirk Appleton."

"Right now?"

"Yes. He's dressed up like Brave Sir Dickie, and he's hopping around on a stick with a horse's head on one end."

"What?"

"You know, like a kid's toy horse."

"A hobby horse?"

"Is that what you call it?"

"Listen, Sequoia. Stay put and keep an eye on what happens. I'll be right over."

"Kirk wants to interview me too. Is that okay?"

"No!" shouted Duffy. "Do not say anything to him that could be construed as an interview. Promise?"

"Okay, okay. You don't have to be such a grouch about it."

Duffy hung up and hustled out the door. As he made his way through the protesters in Blunt's waiting room, Fifi said, "Hey pal, what's the hurry?"

"I have to see a man about a horse," replied Duffy.

As he neared the quad, Duffy heard what sounded like a heavy gong being repeatedly struck in a long, measured beat: *bonnnggg … bonnnggg … bonnnggg….* The sombre resonance bounced off the surrounding buildings, reverberating with an apocalyptic solemnity.

As Duffy drew closer, he spotted the source. Rebel—the student with the shaved and tattooed head—was striking the hollow testicles of Sir Dickie's horse with a hammer.

Bonnnggg … bonnnggg … bonnnggg….

Two small crowds were gathered near the statue. The members of one group sported the red liberty caps of *Le Collectif radical*; the members of the other group wore beige overcoats and carried placards that proclaimed a variety of slogans: *Protect Free Speech! Respect History! Down with Affirmative Intolerance!*

Between the two groups stood Kirk Appleton. His cameraman stood next to him, adjusting a tripod. Nearby was Rufus Lillidew, dressed in a cavalry uniform: calf-high riding boots, jodhpur-style pants, khaki tunic and tropical pith helmet. A long pole protruded from between his thighs. At the end of the pole was a horse's head, made of plush and sporting a golden mane. Lillidew gripped the pole with white-gloved hands as he pranced about in tight little circles for the benefit of the news camera.

"Good Lord," said Duffy.

Sequoia Tush joined him at the edge of the spectacle.

"Great photo op, eh?" she said.

"Yes, if we were going for a Monty Python look."

"Why is that girl whacking the horse's balls?"

"Good question. Probably to mess with the sound quality of Lillidew's interview."

As Duffy and Tush looked on, J.J. Jones joined them.

"What a goddamn disgrace," he said. "Those balls are sacred!"

"Students paint them all the time," Tush pointed out.

"That's different," replied Jones. "That's tradition."

Before Duffy could stop him, Jones ran towards Rebel like he was rushing a quarterback. He chased her around the statue, grabbing for the hammer that she clutched in her left hand. After two laps, Rebel climbed up the plinth and took shelter directly beneath the horse's dented scrotum.

"Fascist creep!" she cried. "Help! Help!"

Jones grabbed hold of an outsized bronze hoof and thrust himself upwards. He managed to wrest the hammer from the young woman's grasp. Lowering himself back to solid ground, he turned the hammer over several times, examining the tool as if it were an ancient artifact. It was a ball-peen model: one end had a flat face, the other was rounded.

"My grandpa had one just like this," said Jones, looking up with a dopey, nostalgic grin.

Appleton directed his cameraman to focus on Jones and Rebel. Lillidew slid into the frame, one hand on the pole of his hobby horse and the other gallantly reaching up to assist the terrified student.

"Fret not, young woman," said Lillidew. "The cavalry has arrived."

Rebel, who moments earlier had been Lillidew's sworn enemy,

leaned into the tall professor like a damsel embracing a knight. Lillidew lifted his chin and presented the TV camera with a look of stouthearted righteousness.

The cameraman then zoomed in on Jones.

"What's your name?" Appleton asked.

"None of your business," snapped Jones. "That bald-headed freak was vandalizing a treasured piece of art."

"His name is J.J. Jones," offered Lillidew. "And he is a senior member of the university administration."

Duffy strode up just as Jones began shaking the hammer at Lillidew. The professor raised the pole of his hobby horse to parry the impending blow. Duffy reached over and, with a surprisingly deft movement, grabbed Jones's wrist with his left hand while taking possession of the hammer with his right. He then hid the ball-whacking implement behind his back before turning to Appleton and the video camera.

"Hello, Kirk," he said. "What brings you to our fair campus today?"

"Isn't it obvious? The Sir Middling protests have turned violent."

Duffy gave an amiable chuckle. "I think that's overstating things a bit," he said. "Emotions are running a little high, perhaps. But the Sir Middling community is known for its feisty spirit. Our faculty and students like nothing more than a respectful exchange of views. And frankly, isn't that what a university is all about?"

Behind him, Jones had grabbed Lillidew's hobby horse. The two men were wrestling for a tighter grip on the pole. All the while, Rebel was kicking feebly at Jones from behind Lillidew's protective arm.

"This is more than a spirited debate," said Appleton, pointing to the chaos behind Duffy. "You've got a professor prancing around on a hobby horse, a student vandalizing a statue and a senior administrator threatening a faculty member with a hammer."

"We could debate semantics all day," countered Duffy. "Let's not get distracted from the real issues at play here."

Just then, Jones managed to grasp the golden mane of the hobby horse. He gave a sharp tug and the head popped off. Jones held it high like a battlefield trophy while Lillidew and Rebel gasped in horror.

Duffy, meanwhile, had launched into a monologue about the real issues at play. Appleton's cameraman shifted his lens from the communications director to the drama unfolding behind him. As Duffy droned on about Sir Middling's freedom of speech policy, Jones gave Lillidew one last shove and ran off with the head of the hobby horse.

"So, you see, Kirk," concluded Duffy, "Sir Middling U is doing exactly what any good university should be doing: staying relevant by fostering a civil exchange of ideas."

Appleton was no longer paying attention to Duffy. He was interviewing Lillidew, who waved his headless stick like a piece of courtroom evidence.

Confused, Duffy turned to Sequoia Tush.

"What's going on?" he asked.

"It's hard to explain," replied Tush. "But I think Appleton got the visuals he was looking for."

Chapter 34

The six o'clock news led off with Kirk Appleton's report on the protest. Duffy's jaw hung slack as he watched the footage of Jones chasing Rebel around the statue, followed by the struggle for Lillidew's hobby horse and a shot of Jones running away with the severed head.

Terri Coyne, who had stayed late to watch the news with Duffy and Tush, tried to give her boss a sympathetic look. Her efforts collapsed in a burst of laughter. "Oh my God!" she shrieked. "What a train wreck!"

Overcome with giggles, Tush fell sideways in his chair. "Oh, man, we got smoked!"

Duffy didn't share in the hilarity. "At least I stopped J.J. from killing Lillidew on TV."

"That's a pretty low bar, even for this office," said Coyne.

Duffy's phone began to vibrate and dance across his desk. Emails, text messages and social-media alerts were pouring in.

Tush and Coyne pulled out their phones and began scrolling.

"How bad is it?" asked Duffy.

"On a scale of one to ten, I'd say fifteen," said Tush.

"Look at this!" Coyne said with undisguised delight. She held up her phone to show an animated GIF of Rebel hammering the testicles of Sir Dickie's horse, again and again.

Another meme portrayed Jones, naked except for a primitive loin cloth, as he ran off with the horse's head held high.

"Jesus, Joseph and Mary," muttered Duffy. "Sir Middling U is going to wear this forever."

His phone began to ring with the Darth Vader music that Duffy had recently assigned to Clive Blunt's number.

"I've got to take this," he said, waving Coyne and Tush out of his office.

He took a deep breath.

"Good evening, Dr. Blunt."

"There is absolutely *nothing* good about this evening, Duffy! I just got off the phone with the chancellor. She's furious. So are the university's biggest donors and the head of the alumni association. Sir Middling U is a laughingstock. How on earth could you let this happen?"

"This is bad, sir. No question about it. But on the bright side, I did stop J.J. from killing Professor Lillidew. And right now, our immediate priority is finding a way to resolve the sit-in and end the story."

"I'm way ahead of you, Duffy. While you were frolicking in the quad, I engaged the services of an outside media consultant."

Duffy was gobsmacked. "May I ask why you would do that?"

"We need an experienced hand."

Duffy let his forehead drop to his desk. Then he took another deep breath and asked, "What did your media consultant suggest?"

"She thinks I should meet with Morris Hill and hear him out. By just listening, without giving in, we could very well bring the sit-in to an end. After that, the media will lose interest."

Duffy considered throwing his phone at the wall. Instead, he said, "With all due respect, sir, that's exactly what I've been recommending for the past two weeks."

"Not from my perspective," said Blunt.

"I disagree," replied Duffy. "But I guess the important thing is that you'll be meeting with Dr. Hill, Dr. Dubé and Tessa Burns. Would you like me to set that up?"

"I am going to meet only with Morris Hill," said Blunt. "Tessa is still a student, and Dr. Dubé is not a tenure-track member of faculty."

"But Dr. Dubé is the one organizing the alternative panel discussion. She and Dr. Hill are equal partners in this."

"Don't push me, James. Hierarchy is essential in the academy."

Duffy hurled his pen against the wall. It exploded like a firecracker, leaving a messy blue smear on the cheery young faces featured in a Sir Middling U recruitment poster.

He then let out a long sigh. If this is what it takes to end this friggin' nightmare, so be it.

"Duffy, are you still there?" barked Blunt.

"Yes," replied Duffy. "I can set the meeting up for ten o'clock tomorrow morning."

"I can't meet before three p.m."

"All right, three p.m. I suggest we use the auxiliary meeting room in the basement of Founders Hall. That way we can avoid the protesters and the media. I can meet you at the back of the building tomorrow at two fifty-five. We can go down to the meeting room via the fire-exit steps."

"Is that necessary?"

"The only other route to the auxiliary meeting room is through the main corridor—and that's full of protesters and reporters."

"Well, that won't work."

Duffy felt his anxieties spike. He wondered which campus constable had seized the hash brownies, and if there were any left.

"That's why I suggest we use the fire exit," he said with exaggerated patience.

"Very well, then. Just make sure there are no paparazzi hiding in the bushes."

Duffy couldn't tell if Blunt was serious. But since he had never heard his boss crack a joke, he assumed that he was.

"Don't worry, sir. I'll task Comms Team One to sweep the area beforehand."

Silence.

Duffy wondered if he'd gone too far.

Fuck it, he thought.

"That arrogant dickhead!"

"I'm sorry, Feef."

"I should be there."

"Of course, you should," said Duffy. "But let's just get this done."

"Morris, what do you think?"

Hill looked from Duffy to Dubé.

"Fifi, I can't stop you from quietly slipping into the room after the meeting starts."

Duffy's head dropped; Fifi hugged Hill.

"I can't be part of this," Duffy said wearily.

"Oh, come on, you love this bad-boy shit!" said Fifi.

"Blunt will blame me. I'll never become assistant vice-president."

"He's going to blame you anyway. You might as well join the troublemakers and have some fun."

Duffy turned to Hill. "Morris, can you break the news to Tessa? And can you be in the auxiliary meeting room by three o'clock? I'll bring Blunt down shortly after."

Hill nodded.

Fifi stood up. As she prepared to leave, she reached out and tousled Duffy's hair with her right hand.

"See you at three, comrade!"

"Shouldn't you be working on your next book?" replied Duffy.

"I am. Today's events will feature prominently."

Chapter 35

Blunt arrived at the back of Founders Hall wearing an overcoat and sunglasses. His chin was buried in a Sir Middling Muskrats scarf, which was tied in a surprisingly stylish knot. Duffy wondered if the media consultant had tied it for him.

"Just through here," said Duffy, guiding his boss towards a fire door and down a flight of concrete steps.

"I've never been in the auxiliary meeting room," said Blunt.

"It's pretty basic. I cleared out some of the storage boxes and made some space at the table."

When they reached the room, Blunt said, "I can take it from here."

"What do you mean?" asked Duffy. "It would be useful for me to sit in on the meeting."

"That won't be necessary."

Blunt removed his sunglasses and entered the room.

When the door shut, Fifi stepped out from around a corner.

"Here we go!" she said.

"Whoa, Feef! Let them get comfortable first. You'll spook Blunt."

233

"Are you coming in with me?"

"No way. You can tell me all about it after Blunt fires me."

Fifi kissed Duffy on the cheek. Then she opened the door and slipped inside as quietly as a cat.

Duffy listened closely. He expected to hear Blunt's protests, but the only sound was a steady, low murmur. He waited a few minutes. All seemed calm. He walked down the dimly lit corridor and flopped onto an old couch. He felt tired and worn out. His anxieties had been running high for the past week, and he hadn't been sleeping well. The afternoon light was slanting in through a ground-level window. He slipped an antacid tablet into his mouth and stretched out on the couch.

"I'll just rest my eyes for a few minutes," he said.

When Duffy awoke, the window was black and the door to the auxiliary meeting room was open.

"Oh, shit."

He leapt up and sprinted down the corridor. The room was dark. Duffy looked at his watch: five-twenty.

"Shit, shit, shit!"

He reached into his coat pocket for his phone and found a sheet of carefully folded notepaper. He held it up to the light:

"Didn't want to disturb your beauty rest," it said. "All's good. We're calling off the sit-in. Message me when you're done napping. Feef."

Duffy could feel a heavy weight lift from his shoulders and evaporate. He was still overwhelmed and struggling, but at least something had gone right.

He walked home and put the kettle on for tea. As it boiled, he put on his housecoat—green plaid flannel, a gift from his Nana in Donegal—and curled up in his favourite reading chair. He sent text messages and left voicemails for Fifi and Blunt. Neither replied. He made a tuna sandwich to go with the tea, nibbling and sipping while he scrolled through the day's news on his phone.

There was another social media post from Mittens' publicist: *"Shall we tack or jibe?/ The sultry vapours luff our sails/ And love unfurls in breezy splendour. @MoreShittyWeather, @SirMiddlingU, #poetrylovers."*

Duffy wondered if Mittens was trying to make some kind of satirical statement. The man had a PhD in English lit, after all. Surely he knew how terrible his poetry was. Then again, maybe he didn't. In Duffy's experience, delusion thrived in the rarified hothouse of academia.

He set his phone down and pondered the day's events. His thoughts kept returning to the media consultant. Why did Blunt hire an outsider? What's going on behind the scenes? Am I really no good at my job? The same three questions raced through his mind, repeating again and again like a carousel he couldn't turn off. His psychologist called it "rumination." Duffy called it torture.

He popped fifty milligrams of trazodone, which he took to augment the sertraline. Duffy was only supposed to use the backup meds when his anxieties were particularly severe. It was always a judgement call, but he felt the need for a serious time out. He went to bed and waited for the drugs to subdue his frenetic mind, hoping for a few hours of precious sleep.

Sometime towards morning he drifted off.

Chapter 36

The incessant ring of his mobile phone drilled deep into Duffy's medicated brain. It poked at his thalamus until it woke up and roused the rest of the grey-matter gang. Duffy floated up from the drowsy depths like an old log pulling free from a muddy lake bottom. He fumbled for his phone, which lay somewhere on the night table. Through filmy eyes he saw the name of the caller and felt relief.

"Hey, Feef."

"Jesus, Duffy. You sound terrible!"

"I overslept. What time is it?"

"Nine-thirty. You okay?"

"Yeah, just tired. I took a pill last night."

"What kind of pill?"

"Anti-anxiety."

"You sound pretty doped up."

"That's the idea."

"You should try meditation and exercise."

"They're on my to-do list."

"Sorry I didn't get back to you last night. I received some big news and got side-tracked."

"Bigger than telling me how the meeting with Blunt went?"

"Much bigger. I got a call from the Confederation Society. My book's been shortlisted for the Macphail Prize for Public Policy!"

"Wow," said Duffy, struggling to give Fifi the reaction she deserved. "That's amazing."

"We have to coordinate our communications with the Society's media people, so no need for a news release yet."

"Sure. Just let me know when."

"Thanks, Duffy."

"So, what happened with Blunt?"

"He didn't tell you?"

"He hasn't returned my messages."

"It was weird. First of all, he didn't seem annoyed when I joined the meeting. He didn't exactly pay any attention to me either, but that's Blunt. And second, when Morris explained what we wanted, Blunt said yes."

"Really? What did he agree to?"

"He said he'd issue a statement prior to Dewlap's lecture that mentions the panel discussion and the university's support for freedom of speech."

"I'm stunned," said Duffy. "I thought he was just going to hear you out as a courtesy."

"I don't know what you said to him, Duffy, but thank you."

"Don't thank me. Thank Lillidew, Jones and that weird girl with the tattooed head. The show they put on is what finally got through to Blunt."

"Don't sell yourself short. You helped too. I left you a thank-you gift on your desk."

"Not necessary, but I appreciate it."

"By the way, there's something seriously wrong with your office door."

"What do you mean?"

"It's hard to explain. Just be glad you don't have boobs."

Duffy got to the office at ten-thirty. The first thing he noticed was the nameplate on his door. It read: *James Daffy*. The second thing was that the door swung inward, not outward as before. This created a problem. Duffy's office was so cramped that the door now hit his desk before it was halfway open. To get inside, he had to squeeze through the narrow opening, press himself flat against the wall and slide his body along for a foot or two—a series of maneuvres that made him feel like a mime in a glass box.

When he finally got inside, he turned the lights on and threw his leather jacket over the back of his chair. He glanced at his desk and saw two things that hadn't been there the day before. The first was a package, about twice the size of a shoebox. A note rested on top.

> *Thanks Duffy for all your help. Here's a little something (and I do mean little) for you to wear to Rocky.*
> *Feef*
> *PS: You're on your way to becoming a good man ... and to getting laid. Don't mess it up.*

Duffy unwrapped the package. It took a moment for his brain to compute what his eyes were seeing. On top were a pair of black platform heels. He took them out and set them on the desk. Next was a skimpy black corset with a lace-up front. Below this was a curly black wig and a dollar-store makeup kit. At the very bottom was a pair of black panties, a garter and fishnet stockings.

Duffy laughed until it sank in that this was *his* costume for tonight.

He pushed the outfit aside and turned his attention to something else that hadn't been on his desk yesterday. A thick packaging envelope. It too contained a note.

Hi James! We ran out of proof copies of Dr. Mittens' book for the second print run, so I took yours back. Hope you don't mind (Terri said it was okay—she's so helpful!)

The signature was illegible.

Duffy stood up and folded himself around his door again, sliding through the narrow opening that led to the rest of the communications office.

Terri Coyne was waiting for him with a coffee.

"Thought you could use this," she said, handing him an extra-large mug.

"Do I look like I need it?"

"Well, you came in late, your door is *tout fucké* and the video of Jones attacking Lillidew is all over social media. I just thought you could use some real caffeine, not that decaf crap you normally drink."

"Thank you. What's the story with my door?"

"Don't worry about it. I called Lloyd and gave him shit. He's coming over to fix it personally."

"Isn't that the problem? Maybe someone else should fix it."

Duffy sipped his coffee. He had to admit, it was much better than the decaf crap he usually drank.

"Hey, Terri," he said. "What's the name of that publicist over at SIRMUP?"

"The one who keeps popping in and out of your office?"

"Yes."

"Mazie? Shasta? Something like that."

"You don't know?" asked Duffy.

"I know a lot of things, but I don't know that."

"Do you think you could find out?"

"Probably. You got a crush on her?"

"No, it's university business."

"Good. Because Sophie Munn is one sweet gal. You treat her right, okay?"

"I'll do my best. In fact, I'm going over to Founders Hall right now."

"If I don't see you later, have fun at *Rocky* tonight!"

"How do you know I'm going to see *Rocky*?"

"I peeked at the package on your desk."

"Terri, am I allowed no privacy?"

"Hey, mister, if you wear an outfit like that in public, you can kiss your privacy goodbye."

"I heard Fifi bought you a costume for tonight," said Sophie.

"She told you, did she?" replied Duffy, who had perched himself on the edge of Sophie's desk.

"Of course. But she thinks you lack the confidence to wear it. We actually have a bet."

Oh, no, thought Duffy. The sisterhood at work!

"What do you mean?" he asked, not sure he wanted to know the answer.

"Fifi bet me that you won't wear the costume tonight. I said you would."

Duffy was pleased that Sophie had bet in his favour.

"What does the winner get?" he asked.

"A large popcorn at the Art Haus Theatre."

"That's it?"

"Hey, we gamble responsibly."

Duffy smiled. He liked that Sophie always had a cheeky comeback.

"So, why are you so sure I'll wear the costume?"

"I didn't say I was *sure*," said Sophie. "But when push comes to shove, I think you'll wear it."

"Okay," said Duffy, a little deflated. "So why do you think I'll don the skimpy costume?"

"Because I know how your mind works."

"And how does my mind work?"

"You think that if you do something daring, like dress up in a corset and panties in public, it'll impress me so much that I'll sleep with you."

"I wasn't thinking that," said Duffy, "but now I am."

"See? I know how your mind works."

"I think you're giving my mind too much credit."

"Just wear the costume, fella, and see what happens."

"I really hate to change the subject," said Duffy, "but what's up with Meriwether?"

"What do you mean?"

"He was AWOL from the whole sit-in situation, and he's handed control of amalgamation over to Blunt. That's not like him."

A look of concern crept across Sophie's beautiful face. "I can't betray the president's confidence," she said, "but, yes, his plate is very full these days."

"I'm sure it is. There must be a lot going on behind the scenes with amalgamation."

"It's taking a lot out of him."

"Anything else?"

"Stop asking, James," Sophie said firmly. "Dr. Meriwether trusts me to protect his privacy, and I take that trust seriously."

"Sorry, I was out of line. Can I ask if you've heard anything about my assistant VP proposal?"

"James! Now that's *really* going too far. I am not impressed."

"*Mea culpa.*"

Sophie put her hands on her hips and looked at Duffy like she was trying to figure something out. "Aren't there more important things going on right now?" she asked. "I didn't think this promotion meant so much to you."

Duffy was embarrassed. He respected Sophie's opinion, and it stung him to fall short of her expectations.

"You're right, I'm being shallow and selfish," he said. "I don't remember when I became that kind of guy. I'll rein it in."

"For your sake, I hope you do. And I want you to cut Dr. Meriwether some slack."

"What do you mean?"

"I mean, don't judge him too harshly."

"Okay," said Duffy. "But now I'm really worried about what's going on."

"I'm sure the president will tell you himself when he feels the time is right. Meanwhile, I'll see you tonight, yes?"

"Given the skimpiness of my costume, you're going to see a lot of me tonight."

Chapter 37

Duffy called Clive Blunt one more time. It was four o'clock on a Friday afternoon; the campus was a ghost town. Even a workaholic like Blunt would sometimes cut out early on the last day of the week. Duffy didn't really expect him to answer, not after ignoring his calls and texts for the past twenty-four hours. So he was startled when his boss picked up.

"Blunt here."

"Oh…. Is that Dr. Blunt?"

"Yes, James. Who else would answer my mobile?"

"Right. I was just calling to ask how your meeting with Dr. Hill went?"

"And Dr. Dubé."

"Uh … yes," said Duffy. "She was quite determined."

"The meeting went as expected," Blunt said curtly.

"Is there anything I should know? I mean, we should probably put out a statement, given the media coverage of the sit-in."

"The statement has already been written. It's scheduled to go out at four-thirty."

Duffy's anxiety, simmering all day, began to boil. "Who wrote the statement?"

"My media consultant."

"Really? I have to say I'm disappointed, Dr. Blunt. I have a lot of experience with this sort of thing, and it's a key part of my job as director of communications."

"You're juggling a lot of things, James. To be frank, I think we need outside help on the amalgamation issue going forward."

"If you have concerns about the quality of my work, sir, I'd be happy to hear them."

There was silence on the line.

"Dr. Blunt, are you still there?"

"Of course, I'm still here!"

"With all due respect, it seems that the media consultant gave you the exact same advice that I've been giving you all along. Perhaps you can help me understand how I could have been more effective at communicating my counsel to you?"

"I disagree with your premise," said Blunt. "I don't think your advice was at all similar to what the consultant suggested."

Sometimes down is up, thought Duffy, recalling a line from *Alice in Wonderland*.

"Does Dr. Meriwether know about your media consultant?" he asked.

"Not that I need to explain myself to you, James, but the president asked me to take charge of both the sit-in issue and amalgamation. I am exercising my judgement on both files."

Duffy's guts began to roil; the anxiety rose from his belly to his chest like hot, choking smoke.

"May I ask if Dr. Meriwether is on some sort of leave?"

More silence.

"Dr. Blunt?"

"Alex needs to step back for a bit. That's all. The Board of Governors has agreed to reduce his workload for a few weeks."

"I'm sorry to hear that."

"Alex is still the president, James. He'll still be on campus."

"Well, let me know what I can do to help."

"You can post my statement to the website. I'll send it to you now, but don't post it until after it gets emailed to staff and faculty at four-thirty."

"Of course. Would you like me to review it before it goes out?"

"No. It's been reviewed and approved. Just post the statement to the website exactly as it is, do you hear me?"

Duffy rapped the phone against his forehead several times. "No, sir, I didn't catch that last part. Could you repeat it?"

"Just … post … the … statement … to … the … website … exactly … as … it … is!" Blunt said with exaggerated enunciation.

"Oh, right. I heard you that time."

Blunt hung up.

"Wanker," muttered Duffy. A moment later, his laptop pinged. It was the statement from Blunt.

> *From: The Vice-President of University Services*
> *To: Faculty, Students and Staff*
> *Subject: Statues and Critical Dialogue*
>
> *It has come to my attention that there may be some concern among the Sir Middling community regarding an upcoming guest lecture.*
>
> *As a member of the University's Executive Team, I wish to assure you that we have reflected deeply on this matter and consulted with the relevant stakeholders. As a result, allow me to share a few thoughts.*
>
> *First, I want you to know that "I hear you."*
>
> *Second, freedom of speech is IMPORTANT to the University.*
>
> *Third, in addition to the guest lecture, there will be a*

separate multi-scholar panel to discuss a similar topic. I trust that this timely and candid email will allay all concerns regarding the above matter.

Yours in scholarship and learning,
Clive Blunt, PhD
Vice-President of University Services

Duffy read the statement twice.

"What a pompous tool!" he shouted out loud. "No empathy, no humanity, no comfort for those who might be feeling hurt by the Dewlap lecture!"

He opened the drawer on the left side of his desk and rummaged through the detritus: paper clips, sticky notes, batteries, antiseptic wipes, plastic cutlery, a packet of soy sauce. Finally, beneath a snarl of computer cords, he found what he was looking for: a nearly full mickey of whiskey, left behind by his dipsomaniac predecessor three years earlier.

Duffy, who had never acquired a taste for hard liquor, studied the bottle. He recalled his father saying that whiskey improved with age. "Like a liquid violin," the old man had said. Duffy unscrewed the cap and took a tentative swig. The alcohol burned deliciously all the way down his throat.

As he posted the consultant's statement to the Sir Middling website, he raised the whiskey bottle and said, "Here's to mediocrity … and to those feeble souls who neither lead nor trail!"

Duffy's doctor had told him to abstain from alcohol while taking anxiety medication. Not being much of a drinker, Duffy had given little thought to the physician's warning. Even now, as he drained the bottle of whiskey, he thought, What harm could a little nip do? He soon found out. A little nip might have been fine; six ounces was definitely too much. The booze mixed with the sertraline and trazodone in his system, causing a chemical reaction that lit up Duffy's brain like Canada Day fireworks. He was soon reduced to a slurring, slobbering mess. When he showed up at Sophie's door two hours later, he terrified even the most hard-core *Rocky* fans within. A smear of red lipstick circled his mouth like a wound; the black corset was on backwards; and despite his skinny hips, the tiny panties left more crack above the waistband than below it.

"Duffy, are you drunk?" said Sophie, a mix of anger and astonishment in her voice.

"And stoned," he mumbled.

"What?"

"Whiskey … an' meds."

"What meds?"

"Anxieties.… I have anxieties."

Duffy leaned against the doorframe like a cartoon drunk. His pupils were wide and vacant, and his slack body shuddered as if it were about to fold in upon itself.

"Someone give me a hand," Sophie yelled over her shoulder.

Several women—all dressed in short, sparkly outfits and thick gobs of makeup—dragged Duffy towards the couch. They lay him in the recovery position with his mouth drooling over the side of a pillow. Someone positioned a cooking pot directly below his chin to catch the drips.

"You guys go to the movie," Sophie said with a sigh. "I'll stay here and babysit the man of my dreams."

Deep within his medicated brain, Duffy heard squeals of laughter. Strange people in even stranger costumes seemed to be hovering all around. They drifted away, replaced by a cat with enormous white teeth. The cat soon disappeared too, leaving only its teeth behind. Next came a caterpillar, and a rabbit, and then someone dressed as the Queen of Hearts. There were voices and chants: "Sometimes down is up," and "We're all mad here!" Things came into focus and then dissolved. Duffy was suddenly filled with self-reproach, as though he had done something repugnant. Remorse flooded every cell in his body like a poisonous dye. *Forgive me, Father, for I have sinned.* He wanted to vomit, to get everything out of his system, but he could manage only a miserably dry retch.

Duffy passed the entire night in muddled torment. Near dawn, he felt as though he was floating up through water—a long, slow ascent towards the light. His head ached, and he was wracked with shame and self-loathing. He tried to focus on a comforting phrase from long ago: *This too shall pass.*

Eventually, he managed to sit up. He was in an apartment—the upper floor of an old house, by the look of it. Through a bay window, he could see the sun peeking over a row of leafless trees. He checked his watch: seven-thirty. He could smell the soothing aroma of fresh coffee, a cure in itself. He stood up and tested his legs. They were a little wobbly, but they held. He took several steps before he noticed the tiny black panties that clung to his narrow hips.

"Shit!"

He looked around and spotted the washroom. He stumbled over, slipped inside and shut the door. A large mirror filled the wall to his left. Turning to face it, Duffy was horrified by the freakish ghoul who gaped back at him. Ten hours of tossing, turning and night sweats had smeared the lipstick and mascara together, creating a zombie mask that would have frightened even a horror-film makeup artist.

Duffy began splashing his face with cold water. Then he took a bar of soap and a washcloth and began scrubbing the lurid colours off his cheeks and forehead. He rinsed the washcloth a half-dozen times and went back to scrubbing, as if he were washing away a mortal sin.

When the makeup was finally gone, his face glowed like a ripe strawberry. The washcloth, once the colour of ivory, was now maroon. He rinsed it with soap and hot water; it lightened a little, but would never be described as ivory again. He dropped it into a hamper and pushed it down below the layers of towels, bras and panties.

When he finished, he poured a glass of water and gulped it down. He found a bottle of aspirin, popped two in his mouth and washed them down with another shot of water.

Duffy stared in the mirror and saw his pale nakedness reflected back. The panties mocked him as he tried to remember why he was here—wherever *here* was. Bits of memory were coming back: the whiskey, the *Rocky Horror* costume, the makeup, a long walk through the cold night and then stumbling up to a door.

Sophie's door.

As if on cue, he heard her voice.

"Hey James, are you okay in there? I have coffee."

"Great, thanks," he said. "Just a minute."

Duffy grabbed a towel and draped it around himself. It was short, but at least it covered the panties. He opened the door. Sophie was wearing a soft blue housecoat and holding two steaming mugs. An angel of mercy.

"The good news is you're alive," said Sophie, handing Duffy a coffee. "The bad news is, well, you've already looked in the mirror."

She pushed past him and sat on the edge of the bathtub, crossing her long legs in a way that made Duffy nearly forget his pounding headache.

"So … What the hell, pal?"

Duffy sipped his coffee and let the milky liquid warm his throat.

"I messed up. I'm sorry"

"You said something last night about whiskey and anxiety meds. Why don't you start there?"

Duffy told her the whole story, or at least as much as he could remember: the demoralizing call with Blunt, the media consultant, the meaningless statement, the whiskey and his struggles with anxiety.

"Well," said Sophie, "it was pretty stupid to mix booze and pills. But I am sorry about your anxieties. I had no idea."

"It's not something I talk about."

"You do have a pretty stressful job," she said. "You're always dealing with negative stuff, and I bet it's pretty thankless."

Duffy took a sip of coffee. "I've always struggled with anxiety," he said, leaning against the vanity. "But working at Sir Middling U seems to amp it up."

"Sounds like you need some healthier ways to amp it down."

"Yes," agreed Duffy. "Getting drunk and prancing around town in woman's panties doesn't seem to be working for me."

Sophie laughed.

"You look surprisingly good in panties," she said. "You better be careful or Fifi's going to recruit you for her burlesque show."

"Please don't give her any ideas."

"Hey, she and the troupe got an eyeful last night. I bet they're preparing an offer for you right now."

"Oh, God," groaned Duffy. "Were they all here?"

"Yup."

Duffy let his head drop to his chest. "Listen, Sophie," he said. "I'm really sorry about last night. I made a fool of myself, and I probably embarrassed you in front of your friends."

"I *was* embarrassed," replied Sophie. "I thought you were being selfish, getting drunk and high for our date. But I understand now—at least a little. I mean, I don't doubt that anxieties are a real health condition. I'm just not impressed that you mixed booze and meds."

A wave of nausea swept over Duffy. The shame of disappointing Sophie was far worse than the wretchedness of a Class-A hangover.

"It was just a lapse in judgement," he said, almost pleading. "I know I've let you down, but I hope I haven't blown it completely. Can you forgive me?"

Sophie stood up and put her coffee mug on the counter.

"Are you still wearing those black panties under that towel?" she asked.

"Yes, I am," he replied sheepishly. "They're actually pretty tight. And scratchy. I'm not sure how I'm going to get them off."

"Let me see what I can do."

Sophie looked deep into Duffy's eyes while gently pulling at one corner of the towel. It came free and fell to the floor. Her gaze drifted downward over Duffy's slim torso to the strip of black polyester that clung to his white hips. She smiled, then giggled, and then laughed so hard that tears rolled down her cheeks.

"Oh, Duffy, I'm sorry. It's not what you think. It's just the panties. They're hilarious!"

Duffy laughed too. "I think Fifi bought them in the tween department at Walmart."

Sophie hugged Duffy and pressed her face against his chest. He felt her warm tears on his bare skin and the shudder of her body as she laughed.

He hugged her back. He still felt terrible, but the hangover was fading. After a few moments, Sophie pulled away and let her housecoat fall to the floor.

Duffy gazed shamelessly at her naked body.

"Oh, Sophie … you're *so* beautiful."

She stopped laughing and just smiled.

"Let's get you out of those panties, mister, and into the shower."

Chapter 38

The sun poked out briefly on Monday morning. It was the first of December. Fall was over—if not by the calendar, then certainly by the feel of the crisp air. Duffy had begun monitoring the weather forecast several times a day. There were flurries in the offing, but the only storms brewing involved amalgamation and the Dewlap lecture.

His first call of the day came from Sophie.

"What a pleasant way to start the week," he said.

"Yes, it is. Have you recovered?"

"From mixing alcohol and meds, yes. From the sex, not quite."

"We'll have to get you into a training regimen."

"Where do I sign up?"

"Invite me to your place for dinner tomorrow night and I'll bring the paperwork."

"Consider yourself invited."

"Good. Now, down to business. Dr. Meriwether is in the office this morning and he'd like to see you. Can you come by in half an hour?"

"Sure. What's it about?"

"He didn't say."

"Is he okay?"

"Ask him yourself when you get here."

"Right."

Once he'd hung up, Duffy pushed his jacket and satchel through the narrow opening in his office doorway and then squeezed out after them. Terri Coyne was waiting on the other side.

"When is maintenance going to fix this?" Duffy said, slapping the door. "If I gain half a pound of winter fat, I won't be able to fit through."

"God knows," said Coyne. "I'll call Lloyd again. In other news, that publicist over at SIRMUP is pretty angry with you."

"Why?"

"It's about the edits you made to Dr. Mittens' book."

"I didn't make any edits to his book."

"The publicist seems to think you did. Something about the title."

"That wasn't an edit; it was a doodle. Besides, it was my copy."

"She took your copy, remember? Maybe it got sent to the printers."

"Jesus Murphy! What's her extension?"

"I'll text it to you."

Coyne watched Duffy as he slid into his jacket and pulled on his watch cap.

"Did you really play in a Springsteen cover band?" she asked.

"Yes. For about three years."

"I've never heard you sing."

"If we ever get the band back together, I'll comp you front-row tickets and a VIP pass."

"Ha! I won't hold my breath."

"I'm off to the president's office," said Duffy.

"Oh, yes. Poor Dr. Meriwether."

"What do you mean?"

"You know, first his dog gets sick and then his wife."

"What are you talking about?"

"His wife, Marilyn. She has breast cancer."

"Oh, geez. I had no idea."

"That's why he cut back on his workload."

"How do you know more about this than I do?"

Coyne waved her hand as if Duffy was the most hopeless person on campus. Then she returned to her desk and got back to work.

Duffy didn't bother to ask for more details; he hoped Meriwether would confide in him when they met.

He walked the familiar route to Founders Hall. The balls on Brave Sir Dickie's horse, along with the rest of the statue, wore a coat of red dye from the recent protests.

As he started up the steps of the old administration building, he met Kerri Quartermain coming down.

"Are you lost?" he asked.

"Nice to see you too."

Duffy didn't bother to apologize. "What brings you to our humble campus?"

"Another meeting with Clive Blunt."

"What do you mean, *another* meeting?"

"Clive asked for some communications help with amalgamation. Rose volunteered my services."

Duffy looked like a kid who'd just learned that Santa wasn't real.

"Oh, dear," said Quartermain. "Clive didn't tell you."

"*You're* the outside media consultant?" said Duffy, outrage building in his narrow chest.

"Rose thought that Clive and I should start getting used to working with one another."

"Why?"

Quartermain hesitated. "It's not really my place to say. But Clive and Sylvia Kiljoy have been negotiating with Rose about faculty and staff ratios. I think the Clive-meister smells a promotion for himself when all the dust settles."

"Like what?"

"I don't know, maybe provost of the amalgamated universities?"

Duffy let this sink in. "So, you're the one who got Blunt to meet with Morris Hill?"

"Rose and I, yes. The sit-in was getting in the way of our amalgamation talks. We thought it was best for Clive to end the protests as soon as possible."

"And you wrote his statement about freedom of expression?"

"I gave my advice and held the pen; Clive signed off on it."

"It was gutless," said Duffy. "There was no mention of support for those who might be hurting from the whole Dewlap and statue discussion. The Sir Middling community expects more from its leaders."

"Well, they're soon going to be part of the HIPE community. Or at least the faculty will be."

"What do you mean?"

"Let's just say that Clive and Sylvia seem more protective of Sir Middling's faculty than they are of staff and managers."

Duffy didn't realise until just then that, at some point over the past few months, he'd come to feel like a real member of the Sir Middling community. Not as much as those colleagues who had attended the university as students and considered themselves honest-to-god Muskrats, but still part of the extended family. He knew that faculty members like Blunt and Kiljoy regarded staff and managers as lesser colleagues—the servants who attended to the royal family. Still, it shocked him to think they would sacrifice non-academic employees to save a few faculty jobs.

"So, Blunt and Kiljoy have met with Samaroo since the bigger group met at the Olde Hen?" asked Duffy.

"Yes, several times."

Duffy shook his head. "I guess I shouldn't be surprised."

"I'm sorry you didn't know," said Quartermain, her tone hovering between pity and sarcasm. "You should probably talk to Clive yourself."

She patted Duffy's arm and smiled brightly. "Who knows? Maybe we'll end up working together again—me developing strategy and you putting it into action, just like the old days!"

Duffy had no recollection of such days. During his time at the Ministry of Higher Education, he'd never known what Quartermain did. Her main talent seemed to involve flitting from one meeting to another, giving her opinion on whatever topic was being discussed and making a quick exit before the hard work was assigned.

As he watched Quartermain skip blithely down the steps of Founders Hall, he shook his head. Some things never change.

Duffy was tempted to barge into Blunt's office and ask what the hell was going on, but he didn't want to be late for his meeting with Meriwether. He soon reached the intersection of the two main corridors in Founders Hall: one led left to the Office of the Vice-President of University Services; the other led right, to the Office of the President. Duffy stood there for a moment, pondering which way his destiny lay.

The door to the president's suite opened and Sophie's head popped out. "There you are! Get a move on. Dr. Meriwether is waiting."

Duffy turned right and walked swiftly towards the open door.

"Sorry," he said. "I ran into Kerri Quartermain."

"Who?"

"I'll tell you later."

"Hang up your jacket and go right in," said Sophie. "Dr. Meriwether has ten minutes before his next meeting."

Inside the president's office, Duffy found Meriwether pacing back and forth, his mobile phone close to his ear.

"Let me be clear, Hugh," he was saying. "I will not let Sir Middling U sink below the waves. It's one thing to compromise; it's another to capitulate."

Duffy couldn't make out the president of HIPE's response, but it was brief.

"Fine," Meriwether said firmly. "Let's meet with Prigg and make our respective cases."

He put down the phone. "Ah, James! Good to see you. Come in, come in."

There were dark circles around Meriwether's eyes, and despite his usual *bonhomie*, there was a lack of vigour in his voice. He motioned for Duffy to take a seat.

"Sorry I haven't been in touch sooner," he said. "You've probably heard that I've cut back on my workload for a few weeks."

"Yes, sir. How are you?"

"Oh, it's not me, James. It's my wife. Breast cancer, Stage Two A. Doesn't seem to have spread to the lymph nodes, but it's still damn worrying. Marilyn's a trooper, but the whole thing takes its toll. She's still deciding on treatment."

"I'm very sorry to hear that, sir. If there's anything I can take off your plate, or help with in any way, just let me know."

"That's kind of you," said Meriwether. "What I really need is for you to support Clive with this amalgamation business. I've asked him to lead the file. He's a good negotiator but hopeless at communications."

"I'm happy to help. But to be frank, Dr. Blunt isn't keen on my advice these days."

"What do you mean?"

Duffy explained Blunt's decision to tap Quartermain for communications advice.

"For heaven's sake!" said Meriwether, genuinely annoyed. "I had no idea. Let me talk to him and get you back on the job."

"Sir, are you aware that Dr. Blunt and Dr. Kiljoy have been

meeting with Dr. Samaroo?"

"Yes, of course. As I said, I asked Clive to lead Sir Middling U through the early chit chat. If it goes beyond that, I'll step in and make our opposition clear to the premier. I was just telling that to Hugh Endicott when you came in."

"Did you know that Dr. Blunt and Dr. Kiljoy plan to save faculty jobs by letting staff and managers fend for themselves?"

Meriwether cleared his throat and leaned back in his chair.

"That may be overstating it a bit, James. My understanding is that Clive and Sylvia are just testing the other guy's front lines, so to speak."

"With all due respect, sir, it sounds like they're trying to save more faculty jobs at the expense of nearly all of Sir Middling's staff and managers."

"It's early days, James. Amalgamation is just a proposal right now. The government has made no official comment. If it gets as far as negotiations, rest assured that I'll do my very best for every member of the Sir Middling community."

Duffy was anything but assured. Until this minute, he'd had complete trust in Meriwether's judgement. But with the president handing command of the bridge over to Blunt, and with Blunt and Kiljoy scheming privately with Samaroo, Duffy was beginning to feel that Meriwether had left the university far more vulnerable than he realized.

"I'm sure you will, sir," he said. "And I'd like to help wherever I can. I still have connections with the Ministry of Higher Education. And if I may say so, I know a lot more about communications than Kerri Quartermain."

Meriwether laughed. "I have no doubt that you do, James."

Duffy appreciated the president saying so, but it brought him little comfort.

"Was there anything else, sir?" he asked.

"Yes, as a matter of fact there is. Bertie hasn't had a walk this morning, and I hate to ask Sophie. Just between you and me, I don't think she's a dog person. Would you mind taking Bertie for a little stroll, out to the quad and back?"

"Not at all."

When Duffy had entered the room, he'd smelled the basset hound, but come to think of it, he hadn't seen or heard the old dog.

"He's just snoozing behind the desk," said Meriwether, who stood up to fetch the dog and its leash.

"There you are, Bertie," the president cooed. "James is going to take you for a nice little walk. You remember James? The red-headed chap?"

Duffy heard some snuffling and grunting, followed by what sounded like a zipper being pulled sharply.

"Oh Bertie, couldn't you have held that till you got outside?"

Meriwether smiled at Duffy. "I don't know what's worse: dog toots or sailor farts."

The president handed the leash to Duffy and gave the inert pooch a little nudge with the toe of his polished black brogues.

"Off you go, Bertie. James hasn't got all day."

Bertie made several attempts to roll onto his paws. The diaper he wore all but immobilized his hind end. Meriwether removed the sodden pull-up, lifted the dog off the ground and set him down on his short, shaky legs.

"Off you go," said the president, giving Bertie another nudge.

Out in the waiting room, Sophie was hanging up her phone when Duffy exited the president's office with Bertie in tow.

"Oh, isn't that cute," she said. "A man and his dog-thingie."

"Be kind," said Duffy. "I'm just taking old Bertie out for his morning constitutional."

"You better take one of these," said Sophie, handing Duffy a green poo bag.

With the leash in one hand and the bag in the other, Duffy pulled a goofy face and said, "Look at me, Ma! All that education finally paid off!"

Sophie laughed. The sound delighted Duffy and lifted his spirits.

"Thanks," he said. "I needed that."

"You're welcome. Now, get out of here before that dog poops on the carpet."

It took a full minute for Bertie to shuffle himself to the door. Out in the hall, he slowed down even more. Duffy winced when he realized that the dog's immense girth caused its privates to drag unprotected along the carpet.

You poor wretch, he thought.

Bertie had waddled less than a metre when a dark, moist stain started to grow on the carpet around him. Duffy was tempted to drag the leaky dog back to the office, but he thought that the pee might be a prelude to nastier things. He bent over and tried to pick Bertie up. The dog was massive—eighty pounds at least. Duffy rethought his approach. He squatted, then slid both of his arms like a forklift under Bertie's flabby stomach. Using his knees rather than his back, he stood straight up. Bertie was both heavy and awkward, but Duffy thought he could carry him the last ten metres down the hall. When he reached the front door, he pushed the accessibility button with his elbow and shuffled out to the top of the steps.

Snow was falling.

" 'Yes,' " Duffy pronounced theatrically, " 'the newspapers were right: snow was general all over Ireland.' "

Bertie didn't get the reference, and Duffy didn't bother to explain. It was a line from Joyce, one of his father's favourite authors. Despite the melancholy story from which it came, Duffy recited the line as a sort of mindfulness exercise whenever he found himself blessed by the tranquility of a quiet snowfall.

He proceeded carefully down the steps, with Bertie's weight shifting like loose cargo in heavy seas. As Duffy navigated the last step, his right shoe landed on a patch of black ice. His feet flew out from under him. He felt like a figurine in a snow globe—the world gone topsy-turvy, with him floating through it in slow motion. The dream-like quality was shattered by the pull of gravity. Duffy plummeted to the icy sidewalk with a painful wump. Winded, he lay on his back, waiting for his senses to re-engage. When they did, he was relieved to see that he'd hung onto Bertie like a wide receiver catching a Hail Mary pass. The football, however, felt wet and gooey. Duffy examined the old dog: its long pink tongue flopped out through its jowls, and the bloodshot eyes were lifeless. The last thing Bertie had done before dying of fright was shit himself.

Chapter 39

"Jesus, Duffy, are you serious?" asked Fifi.

Sir Middling U's director of communications was lying flat on the floor of his office, his mobile phone propped next to his left ear.

"I am, Feef. Old Bertie died in my arms. I'm lucky that Lloyd from building maintenance saw the whole thing. He was on his way over with a bag of salt to melt the ice."

"You fell on your back and killed the president's dog. I wouldn't call that lucky."

"True. But Meriwether doesn't blame me. In fact, he's relieved. The vet wanted to put Bertie down weeks ago, but Meriwether couldn't bring himself to do it. He says I've done him and the dog a huge favour. He was glad that Bertie died quickly, and with someone holding him close."

"That's one way to look at it, I guess. How's your back?"

"Sore. Sophie's coming over tonight to give it a rub."

"I guess you *are* lucky, Duffy. Who else could show up wildly intoxicated for a date, then kill the boss's dog and still have the chick fall in love with him?"

"Luck of the Irish, Dr. Dubé."

"Well, I could sure use some of it. The poli-sci department delayed its decision again on whether I get a tenure-track position."

"That sucks. Did they say why?"

"Some horseshit excuse. The chair didn't like the sit-in, and he's waiting to see if I win the Agnes Macphail Prize."

"Isn't making the shortlist good enough? I doubt any of the hiring committee has ever been nominated for something as prestigious as the Macphail Prize."

"I know, right? But I did get a call back from the Chadwick School of International Policy in London. They want me to interview for a position in their political economy program."

"Wow, that's great!"

"Yeah, well, we'll see. If I can't get a tenure-track appointment at Sir Middling U, what chance do I have in the big leagues?"

"Just focus on the fact that you've got an interview with one of the best universities in the world."

"You're right. Thanks, Duffy."

"Besides," he added, "who knows what Sir Middling U is going to look like after Blunt and Kiljoy sell it out to HIPE."

"What do you mean?"

Duffy told Fifi about his conversation with Kerri Quartermain. "And the worst thing is," he said, "I don't think Meriwether understands what he's done by putting Blunt in charge of the amalgamation file."

"That's definitely bad," said Fifi. "But I'd rather hear about Meriwether's wife. How is she doing?"

"Alex says it's breast cancer, Stage Two A. It sounds like Marilyn's doing as well as can be expected, but they're still trying to decide on a course of treatment."

"That poor woman. No wonder Meriwether has been away from campus so much. At least he's got his priorities straight."

Duffy agreed but said nothing. His attention was seized by a twinge in his lower back. He tried to roll onto his side, but the pain prevented him from doing anything but groan.

"Duffy, you should see a doctor," said Fifi.

"It's just sore. All I need is a hot bath."

"The timing sure sucks."

"What do you mean?"

"Just when you and Sophie finally get together, you hurt your back. That's got to impact the old hanky panky."

"Geez, Feef," Duffy said sarcastically, "I hadn't thought of that."

"Sorry. But, hey, I know a website with sex tips for people with chronic back pain. Want me to send it to you?"

"No! Well, maybe. Is it legit?"

"You decide. I just sent you the link."

"Not to my work email?"

"Yup. Enjoy!"

CHAPTER 40

The story appeared in *The Daily Clamour* on a Tuesday morning in early December.

Ministry Mulls Sweeping Reforms to Higher Education
Plan would cap salaries, hike teaching loads and require cost-cutting plans

Quoting a leaked report and an anonymous source, the story said that the Minister of Higher Education, Anne Moreno, was considering a set of recommendations to make universities "more relevant, more accountable and more efficient." It also said that the concept of amalgamation—starting with Sir Richard Middling University and the Henfield Institute for Polytechnical Education—was just one piece of a larger plan to improve productivity and cut costs right across the post-secondary system.

" 'Our government thinks universities should be more accountable for student success and the spending of taxpayer dollars,' said one source familiar with the recommendations. 'We think academic leaders should modernize their curricula to help students secure well-paying jobs.' "

The story went on to say that Minister Moreno had been invited to comment on the leaked report, but as of press time she had not replied.

"That's because you gave us thirty fucking minutes to respond before you posted this bullshit!" shouted Jill Kaiser as she read the article online.

The chief of staff to the minister of higher education then looked at her phone and saw message after message popping up.

"Eric! Get the hell in here!" Kaiser yelled to her deputy.

A young man in beige chinos, a pink button-down shirt and suede lace-ups raced in.

"Yes, Jill?" he said, his body shimmying like a puppy that was desperate to please.

"Read the story on *The Daily Clamour* website and start drafting a statement."

"Sure. Which story?"

"You'll know the fucker when you see it."

"Okay. What do you want the statement to say?"

"That the minister is always looking for ways to improve student success and save taxpayer dollars. But don't commit her to anything."

"So, you want an Easter Bunny?"

"A what?"

"An Easter Bunny. You know ... hollow but tasty."

"Did you just make that up?"

"Kind of."

"Hop the fuck out of here before I bite your goddamn tail off!"

As her deputy hustled out the door, Kaiser called Anne Moreno's executive assistant.

"I need ten minutes with the minister right now!"

"Oh, good morning, Jill," said the assistant. "Hmmm, let me see . . . I could squeeze you in later this morning, say ten-fifteen?"

"What part of 'right now' wasn't fucking clear?"

"Oh, dear. I see. Okay, I'll let the minister know you're coming over."

Kaiser speed-dialled Dev Sharma.

"Good morning, Dev speaking."

"It is definitely *not* a good morning, Sharma. In fact, it is a shitty morning, and it's going to get worse."

"Oh. Hi, Jill. What's the problem?"

"The story in this morning's goddamn *Daily Clamour!* That's the problem!"

"I haven't seen the news yet," said Sharma. "It's seven-fifteen. I just got out of the shower."

"Then let me give you the highlights," barked Kaiser. "Some deceitful little shit drafted a report on higher-education reform without bothering to tell the minister in charge of higher education. Then this little shit leaked it to Shelly Katz at *The Daily Clamour*, who then wrote an anonymously sourced piece of crap, which the *Clamour* splashed all over its website. And the thing is, the recommendations in this bullshit story are the same recommendations that you, Dev Sharma, have been peddling for years."

"Let me read the story and I'll get back to you."

"No, Dev. I don't care if you're dripping water all over your carpet. Tell me right now: Who put you up to this?"

"I had nothing to do with any story in the *Clamour*. Yes, I was commissioned recently to write a briefing note on system reform. But I didn't say anything about the minister of higher education. I just provided an overview, three recommendations and the data to support them."

"Who commissioned you?"

"Jill, you know I can't reveal client names."

"Who, goddammit?"

"Back off, Jill. I'm not going to tell you. What I am going to do is dry off, get dressed and read the article in *The Daily Clamour*. Goodbye."

Kaiser looked at the "call ended" message on her phone.

"Motherfucker!"

She took a sip of water, ran a hand over her cropped black hair and strode down the hall to the minister's office.

Anne Moreno was standing beside the desk of her executive assistant, talking on her mobile. She motioned for her chief of staff to go on through to her private office, which Kaiser did. The room was spacious, with a large desk, a conference table, several padded chairs and floor-to-ceiling windows on two walls. Kaiser was too pumped to sit down. She paced back and forth behind the minister's desk, looking out over the small slice of city park that was visible between two office towers.

Moreno walked in and closed the door. "Take a deep breath, Jill, and tell me what happened."

Of all the ministers Kaiser had worked for, she liked Moreno the best. The woman was a former Olympic rower and national champion in four-person sweeps. She'd earned her master's degree and PhD in sports psychology. She used her smarts, training and broad-shouldered physique to impress others and earn leadership roles in whatever she did.

"We got screwed," said Kaiser.

"No kidding. Who did the screwing and why?"

"Dev Sharma admits writing the report, but he won't say who commissioned it. I doubt it was an opposition party; this has the feel of an inside hit."

"Giles Prigg?"

"That's my guess. He's got his eyes glued on the policy convention and the election. We know he's worried that you're going to suck up all the media coverage and make the premier look like the empty little turd that he is."

"So, Prigg creates a crisis in my portfolio to tie me up and keep me on defence?"

"That's a good bet. He's the one who's been working with Bud Walters and floating rumours about amalgamating HIPE and Sir Middling U."

"How's that polling?"

"There's interest out there, but the mayors of all the university towns are worried. They see a HIPE-Sir Middling merger as just the beginning. None of them want to lose a goose that lays golden eggs for the local economy."

"Put some polling in the field about Sharma's recommendations. Let's get our own data on higher-ed reform."

"If voters like it, would you consider taking it on?"

"Possibly," said Moreno. "It should have been done years ago. If voters agree, why not embrace it? Prigg floated the trial balloon, but he doesn't own it."

"And if voters *don't* like it?"

"Prigg floated the trial balloon; we'll make *sure* he owns it."

The story in *The Daily Clamour* rang through the groves of academe like an air-raid siren. Inter-university email lists that hadn't been used in years sprang to life; social media hummed with outrage and panic; and faculty union leaders re-read their collective agreements with particular attention to workload and compensation clauses.

Hugh Endicott and Rose Samaroo were pummeled with angry messages from professors and administrators right across the province.

- "Couldn't leave well enough alone, could you?"
- "When the timbers are dry, don't strike a match!"

- *"What rough beast, its hour come round at last, slouches towards Academia?"*

"Rose, I put you in charge of stickhandling this," said Endicott. "How could you not know about this report on system-wide reform?"

"Prigg never breathed a word about it."

"What about your contacts in the Ministry of Higher Education?"

"You're the one who told me to work with the premier's office, not the ministry."

"But you still have to know all the pieces in play. This is amateur hour!"

"I disagree," said Samaroo. "The ministry recommendations are clearly a trial balloon. There's an election in the fall; someone in government is testing higher-ed reform with voters. It could be Anne Moreno herself. It's no secret she's got her sights on the premier's job."

"She'd do a hell of a lot better than that clown Teddy Banks."

"Hugh, let me talk to Giles. Once I know what's going on, we can recalibrate our strategy."

"Go ahead. But if you've been outfoxed, we have to think seriously about ditching amalgamation and finding a way to hang this whole fiasco around Prigg's clever little neck."

"Agreed. But we're not there yet."

"Make your call, Rose. I've got a one o'clock with the other presidents. I need you to get back to me before then."

"I've got this, Hugh."

"You better, or you'll be teaching English 101 for the rest of your career."

Chapter 41

Meriwether asked Sophie to arrange a meeting for ten o'clock. He wanted the original trio in his office: Blunt, Kiljoy and Duffy.

Duffy hadn't responded to Sophie's email, so she called him. He was lying on the floor of his office when his phone rang. He rolled over, his back stiff with pain, and hit the speaker button.

"Hello?" he groaned

"Hey, James, it's me. Did you get my message about this morning's meeting in the president's office?"

"Yes. I'll be there. Just resting my back right now."

"Oh, poor you," said Sophie. "The massage didn't help?"

"The massage was great, but we probably should have stopped there."

"Blame Fifi and her special website."

"I'm not blaming anyone," said Duffy. "Last night was wonderful, until it wasn't."

"If your back is that sore, you could phone in to the meeting."

"No, I better be there in person. I'll get going now to give myself time."

"You've got an hour."

"You're right. I should have left ten minutes ago."

As Duffy was stepping gingerly down the steps of Alumni Manor, the young publicist from SIRMUP was charging up to meet him.

"James, how could you?" she cried.

"How could I *what*?"

"Sabotage Dr. Mittens' book with that mean-spirited subtitle!"

"It was a doodle on a proof copy, which I thought was mine to keep," said Duffy.

"Well, that's the copy that got sent to the book printers. They did the whole run—two hundred copies—with your subtitle."

"You only printed two hundred copies?"

"It's a book of poetry."

"Right. So, no one proofed the proof copy?"

"No," the publicist admitted. "I should have, I know, but we were late and I just wanted to move things along."

The young woman looked like she was about to cry.

"Well, I *am* sorry," said Duffy. "What are you going to do?"

"There's no budget for another run. My editor thinks we should try to sell them as is. Who knows? They might become a collector's item."

Duffy felt bad for the young woman, but oddly for him, he didn't feel guilty.

"Is Mittens' poetry any good?" he asked. "I mean, you have to admit that *More Shitty Weather* sounds like a parody."

The publicist smiled and wiped a tear from her cheek.

"No, his poetry isn't very good. It's getting ridiculed on social media. And yes, the title of the book does sound like a send-up."

"Well, this will make for a funny story someday."

"If I keep my job."

"I'll call Dr. Mittens and your editor and tell them it was my fault."

"No need. I've already thrown you under the bus."

Duffy smiled. "You'll go far around here."

"Thanks. Say, does the Communications Department have the budget to buy two hundred copies of a book of bad poetry?"

"No. But I'll spring for my own copy."

"You can get one at the campus bookstore. They should be on the shelf by the end of the week."

"I'll mark it in my calendar," said Duffy. He looked at his watch. "I'm sorry, but I've got to get to a meeting."

He hobbled down the rest of the stairs. As he opened the front door and stepped out into the chilly morning, he started to laugh. He knew what he was going to buy Sophie and Fifi for Christmas.

Duffy was still hobbling when he arrived at the president's office.

"You should get your back checked out by a doctor," said Sophie as she helped him off with his jacket.

"Maybe this afternoon. Has the meeting started?"

"Dr. Blunt and Dr. Kiljoy just got here. Go on in."

Duffy gave Sophie's hand an affectionate squeeze as he opened the large wooden door to the president's inner office. The room still smelled of urine and wet dog. Bertie's plastic-covered bed was gone, but Duffy spied a few chew toys beside the sofa.

"I've got a sturdy chair for you here, James," said Meriwether. "Best thing for a sore back."

Blunt and Kiljoy watched Duffy shuffle over. He hoped they wouldn't say anything about his fall or the demise of the old basset hound.

The bags under Meriwether's eyes seemed a little puffier than they had two days earlier.

"Let's get started," said the president. "We all know the bad news, so let's not waste any time on it. The good news is that we're no longer alone in this fight."

"Have you heard from the other presidents?" asked Kiljoy.

"A few. The heads of all the universities in the province are getting together for a conference call at one."

"The faculty association presidents are doing the same at eleven thirty," said Kiljoy.

"Good. Let's all reconnect at two o'clock. In the meantime, let's do what we can. James, what do you propose on the communications front?"

"We need to get a statement out right away to faculty and staff, and a similar one for the website and the media. I've got both started. I can rework messaging for J.J. to send to alumni and donors, and for Sophie to send to the Board of Governors."

Blunt made a huffing noise, like a wild boar protecting its truffles.

"Oh, Clive, just spit it out," said Meriwether.

Blunt smoothed his tie and raised his chin. "How can we issue a statement when we know so little?" he asked, as if it pained him to point out something so obvious.

"We know that faculty and staff will be worried," said Duffy. "They'll want reassurance. We can issue a statement that says the administration is just learning about the proposed reforms now, and we'll provide more information as soon as we can."

"Is that really necessary?" asked Blunt, looking to Meriwether.

"Yes, it is," answered Duffy. "It's Communications 101. If you don't trust me, ask Kerri Quartermain."

Blunt scowled. "You're walking a fine line, James."

"I'm not the only one, am I?"

"What's that supposed to mean?"

"Kerri told me all about your deal with Dr. Samaroo to sacrifice staff to save more faculty jobs. If she told me, she's told others. It won't be long before it hits social media."

"Clive, you better give us the gory details," said Meriwether.

Blunt looked to Kiljoy. The head of the faculty association said nothing, her face a warrior's mask of brazen composure.

Duffy was impressed. Never explain, never retract, never apologize.

Blunt turned to Meriwether. "It's nothing I didn't tell you about, Alex. Sylvia and I have been testing the waters with Rose to see where HIPE might be willing to give an inch or two. It sounds like this Quartermain person has exaggerated our intent. I assure you that we've made no commitments."

"You've been taking communications advice from this 'Quartermain person' for the past two weeks," said Duffy. "She works for HIPE. That's her first and only priority!"

"James, that's enough," said Meriwether. "We're wasting time. Finish the statement that you've started and get it out *pronto*. We'll meet back here at two o'clock."

Blunt and Kiljoy hustled out of the room. Duffy eased himself up off his chair.

"How's the back?" asked Meriwether.

"Stiff, but it'll be fine."

"James, a little advice if I may," said the president, putting his hand on Duffy's shoulder. "Keep your emotions in check. I know Clive irks you. He irks all of us. But one thing I've learned over the years is to focus on the issue at hand, not the personal resentments. It's something to keep in mind if you're serious about moving up to an assistant vice-president role."

Duffy nodded and inched his way towards the door.

As he was about to leave, he said, "Sir, I'm really sorry about Bertie."

Meriwether nodded.

"I know you are, James. Now go finish that statement."

Chapter 42

Hugh Endicott was on the defensive. The other presidents on the video call had been itching for years to take a swing at their colleague from HIPE, a man who paraded his institution's growing reputation with all the modesty of a Vegas showgirl.

The one exception was Alexander Meriwether.

"Ladies and gentlemen," said the president of Sir Middling U. "No one is more disappointed with HIPE than I am. But we're all in this fight together now. What we need is a common strategy and a united front."

"What do you suggest, Alex?" asked the president of one of the more vulnerable schools, a small university in a northern community.

"A three-tier strategy," Meriwether said in the confident tone of the naval officer he'd once been. "First, we draft a statement—a strongly worded show of solidarity. Second, we marshal an evidence-backed argument, something to demonstrate that higher education is the backbone of the knowledge economy. And third, we get our mayors, business leaders and other champions to make a helluva racket on our behalf."

A murmur of approval rippled across the fibre-optic cables that connected the group. One dissenter—the president of the largest research university in the province—spoke up.

"I suggest a wait-and-see approach," said Ziba Ahmadi, whose institution's research funding, donor support and industry clout protected her from the kind of financial worries that kept the other presidents awake at night.

"That's easy for you to say, Ziba," replied the president from up north. "My biggest donor is the local snowmobile dealer."

A rumble of "hear, hear" from the others suggested agreement if not sympathy.

"I like Alex's approach," said the chair of the presidents' group, a business-strategy scholar. "Leave it to me. I'll organize a small working group. We'll get you a draft statement later this afternoon, and we'll hammer out our knowledge-economy argument by end of day tomorrow."

There were chirps of consent from a majority of the presidents. One by one, they began ringing off until it was just Endicott and Meriwether on the call.

"I appreciate you taking the high road, Alex."

"I meant what I said, Hugh. We need to move forward and put this whole episode behind us. Like it or not, we're neighbours."

"You know, Alex, I suspect that it's Giles Prigg behind all of this, not Anne Moreno. He's the one we've been dealing with all along."

"Has Prigg gotten back to you?"

"No. But I'll reach out to him again and insist on a meeting for tomorrow afternoon. Who do you want on the call?"

"Myself, Clive Blunt and my communications director, James Duffy."

"Right. I'll bring Rose Samaroo and Kerri Quartermain."

"And Hugh, I have no more patience for media leaks or other shenanigans. Please let Rose and your communications person know that from now on we must work as a team."

"I'm not sure they're familiar with the concept," said Endicott. "But I'll keep them on-side."

While the university presidents plotted their response, the heads of the faculty unions were engaged in a fierce disagreement over solidarity.

"How can we trust our HIPE colleagues?" asked one.

"Sanction them!" said another.

"We could withdraw love," suggested a third, who, as the representative of a religious college, wrapped her aggression in a soft outer layer.

The chair of the group called for order.

"All right folks," she said. "What's done is done. We've got to stick together. I now invite suggestions for how we fight the reforms."

"Strike an action committee!" said one.

"Activate a strike committee!" said another.

"Pray for divine retribution!" urged the religious college rep.

Kiljoy grew more impatient by the minute. She was committed to the labour movement but not to the petty squabbling and tedious discussions that went with it.

"Listen up!" she barked. "We need a plan, and we need it now. Here's what I suggest: First, we put out a statement saying that any kind of post-secondary reform is an intolerable assault on students, education and academic freedom. Second, we mount a work-to-rule campaign—tie up marking, exams and graduations for months. And third, we down tools and hold a general day of protest across the province."

"Hear, hear!" shouted her colleagues.

"Thank you, Sylvia," said the chair. "We'll ask our communications committee to draft the statement, and we'll get the direct-action committee to organize the protests. If that's all, I suggest we convene again tomorrow at noon."

As the union leaders began to ring off, Kiljoy asked Ed Palavoy to stay on the line.

"Ed, I've got to know where you stand on this," she said.

"I stand with my faculty colleagues."

"Your HIPE colleagues or all of us?"

"Both, I suppose," said Palavoy.

"That's pretty damn wishy-washy," said Kiljoy.

"It's all I've got right now. Let me touch base with Rose and Hugh and see what they're thinking."

"They're not your friends, Ed. They'll screw you over the minute it helps them."

"Maybe that's how things work at Sir Middling U. But at HIPE, we support one another."

"Oh my! It sounds like little Eddie has made a deal to join management."

Palavoy was silent.

"That's what I thought," said Kiljoy.

Meriwether shared the substance of the presidents' call with Blunt, Kiljoy and Duffy.

"Hugh Endicott is setting up a meeting with Giles Prigg for tomorrow afternoon," he said. "Just us and the HIPE team."

"Will the minister of higher education be there?" asked Duffy.

"I don't think so. Hugh seems to think this whole mess is Giles Prigg's doing."

Blunt turned to Duffy. "What about your contacts in the minister's office?"

"What about them?"

"Could you give them a call and ask what the minister is thinking?"

Yes, thought Duffy, I could. But do I want to? He had been thinking a lot about the proposed reforms leaked to *The Daily Clamour*. They reminded him of his early days in the Ministry of

Higher Education, back when he had been a champion for change. The reforms outlined in the newspaper story—accountability, workloads, compensation restraint—made a lot of sense to Duffy, especially after three years at Sir Middling U.

"I'm afraid it won't do any good to ask my contacts," he told Blunt. "This is a crisis for the minister too. Her staff are not going to risk further damage by sharing inside information with the universities."

A pout formed on Blunt's plump lips. He folded his arms across his chest and slouched farther down in his chair. His posture reminded Duffy of a petulant child. If I were Blunt's teacher, he thought, I'd give him a detention and make him write a hundred lines on the blackboard: "I will not be a whiny dork; I will not be a whiny dork…."

The image raised a Mona Lisa smile on Duffy's tired face.

"What's so funny?" asked Blunt.

Duffy ignored him.

"Listen, James," said Meriwether. "Are you sure you can't just make a call to your friends in the minister's office? Any bit of insight would help. I'd like us to know as much as we can before we meet with Giles Prigg."

Duffy hated to the let the president down. Despite Meriwether's decision to let Blunt lead the amalgamation file, the old man was a caring person and a generous mentor.

"I'll give it a shot," said Duffy. "But I don't want anyone to get their hopes up."

"No worries on that front," huffed Blunt.

Two detentions, thought Duffy, and a wedgie.

Chapter 43

Nine years as a university student—four as an undergraduate and five in grad school—had taught the Honorable Anne Moreno, PhD, all about the good, bad and in between of academia. She respected higher education but was convinced that systemwide reform was long overdue. She hoped it would come from within but was not optimistic. So, when the first overnight polls came in, Moreno wasn't surprised to see how popular Dev Sharma's recommendations were with the public.

"You could ride this horse all the way to the premier's office!" said a gleeful Jill Kaiser. "Most voters don't understand higher education, but they sure as hell think it's cushy."

Moreno studied the top-line summaries.

"Prigg has to be polling too," she said. "What's he going to make of these results?"

"Given that you were part of the academic tribe, he's going to assume you'll distance yourself from Sharma's recommendations."

"What do you think?"

"I think you embrace them. I think you take credit for them. I think you say to the party and the voters, 'Hell yeah! It's high time we rein in those ivory-tower know-it-alls.' "

"Why would I do that?"

"To become the next premier."

"I don't follow."

"The party grassroots will eat this up and treat you like the Second Coming. Prigg will shit his pants because all of a sudden, you're a real threat to replace Teddy Banks. The minute Prigg hears that you're going all-in on reform, he's going to try to bury the plan a mile deep in lead and reinforced concrete."

"But I *want* to take over the party leadership and become premier."

"And you will, but on your own terms. I'll talk to Prigg and let him know that you're super keen on higher-ed reform. In fact, you think it should be the Number One plank in the party's re-election platform. He'll go, 'Oh, fuck!' and want to deal. That's when you demand a more influential cabinet post—finance or treasury board—and start charting your ascent to the premier's office with your own agenda."

"You make it sound easy."

"Not easy, but do-able."

"If I embrace reform, I'm in for a rough ride with the universities until I move over to finance or wherever."

"Maybe. But they'll love you when, in a more senior cabinet role, you put higher-ed reform on hold and encourage change from within."

Moreno looked through the poll summaries one more time.

"Okay, I'm in. Go turn Prigg's world upside down."

While Anne Moreno and Jill Kaiser were planning their counter-attack, Giles Prigg was preparing for his video call with HIPE and Sir Middling U. He asked Dev Sharma to join him.

"Bring your facts and figures," said Prigg. "I may need to shame our university friends into submission."

The call from Jill Kaiser had dampened Sharma's enthusiasm. "Listen, Giles, I'm not comfortable with any of this," he said. "How did my report get leaked to the media? Jill Kaiser said the minister had no idea I'd written it."

"It's politics, Dev. You believe in these reforms, right? Well, this is how change happens, my friend."

"Why not just have a straightforward policy debate in cabinet? Why not just push the reforms forward because it's the right thing to do for the people of this province?"

Prigg gave an indulgent chuckle. "Dev, Dev, Dev. You've worked in government. You know that politicians are driven by poll numbers. In fact, they're driven by the very data that you claim to revere."

"My data is intended to help politicians make good decisions," said Sharma.

"And my data," replied Prigg, "helps them stay in office so they can continue to make those good decisions."

The HIPE team joined Sir Middling U in the Old Boardroom in Founders Hall.

"I like what you haven't done with the place," said Hugh Endicott, gazing at the wood paneling. "Very Dickensian."

"It links us with tradition," said Meriwether. "Call me old fashioned, but I prefer limestone and wood to steel and concrete."

Meriwether, Blunt and Duffy took seats on the window side of the table while offering their guests—Endicott, Samaroo and Quartermain—the side looking directly into the afternoon sun.

"Could we draw the blinds?" asked Quartermain.

"They don't work," said Duffy. "Too Dickensian."

Sophie glided into the room and set up the video-conferencing unit. A giant closeup of Prigg's face appeared on the two-metre-wide screen as he leaned forward and adjusted the monitor at his end.

"Good day, Giles," said Meriwether. "How's the weather in the big city?"

"Never better," said Prigg, all smiles and charm. "The freezing rain has stopped; now we just have sleet and snow."

There were polite chuckles all around.

"I think you know everyone at our end," said Meriwether. "And I see you have Dev Sharma with you. Hello, Dev."

Sharma gave a shy wave and averted his eyes, like a husband caught exiting a strip club.

"So, let's get down to business," said Endicott. "Giles, what the hell is going on?"

"Well, Hugh, as you and I have discussed many times, our government happens to think that universities should be more accountable to taxpayers and more attuned to student needs. We think the post-secondary system tilts too much towards academic self-interest."

"When did our amalgamation proposal turn into a total overhaul of the system?"

"Our discussions were always about controlling costs and improving higher education," said Prigg.

"Yes, but at no point did you mention salary caps, workload minimums or cost-cutting plans."

"Our talks, Hugh, were but one piece of a larger modernization strategy. It's a strategy that, quite frankly, university leaders should have proposed and implemented a long time ago."

Endicott's face was turning the colour of his crimson tie. "Then why the hell didn't you just tell us that? Instead, you've had us chasing our tails up here trying to set the table for amalgamation."

"Oh, come now, Hugh," said Prigg. "We've been pleading for reform for years. Remember the Strategic Program Reviews? Tell me, whatever became of those?"

The academics at the table blanched as if Prigg had found a dead body in the trunk of their car. The Strategic Program Reviews, or

SPRs, had been a much-hated government directive that required each university to conduct a detailed examination of all its programs and expenses. It was a kind of spring housecleaning, the goal of which was to get rid of outdated and redundant activities. Faculty and administrative leaders had fiercely resisted the exercise, stonewalling and ignoring the directive until the government had quietly abandoned the initiative.

No one responded to Prigg's question, so he turned to Sharma.

"Dev, did any university in the province complete an SPR?"

"Just two, but neither implemented their plans."

"Hmmm," mused Prigg. "I bet the media would be interested in a fact like that."

Samaroo spoke up, hoping to move the conversation to safer ground.

"Hi, Giles. Correct me if I'm wrong, but the article in *The Daily Clamour* had all the markings of a political trial balloon. What's your polling telling you?"

"Voters love the idea of higher-ed reform," replied Prigg. "Parents and students think universities should be doing more to prepare young people for lucrative careers. Business leaders want employable graduates and research that has practical applications. If you ask me, the government would be irresponsible to ignore this cry for change."

"So, how do we help, Giles?" asked Samaroo.

Blunt shot her a flamethrower of a look. The others all leaned forward, suddenly more engaged in the conversation.

"Same as always, Rose," said Prigg. "Follow the government's lead. Push back if you must, but not too much. Keep your eyes on the long game."

"That game seems pretty dangerous," said Meriwether. "Cutbacks and amalgamations don't just affect those of us who have the privilege to work in higher education; they hurt the communities that depend on us for jobs and economic spinoff. A university injects millions of dollars into the local economy each year. You might be surprised by the alliances that that kind of money creates."

"Water finds its own level, Alex," said Prigg. "Rest assured that we'll keep a close eye on public opinion. I'm confident that we'll all end up where we need to be."

"Is that a threat or reassurance?" asked Meriwether.

"That's politics," replied Prigg.

Chapter 44

"Where does this leave us?" asked Samaroo.

"We're sailing into heavy weather and unpredictable seas," replied Meriwether. "We need to keep a steady hand on the tiller and our eyes firmly on the horizon."

"Okay, Captain Ahab, what does that mean in plain English?" asked Endicott.

"The risks are real. Governments need to get re-elected, and this one seems to have found a popular issue. I think we need to make our case to the public without sounding inflexible and without giving the politicians more ammunition to shoot back at us."

Duffy struggled to contain his frustration. What had Meriwether told him? Keep his emotions in check? Well, screw that!

"Shouldn't we be thinking about what's best for students?" he said tersely. "The university system seems outdated and self-serving. Maybe *we* should be the ones who open the windows and let in some fresh air."

Blunt looked appalled. "Whose side are you on?" he demanded.

"Good question, Clive," said Quartermain, giving Blunt a supportive nod.

Duffy looked to the others around the table.

"It's not a question of taking sides," he said. "It's about acknowledging the need to reimagine higher education and committing to what's really important."

"The faculty in this room know what's important, thank you very much," said Blunt. He turned away from Duffy and addressed Endicott and Samaroo: "If we work together to push back on system-wide reform, will you drop the amalgamation plan?"

Samaroo was about to respond; Endicott beat her to it.

"Yes," he said. "The priority now is to preserve what we've got."

"If I may speak," said Samaroo. "It's not just Prigg we need to worry about. If what he told us about the polling numbers is true, Anne Moreno has seen them as well. And that's good news for her. It's no secret she wants to become party leader and premier. This issue is tailor-made for her. She's going to push it hard at the party convention, and then right through the election. And if you think Prigg is tough, wait till you see Anne Moreno in action."

Silence fell upon the group.

Duffy glanced around the Old Boardroom. The attitudes and opinions expressed in this space probably hadn't changed much over the last hundred years. Looking at the paintings of past presidents and governors, Duffy felt as if the old ghosts that haunted the room were mocking his feeble crusade for change.

A chorus of ring tones shattered the silence. Everyone reached for their phones.

"Good Lord!" said Blunt.

"What is it?" asked Meriwether.

"The HIPE and Sir Middling faculty associations have put out a news release. They're holding a joint rally tomorrow to protest the proposed reforms. They're blaming the administrations at both institutions for mishandling the whole amalgamation business."

"Damn!" said Endicott.

Meriwether looked at Duffy. "James, have you had a chance to speak with your contacts in the minister's office?"

"Not yet," he said wearily. "I'll call as soon as we wrap up here."

"Good. We're shipping water and need all hands on deck."

Aye aye, Captain, thought Duffy.

Chapter 45

Prigg's executive assistant told Jill Kaiser that his boss was too busy to meet with her.

"Your zipper is down," said Kaiser as she breezed past the young man and entered the office of the premier's chief of staff.

Prigg, who was sitting at his desk, looked up.

"Oh, dear," he said. "Todd failed to keep you out. Well, I suppose I'll have to fire him now."

"He's young and cute; he'll find another job."

"Yes, indeed," said Prigg. "Well, now that you're here, Jill, why don't we have a chat?"

Kaiser grabbed a hardback chair, swung it around and straddled the seat. She took her phone out of her hip pocket, checked the screen, then slid it into the breast pocket of her suit jacket.

"So, Giles, what the fuck are you up to?"

"It's simple, Jill. Your girl is threatening my boy."

"Your boy is a bonehead with absolutely no vision."

"That's why he's the perfect premier. He lets those of us with vision and talent get things done."

"Anne Moreno is a hundred times more fit to be premier than Teddy Banks."

"No argument there," said Prigg. "But if Anne Moreno were premier, she wouldn't listen to someone like me. Someone who knows how to get things done. She'd fight the good fight and lose. Four years would go by and this province would be exactly where it was when Moreno took over. Every successful leader has someone like me behind the curtain."

"You're *so* fucking arrogant."

Prigg smiled. "Guilty as charged," he said. "But I'm also right. And as long as I'm chief of staff to the premier, I'm not going to let some do-gooder from the truth-and-light brigade run this province into the ditch."

Kaiser bristled at the smug look on Prigg's hawk-like face.

"So, you created this whole university reform shit just to tie up Moreno and take her out of the game?"

"Politics is indeed a game, Jill. And that game is called 'Bugger Your Neighbour.' I play it with my left hand, while my right hand gets things done."

"When this gets out, you're screwed."

"I don't think so. If this gets out, Bud Walters, Rose Samaroo and Dev Sharma are screwed. They each have agendas they want to push; I've just facilitated the pushing."

"And what does Moreno get if I keep this to myself?"

"I don't care if you keep it to yourself. Anything you say is just your spin on things. I have my version well-documented."

"What if I have my own documentation?"

Prigg leaned forward. "Oh, Jill, have you been a clever little politico?"

Kaiser ignored the question. "Like I said, what does Moreno get if I keep this to myself?"

"What would she like?"

291

"Move her from higher education into the big leagues: minister of finance."

Prigg took a sip of tea. It was tepid.

"Let me give that some thought."

"Listen, Giles. The party is going to give Teddy Banks the heave-ho sooner or later. When they do, Moreno has a real shot at the party leadership. If you support her now—make her minister of finance—you might just get a chance to stay in the premier's office for the long term."

"My, my, Jill, you're starting to see how things work."

"So, what do you say?"

"I say you're bluffing."

Chapter 46

It was dark outside as Duffy made his way back through the quad towards Alumni Manor. Lamplight illuminated Brave Sir Dickie and his horse. Both wore a light coat of snow. A long red scarf was knotted around the animal's testicles, which were painted ivy green. Someone had completed the look with a sprig of holly.

Merry Christmas, thought Duffy.

When he reached Alumni Manor, he opened the door with his security card and climbed the stairs to the second floor. The building was empty and the lights in the Communications Department were off. He switched them back on and saw that the door to his office was gone again. Just as well, he thought, giving the lower part of his back a rub with his right hand.

He lay down on the floor and took out his phone. He found Jill Kaiser in his contacts list and clicked on her number.

It rang once and Kaiser picked up. "This is a coincidence," she said. "Maybe even fate."

"It's Duffy."

"Yes, I know. I was just about to call you."

"Really?"

"You don't sound great."

"I threw my back out."

"Having wild sex, I hope."

"Well, kind of. But it really started when I slipped on some ice and killed the president's dog."

"Oh, my god, Duffy—I have to hear the whole story! But another time. Right now I have a question for you: How badly would you like to make amalgamation and higher-ed reform go away?"

"Personally, I think the reforms are long overdue. But my boss would definitely kill to make them disappear."

"Well, I'm about to make you a hero with your boss. I have a recording of Giles Prigg admitting that the whole amalgamation and reform plan is just a ruse to keep the minister of higher education from making a run for the premier's job."

"You're shitting me," said Duffy.

"I shit you not."

"Where did you get this?"

"I recorded it on my phone this afternoon when I met with Prigg."

"Is that legal?"

"It's politics."

Duffy squirmed himself into a sitting position. "How do I fit in?"

"I'll send the recording to you so that you can send it to Prigg. Say someone shared it with you, but don't mention my name."

Duffy closed his eyes and groaned.

"I heard that," said Kaiser. "Don't wimp out on me, Duffy."

"Come on, Jill. Prigg is going to know that the recording came from you."

"Of course he will. But the fact that I shared it with you will show him that I'm serious. It's a shot across the bow."

"The president of Sir Middling U would like that metaphor."

"What do you mean?"

"Never mind," said Duffy. "Listen, I don't know if I want to get mixed up in this. It's the kind of thing that could backfire and get me canned."

"Don't go all scruples on me," said Kaiser. "You owe me for the Walters Report, remember?"

Duffy groaned again and lay back down on the floor. "What would I have to do, exactly?"

"I'll email you an audio file. You copy it and email it to Prigg. Say something brief like, 'Hey, Giles. This got sent to me. Thought you should be aware of it.' That's it. Done and dusted."

"And you think that will make Prigg drop amalgamation?"

"Like a hot potato," said Kaiser. "And when he backs off, my office will put out a statement saying that higher-ed reform is an interesting concept that deserves more thought, but that we have more pressing priorities at the moment. Life goes on for everyone, and you're the hero of Ass-scratch U, or wherever it is that you work."

"It's Sir Middling U," said Duffy.

"Whatever. Will you do it?"

"If I have to. But if I get fired, I hope you can get me a job in the minister's office."

"If this works out, I'll get you a job in the premier's office."

Duffy called Fifi and told her about Kaiser's request.

"Holy shit, Duffy! This is like Watergate!"

Duffy winced. "Do you think so?"

"No, not really. But it's going to take some balls."

Duffy had hoped that Fifi would tell him flat out not to get mixed up in political skulduggery. Instead, she seemed to be encouraging him to man up and send the tape to Prigg.

"The thing is," he said, "I think some of the reform recommendations are reasonable."

"You're not killing reform, Duffy. You're just making sure it's done for the right reasons, not for some backroom political bullshit."

"Maybe," he said, wriggling on his back to find a comfortable position. From where he lay, Duffy had a floor-level view under his desk. He spied the old Sir Middling Muskrats mascot that Bertie had liked to chew. He reached out and grabbed the plush toy; it was crusty with dried slobber.

"Yuck," he said.

"Yuck?" asked Fifi.

"Sorry. I just found something gross under my desk."

"Duffy, what the hell are you doing?"

He explained what he had found and how he had come to find it.

"God, Duffy!" yelled Fifi. "Put that thing down and get up off the floor before you catch some kind of bacterial infection."

Duffy did as he was told.

"Okay," he said. "I'm standing, and the only thing I've got in my hands is my phone."

"Sometimes I worry about you," said Fifi.

"Thanks, Feef. I'll be okay."

"Good. So back to this recording.... What are you worried about?"

"Well, if I do this, I'm helping Blunt and Kiljoy," said Duffy. "They're willing to throw me and the other staff under the bus to save a few faculty jobs."

"Consider it acceptable damage," said Fifi. "If you send the recording, *no one* loses their job. And you'll be a shoo-in for that assistant vice-president's title."

"Aren't you the one who told me not to let a promotion influence my better judgement?"

"Yes. And I stick by it. But in this case, the promotion isn't the driver. It's simply a collateral benefit."

"Sounds like flexible ethics to me."

"Well, at least you're talking about ethics now. You weren't before."

"Another collateral benefit, I guess."

Duffy tried bending over at the waist to stretch out the muscles in his lower back.

"You still there?" asked Fifi.

"Yes. Just stretching."

"Well, let's change the subject. How are things with Sophie?"

"Pretty good. I saw her in the president's office today. We didn't have much time to talk."

"Make sure you give her the attention she deserves."

"What's that supposed to mean?"

"It means that Sophie is smart, kind and attractive. And you're competing with men *and* women for her affections. Just make sure she feels appreciated."

"Are you trying to tell me something?"

"I just *did* tell you something: make Sophie feel appreciated."

"That's it?"

"That's it. Now, go put an end to amalgamation."

Chapter 47

Duffy decided to sleep on it. He had a restless night, capped off with a stressful dream. It was all a muddle, as dreams often are. Someone was drowning. Duffy swam out to save them. The waves were high and dangerous. No matter how hard he swam, the tempest prevented him from reaching whoever it was that needed help. Duffy saw Fifi on the beach, laughing and horsing around with her friends. Sophie was there too, separate from the hijinks, her eyes focused on Duffy. He tried to call to her, to say he'd be all right, but he had no voice. Then Bertie appeared in the water, grabbing Duffy's shirt in his floppy jowls. Duffy grasped the basset hound's long ears, and Bertie began dragging him farther out, towards a small rowboat on the horizon. When they reached it, they found Meriwether, Blunt and Kiljoy on board. The trio pulled Bertie into the boat but left Duffy to bob up and down in the violent waves. No one seemed to see him except Sophie. The last thing he remembered was Bertie floating above him like a diaper-wearing sprite and muttering something about a "sea change."

Duffy woke up anxious and exhausted. He looked at his phone.

It was nine-fifteen.

"Shit!"

He got up, showered, dressed and walked to campus. The sky was dark, and the cold seemed to be settling in for the long haul. Duffy's back was still sore, but the walking helped. As he neared Alumni Manor, he decided to swing by the university bookstore and buy several copies of Percy Mittens' new book. There was a display in the window with a giant poster of the author. It featured Mittens—a baby-faced man in his early thirties—wearing a knit sweater and a Greek fisherman's cap. A pipe was clenched between his teeth, and his eyes stared broodingly towards a turbulent sea. Below this picture ran the words:

More Shitty Weather
A Poetic Parody
Available here.

Duffy entered the bookstore and walked over to the display. There were no copies of the book. He looked under the table and at the closest shelves. Nothing. He asked a salesperson for a copy of *More Shitty Weather*.

"Sold out," the woman said. "We'll be getting more tomorrow. Would you like to place an order?"

Duffy was mystified. "When did the book go on sale?"

"Three days ago."

"How many copies did you sell?"

"Hmmm, must have been at least fifty. They went quickly."

"Really?" said Duffy.

"Yeah, I know, right?" said the saleswoman, sounding as surprised as Duffy.

He placed an order for two copies and left. As he walked back to his office, he ran into the SIRMUP publicist.

"Hey," he said. "I just tried to buy a copy of *More Shitty Weather*.

The bookstore was sold out."

"Yes. Isn't it amazing?"

"I thought I'd ruined things."

"You did, but fate stepped in. A book reviewer loved the title and wrote a wonderful piece online about how daring it was for Dr. Mittens to spoof his own poetry."

"You're kidding?"

"I'm not. The review went viral. I've had half a dozen other reviewers ask for a copy, including a woman from *The Guardian* and a man from *The New York Times*. We've ordered another print run of three hundred copies!"

"Wow. How does Dr. Mittens feel about it?"

"He was a little depressed at first. But he's a poet with a book that might sell five hundred copies, so I'd say he's feeling pretty good."

"Well, I'm happy for you both," said Duffy.

"Happy enough to interview him for a story on the university website?" asked the publicist. "He has an opening today at two p.m."

Duffy had to admire the woman's pluck. If I ever write a book, he thought, I've got to get her to promote it.

"I'm tied up this afternoon," he said. "But I'll ask my assistant manager to do it."

The publicist typed something rapidly into her phone.

"I just sent you a reminder!" she said with a cheeky smile. "Now, I've got to run. *The Rat's Ass* wants an interview too!"

As Duffy continued towards Alumni Manor, his phone rang.

"Hey, Duffy, it's Feef. Did you hear about Rufus Lillidew?"

"What now?"

"He cancelled the Harrison Dewlap lecture … *and* he's taking a leave of absence."

It took Duffy a moment to process the news.

"You still there?" asked Fifi.

"Yes," said Duffy. "Just surprised. Why is he taking a leave?"

"I don't know for sure, but there's a rumour he lifted a section from a grad student's research paper and included it in an article he wrote."

"Lillidew *plagiarized* a student's work?" said Duffy, the shock lifting his voice a full octave.

"No one's going that far," said Fifi. "But the journal removed the article from its website until it sorts it out."

"Why hasn't the university fired Lillidew?"

"Who knows?" said Fifi. "Plagiarism is a bitch to prove, even with students. Most people claim it was an honest mistake—you know, cutting and pasting notes, forgetting where certain paragraphs came from. It happens."

There was silence on both ends of the phone. After a moment, Duffy asked, "Do you think this is why Blunt finally agreed to meet with Morris? He probably knew that Lillidew would have to cancel the Dewlap lecture."

"Maybe. But the important thing is that Dewlap no longer has a platform at Sir Middling U."

"*Is* that the important thing?" asked Duffy, feeling more dispirited as the conversation went on. "I mean, what if Lillidew did take credit for a student's work? What the hell does Sir Middling U stand for anyway? Maybe it deserves to be amalgamated."

"Whoa, my friend, take it easy. Life is messy. Focus on the good that comes out of the bad."

Duffy let out a long sigh. "I don't know, Feef. I'm feeling pretty bummed about this whole lousy business."

Fifi could feel the depth of her friend's exhaustion, even over the phone.

"Cut yourself some slack, Duffy. You've been through a lot. The holiday break is coming up. Maybe you and Sophie can get away for a few days. You know, rent a cabin in the woods, forget about everything and just screw like minks."

"That's not a bad idea. Do minks really screw a lot?"

"They mate with multiple partners."

"That's not necessarily the same thing, is it?"

"No, I suppose not. But don't overthink this, Duffy. Just go away and spend some quality time with Sophie, okay?"

Duffy suddenly realized that with all his walking and talking, he'd overshot Alumni Manor. His back had also reached the end of its upright limits.

"Listen, Feef, I better talk to Blunt about Lillidew's leave. It may get leaked to the media, especially now that the Dewlap lecture has been cancelled."

"I'd be surprised if Blunt talks to you about it."

"You're right," said Duffy. "It'll probably piss him off."

"Ha!" said Fifi. "All the more reason to make the call."

Duffy laughed. "Dr. Dubé, you have a wicked streak."

"Yes, I do," she said. "Now, go get under Blunt's skin."

Duffy decided to call his boss right away. He was startled when Blunt picked up on the first ring.

"What do you want, James?"

Duffy was used to Blunt's cranky manner, but this was the first time he'd enjoyed hearing irritation in the man's voice.

"Hello, sir," Duffy said cheerily. "How are you this morning?"

"Cut to the chase, James. What do you want?"

"Well, sir, I just heard that Dr. Lillidew has cancelled the Harrison Dewlap lecture."

"Yes, I'm aware of that."

"I also heard that Dr. Lillidew is taking a leave of absence."

"Where did you hear that?" demanded Blunt.

"There's chatter among the faculty," said Duffy. "Is there anything I should know from an issues-management perspective?"

"What do you mean?"

"Well, sir, universities are rumour mills. The fact that Dr.

Lillidew cancelled a controversial guest speaker and then took a leave may prompt people to ask why."

"Just what are you getting at?" asked Blunt.

"Well, I've heard that Dr. Lillidew's leave might be related to an article he published recently."

"Don't go there, James. Faculty members *and* support staff are eligible to take leaves of absence. There's nothing unusual here. Just be glad the Dewlap lecture is cancelled."

"Yes, of course. But I'd still like to be prepared in case this hits social media."

"Do I really have to do your job for you?" huffed Blunt. "This is a personnel matter—a perfectly above-board agreement worked out between Rufus Lillidew and HR. The university is precluded by privacy legislation from saying anything more. End of story."

There was a click followed by a long buzz.

Well, that was fun, thought Duffy.

He was about twenty metres from Alumni Manor when his phone rang yet again.

"Hello?"

"Hi, James. It's me."

"Me who?" teased Duffy.

"Me Sophie."

"I was just thinking of you," he said, sitting down on a bench to ease his aching back.

"And I was thinking of you. And so was Dr. Meriwether. He wants to meet with you, Sylvia and Clive. Can you come over?"

"Right now?"

"Yes, right now."

"Can I drop some things off at my office first?"

"If you have to. But make it quick."

Duffy felt a twinge in his back. He decided to put what little strength he still had into the walk to Founders Hall.

"Listen, I'll skip my office and come straight over," he said. "There's something I need to ask you when I get there."

"Better ask me now," said Sophie. "I have a meeting with the university secretary in five minutes, and I won't be back for at least an hour."

"Okay, I'll talk while I hobble along."

Duffy explained Jill Kaiser's scheme and his reluctance to get involved.

"What do you think I should do?" he asked.

"Follow your conscience."

"That's it?"

"Isn't that enough?" said Sophie.

Duffy felt naked, as if his clothing had been ripped off, exposing his pale body and the meagreness of his soul. He had been tested and found wanting.

"I didn't mean that the way it sounded," he said. "Of course it's enough."

The silence on the other end of the phone made Duffy ache with shame.

"I guess I'd better let you get to your meeting," he said. "See you later?"

"Yes," said Sophie. "I think we've got a few things to talk about."

Duffy's heart sank. His relationship experience was limited but he knew that when a woman said you had "a few things to talk about," it would likely involve an examination of his shortcomings.

Just like confession.

Duffy felt exhausted. All the walking and talking had disoriented him. He found himself in the quad, next to Brave Sir Dickie and his horse. The bronze statue was surrounded by members of *Le Collectif* and a passel of student acolytes. They were all wearing red liberty caps and handing out leaflets. Duffy grabbed one from the hand of a baby-faced student whose cafeteria-fed body was squeezed into an undersized down jacket. The kid, who gave every appearance of a middle-class upbringing, tried to disguise his suburban origins with a nose ring and a mop of green hair.

"Stick it to the Man!" the student said with an unconvincing snarl.

"Every chance I get," replied Duffy.

The leaflet urged him to join the faculty association's Rally Against Reform later that day. The headline exhorted: "Protect education! Protect academic freedom! Protect our students!"

And above all, thought Duffy, protect tenure, sabbaticals and the four-month summer break!

Just then Morris Hill walked by.

"Hello Dr. Hill," said Duffy. "Are you handing out leaflets too?"

The professor chuckled.

"I pick and choose my battles," he said. Then, as if he'd been reading Duffy's mind, he added, "Besides, I've got a busy day—teaching, marking, a meeting with my tutorial assistants, writing a reference letter for a grad student and finishing a grant application."

Duffy nodded. "That *is* busy."

Hill responded with an enigmatic smile. He patted the communications director on the shoulder and walked off.

Duffy watched the professor make his way through the crowd of protesters, exchanging greetings with colleagues and students. Morris Hill was one of the good ones. He treated everyone with respect and courtesy, making them all feel part of the university community.

I should spend more time with him, thought Duffy.

Then he remembered his meeting with Blunt, Kiljoy and Meriwether.

A lot more time.

Chapter 48

By the time Duffy reached the president's office, Blunt and Kiljoy were already there.

"Come in, James, and take a seat," said Meriwether, pointing to a hard-backed chair.

Duffy removed his jacket and scarf and carefully eased himself down.

"So, what do you have for us?" asked the president.

"What do you mean?" asked Duffy.

"Your contacts in the minister's office. What did they tell you?"

Duffy looked from face to face to face. All three were staring at him in their own intense way. Blunt resembled a jealous older sibling, resentful that his kid brother got to tag along; Kiljoy had the inscrutable look of a resistance fighter who hadn't decided which side she was on yet; and Meriwether gave the appearance of a kindly uncle, hopeful for good news from his favourite nephew.

Duffy recounted, for the third time, Jill Kaiser's proposal.

"That's wonderful!" said Meriwether, clapping his hands together.

Blunt and Kiljoy both gave grudging nods of approval.

"When do you send the email?" asked the president.

"I'm not going to send it," said Duffy.

The others stared at him in astonishment.

"What do you mean?" demanded Blunt. "You *have* to send it!"

"No, I don't. What I *do* have to do is follow my conscience. I've thought it over and I've decided that I don't want to be involved in this kind of back-room politics. It feels cheap and sordid. I also happen to think that higher-ed reform is worth discussing."

It took a moment for Duffy's words to sink in. The first to react was Blunt, whose whole body shook like a lumpy volcano.

"For God's sake, James, don't be so high-minded," he scolded. "Do you know what's at stake here?"

"As a matter of fact, I do. And it's not faculty jobs or cost savings or amalgamations. It's my self-respect."

They all sat in silence. Duffy detected a strong smell of Bertie, as if the old basset hound was nearby, squeezing out soundless farts from beyond the grave. The odour grew stronger. It struck Duffy that perhaps it was never Bertie who had fouled the air in this room. He glanced at the three people seated around him; none looked completely innocent, but no one stood out as the obvious culprit. Perhaps it was just Bertie passing judgement, not wind, on all of them.

Duffy suddenly pictured the mournful old basset hound floating above them in doggy heaven, his long leathers flapping like the wings of an angel and his hind end finally free of diapers. The image ignited a giggle in Duffy's throat. It was like the time at his uncle Liam's funeral when he'd struggled to stifle the urge to laugh out loud. He'd loved his uncle, but the solemnity of the service—and the prodding toe of his cousin, Mary Elizabeth—had provoked a powerful giddiness inside him. At the time, Duffy had restrained himself by closing his eyes and biting his lip until it bled. He didn't think that would work in his present situation, so he decided to head off the giggles by breaking the silence another way.

"I'm willing to submit my resignation," he said.

Blunt looked to Meriwether, beaming with hope.

"Not while I'm at the helm," said the president. "I respect your decision, James. We'll find another way to fight the good fight."

Duffy was relieved, but the silence that followed was too painful to bear.

"Listen," he said. "The statue panel is tomorrow night and I've still got work to do. If it's all right with you, I'd like to excuse myself and get back to my office."

"Of course, James," said Meriwether.

"I'll walk you out," said Kiljoy.

Duffy eased himself off the hard chair and made his way to the door. In the foyer of the president's suite, Kiljoy put her hands on her hips and stared Duffy in the eye.

"That took balls, Red," she said. "If Clive fires you, I could put in a word with a few unions. They're always looking for a good PR hack."

"Thanks, Sylvia. I may take you up on that."

Kiljoy reached out and put a hand on Duffy's shoulder.

"Never explain, never retract, never apologize," she said.

"Nellie McClung, right?"

"She was a complicated woman, but when she said that she got it right."

Kiljoy returned to the president's office. It wasn't until then that Duffy noticed Sophie standing by her desk.

"You're back early," he said.

"The university secretary stood me up. What did Kiljoy say to you? It sounded almost kind."

"I told her and the others that I wasn't going to send the audio recording to Giles Prigg. Blunt is pissed, Kiljoy seems okay with it and Meriwether says he respects my decision, but I'm pretty sure he's disappointed too."

"How do you feel?"

"Not bad for a guy who's probably going to get fired."

"You did what you thought was right. That's what matters. I'm proud of you."

"I don't know why," said Duffy. "You gave me great advice, and I responded like a jackass."

"Yes, you did," said Sophie. "But you recovered quickly and followed your conscience. I'm happy for you."

She smiled and opened her arms wide. "Come get a hug."

Duffy did as he was told.

"Careful," he said. "My back's killing me."

"Some things are worth the pain."

They held one another for a long, tender moment. When they finally pulled apart, Sophie said, "You better rest up before tomorrow night."

"Why?"

"The student Equity and Diversity Club is holding a party in the auditorium after the panel discussion. Fifi says there's going to be a live band and free food."

"Is her burlesque troupe performing?"

"Sorry to disappoint you, but no. It's not quite the right venue for burlesque."

"I suppose not. What was I thinking?"

"What every man thinks."

Duffy squeezed Sophie's hand. "I've got to get back to my office," he said. "We're going to get questions about why the Dewlap lecture was cancelled. I'd better draft a response."

He pulled on his leather jacket and started for the door.

"Hey, Red," Sophie said with a smile. "You did well."

Chapter 49

When he reached his office, Duffy lay down on the floor. He soon found himself squirming once more in search of a comfortable position. With his door still in the maintenance shop, his writhing and wriggling was on full display for anyone in the outer office to see.

"Do the worm!" Coyne shouted each time she walked by.

Duffy ignored her. He thought about taking muscle relaxants, but after his fiasco with whiskey and anxiety meds, he decided against it. Still, he wasn't getting any work done, so he decided to get up. He grabbed hold of his desk and pulled himself to his feet with a grunt. He scrounged up a hard-backed chair from the forest of derelict furniture at the back of his hallway office. Sitting wasn't much better than lying down, but if he perched his bum just right the pain was manageable.

Duffy powered up his laptop. He didn't feel like drafting a response about the Dewlap cancellation, so he opened his To Do file. There were a dozen tasks on the list; he started applying his Shitstorm Decision Matrix to each one to see which could be ignored or delegated.

A few minutes later, Coyne appeared in his doorless doorway.

"Don't you ever knock?" he said.

Coyne looked startled, but just for a moment.

"Hardy har, har!" she said. "No door to knock on. Very funny."

"What can I do for you, Terri?"

"Sophie's been trying to get hold of you. Your ringer must be turned off."

"Thanks. I'll call her now."

"By the way, what's the story with Dufus Lillidew?"

"What have you heard?"

"That he cribbed from a grad student."

"Blunt hasn't told me why Lillidew is taking a leave," said Duffy. "It's a personnel matter."

"Is he still going to sue you?"

"Good question."

"Well, you better call your gal pal. Sounded kinda urgent."

Coyne returned to her desk, leaving Duffy to call Sophie. He clicked on her number and was stretching his back when Sophie picked up.

"I hear you were trying to get hold of me," he said.

"Yes! Did you hear the news?

"What news?"

"The minister of higher education has shelved amalgamation *and* the systemwide reform plans."

"You're kidding?"

"No! Anne Moreno just sent a memo to every university president in the province. It says the ministry is issuing a news release within the hour."

"What happened?"

"I have no idea. Listen, I've gotta go. I just wanted to let you know. It looks like the crisis is over!"

Duffy hung up and called Jill Kaiser.

"Jill, it's Duffy."

"I know. There's this crazy thing called call display."

"I just wanted to tell you that I didn't send the recording to Prigg."

"I know."

"Then why did you call off the reforms?"

"After we talked last night, I figured there was a fifty-fifty chance you'd wimp out. So I gave the recording to Kerri Quartermain. She's the kind of shameless suck-up who'd have no qualms about sending it to Prigg. She's already hitting me up for a job, for Chrissake."

"Sounds like Quartermain," said Duffy. "So, I guess I can forget about working in the premier's office?"

"That's right, bucko. This is no place for wusses."

"I think I'm okay with that."

"Good for you—not that I give a shit."

"It's always nice to talk to you, Jill."

"I'm sure it is, but I gotta go. My gal is about to be sworn in as the new minister of finance."

Duffy's back felt slightly better. He tried bending forward from the hips in a short, shallow stretch. Not bad, he thought.

He slid carefully into his jacket and walked out of his office.

"Terri, this day is turning out pretty well after all," he said.

"Yeah?" Coyne replied without looking up from her computer.

"The government has scrapped the amalgamation proposal. Looks like we all get to keep our jobs a little longer."

"Woohoo!" yelled Coyne, suddenly engaged. "God bless public-sector employment!"

Duffy zipped his jacket and checked his pockets for his gloves.

"I'm going back over to Founders Hall to see if Sophie wants to celebrate over lunch."

"What about your back?"

"It's feeling better."

The words had barely left Duffy's lips when Sophie walked into the office.

"Hey!" said Duffy. "I was just coming over to—"

The tears on Sophie's face stopped him mid-sentence.

"What's wrong?"

Sophie hugged Duffy and buried her face in his jacket. "Alex had a heart attack. They've rushed him to the hospital in an ambulance."

"Oh, man," said Duffy. "How is he?"

"I don't know. I'm going to the hospital now. Will you come with me?"

"Of course."

Duffy's old car was giving him trouble, so he'd left it in the parking lot behind his apartment building. Sophie offered to take her car.

"Would you mind driving?" she said, handing Duffy the keys. "I'm too upset."

"Sure."

Duffy pressed the key fob and the lights on a small, red hybrid blinked on and off. He pushed the driver's seat as far back as it would go and folded himself in. A spasm of pain cramped his back; he tried to stretch it out, but his head hit the ceiling. He wondered if he would be able to get out again once they reached the hospital. Sophie was crying into a tissue and didn't notice his struggles. Duffy shifted in the seat until he found a position that was tolerable. He pressed the ignition button, put the transmission in gear and drove slowly out of the parking lot.

"So, what happened?" he asked as he navigated his way towards the Yawnbury Community Hospital.

"After you left, Clive and Sylvia stayed on for another twenty minutes. I was busy with the month-end budget. I didn't think about Alex until I looked at the time and saw that he'd missed an eleven-o'clock phone call. When I went in to check, he was slumped on the floor."

"I know he's had a lot of stress lately, but was he having health problems too?"

"Just fatigue, I think. That's all he shared with me."

"I'm not surprised. The president's job is 24/7, even when things are normal. I can't imagine what it's like when you've also got amalgamation and a social-justice revolt on your hands, not to mention his wife's cancer."

The hospital was located in the old-money part of town, a neighbourhood with large stone homes, mature trees and wide boulevards. Duffy found a parking spot on a quiet crescent. As Sophie sprang out of the passenger door, Duffy wriggled and squirmed in the driver's seat like a man trying to escape a straitjacket. It took him a minute or two, but he finally got his lanky frame into a position where he could withdraw his legs from under the steering wheel. He grasped the upper edge of the door frame, and with shards of pain stabbing his back, hoisted himself up and out of the driver's seat.

"Back still sore?" asked Sophie.

"Not too bad," Duffy fibbed.

Sophie slid her arm through his and they began walking down the tree-lined street towards the hospital. Snow was falling—big, fluffy flakes floating serenely through the air. If they were headed anywhere else, or nowhere at all, it would have been a wonderfully romantic stroll.

They left the residential area and crossed a busy street to the hospital. At the reception desk, Duffy asked for Alexander Meriwether. The attendant typed the name into her computer.

"Looks like he's still in Emerg," she said. "I think his wife and son are in the visitors' lounge. It's just down the hall on the left."

They found Marilyn Meriwether and a young man seated in a small, fluorescent-lit room.

Sophie gave the woman a hug and they both began to cry.

"Oh, Marilyn, I'm so sorry. I should have checked on Alex right after his meeting."

"Oh, come on, Sophie. It's not your fault. I'm just glad you found him when you did."

"How's he doing?"

"One of the doctors said it looks like a mild heart attack or maybe just exhaustion. Anyway, he said Alex is resting comfortably, whatever that means."

Sophie introduced Duffy. "James is the university's director of communications."

"Oh, yes, I've heard a lot about you. Alex says you and Sophie make a cute couple."

Duffy's cheeks flushed. "We've only just started dating," he said, giving Sophie's hand a discreet squeeze.

"Really? Alex seemed to think you two have been an item for some time."

"Well, James and I work together a lot," said Sophie.

The young man who'd been standing off to one side stepped closer.

"Hi, I'm Malcolm, Alex's son. I'm going to see if I can get an update from one of the nurses. I'll be back in a minute."

As they watched Malcolm go, Sophie clasped Mrs. Meriwether's hands in both of hers.

"How are *you* feeling, Marilyn?"

"Better, at least until this morning. I'm scheduled for a lumpectomy, so at least that decision's been made. But I've got to tell you, it sucks getting old. I've been bugging Alex to retire for years. Maybe now he'll pass the baton to someone else."

Duffy felt a rush of anxiety. Without Meriwether, life at Sir Middling U would be unbearable. Just as quickly, he felt the familiar jolt of self-rebuke. Alex was seriously ill—struggling for his life perhaps—and his wife had cancer. Duffy's troubles were trivial by comparison.

Malcolm appeared in the doorway. "The nurse says we can see Dad for a few minutes. He's in the hallway waiting for a room."

"Go on," Sophie said to Marilyn. "We'll wait here."

When the president's wife had joined her son, Duffy took Sophie's hand and kissed the back of her fingers.

"How are you?" he asked.

"I'm still getting used to Bertie being gone; I have no idea how I'll get by without Alex."

"Oh, come now, Moneypenny," said Duffy, his Scottish accent as lame as ever. "Stay strong for king and country."

He kissed Sophie on the cheek.

"What will we do without M?" she said.

"We'll go visit him out at that big country house of his. I hear he keeps a great bar."

Sophie smiled weakly and wiped her eyes with a tissue.

Duffy put his arm around her shoulder. "Alex is all about duty," he said. "He's got a loving wife, a son, two daughters and a grandson. He'll bounce back for them."

Just then, Malcolm rounded a corner and beckoned them over.

"It looks like Dad is going to be okay," he said. "He wants to see both of you. But please just stay for a minute. I don't think he's as strong as he lets on."

Sophie and Duffy followed Malcolm through a maze of identical, fluorescent-lit corridors. When they reached Meriwether, he was lying on a gurney with a pair of oxygen tubes up his nose. An orderly appeared to be getting ready to move him.

"Ah, Sophie and James," rasped Meriwether. "Thanks for coming."

Sophie took his hand. "You scared me, Alex," she said. "Don't ever do that again."

"I'm sorry, my dear. I should have listened to Marilyn. She's been urging me to hand the bridge over to someone younger. And now I must."

"I won't ask how you're feeling," said Duffy. "But I hope it's better than you look."

"Ha!" said Meriwether. "Just the tonic I need."

The orderly unlocked the wheels on the gurney.

"Sorry, folks. I've got to get this fella back in for some tests."

"Just another minute," said Meriwether. "Sophie, James, I want to let you both know something. The Board of Governors will need to appoint an acting president. That would normally be the provost, but since we don't have one of those at the moment, the next best thing is Clive. I know that won't thrill either of you, but he'll keep the train on the tracks until the board can do a full search."

"But you'll be coming back?" asked Sophie. "You just need to convalesce a while, right?"

"I'm afraid not," said Meriwether. "This is my wake-up call. Time to slow down and be a proper husband to Marilyn."

Duffy's heart sank. "I'm going to miss working with you, sir."

"I'll miss you too, James. I admire what you did, or didn't do, this morning. That took real courage. I've instructed Clive to give you responsibility for community relations and a new title—acting assistant vice-president. Clive will need the board's approval to make it permanent, but he knows I want it to happen."

Duffy nodded, but the news gave him no joy—no emotion of any kind, really.

"That's it, folks," said the orderly. "It's time to rock 'n' roll."

Duffy grabbed Meriwether's right hand in both of his.

"Fair winds and following seas, sir."

As he was rolled away, Meriwether struggled to give Duffy a salute but he could only manage a weary smile.

Chapter 50

The panel discussion on the use of statuary to honour historical figures was scheduled for that evening. The weather forecast was both ominous and vague: a significant "snow event" appeared to be blowing in from the northwest, yet the government weather office hedged its bets with woolly terms like "probability," "varied conditions" and "rapidly evolving." The local radio station, which loved to report a good storm, gleefully torqued the forecast into a full-on catastrophe. "Winter blast poised to strike Yawnbury!" the announcers gushed. Duffy spent much of the day monitoring the weather and preparing to convene a snow-closure call if necessary. By late afternoon, however, Environment Canada downgraded its alert to "isolated flurries." Duffy relaxed and gave Fifi a call to let her know that the panel discussion wouldn't be affected by the weather.

"I never thought it would," she said. "You worry too much, Duffy."

The statue talk was held in the Pike Auditorium, an odd-duck space that had originally been built for reserve-officer training in the 1920s. It had once housed a rifle range and parade square; for the past half-century, it had been used for theatre productions and blood-donor clinics.

The moderator of the discussion was a national television anchor who doubled as a reliably inoffensive host for fundraisers and award ceremonies. The panel included a social anthropologist who specialized in systemic racism, a civil liberties scholar and an art historian who had published a book on political statuary.

They each brought thoughtful, measured insights to the discussion. There were a few disagreements, including one over the destruction of controversial statues, but the verbal sparring was tame and respectful. Duffy wondered if Lillidew had been right: maybe a provocateur *was* needed to fire people up and push them to give a more articulate defence of their opinions.

The event ended with polite applause. The audience chairs were pushed to the side, tables of food were rolled in and a rag-tag band launched into an old Bob Marley tune. The guitarist whiffed the opening chords, but she plowed on and eventually caught up to the drummer and base player.

Good for you, thought Duffy.

After the band's fourth song, the lead singer made an announcement.

"There's a rumour on campus that Sir Middling's director of communications plays a mean guitar," he said. "Who wants to hear James Duffy shred the axe?"

The small crowd cheered as if someone had announced free beer. Duffy shook his head. His back was better but not great, and he hadn't picked up his Fender in nearly two weeks. The crowd began to chant, "Duff-y! Duff-y! Duff-y!" The band's guitarist unplugged, jumped off the stage and ran towards him. She handed over her guitar and draped the strap around his neck. Duffy held up his hands in surrender and took to the stage.

"You fellas know 'Born to Run?' " he asked.

"Springsteen?" asked the singer. "Absolutely!"

Duffy launched into the hard-charging intro like a crack of thunder. He raced through the chords and repeated the signature riff with lightning speed. The band caught up and off they went. The music roared through the auditorium, sweeping the crowd along on a wild, joyous ride. Duffy raked the strings like he was trying to break them. A man transformed, he plunged into the music, forgetting the pain in his back and the disappointments of the past few weeks. His fingers flew up and down the fretboard, eyes closed, a smile stretching from ear to ear. He jumped, danced and spun around, lost in the gloriously wild rock anthem.

The final bars came too soon. Duffy lingered on the last few chords, stretched them out and savoured the intoxicating rush of performing in front of a raucous crowd. When it was over, the audience cheered and whistled. Duffy took a bow, his pain temporarily forgotten, and handed the guitar back to its rightful owner.

People shook his hand and slapped his ailing back as he made his way to the far side of the auditorium. He looked for Sophie, but the crowd was too thick. He found a secluded space on a riser next to the rollaway bleachers. It had a good view of the dance floor. Duffy sipped from his water bottle and scanned the room. He spotted Sophie at the centre of a small vortex of dancers—all women, including Fifi and Tessa Burns—whirling, jumping and laughing like kids on the last day of school.

Off to one side was Morris Hill, chatting amiably with several professors, one of whom was Rufus Lillidew.

"Are you kidding me?" Duffy muttered.

"My thoughts exactly," said a husky voice to his left.

It was Kiljoy.

"Jesus, Sylvia, you scared the crap out of me," said Duffy.

"I have that effect on people."

Duffy took another drink from his water bottle.

"I didn't know you were a rock star," said Kiljoy.

"A misspent youth," replied Duffy. He nodded towards Lillidew. "I thought Rufus would've scurried away with his tail between his legs."

"He should have. The man is shameless. And a fool. Bigots like Harrison Dewlap take advantage of people like Rufus Lillidew to normalize their racism."

Duffy thought about the remark. Kiljoy could be harsh, but she was a shrewd observer of people and politics.

"I hear that Blunt is going to be the interim president," he said.

Kiljoy nodded. Then with a smile she said, "When you told Clive you wouldn't send that audio recording to Giles Prigg, I thought his eyes were going to bleed."

"Me too."

They both laughed.

"I spoke to the chair of the Board of Governors earlier today," said Kiljoy. "She plans to keep Clive busy with some kind of institutional-review baloney."

"I expect you'll keep him busy too."

"That I will. Contract negotiations start in the new year. With the government backing off reform, it's time to swing for the bleachers and make up some lost ground."

"Ah, *plus ça change*," said Duffy.

"*Plus c'est la même chose,*" said Kiljoy, completing the old saying. "Don't you find that depressing?"

"That we're right back where we started?"

"Yes," said Duffy. "Nothing has changed."

"I disagree. Maybe the things you hoped for haven't changed, but things are different."

"Like what?"

"Like you and me standing here having a heart to heart."

Duffy smiled. "That's true."

"And then there's Alex. He's finally getting the break he should have taken years ago. That's a change—a good change—for him and his wife."

Duffy nodded.

"And then there's you. I heard you were gunning for a promotion. It took backbone to stand up to Clive."

Duffy didn't reply. He was thinking of his actual spine. It was aching again. He shifted his weight from one foot to the other.

"Who do you think will replace Meriwether full time?" he asked.

"Who knows. President searches take a long time. I hear Rose Samaroo is interested."

"Really? She hired me for this job, but I never got a chance to work with her."

"That's too bad. You would have learned a lot. I'm not crazy about Rose personally, but I admire her intelligence and drive. She'll make a good president somewhere."

Kiljoy wrapped a scarf around her neck and slipped into her parka. She gave Duffy a long, appraising look.

"Is it true you're dating Sophie Munn?"

"Yes," said Duffy.

"Hmmm," said Kiljoy. "Just my luck."

She squeezed Duffy's hand and gave him a rueful smile before slipping away into the boisterous crowd.

Duffy wasn't sure what had just happened, but a tiny shock wave rippled through his body. He was too tired to dwell on it. Instead, he looked out over the crowd, hoping to spot Sophie and Fifi again, but they were no longer part of the whirling dervishes.

Exhaustion hung on him like a heavy quilt; he lacked the strength to resist its downward pull. Bed, he decided, was where he needed to be. He made his way along the edge of the crowd, stepping out through the auditorium's emergency exit. He looked across the campus sports fields to the Yawnbury River. The surface of the slow-moving water shimmered with the reflection of a million stars. Duffy looked up into the clear night sky. Ursa Major was easy to spot above the northern horizon, with Polaris—the pole star—gleaming like a beacon to the upper right. Duffy was entranced by the celestial panorama. The sheer vastness of the universe soothed his anxieties, putting his fears and worries into perspective, if not completely out of mind.

The reverie was broken by a hand clutching at his elbow.

"Ow!" he yelped, reaching for his back.

"Sorry, Duffy," said Fifi. "Growing a spine after all those years in PR must hurt."

"More than you'd think."

"Nice guitar work tonight."

"Thanks. Was it you who put the band up to that?"

"Of course. And it turns out you really can play."

"Did you think I was lying?"

"No, just exaggerating," said Fifi. "Either way, it was more impressive to hear you play than listen to you blab on about it."

Duffy laughed. "Well, on that strange note, let me say goodnight."

"Where are you going? It's only nine o'clock, for God's sake."

"I'm dead tired, Feef. My back is sore and I think Kiljoy just made a pass at me. Long story short, I've had enough of this place for one day."

"Kiljoy made a pass at you?"

"I think so."

"Jesus, Duffy—you're a magnet for weird shit."

"What do you mean?"

"Think about it: Mittens' poetry book, your *Rocky Horror* bender, killing the president's dog and now getting hit on by the head of the faculty union. You're the common denominator in a lot of strange stuff."

"You forgot to mention that my best friend is a noted scholar *and* a burlesque queen."

"Yes, I suppose there's that too."

"Even so, *post hoc ergo propter hoc* is a flawed line of reasoning."

"And you thought four years of philosophy was a waste of time."

"I never said that."

"No, I guess that was me. But before you go, you have to hear my news."

"Okay, hit me."

"My book won the Agnes Macphail Prize!"

"That's awesome!" said Duffy. "We've got to get a news release out."

"It can wait till Monday."

Despite his exhaustion and sore back, Duffy beamed with joy for his friend. "I'm really happy for you, Feef. Sir Middling U has to give you a tenure job now."

"We'll see. Anyhow, I'm glad I caught you before you shuffled home for a cup of hot cocoa."

"Me too. If you see Sophie, tell her I left."

"Tell her yourself."

"She's having too much fun. I don't want to drag her down."

"Okay, Gramps. But a word of advice: communication is the key to a successful relationship."

"Would a text message do?"

"Not great, but acceptable."

"Honestly, it's all I can muster."

"Then send it now in case you collapse on the way home and get eaten by coyotes."

"You should write an advice column."

"You're right. I could call it, 'Tough Love.' "

"Perfect."

It took Duffy twenty-five minutes to hobble the five blocks to his apartment. As he opened the door, he heard Bruce Springsteen on the sound system playing one of Duffy's favourite songs, the slyly seductive "Fire."

"Hello?" Duffy called out.

"In here!"

Duffy peeked his head into the bedroom. Sophie was lying there, wearing his plaid housecoat and reading one of his newly purchased copies of *More Shitty Weather*.

"How did you beat me here?" asked Duffy.

"Fifi said you'd headed home, so I got in my car and drove."

"Did you get my text?"

"No. What did it say?"

"Nothing, really."

Sophie held up Mittens' book. "A poetry fan, huh?"

"Just the classics."

"I see you bought two copies."

"I'm thinking of giving them as Christmas gifts."

"And to think I was hoping for sexy lingerie."

"Play your cards right and you might get both."

Sophie laughed. "You're quite the charmer, Mr. Duffy. By the way, great work on the guitar tonight. I had no idea you were that good."

"And yet you still went out with me."

"Hey, I can spot a diamond in the rough."

"Thank goodness."

"Seriously, I loved seeing you on stage. You looked comfortable, like that's where you belonged."

It was Duffy's turn to laugh. "I'm just a garage-band amateur."

"If it gives you joy, that's all that matters."

Duffy thought about it. "You know, it does give me joy. I'd almost forgotten that."

Sophie tilted her head and smiled. "Have I ever told you how sexy you look in that leather jacket and watch cap?"

"Yes. But tell me again."

"Come over here and I'll whisper it in your ear."

Chapter 51

A week later, Duffy received a message from Fifi.
"Meet me at Sir Dickie's at three."

He bundled up for the walk to the pub. Fluffy snowflakes were falling in a gentle cascade, muffling the sound of cars and buses on neighbouring streets. With exams nearly over, the campus was all but empty. Duffy entered the quad and paused at the statue of Sir Richard Middling. The balls on the great horse were still painted red and green, but the sprig of holly had been replaced with a garland of popcorn.

"You may have survived the battle," Duffy said to horse and rider, "but I doubt you'll survive the war."

He carried on, shuffling his boots through the snow like a kid dawdling his way to school. The turmoil of the past six weeks had died down and his back pain was all but gone. With any luck, the Christmas shutdown would provide two weeks of peace and relaxation.

When he arrived at Sir Dickie's, he found the pub decorated for the holidays. The sound system was playing the Pogues' "Fairytale of

Sir Middling U

New York," a Christmas classic for fans of Irish punk. Alone at the bar, in contrast to the down-and-outers in the song, stood a tall woman with high cheekbones, full lips and a mane of auburn hair. She wore a luxurious Melton trench coat, and her long legs were clad in black tights. A pair of brown leather riding boots completed the casually elegant look.

Duffy knew there was only one person in the world who could lure such a Vogue-like goddess into Sir Dickie's Pub. Right on cue, Fifi breezed in from a side door. She approached the bar and wrapped her arms around the woman in a long, intimate embrace. When they each let go, Fifi took a seat next to her friend. The two chatted for nearly twenty minutes, their faces never less than an inch or two apart. Fifi stroked her companion's cheek and touched her well-coifed hair with the tips of her fingers. When the woman prepared to leave, she leaned in and gave Fifi a smouldering kiss. Duffy, who was watching from his table at the back of the pub, lowered his eyes. When he looked up, the goddess was gone.

He gathered his jacket and satchel and walked to the bar.

"Hey, Feef."

"Hey, Duffy."

"It's good to see you."

"You too."

"Let me buy you a coffee."

"Thanks, but I gotta run."

Duffy's smile collapsed in puzzled disappointment. "Really? I thought we were going to hang out?"

"I just wanted to say goodbye."

"Goodbye?"

"I turned down the contract extension."

"You mean Sir Middling U didn't offer you a tenure-track position?"

"Nope. But it doesn't matter. Do you remember that call I had from the Chadwick School?"

"The university in the UK?"

327

"They gave me an interview."

"And?"

"They offered yours truly a tenure-track position *and* a research chair."

"That's fantastic!" said Duffy, his smile rocketing back up to a hundred watts.

"Political economy, with a cross appointment to environmental studies."

"What about your mother?"

"She's better. In fact, the only thing she's sick of is me. Old Iris says I should go away and restart my life."

Duffy reached over and embraced Fifi. They'd never been huggers with one another, and the gesture was awkward. When they pulled away, a lock of Duffy's shaggy red hair caught on Fifi's earring. She tried to yank it free; he yelped in pain.

"Don't be such a baby," said Fifi.

"You were pulling my hair out by the roots!"

"Give me your Swiss Army knife."

"Why?"

"Just give it to me."

Duffy pulled the knife out of his pocket and handed it over. Fifi unfolded the scissors. Before Duffy could stop her, she snipped at his hair, leaving a swatch of red curls attached to the earring.

"Cripes!" he said. "You could have just taken your earring off."

"This was more fun."

Fifi handed the knife back to Duffy.

"Keep it," he said.

"No way, Duffy. This is your favourite possession. It's your security blanket, for God's sake."

"That's why I want you to have it."

"Seriously?"

Duffy nodded.

"Thank you. That's incredibly sweet."

Fifi kissed the red handle and slid the knife into her backpack.

"So, paleface, what are *you* going to do next?" she asked.

"I thought about sticking around for a few months so I could add the assistant vice-president title to my résumé. Then I said, *fuck it*. I'm going to take what I've learned and move on. No one should stay too long in one job. You get cynical and burned out. I told Blunt I'm quitting. He's thrilled. I think the sight of me reminds him of what a dink he's been."

"Let's hope something does," said Fifi. "Anyway, staying at Sir Middling U would be hell."

"More like purgatory. Either way, I need some time off. I'm going to visit my cousin in New Zealand. His band needs a guitar player for a few months. And besides, I've always wanted to see Hobbiton."

"You're too tall to be a Hobbit."

"I could be Gandalf."

"Not yet. You need to acquire more wisdom."

"Fair point."

Fifi poked Duffy in the chest with her index finger. "So, what does Sophie think of your Kiwi trip?"

"She's all for it. In fact, she's going to ask Blunt for an unpaid leave to come with me."

"Wow! I'm happy for you two!"

"Thanks. We're looking forward to really getting to know each other, away from this place."

"I approve."

Duffy smiled. "Thanks. You should come visit."

"I might just do that. Maybe take the troupe on tour."

Duffy's face lit up. "That would be awesome—The Fabulous Ladies down under! My cousin's band could open for you."

"Imagine that: You and me on stage together."

"Sounds like destiny."

They sat in silence for a moment. Each of them was moving on, which was better than one of them being left behind. Still, Duffy's readiness was tinged with melancholy.

"Cheer up," said Fifi. "The only constant is change."

"My father likes to say that."

"I know. You've told me a million times."

Duffy smiled and reached for Fifi's hand. "I'm going to miss you, Feef."

"I'm going to miss you too, kiddo."

They hugged again; it was less awkward this time.

"Well, I've got an office to pack up," said Fifi.

"Hey, you can't leave without your Christmas present."

Duffy reached into his satchel and pulled out a copy of Percy Mittens' book. He handed it to Fifi, who read the title out loud: *More Shitty Weather: A Poetic Parody.* Oh, my God, Duffy, you weren't kidding!"

"I even got Mittens to sign it."

> Dear Dr. Dubé,
> Some friendly advice: Do not let Duffy near your next book.
> Best wishes.
> PM

"Ha!" said Fifi. "You're a good man, Duffy."

She gave his hand a final squeeze and got up to leave.

"Hey, Feef," said Duffy. "Never explain, never retract, never apologize."

Fifi looked at him over her shoulder.

"Just get the thing done and let them howl!"

Acknowledgements

This novel was a long time in the making. It began as a germ of an idea that grew and evolved over the course of many years. Along the way, I received help and encouragement from family, friends and publishing professionals. Catherine Thompson, Paul Thompson, Donna Crowley and Doug Fox—book lovers all—read early versions of the manuscript. The talented Abbie Headon provided a thoughtful developmental edit. And the ever-helpful staff at FriesenPress took care of copy editing, design and production. *Sir Middling U* is a far better book because of their assistance; any flaws and shortcomings are all mine. Finally, to Catherine, thanks for thirty-plus years of love, laughs and support.

Milton Keynes UK
Ingram Content Group UK Ltd.
UKHW011437031123
431729UK00004B/205